SALLY SPEDDING

WRINGLAND

PAN BOOKS

First published 2001 by Macmillan
This edition published 2002 by Pan Books
an imprint of Pan Macmillan Ltd
Pan Macmillan, 20 New Wharf Road, London N1 9RR
Basingstoke and Oxford
Associated companies throughout the world
www.panmacmillan.com

ISBN 0 330 48695 0

Copyright © Sally Spedding 2001

The right of Sally Spedding to be identified as the
author of this work has been asserted by her in accordance
with the Copyright, Designs and Patents Act 1988.

All rights reserved. No part of this publication may be
reproduced, stored in or introduced into a retrieval system, or
transmitted, in any form, or by any means (electronic, mechanical,
photocopying, recording or otherwise) without the prior written
permission of the publisher. Any person who does any unauthorized
act in relation to this publication may be liable to criminal
prosecution and civil claims for damages.

1 3 5 7 9 8 6 4 2

A CIP catalogue record for this book is available from
the British Library.

Typeset by SetSystems Ltd, Saffron Walden, Essex
Printed and bound in Great Britain by
Mackays of Chatham plc, Chatham, Kent

This book is sold subject to the condition that it shall not,
by way of trade or otherwise, be lent, re-sold, hired out,
or otherwise circulated without the publisher's prior consent
in any form of binding or cover other than that in which
it is published and without a similar condition including this
condition being imposed on the subsequent purchaser.

Newport Library and Information
Service

Z352229

Newport Library & Information Service
Gwas⟶ ⟶frgell a Gwybodaeth Casnewydd

WRINGLAND

Born in Wales, Sally Spedding studied sculpture at college, and is still a practising and exhibiting artist. She has won awards for her poems and short stories, and *Wringland* is her first published novel. The author is married to a painter and lives in Northamptonshire, but writes in their home in the Pyrenees.

For Katilie

Wringland From Old English *wringan*, related to Old High German *ringan* and the Gothic *wrungō*, meaning snare.

Make a cross over tomorrow, a final cross with your hand.
from 'The Spade', Émile Verhaeren

Prologue

THE GARGOYLE SQUATS on the gutter of the Mary Magdalene tower: half dog, half man, his greenstone eyes blind to the infinity beyond Black Fen and the vague intermingling of mud and tide.

History has passed unknown beneath him and, as the traps spring below Morpeth Bank and the fishing seals are filled with shot off Cortlever Low, his is the only silence. He is powerless to pluck the herrings from their lunar deaths or the beakless broilers from their crates, for the centuries have softened his jaws, and in that bleak waterworld he is just another conduit to the graves below.

A peewit perches on his ear, silhouetted against a sky so vastly light that the candlewick spread of dyke and drain seems for the moment bleached of all evil . . .

The young woman has green eyes too, but she has the advantage of sight. She sees the bird fly free yet chooses to stay, to feel the wreathing breeze around her hair, binding her to that special place with its feckless sighs of spring. For she is curious and, as the vestry door opens, its handle burns like ice in her palm . . .

January 1841

Even the birds are frozen on to the sky the way goose feathers stick to my coat. And cold so cold my fingers feel nothing. Ma Tully at the Dame School says another Ice Age is upon us and lets us keep our bonnets on. The one good thing this week. The worst is my draw scoop broke. It snapped like a Branta's neck and Mr Hemmings the gang leader says I will have to use my hands instead to clear Slave's Drain. I tell him God is looking down and sees everything, besides, as Moeder says, he's just catchwork with no right to make us suffer . . .

One

A stands for angel who praises the Lord.
B stands for Bible that preaches God's word.
C stands for Church to which righteous men go.
D stands for Devil, the cause of all woe.

EARTH-COLOURED WORDS IN a warped black frame, dated 1862. Abbie shivered in the half-light, but there was more. Six sepia photographs, cracked and buckled like the wintry soil itself, each signed Gabriel Hemmings in a strong square hand. A litany of death without mercy, frozen in time.

She noticed, too, there were no men; just women and children, obviously all his workers, hoeing, twitching, piling bricks, their faces faded against the Fenland sky. Blurred to loam like all the dead Hicklings, Graylings, Saxons and Huguenots resting in their brief borrowed ground, their young hands white like the fronds of a Christmas pine.

Abbie pulled her denim jacket tight around herself, feeling their cold touch her own bones, wondering about the one little girl whose steady, almost defiant gaze met hers when suddenly a voice eddied through the gloom, destroying the moment.

'Is that you, my flower?'

Whoever had called out was coming closer from the darkness of the nave, moving the air, bringing an odd musty smell. Then she saw him: a tall cassocked figure looming in front of her, disappointment lengthening his face.

She recoiled, trying to judge how far she was from the door, then realized that it was impossible. She was trapped.

'I'm most awfully sorry.' He composed himself. 'I thought you might have been *mea mulier florum*. Never mind, I expect she'll be along later. Meanwhile, welcome, my young friend.' A smile stretched his lips, and Abbie was sure he could hear her heart. 'Peter Quinn, Reverend. Pleased to meet you.' A hand extended, marbled like a map, while eyes that swam in their sockets trawled from her brown bobbed hair to her feet.

'I'm not stopping.' Abbie inched away from his waiting fingers.

'Ah, but I could see you were finding these remnants of local history quite riveting. All people of our parish here, you know. And if old Samuel Scott, God rest his soul, of Rievely Hall hadn't been such a Good Samaritan, their fate might have been quite different.'

Abbie shivered again.

'My dear, do you know there used to be a small school held in the chapel which he personally funded?'

'No, I didn't.' She needed to be out beyond the sliver of daylight that edged the door. Away from the catacomb smell and the creepy smile that hid the man's teeth.

'Mind you, not all the poor had the good fortune to be educated. Only those truly committed to the Lord . . . Would you like to come and see?'

'I've got an appointment, actually.'

But he ignored her lie, his nose now almost touching the tallest figure dressed in black in the first picture.

'"Martha Robinson, who now lies cold, possessed a gift worth more than gold." What d'you think that meant?' Quinn turned for their eyes to meet, and with a shudder she noticed the red of each eye corner.

'Looks like she possessed precious little.' Abbie tried to back away.

'Ah, that's where you're wrong, young lady. The strength of four men isn't given to everyone, least of all a woman. She was by far and away the best labourer on the estate, and –' his voice changed in a way she couldn't quite fathom '– the kind of mother we'd all like to have, until, that is, she strayed from the Lord's path . . .'

'What do you mean?' Abbie searched the image for even the smallest expression, but the light on the old plate camera had kept her face a mystery for all eternity.

Quinn ignored her question. 'And this is little Harriet, one of her daughters.' Pointing at the same child whose eyes never flinched, like black pebbles uncovered by snow. 'Until the Gangs Act of 1868, she'd have worked from eight to five-thirty for four pence and out in all weathers. My goodness, can you imagine that, these days? Still, it all came too late for her anyhow . . .'

'It's shocking.' But Abbie wasn't going to tell him she'd studied nineteenth-century social history for Paper II, or anything else for that matter.

'Do you know –' he half turned '– I always liked the name Harriet myself, but my wife insisted on Rosie for ours. Still, anything for a simple life, say I. Now, if it had been a boy, I'd have been quite tempted to plump for . . .'

But his audience had slipped outside and his voice was drowned by the rooks and starlings settling in the trees.

Everything was bright. Too bright for a graveyard, she thought, glimpsing the army of stumps angled haphazardly into the distance, across land deep below sea level. Late daffodils lay strewn over recent soil. Raw and brown, the graves were unmarked, save for a succession of landlord Scotts and their last loyal retainer Gedney Stimpson, 1919–1968, topped by a tilting Bible.

Abbie was glad to be out of the tower's shadow. Glad to be warm again. She took off her jacket as she walked and pushed her hair back behind her ears. The air had become still and clammy here, below the level of ships and tides, trapped by the dark viridian of Six Mile Bank, which also harboured the acres of Fat Hen Farm. A misnomer, since all its hens had perished when, in 1941, an incendiary bomb meant for the code-breaking depot at Outwold blasted black claws and feathers into the night.

Abbie could hear the tractor in the furthest field. The engine's drone added to the heat and the clinging calm. She wanted to sing, shout, anything unruly just to break the spell, but nothing came, not even that half-expected sudden chill, and in a brief panic she began to quicken her pace.

With relief she reached Six Mile Bank and scrambled up its grassy slope, then looked back to see the church and its gargoyle reassuringly now in miniature, its strange incumbent almost forgotten in the brilliant cleansing light of day. She lifted her face to the sun and took in great gulps of sweet air, then stared at the surrounding open spaces, turning like the gnomon's shadow to take it all in.

To the north lay the eponymous sea, swilling out the marsh channels with fresh detritus from vanished ships. To the south were the chimneys of Snutterwick set among cabbages. To the east, over the Wenn, extended reclaimed acres greening with cattle crops. But to the west, something altogether different sprouted from peat bog where West Winch Farm had once stood.

The Kingfisher Rise Development: Holtbury Prestige Homes in London brick, topped by matchstick rafters – skeletal boats beached not anchored, soon to be righted by the warming seas and taken to another shore.

Her territory now, with turquoise flags ranged round a stockade celebrating the victory of fake stone and PVC over slop and water. Plots 1 to 25 all needed to be sold within twelve months. And she would do it for herself, for her dead mother and for Vallender. Strictly in that order, for he was the sort who'd persuade a paraplegic to take a loft conversion and coax the punter to more than they could afford. She'd seen it in his body language – every deal a fix, every lie a truth. He was slick trade and she was different: an academic, from a professional background. But she liked his body and the way he moved, so it wasn't that simple . . .

Now, on this Easter Bank Holiday Monday, number 1 Kingfisher Rise was ready. Newly cleaned up and fleshed out with floral borders to disguise the meanness of its rooms. Taiwanese trinkets on every surface and each plain window overdressed with voluminous swags and sashes. Her daytime home, the Willoughby, a middle-of-the-range house for middle-management, boasted four beds (two for teenagers in ultramarine and red), study, cloaks and en-suite, own-choose tiles, aqua carpet and double garage. One thirty-nine nine-fifty – no offers, but part-exchange possible to make a sale.

The only drawback to the site had been the existing names of the adjacent roads. Piddle, Turncoat, Widows' Droves . . . all of them once trackways round the fields. Vallender had tried offering Snutterwick Council a back-hander to change them – to no avail.

'Names allotted at the time of the Enclosures are to stay,' they'd said in unison, to this man who could easily have stepped from the set of *Carlito's Way*. 'We must endeavour to keep the soul of the area alive for future generations living on Black Fen.'

'So try and make a bit of a joke about it if the subject comes up.' He'd steered Abbie with more than a paternal arm towards drinks afterwards. 'Widows won't like it, nor the incontinent, but tough shit.'

'Or the turncoats either,' she'd added wrily, immediately feeling a slight chill touch her skin.

Abbie finally reached her car, which was still stuffed with luggage. Inside was as hot as a coffin facing the cremation fire and having the window open made little difference. She checked her watch. There was still time to get back to the cottage and sort things out, have a shower, change into slobbing mode.

Then, as she stopped to let an elderly couple cross the road, she thought of Simon, who after his degree with her in Leicester had gone off to Osnabrück. And now he was on stand-by in Rheindahlen for Kosovo when he

could have been here instead. On their day of goodbyes,
she'd held him tight, told him she wanted him more
than anything. She'd hoped against hope he'd change his
mind, but no, and it hurt – hurt like that day when he'd
posed in uniform for his proud parents at Dan y Parc,
then something inside her had broken.

If anything, she'd found his absence had made the
heart grow bleaker, not fonder. It was bad enough being
second best to this Man Thing, but worse was the
stomach-churning worry every time she opened the newspaper or listened to the news. Simon was due back on
leave soon, he'd promised. That was when they could
talk. No, would *have* to talk. And less than a mile away
now was Goosefoot Cottage, where she would deliver her
ultimatum.

A grey and frail Mr Mower, in Chatteris, had handed
over the key after one month's payment in advance. He'd
looked at her with a strange fearful expression that never
left his face, so she'd wondered what was wrong. There
was something else too. His hand holding the key had
shaken as though he couldn't part with it quickly enough,
but on that sunny afternoon optimism had prevailed.

At least the place was cheaper than the Domesday
Motel in Walsoken or the St George's Sails by the Wenn.
Besides, she'd reasoned when she'd first phoned him,
having somewhere in the middle of Black Fen would be
handy not just for walks but for work as well. Now,
having encountered that weirdo vicar, she wasn't so sure.

Abbie drove up the rest of Smithy Lane, from tarmac
on to chippings, then cinder to grass an unnerving
distance from the last house. She left the Polo parked
outside and looked round to get her bearings. But the
wind was king and it took her hair, blinding her to the

swaying line of poplars along Morpeth Bank and, beyond still, the slurry spread of marsh.

The gate, with its wooden plaque in the shape of a goose's foot, was embedded in weeds, the path a line of ill-fitting slabs. The door, stiff in its frame, sprouted brittle strands of paint which fell away at a touch, leaving patches of old wormholed wood.

Dismay gripped her as she wrestled with the key. Maybe she wasn't meant to be here. Maybe everything had been too easy. After all, finding a flat in Leicester had taken most of the summer vacation and her last house-share in Northampton all of three months. She suddenly missed her girl friends and that roomy Edwardian semi opposite the park, and found herself wondering if Monday was still take-away night, and what they'd be ordering to eat by the telly.

'Can I be of assistance?'

She spun round. The Reverend Peter Quinn was by her car. His snatch of dog collar was white as ice against his worn jacket, his skin like flour in the daylight.

'I'm fine, really.' Abbie returned to the lock. She tried again and swore for his benefit, but he wasn't reading her body language.

'It's been left some time, I'm afraid. Our Mr Mower's not well by all accounts.'

She heard him push open the gate and dreaded his step.

'I'm quite used to this sort of thing. No problem,' she said. Keys, after all, were to be her speciality.

'Here, let me try.' His breath was close behind her, tainted like old fish.

'Quite a bit of history here, too, did you but know.' But before she could argue, the key connected.

Quinn shoved the door open with surprising strength. The reek of wet walls escaped and he sniffed the darkness like a dog after meat.

'Better see if we've got any electricity.'

She didn't like the 'we' and stayed well behind him.

'How long are you here for?' he asked, reaching up, and she noticed how the back of his neck lay in folds, spiked by grey hairs.

'Not sure. It depends.' She wanted him gone, to have her own space, however dismal. She had to think quickly. 'My fiancé'll be along any minute.'

'I see.' His gaze switched to her ringless hand. 'Lucky chap.'

Damn you. Damn you. He wasn't missing a trick.

Suddenly the lights were on, turning everything yellow, from lemon to mustard.

'Thanks,' Abbie said sourly, making for the car.

'Any time, Miss . . . er . . .' He followed her.

'Longman. Stella Longman.' Hoping her mother's friend, far enough away in Berwick, wouldn't mind.

'Never know nowadays whether you young ladies prefer Ms to Miss. Not that it worries me, you understand.' Her suitcase caught his thigh and he moved aside, still staring at her. 'Remember we have a special service for newcomers the first Sunday after May Day – such a pleasant time of the year, don't you think? – just to make people like yourself feel more at home.'

So far she'd neither felt at home nor seen anyone else remotely like herself. The few locals huddled near the terraced cottages further down Smithy Lane might easily have stepped from those old photographs she had seen: hunched, rickety, all in dark clothes.

'I'll do my best.' Abbie pulled a hold-all from the

boot, realizing finally that acquiescence was the best way to shift him.

'Can't say fairer than that, I suppose. Well, *vale, mea amica.*'

She watched him head on for the church, and coloured as he suddenly glanced back and caught her stare.

Then she noticed what lay on the step.

I took two weeks to get over the beating so it's only my uncles who get the fat rind while the one loaf from Scotts bakehouse has to last the week . . . I hate Mr Hemmings and when I'm dead I'll push him down to Hell myself . . .

February 1843

I've discovered the only thing I've got what's really mine is my name, Martha. Do you like it? Would you ever call yours that? I doubt it, not after what I'm going to tell you. But as the Devil's my witness, I don't give a fig. Try me . . .

Two

I T WAS A PRAYER BOOK, old and weathered, its corners smoothed down by unknown hands. Abbie opened it gingerly to see if there was any inscription or dedication on the fly leaf. There was a name – Esmond P. Downey – carefully scripted, barely legible, on a page as thin as rice paper. Thin as the air itself.

She snapped it shut. 'Bloody vicar! I'll believe what I want to believe and it's not this stuff.'

Her anger then dealt with the one downstairs room and the dune of droppings round the grate, her despair with herself. 'Bloody Mr Mower too,' as the third giant rubbish bag squeezed its exit to the gate in the wild hope of attracting a stray council operative.

She hunted for the phone. No phone. The landlord had lied and she'd never checked the place out earlier. She'd let her father have her mobile, expecting the Holtbury one to be at the Show Home in the morning.

'What in hell's name am I doing here? I must be barking.'

But the advert in the Northampton paper had seduced: 'Historic cottage, ½ mile from sea. All mod cons, and amenities close by . . .'

Cons is right, she thought, looking at where a washing

machine and fridge should have stood. This dump had
no possibilities whatsoever.

She slipped out of her filthy skirt and tights, trying
not to let so much as a bare toe touch the floor, then she
pulled on jeans and trainers and slammed the door on
her way out.

There was a call box at the end of the lane, in front
of the church, and irritatingly the Reverend Peter Quinn
was there again, standing among a group of teenagers
with pushchairs. The babies and toddlers she noticed
were all girls.

She got her speech ready for the landlord, Mr Mower,
keeping her back to the vicar. A woman answered the
call, flustered and breathless over other voices and a
barking dog. 'I'm afraid Mr Mower passed over this
morning,' she rasped.

'What?' Abbie remembered his frightened eyes, his
tremulous fingers.

'He'd been very poorly, you know, but this was so
sudden. Only last week Dr Bristle said how he was
picking up nicely . . .' Her voice faltered. 'I can give
you his sister's number if you like. She'll be coming
over from America as soon as she can, to sort things
out . . .'

'No, no, that's all right. I'm really very sorry.' Abbie
felt a chilling numbness creep through her clothes.

'I'm just the meals on wheels, me. I found 'im, you
know. He'd have had 'is favourite today: sausage and
mash with apple dumpling to follow. Such a shame . . .
You still there?' the voice asked.

'Yes, er, no, look, I'd better be going.' Abbie put the
trembling receiver down on that distant Tower of Babel
and turned to see Quinn smiling.

'Hello again.' He waved to her, and the young mothers looked her way.

'Thanks for the prayer book,' was all she could think of.

'Pardon?'

'Your little gift.'

'My dear, I really don't know what you mean.' He seemed genuinely puzzled.

'Never mind.' Abbie sighed. She wasn't going to push it, not with them all staring at her like she'd got two heads. She secured her sweatshirt hood and gritted her teeth for the return to Goosefoot Cottage and its ghosts, wondering – if Quinn wasn't playing tricks – who on earth had left the prayer book there and why.

Abbie finally made some Earl Grey tea with her own electric kettle and cleared a space for her papers. In control again, with files neatly stacked, a list of memos for her first day's work in the Show Home and instructions for the complex alarm system on site. Then she put to memory all the variable specifications and the array of deals and freebies available on the Ripton, the Ramsey, the Willoughby and the Somersham, homes for the 'outwardly mobile'. Locals moving up conspicuously from terrace or council house sale? Homes for birdwatchers and gazers at water? The last stop before the graveyard?

She shivered again. That same abnormal chill she had felt in the church reached her nerves, as if she was naked, and she clenched her fingers to stop them shaking. Even the warm cup she held made no difference.

She looked round the room, her jaws tapping out their own Morse code. She studied the grate: clean now at least but, without a fire, black and empty, like a dead mouth. She had no kindling, no matches, so how long could she endure it? One night? Two at a push?

It was seven o'clock and getting dark. Too late now to find anywhere else to stay. Besides she'd parted with rent money, and that decided her. The Book of Common Prayer followed the tea bags into the rubbish bin, then it was time to go and sort out her clothes. She dragged her case and holdall upstairs to the landing.

Here it was marginally lighter, if only by dint of the curtains not meeting and the glimmer of the dying sun spreading in from the south-west over Canal Farm's fields. It caught the cross-stitched sampler simply framed, hanging askew . . .

> The people here have neither horse nor cowe
> Nor sheep nor oxe
> Nor asses, pig, nor sow.
> Nor cream curds, whey,
> Buttermilk or cheese,
> Nor any other living thing but geese!

She set it straight, dislodging the long-dead woodlice behind. Curled up like bullets, they sprayed her feet, and she pushed them to oblivion between the shifting floor-boards.

It was even worse in the bedroom, where more of their relations crunched like gravel under her trainers the moment she entered and an invisible cobweb clung to her nose. The ceiling was even lower than downstairs, with a single rotted beam along its length. Bad Feng Shui, she remembered from somewhere: 'A killing energy pressing on anyone sleeping below . . .' Abbie shivered again, biting her lip in the tense silence as she looked around.

The plaster walls bulged and sagged like old sails. She thought of the Show Home's perfect surfaces and neat coving, how this dwelling and others like it in Victorian England had been barely fit for animals, let alone humans piled together above the heat of a single fire.

The wardrobe door hung open and she stopped dead, her heart pumping in her chest. For something very strange was reflected in its old freckled mirror.

Dolls. But not set out at all like normal childhood companions. She went closer. There were three altogether – obviously all quite old – two girls and the largest, a boy, wearing a sailor suit which looked more recently made than the others' clothes. He was lying on top of the one whose frayed muslin dress was pulled up to the chin, while the doll in pink with a china head had been positioned to watch them.

'This is so bloody weird,' Abbie whispered, seeing their downturned mouths and heads as bald as marbles. She turned the sailor doll over, only to discover his painted eyes had almost been worn away. His face was a sad mix of dirt and cotton, much loved obviously, she thought, but by whom? She rearranged him, propping him up, trying to fathom what disturbed mind had been at work here, convinced that whoever it was might be coming back. Then she noticed something black crawling from one of the doll's cuffs.

She screamed and, without waiting for the rest of the beetle to emerge, smothered all three toys in the bed-spread. Then she wrenched open the window and hurled the whole bundle to the path below.

She leaned out and checked to the left then the right,

but there was no one visible. Only the blowing trees and a pair of grey-necked geese tearing towards the sea.

She finally sat down and wrote to Simon, giving away nothing of recent experiences, and left a half-hearted impression of her lips on the last page. Then, with a bath towel covering the old settee below, settled down there for a hungry and restless night.

All her possessions were safe downstairs again: her suit for the morning in its dry-cleaner's bag behind the door, Clinique ready on the draining board and shoes sitting on a square of kitchen roll. Upstairs lay empty, a playground for the dolls and the wind from the eaves that tinkered with the windows and nudged the doors.

Abbie shivered repeatedly, squeezing her eyes shut, pretending Simon was lying close to her and breathing into her hair. Trying to imagine what he looked like now, over and over again, while from the far end of Smithy Lane the church bells chimed two.

Their melancholy permeated all the hearths of Black Fen and was the last sound Abbie heard before sleep descended.

Moeder says my name's very old, from the Bible. Same as that Martha whose sissen wiped Jesus' feet with her hair, but so far thank the Lord that's the only thing my uncles haven't made me do. What I do mind though is having to share the other bit of my name, Church, with the new brat who has increased our number. Even the same birthday. November first. If you want to know, and I tell God this sometimes, I cannot share anything.

Three

THE DOLLS SHE had thrown outside had vanished without trace.

Abbie took a quick look through the neglect around the cottage, wondering if the wind might even have moved them, but there was no time to speculate further. The day was bright and full of promise, the sky strewn with gulls heading for Buckley's Farm – and she was ready.

Despite the deprivations of the night, she felt smart, looked smart. Something of a miracle, she thought, parking in the Show Home drive, and if she'd managed that crisis she could manage anything . . .

She waved to the men working over on the site and one of the pipe-layers whistled his approval as she walked up to the garage conversion. Abbie took a deep breath to calm the first-day flutter of nerves, the security system's alarm code ready on her lips.

Then she stopped. The door was already ajar and, although a lamp on the desk was softly glowing she froze.

'Who's there?'

She sniffed as an unusual smell reached her nose which was nothing to do with cleaners or even faulty drains, more like the earth near Fat Hen Farm. She peered in, still gripping the door handle, her knuckles white through the skin.

O Jesus, shit!

Someone had got in first and was already waiting.

It was a dark-haired woman with clothes to match and an aura of stillness that grew cold as Abbie went over to her desk. What was up with the alarm system then? The sensor in the corner was dead. Her anxiety reached overdrive. The stranger wouldn't have known the code, surely?

Abbie tried not to look at her. Maybe the cleaner had forgotten to set the alarm last night – that was the most logical explanation. A shiver passed through her new suit and through the viscose blouse tucked into her skirt. A shiver that seized her hands and made her drop her briefcase to the floor.

'Damn it.'

As she bent to pick it up she sneaked a look at the brown tide mark on both the woman's boots, and her ankles that were little more than skinless bone.

Puzzled, Abbie tried to reassert herself, and she clicked open the case with some irritation. She'd wanted a coffee first, time to use a decent loo, and a chance to get her desk organized. All her 'make the punter feel at home' pitch, so carefully rehearsed ad nauseam, had now evaporated. For this person had quite clearly made herself at home, her hands resolutely crossed in her lap. They were heavy and red, at odds with her face.

'How can I help you then?' Abbie asked, suddenly noticing that the woman didn't look at all well. Her lips were colourless, her skin sallow and jaundiced, especially around the eyes, while a black woollen scarf lay tight around her throat.

'We need a home.'

Abbie met her gaze for a moment as she picked up the glossy Kingfisher Rise brochures and fanned them out to show the complete product range.

'Well, you've got a choice of twenty-five houses to be precise. Each of them with either three beds or four, and all with full gas central heating and en-suite facilities . . .' She unfolded the crisp new site plan, which took up the whole desk. Bubbly green trees, slight enough to lift away on a breath, fancy walling in arcs and curves where rubble still reigned, and figures without shadows rendered in a light swift line. Lost souls of a Never Never Land, with the sea echoing to eternity under their feet.

The woman leaned forward, clearly not listening to her spiel, her eyes as still as beck water, as if focused on one plot.

'That one there.' She pointed with a broken nail.

'Right.' Abbie hunted for a pen. 'That's a Ripton. Top of the range at a hundred and eighty thou. To include kitchen/breakfast, patio doors, Victorian conservatory . . .'

'Makes no difference.'

'I beg your pardon?'

'Like I said, means nothing.'

'Are you a cash buyer then?' Abbie ventured, recognizing a cul-de-sac when she saw one. 'Have you sold a property?'

'Oh yes, I've sold all right. Everything.'

Abbie blinked in surprise, then reached up to the heating switch behind her. Feedback to Vallender was looking promising, she told herself.

'Well, that's just great. Most purchasers these days would give both arms to be in your position.'

'I did.'

Abbie stared again, but was diverted by the digger driver outside giving her a grin and the thumbs-up sign.

'I'd better take your name . . . Mrs . . . er?'

'No name. Just me and my boy.'

'I do need a name – for my records,' Abbie persisted tactfully.

'You'll have it soon enough.'

'Your solicitor then. That'll be handy for later on.'

'I'll sort it myself, if it's all the same to you.'

Abbie sighed. She'd always been good with the tricky ones in Mortgage Advice – the ones who wanted something for nothing or lied about their incomes. This, though, was different. Something wasn't quite right. Was the woman ashamed of her name for some reason or did she just not want it known? Whatever the reason, she wasn't going to let this client slip away without a fight.

'I know someone who can help with self-conveyancing. He's very reasonable and based in Wellingborough, which isn't far,' she said.

'No thanks.'

'Perhaps a holding deposit then? Say 5 per cent. That's well below what other developers are asking.'

The woman's lips pursed into a stubborn line, but Abbie persevered.

'There'll be a lot of demand come the summer . . .'

'It'll be mine, you'll see.'

'Yes, that's all very well, but there are procedures we must go through. First, there's the question of—'

She suddenly looked up from her pad. Her voice died in her throat. The client had disappeared. Her chair was empty.

Abbie got up, her mouth fixed open. She checked at

the door to the hallway, only to return confused and
bewildered. She was on her own, no question of that,
and the leatherette seat the woman had just sat on was as
smooth and cold as black ice.

Abbie's pulse quickened as the thermostat cut out.
She realized it had made no difference at all to the temperature. And even though she flung the office door wide,
for the sun to reach her legs and let new air in, the smell
of turned earth remained.

After making some shaky notes, Abbie composed herself
and then dialled her boss in Northampton. This was
tricky, but she wasn't in the mood to lose face.

'Yes?' The sales director sounded different – stressed?
– and that helped. It meant he was human too.

'Mr Vallender, it seems we do need to check security.
Who's the cleaner on this site?'

'Why?'

'The Willoughby's door was open when I arrived this
morning. Not only that, but a client was already waiting
in the office.'

She heard him blow his nose. Then a ballpoint rolling
on teeth.

'A client, you say?'

'That's right.'

'Well, they're not exactly growing on trees at the
moment, are they?'

'That's not the point. Anyone could have come in
and the stuff's not been tagged yet. So do I have
authorization to (a) contact the cleaner and (b) get the
alarm sorted?' She didn't tell him it was now completely
dead: no lights, no response.

'Let's prioritize, shall we, Miss Parker? The main thing is, you had a bum on a seat, *n'est-ce pas?*'

Stung by his attitude and this terse use of her surname, she moved the phone further from her ear, but he was back with a vengeance, like sudden lightning.

'So what were they interested in?'

Abbie sighed. There was no pleasure in this at all.

'She says she wants plot 2.'

An excavator growled past the window.

'Can we get top whack on this, d'you think? Is she cash?'

'I think so, but—'

'No ifs, no buts, Miss Parker. Definitely no buts. Think targets. Sit on her. Phone her this afternoon, then get back to me. Understood?'

Abbie looked at the receiver, her breath condensing round the perforations of the mouthpiece. The nameless woman had picked the slowest-progressing plot of all, the poor relation of its faster-developing neighbours, still dotted with breeze-block markers like small mean graves. She'd also managed to spoil the day, turning the cosy welcoming Show Home into a nest of anxiety for the rest of the week, while Rodney Vallender, who'd still not sent her mobile, was sitting fifty miles away and didn't give a shit.

'Bastard.'

With the outer door secured, Abbie explored the fridge, downed a hospitality gin and tonic in one go, and then went outside to see if she had a witness.

The rain set in just after five. Striking from the north, it beat the flags into submission and left huge ochre pools in the unmade road.

Inside the designers' pink paradise it was closing time. Abbie had spent the day dealing with half a dozen telephone enquiries and fixing follow-up appointments. The site men she'd talked to earlier had seen nothing unusual, for there were people coming and going all the time, and not necessarily into the Show Home. She switched off the lights and pulled the blinds down, then automatically set the alarm code, before remembering it was dead. She punched the numbers in frustration.

The contractor's team had long gone. Their earth movers slumbered together in chains, clogged up with mud. Thank God for the car, she thought, and whoever it was had invented the wheel. Abbie set the wipers on full and water splayed from the blades as she edged forward. All clear. But not quite. Something was in front of her, and the warmth of the car became frosty. She screamed as a shadow darkened the glass like a black veil that hung over it until she hit third and screeched through the gates.

In Walsoken Road, still shaking, she collected milk, four Mars Bars and the *Morpeth Record*, before braving the downpour on the way towards Black Fen. As she drove, cocooned by the thudding rain, with headlights that made little difference to the infinity ahead, another surge of fear made her hit central locking.

The cottage seemed worse second time round. Just one day spent among clean skirting boards and spotless plumbing was enough to convince her of the need for another billet. She could have used the Willoughby facilities, even the frilled and valanced bed for a while, like her friend Jane had done in the Badgers' Hollow development near Rugby. But not since *that* woman's

visit this morning. Oh no. Just sitting in the office, prey
to all comers, was bad enough, without being vulnerable
between sheets or, worse, in a shower.

Having drawn the dingy curtains as close as they would
go and dragged the one armchair and the settee in front
of each door, Abbie settled down to write up the day's
events, with memos and chasers for those who'd registered
an interest. Then she turned on the small TV that stood
welded in a sea of grease to the kitchen worktop and tried
to tune it. But news of flooding in Humberside looked
more like a snowdrift and the other channels were no
better, so, taking her torch, she shoved back the kitchen
chair and went outside. The rain lashed her face with an
instant soaking and water crept down her neck. What
passed for an aerial lay adrift of the chimney, twisting in
limbo and whitened by bird-slime. 'Goose Arse Cottage,
more like,' she muttered. Then, back indoors in hopeless
wet silence, she changed her clothes again and sat down
with the local paper. Something normal at least, full of
good works and worthy causes.

She opened it out, expecting to find the Holtbury
Prestige Homes advert that should have taken a double-
page spread across the middle. Instead it was monopo-
lized by St Mary Magdalene Church notices, each one
full of mind-numbing minutiae. 'Bloody cheek,' she
thought. The Reverend Quinn was nothing if not pushy.
Trying to squeeze them out, probably not wanting the
site at all. She wondered if he'd guessed she was working
there – and if that was a problem for him. Good, she
hoped so.

Then something caught her eye: between the Fur and
Fancy show in Grimswick on Saturday and the darker
blocks of Births and Deaths.

Black Fen Primary School.
Open Evening. Friday 23 April. 7 p.m.
Refreshments. All welcome.

'If there are bums on seats, go and sniff 'em out,'
Vallender had always said, and that's exactly what she'd
do. But only because someone there might know of that
mystery woman, where she was from – maybe some farm
or other – and whether or not the son she'd spoken of
went to the school.

She ringed the notice in red, then began cutting.
Suddenly her scissors stopped at sounds from the bedroom above. Young voices, she was positive of that,
singing lighter than light . . . She strained to hear, holding
her breath, but the rain had renewed its barrage and the
kettle simultaneously reached the boil.

Then the singing was audible, not sweet exactly, but
purer than anything she'd ever heard in her life, and so
eerie. It was a crystal water-wailing which filled the whole
cottage and which somehow she knew she was meant to
hear.

> *'Matthew, Mark and Luke and John,*
> *Bless the bed that I lie on.*
> *Four corners to my bed,*
> *Four angels round my head.*
> *One to watch and one to pray.*
> *One to bear my soul away . . .'*

It faded as the latest deluge subsided and, with the
moon high over World's End Marsh, casting a liverish
glow through the window rags, Abbie also knew that her
moment had come. She hurriedly locked up, crammed

all her possessions into the car and, without bothering to look back, was out through the gate. Within one frantic minute she'd turned the Polo full-circle and was heading inland towards the distant lights of Snutterwick.

Often at night when I'm lying with Mary in the smoke above the fire and my eyes are so sore I can't sleep I hear the wind moan through the Devil's Mouth which is between the lathe boards by my bed calling Martha Martha as if he wants to take that from me as well. Why is the needy creature always warm when I am so cold? I'll tell you because she gets the softest crust and the best yellow milk from the top. She squeals like the voles under the floor and tries to open my coat to find my chest. She would suck blood from me if she could and sweet Jesus it scares me to death . . .

Four

'SIGN HERE, PLEASE.' The older woman studied the newcomer as she keenly handed her the register. 'So, you decided to honour us after all.'

As Abbie flicked back through its yellowing pages, she could see there had not been many staying at the St George's Sails since she'd first called in. No AA or RAC stars either, just Sheila Jane Livingstone's name displayed as licensee over the door. But so what? Nothing mattered to her except the place was warm and orderly, with solid furniture and a range of sporting prints. Behind her, in the bar area, bottles glinted upside-down, poised to deliver.

'We're a bit quiet at the moment.' It was almost an apology as the hotelier watched Abbie's trembling hand fill the space. 'Still, it was busy over Easter,' she lied, fetching a key. 'Is Abbie short for Abigail then?'

'I've never been called anything but Abbie.'

'Well, I'm Sheila, by the way. Sheila Livingstone. Nothing very special, I'm afraid.' She smiled, her teeth on full show. 'Looks like you've been having some fun out there.' She wiped a drop of rain off the page with her sleeve — and Abbie liked her instantly.

'It's no joke, I can tell you.'

'I'm not laughing.' Sheila handed over the receipt. 'Where've you come from then?'

'Goosefoot Cottage. Escaped, more like.'

Two grey eyes widened. 'No one's been living there for years. It's in a right state. The Sanitary was round to inspect last Christmas, so I heard.'

Abbie recalled the gruesome loo. No seat and the flush into the stained bowl, just a yellow trickle.

'Course, the bin men won't touch it.'

Abbie thought of all the rubbish she'd left and would have asked about the nearest tip, but she was tired and worried about far less tangible things.

'They ought to stick a bomb under the place, that's what.' A sturdy arm pulled on the Guinness pump. 'Look, d'you fancy something to help you sleep?'

'No thanks.' Froth cascaded down the glass and formed a lake on the bar. 'I know it sounds weird,' Abbie continued, 'but there was this prayer book as well. It just came from nowhere. Then some singing . . .'

Sheila Livingstone leaned forward, flecks of stout on her lips. 'I'm telling you, I wouldn't live out there even if it meant I came up on the bloody Lottery. And those kids, they let them roam all over the shop, break times, lunch times . . .'

'Black Fen Primary School?'

'No less.'

Abbie recalled the notice in the paper, then something else. 'There were three dolls on the bed. It was freaky.'

'How do you mean?'

'You know, the dolls were positioned like they were . . . doing it.' Abbie felt an idiot as the words came out.

Sheila picked up a packet of Marlboro Lights and shook one free, preoccupied for a moment. 'Well, nothing surprises me about those kids.' She drove her smoke upwards, targeting a row of earthenware tankards. 'They're a law unto themselves.'

Abbie smiled wanly. Suddenly feeling exhausted, she gathered up her things in slow motion. There'd be time enough tomorrow to ask about her strange client that morning. Now she just needed to stop for a while.

'Room 6. First right after the bathroom.' Sheila led her to the bottom of the stairs. 'See you in the morning.' She touched Abbie's arm, just like her mother used to do.

Abbie found the landing, then the door of her room – at that moment the most welcome sight in the world.

It was an undreamt-of heaven. Not only had Sheila Livingstone accepted her Switch card, but Abbie now had a decent bed. A double one at that, with clean cotton sheets white as Vallender's shirts, covered by an old-fashioned quilt.

The room resembled her parents' home in all its genteel dinginess, with dusty cornices and a huge ceiling rose bearing cherubs and acanthus leaves, while at the window heavy curtains hung in bleached stripes, keeping the night at bay. No killer beams here, no woodlice either, Abbie noted with relief, as outside the river slid inland, black as oil, littered by the past. Old spritsails and luggers nudged newer barges on the current, while here and there figures stalked the decks with torchlight antennae, deserted by the moon. Adrift in darkness.

Time for a bath. She'd thought of nothing else but the bliss of hot water, the comfort of steam ... Abbie scraped back her hair. Suddenly there was a rap at the door.

'Hang on!' She covered herself.

you back.' Abbie kept her eyes on the familiar silhouette that had just appeared, motionless against the daylight.

'No need, no need. Just strut your stuff there, Miss Parker. They'll be in the post tonight.'

'And what about my mobile? It's still not here.' But he'd gone.

She replaced the receiver, her pulse quickening. There was a deeper damper smell this time, of reeds and grass devoured by water, solid enough to eat. Abbie kept her mouth closed to a minimum, trying not to breathe in.

'Bit better today, isn't it?' Her pad flicked open, Holtbury ballpoint at the ready for a fresh start. 'Do sit down.'

'No, thank you. Too much sea, too much silt.' The woman stared at the floor. 'You're not from these parts are you?'

'Not yet.'

'Count yourself lucky then.'

'Why's that?' Abbie thought it best to stand, as if to match her, although she only just reached the woman's shoulders.

'Nothing but malaria and the ague. And the worms all drowned.'

A frown settled on Abbie's face. 'You don't mean here in Black Fen, surely?'

The strange client ignored her and moved over to the laid-out plan, her dress weighted by earth around the hem. Her fingernail, split and etched by dirt, traced the Ripton outline again and again. 'You won't be letting my plot go to anyone else, will you?' The Lincolnshire vowels barely disguised her threat.

'I'm sorry, but until we get some kind of firm

commitment, it's anybody's. That's our policy, I'm afraid.'

The atmosphere suddenly changed, no longer warm and cosy as the thermostat in the corner cut out like it had before. Abbie ignored it. If there was a choice between losing a client and being a bit cold so be it.

'I'm not anybody.'

'Let's just have your name first, please.'

Abbie passed the woman a pen and pointed to the chair. For the first time she noticed a savage red weal on her left cheek that followed down to that same black scarf. In the chilling silence it looked new and sore.

'Can't write. What's the use?'

But Abbie wasn't convinced. Nobody looking at houses in this price bracket could be so backward. The woman was just being difficult.

'Perhaps I can help?'

'No, thank you.' The client's tone made the nego-tiator keep her distance and check who was nearby outside, but all the men were busy over on plot 7.

'I'm under pressure too, you know,' she said. 'I'm not just here as decoration. I've got a job to do: selling.'

'Lucky you got a job, leastways.'

'I know, but I like helping people too . . .'

The woman's lip curled up over her broken teeth. 'You couldn't help no one, stuck here in your pretty little home.'

Abbie stared at the sickly skin stretched over big angular bones, at eyes that reflected only the bleakness of her life.

'What is it you've been doing then?' she ventured.

'Anything to keep a spoon to our lips.'

'Anything?'

'You ever worked peat?'

'Can't say I have.'

'There was ten acres to dig.' The woman pushed both sleeves up to show muscles white and taut like garlic bulbs in their skins, but bruised around the elbows.

'And that's where he used to hit me. Mr "Angel" Gabriel. My girls as well.'

Gabriel Hemmings? Girls? Abbie's stomach tightened as she recalled the photos of that dour and dreadful existence years ago. Surely she was dreaming this? But no, the stranger was still as real as anything else in her office, and gradually curiosity overcame Abbie's fear. She wanted to ask about the woman's boy, to touch her, and to be able to say to Vallender that she wasn't just a hallucination or a shadow. That she did exist and was serious. But all she could hear in her mind was Vallender pushing for a sale.

'I know what you're thinking,' the woman said suddenly.

'No, I wasn't . . .' Abbie spluttered.

'Well, I *am* serious. That plot belongs to me.'

'So, are you buying or aren't you?'

The woman nodded.

'Right, well I can start the ball rolling by getting your address. Let's have that first.'

'Goosefoot, Black Fen.'

Abbie started. Her pen slipped from her hand and rolled to the floor.

'It can't be. O Jesus.'

'I'm telling you, it is.'

Suddenly the air became ice, stinging her face to numbness, while something bigger, like that shadow on her windscreen, was moving close by and Martha

Robinson, with all her rickety strength, bore down on Abbie's shoulders, forcing her into darkness.

'Christ, it's nippy in 'ere. You OK?' Dave 'Gravedigger' Jones had come in from the site, an ox on two legs. 'Looks like you passed out. 'S lucky you didn't hit the desk.'

'It's nothing, really,' Abbie murmured. His dark duffel seemed too close, too smothering, burying her alive. She pushed it away, so he made a pillow of it instead.

'Forgive me saying, but you ain't a very good liar. Someone's given you a shove, haven't they? Was it the same one as you mentioned last time?'

She managed to stand up and avoid an answer to the first question. 'I'd just offered to record her name for her, that's all. But for some reason she didn't want me to know . . .'

He scratched his head. 'Got to be a job for the plods, this.'

'No, I can handle it.'

But Dave ignored her, picked up the phone and dialled Snutterwick. Dried mud showered her neat paperwork.

'Ten minutes? Fine.' He put the receiver down, checked his watch and turned to Abbie. 'Now then, cup of tea for the lady?'

'Thanks, but you shouldn't have done that.'

'All part of the service.'

Despite the warm mug he handed her a few minutes later, her hands shook uncontrollably in the deadening cold, before he reset the heating. 'Weird that. Timer's set on continuous,' he muttered to himself. 'Anyhow, don't you let yourself be intimidated.'

'I'm not.'

'I got a kid like you,' Dave said almost proudly. 'Talk about determined.'

But Abbie was listening for sounds outside and, kind as Dave was, she just wanted him to go. As if he could read her thoughts, he heaved himself into his neglected duffel coat.

'Nature's calling, I'm afraid. Tell the cops everything, mind.'

'I will. But don't spread this around, please.'

'Come on, Holtbury can take it. Might whip 'em up a bit. 'Bout time they came down to see what's really going on. See what the bloody ground's like for a start.'

'What d'you mean?' Her head was still muzzy, not thinking straight.

'I read up on it a bit some time ago. The old farm here didn't last fifty years.'

'Why?'

'The estate wouldn't spend on marling up.'

'Marling up?' Abbie had never heard the term before.

'It's when you add clay to make the land a bit more solid. Stabilizes it, if you get what I mean. This peat we got here just soaks and dries, then starts shifting . . .'

'I didn't know that.'

'Ignorance is bliss, my darlin'. Pity the poor sods now dipping in their pockets . . . These houses'll hardly be heirlooms. Still, not our problem, is it? Take the money and run, say I.'

He left not just an unnerving solitude in his wake but also too many unanswered questions.

Am I going mad? How can that woman possibly be living at Goosefoot Cottage unless she means another Goosefoot? Maybe it's a nearby barn or something – that's it.

And it made Abbie feel better to think so.

And why, for God's sake, is plot 2 so important to her? Why does she want it badly enough to hurt me?

That bruised woman with no name . . . she'd been solid, real, too real for a ghost and yet . . . and yet there was something vaguely familiar about her.

The young housing negotiator, who'd spent her solitary childhood inventing others, subsided into her chair as two Disprin fizzled in the glass. She then wrote to Simon again, begging him to get his leave brought forward, and as she licked shut the envelope the deepest loneliness she'd ever known gripped her soul.

June 1843

My moeder is swelling up again like a pumpkin and I know the signs from last time. Every morning when Uncle Kirton and Uncle Poynton have gone off to Slave's Dyke, she sicks up like a dog with such a noise I am glad to go out to work . . .

Six

SHEILA LIVINGSTONE SAT opposite Abbie, waiting for her to further disturb the mound of mashed potato and sausage, her eyes intent, for there were no other distractions in the bar. 'Off anywhere special?' she asked eventually, squeezing a blob of ketchup on to her finger and licking it before passing over the plastic tomato. But Abbie had set her spoon and fork together.

'Just up to the primary school. They've got an open evening.'

'You must be desperate.'

'I know what you said, but there are always possibilities. Got to be pushy in my job.' Abbie got up and smoothed her skirt. 'Otherwise the company wouldn't survive.'

The hotelier cleared the table in slow motion, giving Abbie occasional sideways glances.

'Tell me,' Abbie began, as she picked up her bag stuffed with flyers and brochures on the houses, 'have you ever heard of a really tall woman round here who wears old dark clothes and who's got a son?'

Sheila put the plates back on the table. 'No, can't say I have. Mind you, I don't exactly hobnob with the locals. But you could ask Amy Buckley at Canal Farm. She's a decent sort and knows a bit.'

Abbie made a mental note to look up Canal Farm on her local map. 'What about Goosefoot then?' She still hovered nearby. 'Is there another place called that in the area?' But her attempt at being casual didn't fool Sheila.

'Now why would you want to know an odd thing like that? I'm worried about you, Abbie Parker.'

'Only asking.'

'No, there isn't one – least not to my knowledge. Don't you think *one* of those shitty holes is enough? Look, just have fun. It seems to me you could do with it.'

'I'll try. Thanks.'

Abbie slung her bag over her shoulder and made for the door. But before going to the school she had one more important thing to do. She made her way towards the church. Its door opened easily, almost inviting her in. The vestry seemed damper, darker than ever, yet the workers' faces in the photographs shone like a row of eerie moons.

Abbie moved closer and, as Quinn had done, peered at the main figure. The boots were the same, so were the hands, and in that instant, with a shiver that racked her whole body, Abbie realized who her client was.

But there was something else. For the first time she noticed how the woman might be pregnant, because of the way her stomach strained the coat buttons, and her feet were set apart on the snow as if to spread the weight. A surge of pity changed what she'd planned to say.

'Martha Robinson,' Abbie said, trying to control the tremble in her voice, 'I can't help what's happened to you. It's not my fault, do you understand?' She stepped back, aware of a dense creeping chill enveloping her, as if the winter all those years ago had begun leaking from the picture. 'So please, leave me alone. Please, I need my job,

I need things to go well. But you can't have the Ripton if you can't pay for it. And that's not my fault either, although I'll try to help if I can—'

Her words broke off as a strange sound filtered in from nowhere. It was faint to begin with but, as Abbie turned to go, it became a hollow grating laugh that followed her out of the door.

A queue had formed outside the low brick building that housed the primary school. Someone was selling masks, another person balloons. She declined both, still disturbed by what she'd just heard in the church.

'Fancy a gingerbread man?' One of the few young boys there pushed a biscuit under her nose and sniggered. Abbie noticed a lump had been added for its genitals.

'That's Charlie Hunter,' someone said giggling.

At that moment, Abbie felt old and alienated. Whose foul kids were these anyway? Then a dark-haired girl tugged her sleeve. '*He's* my boyfriend.' She grinned at the lad with the biscuits. 'He's eight, so am I. And my name's Emma.'

'Really?' said Abbie. The child was all braids and ribbons and a Mabel Lucie Attwell grin.

'Have *you* got a boyfriend?' she persisted, as suddenly the queue shortened and dispersed into the bright hall.

'No.'

Abbie escaped, but not for long. Suddenly a smaller child touched her arm. Her blonde fringe, smooth as silk, framed eyes that were disconcertingly large and earnest.

'I've done some paintings. Do you want to see?' The little girl snatched her hand and led her over to the wall. 'Those two,' she said with pride.

The name ROSIE QUINN 7 YRS in the corner of each

made Abbie scour the hall for any sign of the Reverend as a balloon burst nearby. Then she looked down at the child again. So this was his daughter? There seemed no physical similarities whatsoever, something at least the child could be grateful for.

Rosie tugged at her sleeve, pointing to the first picture. 'Look, that's a daddy and that's a . . .' She faltered.

'You mean a mummy?' Abbie tried to help out, but the child's lips were pursed together and her grip tightened. No more questions, no more answers, and still no sign of the Reverend Peter Quinn. She felt uneasy. 'I've got to go, I'm afraid.'

But the child hung on. 'You can't. You're *my* friend now!' Little nails dug in just as a high-pitched voice pierced the crowd.

'Rosie!'

Abbie stared as a wheelchair powered by strong hands cut a swathe through the room. Whispers followed the disabled woman, whose small strained face was topped by a boater bearing freesias.

'Bedtime.'

Helen Quinn's eyes were focused on her only child, but Rosie buried her head against Abbie's thigh and began to sob. The hubbub of talk around them dwindled and, not for the first time, Abbie felt trapped and helpless.

'Come here,' Helen Quinn said to Rosie, almost under her breath, 'or you'll be put up with the bats.'

The child stood rigid for a moment, then finally went to her mother's knee. By the time the head teacher had mounted the rostrum to announce the prize draw, both of them had disappeared. Abbie desperately wanted to follow, but the crowd had thickened and cut her off.

Enthusiastic clapping filled the hall as the winner was named. Abbie went over to study Rosie's paintings again. They were like nothing she'd ever seen, poster paint applied thick as skin, with writhing pinks and whites dotted by gaping black holes.

Suddenly the head teacher clapped her hands again and an attentive silence followed. An overly made-up woman standing next to her stared down at Abbie from under fearsome black eyebrows. *Her make-up was like something out of a circus . . .* Sheila's words came to mind.

Abbie stared back. Could this be the person who'd delivered that letter? *You will all die . . .* She certainly looked capable of anything, with her hideous Cupid's-bow lips pushed out like that and eyes like a bird of prey's . . .

Abbie began to feel distinctly uncomfortable and moved away just as the head teacher began another announcement.

'I'd like to introduce a group from J6, who'll be reciting excerpts from *Alice in Wonderland* and also some Edward Lear verses. We hope you'll appreciate the hard work that the class and my deputy, Miss Avril Lawson, have put in for this presentation.'

So the woman with the lips has a name, that helps, Abbie thought, finding a seat near the toilets. She was aware of Vallender's flyers still in her bag, but was in no mood now to play at being a saleswoman.

The stage filled up with mainly girls of all shapes and sizes. They were dressed in the latest cheap garish fashions and, while droning through all the set pieces without much enthusiasm, occasionally broke into fits of giggles. They seemed to go on and on, and gradually those parents whose offspring weren't involved surreptitiously began to leave. Eventually, the children and their flustered mentor filed away to subdued applause. The head teacher, aware of a lull, then placed a music stand in the centre of the stage.

'Now, ladies and gentlemen, for your entertainment, and to close this very successful evening, we have "The Gang" as they like to call themselves, from J4. Emma Mason, Darren Greenhalgh, Cherry Pickering and, finally, Charlie Hunter.'

The quartet stepped out from behind the curtain and trooped across to their positions. Abbie recognized two of them from earlier and thought that Charlie Hunter especially looked subversive, not to mention nearer eleven than eight.

'If Mr Silver would come and do the honours.' The head frowned at a titter which rose from the group as a young man struggled over to the piano and began hunting for the music. Someone had obviously hidden it inside the stool.

The four children had meanwhile positioned themselves: two standing, with a red-eared Cherry Pickering and a smirking Charlie Hunter kneeling at the front, hands in mock prayer, until the deeply flushed teacher gave the signal to start.

> 'Matthew, Mark and Luke and John,
> Bless the bed that I lie on . . .'

Abbie gasped and swayed. It was the same eerie refrain that had recently driven her from that dismal cottage.

'You all right, me dear?' a woman next to her asked.

But as the singing continued, Abbie pushed her way through the crush of warm bodies, aware of the stares that followed her. This wasn't part of the plan, to feel sick and shaken in her confident suit, when she could have been fixing that young Mr Silver with a nice little Somersham and the head teacher with a de-luxe retirement place, plying the handouts with a Holtbury smile.

But a smile was the last thing she felt like now. She was losing her way. It was no longer just a matter of eat, sleep, go to work. Other things were beginning to enmesh her. Not least the ubiquitous and frightening Martha Robinson, the pervasive Quinns with their strange little daughter and the death threat that lay in that horrible letter . . . Abbie steadied herself by the main door, and pulled up her collar against the latest rain, wishing with all her heart and soul she'd got more than just her umbrella to protect her.

The lights near the school had been vandalized, and in the blackness to be navigated before the first glow in Walsoken Road what was real and what was unreal no longer seemed clear. She quickened her pace, dreading the shadows more as a hidden puddle sprayed her feet. Her best new tights were besmirched with each step and she continued cursing Black Fen and all its works until she finally reached the hotel.

There'd been no time for her to find anything out. She was still none the wiser about Goosefoot Cottage and the woman in black, and perhaps that's how it was meant to be: herself versus this strange place, not one-to-one in a fair fight but one against many. Too many. Too much.

It was only back in her room that Abbie began to calm down and organize herself. After a small glass of Bailey's from a bottle kept for emergencies, she began to compose a list. First, Snutterwick library. They'd be sure

to have names of any historical societies or records of
public work gangs in the area. Next, the planning offices
to see if other Goosefoots existed and what exactly the
Kingfisher Rise project had been built on. Better that
than picking the Gravedigger's brains, she thought. Also,
she had to find out more about the odd-looking Miss
Lawson, and sometime speak to Amy Buckley at Canal
Farm. Then she vented her frustration for the omission
of the Holtbury advert in a letter to the *Morpeth Record*
editor. As she finished her second glass, she resolved that
the time had come to do something more productive
with her lunch hours than hang around the site.

*I am working on Leakes's Drain now,
with Wednesdays at old Ma Tully's,
but since Mary died she has been looking at me strange and rapping my poor
knuckles for the slightest thing like the
hole in my leggings or not having a
comb in my hair. I would rather go
digging and work with the horses, with
the ones they call Prussians and with
Bep. She is from Holland. No one
knows how she got here and neither
does she. Ma Tully kept her from going
to the workhouse school in Gosdyke,
but when she's finished with her spade
there's the washing and desk scrubbing
to do. Still, she's prettier than me, so
that makes it fair, I suppose . . .*

Seven

IT WAS TUESDAY after May Day, with land and sea bound in a mist, and World's End Marsh, Three Fingers Beach and the Deeps of Lethe muffled in sullen silence.

Abbie was high up on the Herringtoft end of Six Mile Bank, facing Holland, her hair in a pony-tail, ears tuned to every nuance of sound: a foghorn, the chink of the kissing gate as it closed behind her, a curlew deep in the reeds. She made her way down to where shrivelled waterborne things, seaweed sprays and bladderwrack, crunched under her feet, then on through brown, fallow fields, still dark from the rain. She stopped for a moment, listening.

There wasn't a soul around, only birds where cows or even sheep would have been welcome. She was under the poplars now. No rustling there; only stillness and a damp tracksuit. Smithy Lane to the north became nothing. Thin grass became tractor ruts. She could see the cottage now and got her Polaroid ready. Suddenly something brushed her legs.

'Jesus!' she cried out.

A child's hand seemed to come up from the ground.

Abbie looked down to a large hole in the bank, camouflaged by weeds.

'Rosie! What on earth are you doing?'

'I wanted my dollies to live here with me in my hidey-hole,' she whimpered, 'but when I went to get them, they'd gone.'

'What dollies? Where?' Abbie was beginning to feel uneasy.

Rosie pointed a filthy hand towards the cottage. Abbie's heart sank. It was impossible to think this little innocent might have left her playthings in that lewd position. Then she remembered the child's paintings at the school.

'So what do you do with your dollies, Rosie?' she probed as casually as she could.

'I show them the sea. They like that, specially Lazarus.'

Abbie frowned at that old-fashioned name.

'Anything else? Things like games. You know: hide-and-seek, ride-a-cock horse . . .?'

Rosie stared blankly. 'Don't know what you mean.'

'It doesn't matter.' Abbie squatted down beside her. She wasn't used to children, and hadn't even seen her little niece, Flora, since she was a baby. 'So what are the other dollies called?'

'Mary and Abigail.'

Abigail? Abbie felt a tiny irrational shiver pass through her and tried to sound normal.

'Did you name them, Rosie?'

The child's tearful eyes widened. 'Course not.'

'Who then?'

Rosie wiped more mud across her face.

'The old witch. And she made me swear never to change the names.'

'What old witch?'

Rosie screwed up her nose. 'Lilith Leakes. She smells.'

'Well, maybe the three of them will turn up after all,' Abbie said brightly, thinking fast about who this new creature might be.

'They won't, I know.'

'Look, let's get you out of there. You'll catch your death.'

'I don't care.'

'Don't be silly. Come on.'

Abbie watched speechless as the little girl crawled out – all mud, dried tears and pink wellingtons.

'They mustn't see me. I'm so scared.'

'Who's they?'

Silence.

'Talk to me!'

'They'll tell my daddy . . .'

'I can't help you if you don't say.' Abbie hugged her tight. 'I'm your friend, remember?'

'I remember.'

'Well, then?'

'It's the Gang. They're horrible to me now.'

'Who? Those singers at the school?'

'Yes. They're in the cottage.'

Abbie stared at the solitary hovel. She took a few shots with Rosie's head in the way and the prints slipped wet, newborn, into her hand. The little girl's eyes widened.

'Hey, that's magic.'

'Not really.' She blew on them and watched them dry. 'Here, you keep them.'

Rosie beamed. 'Thank you. They're better than what the old witch does, anyhow. D'you know, she said she had a baby once that was cursed.'

'I see.' Abbie checked her watch, anxious to stem the child's imaginings before they got out of hand. 'Come on, let's get you back to school. It's too dangerous out here.'

'I don't want to!'

'You must!'

Abbie tried to drag her, but was rewarded with a kick. She grabbed the child before she ran off, feeling the pent-up terror in her. There was only one way to get back without being seen – up the bank again and down behind Fat Hen Farm.

That was when Rosie stopped screaming.

Abbie was in a dilemma. Should she go into the school and report the bullies or leave her charge at the school gates and get back to her own work, single-mindedly applying herself to bricks and mortar and Vallender's gratification? As they walked the footpath adjoining Ten Barn field, it was Vallender who was winning her reluctant attention.

'What's your *real* name then?' Rosie suddenly asked, her damp blue eyes unflinching, a splice through Abbie's thoughts. 'Daddy says you told him a lie.'

Oh, really. How nice.

'Just call me Abbie.' Apprehension had quickened her tongue, for the mist was thickening and that other little dependent hand burned in hers.

'Is that short for Abigail?'

'No.'

They walked in silence until Fat Hen Farm appeared.

'Guess what. I saw bats last night. Real ones,' Rosie whispered as a tractor lurched out of the farmyard. 'Round my head, like so . . .' She loosened her grip and fluttered her fingers. 'In the bat room.'

Abbie swallowed, remembering Helen Quinn's murmured threat. 'You're fibbing.'

'I swear on Mary's heart.'

'What were you doing in there?' The vehicle loomed up, spraying divots against the sky. 'Rosie, tell me.'

'It's when I'm bad.'

'I can't imagine you ever being bad.'

The little girl pressed close to her, cold, shivering. 'Don't leave me, Abbie.'

'I've got to get back for my job . . .'

'Can I come with you, *please*!'

They were near the school and children were returning from lunch. Abbie looked for any sign of the Gang but recognized no one.

'Tell you what, I'll call for you on Saturday,' she said. 'We could have a picnic out. Ask your mummy if that's all right.' She couldn't bring herself to mention the child's father.

'I never ask mummy anything any more.'

'Oh?'

Then Rosie let go of her hand and Abbie watched her pass through into the playground. Smaller than her peers, but quick, for as soon as her new protector's back was turned, she ran out again and up towards the cottage.

Mary is buried by the geese house. I heard Moeder crying just after that there was nowhere in St Mary Magdalene for her to go. Saying the Reverend Pinkton Downey would not give her hallowed ground because it was not the proper Mr Church's child and by that he meant my Pappy. Sometimes I do not understand it all and when the Beadle comes asking his questions I pretend I am deaf. Ma Tully says we are all God's children and that is the end of it. But she has not heard the Devil's Mouth like I have, so how does she know? So it looks as if I am soon sharing my bed again and just the thought of it is making my head hurt . . .

Eight

ABBIE DIALLED VALLENDER yet again to request a mobile and, equally urgently, a panic button. Then, at eleven o'clock, with a coffee cold in her cup, she pored over the site plan.

The offer on plot 5, the Somersham, wasn't materializing, nor that on 6. What had semed a genuine enquiry about the Ramsey, on plot 9, had evaporated and, worse, the family of four who'd 'loved' one of the other Riptons on 14 had disappeared with the mist.

Abbie'd phoned each client in turn, only to be met with a series of excuses and abstractions. It was Mrs Dobson from Birmingham, pursuer of the Willoughby on 6, who'd been most forthcoming.

'It's not that we don't like the area,' the woman whined. 'We've always fancied the countryside round there. It's just that . . . I don't know . . .'

'Go on,' Abbie urged with a dull ache, as she mutilated her pen.

'There's a funny sort of feel to the place . . .'

'I can't think what you mean.' Ink circled the plot, blacker and blacker, thick as a mourning band. With every syllable uttered, the deal was slipping away. 'I still say, for your money, this is one of the best spots you could get.'

'It's not just me, though. My husband thought so too. And the kids.'

'Well, do come on over again – they've forecast better weather for the rest of the week. It's been pretty foul so far and that has a lot to do with things, I'm sure.'

'I don't know . . .' The voice was more faint, more distant. The rat was tactfully deserting ship.

'You'd kick yourself if you missed it . . .'

'The truth is, we've taken a fancy to something else.'

An awesome pause followed, in which temping agencies and revamped CVs loomed large in Abbie's mind. 'I understand.' By now her pen had bored through several pages. She slapped the receiver down and went outside.

A pale but persevering sun did nothing to lift her spirits and, despite the Kumatsu clawing out a corner garden, very little else was moving. Vallender would be here doing a progress check next week and Kingfisher Rise was looking dire. She negotiated a half-finished kerb, then walked over to plot 2. It looked like the last one to have been started, when in fact it had been the first. The eight-inch foundation mix poured almost a month before was still wet and leached into her shoes. Bewildered, she looked around for a handhold. There was nothing except a pen of cavity-wall breeze blocks, barely begun. They moved and toppled at a touch, their mortar dribbling down to the ground, while next door, in stark contrast, the windows were already in.

Abbie tried to edge forwards, all her muscles straining, but her feet were suddenly held fast.

'Trouble's your middle name, innit?' The fork-lift driver, John Wilkes, had to lift her out of her shoes and on to dry land. 'This lot should be bloody cordoned off till the inspector's been. Can't do nothing with it . . .'

Abbie regarded with dismay her Next creations, stranded like some artwork, while her tights ripped further with every step.

'Damn.'

'I'll second that.' He cupped his hands round a cigarette while lighting it and then let the smoke drift away. 'This is one helluva weird set-up, I tell you. We've tried extra reinforcing, resin and fibreglass, you name it . . .'

'I've got someone who really wants that plot, would you credit it?' said Abbie as she locked up the office.

'Must be a retard.'

That's what she'd like me to believe.

She checked her watch: twelve-thirty. There was still time to kill two worrying birds with one stone. First, to find out if Rosie or any of the Gang were at the cottage, which she still technically rented, and then on to Clenchtoft Farm, where, according to the newsagent, Lilith Leakes was sure to be at home.

Abbie found some old slip-ons in the boot of her car.

'Oh, by the way. Don't say anything, if that's OK.'

'No skin off my nose.' John Wilkes ground his dimp underfoot.

The Polo nudged fifty along Herringtoft Track until the road became unsafe. Abbie parked alongside the trawler *Scheveningen Princess*, where Six Mile Bank reared up to the sky, its outline softened by weeds. The westerly view was perfect.

This time Goosefoot Cottage was in sharp focus, its windows darkly awake, willing her to look at it. But she turned away, ignoring the footpath that crossed the beet field to the top of Smithy Lane. There was no sign of the tractor now, no sign of anything, and, trapped in a rash of bramble with only four more shots left, she was returning the camera to its case when suddenly she heard the rustling of vegetation first and someone's rasping breath.

Abbie crouched down, her heart pumping.

'Oi! What ya doin' of?' came the voice from above. It wasn't Quinn, thank God, or anyone else she knew. She could already feel the wet leaves seeping through her skirt. 'Old Lilith Leakes can see ya. No use pretending.'

So this was the witch. Abbie took a deep breath and, not knowing what to expect, stood up to face her. 'I'm a photographer. May I?'

Her Polaroid fixed the woman's fleshless bones for ever and Lilith Leakes stared back like a rabbit in headlights as the grim pucker of toothless mouth slid into view on the damp prints.

'Thanks.' Abbie smiled. 'That's great. I honestly didn't mean to scare you.'

'Nothing scares me no more and tha's the truth of it.'

'Oh?'

Abbie brushed herself down, then to her surprise saw in the distance someone hanging out of the cottage window. She took another shot, then hid it quickly with the rest.

'And who might ya be?' the old woman asked, squinting disconcertingly.

'Abbie Parker. I've got a show coming up in the autumn. *Fenland Secrets* it's called.' The falsehood had come easily, but she knew the stranger wasn't convinced.

'Too many o' those round here, I can tell ya.'

As the crone lifted up her carrier bag in front of her, the stench of death snaked out. Abbie stepped back, covering her nose.

'Ugh! That smells disgusting.'

'Ah, but at least it's mine, what no one can take from me.'

As her practised fingers parted the polythene, the stink intensified. Just one glance at the contents was enough to make Abbie's stomach heave. Entrails and bird skulls jostled together as the bag moved in the old woman's grip, its sides bulging like normal shopping.

Lilith Leakes took her arm. 'Not pretty, I know, but they tell me things. Things ya'll never read about in books . . .'

Abbie heaved again and turned away – in time to see another child at Goosefoot scrambling up from the lean-to. She managed to use her last shot.

'Ya takin' a picture o' tha' cottage?' The ragged profile looked round.

'It's an interesting example of Fenland domestic architecture, that's why.' Abbie put the camera back in its case. 'Tell me,' she ventured, 'is that the only place called Goosefoot round here?'

Lilith Leakes snorted. 'If there was another, then we'd have hell twice over.'

'What do you mean?' Abbie's skin suddenly felt cold.

'Home of the Devil's Mouth, tha's what.'

The Devil's Mouth?

Abbie shivered and plunged her hands deep into her pockets. It was as if that same heavy shadow had suddenly brushed against her soul. Then she noticed those burrowed eyes following her every move.

'Funny, but ya don't look like no photographer. Not

to me anyways.' The old head, cocked sideways, had sensed something was wrong with her acquaintance.

'What then?' Abbie challenged.

'I can't rightly say, 'cept I see a building. A bank p'rhaps? An office o' some sort?' Her fingers stroked the jacket and Abbie recoiled. 'But that's not where ya want to be, is it?'

'I'm doing all right.'

'Ya mother wouldn't agree.'

Abbie started.

'I see grief and disappointment. It lies just behind.'

'I'm fine. I'm fine . . .' But water came to her eyes and for a moment seemed to blur out her very life.

'Not true, young lady.' She looked down at Abbie's damaged tights, the patches of exposed flesh above the shoe line. 'Ya're already in trouble. My friend here says ya must be careful and only give o' ya' sen to what ya know. Here, feel this.'

Abbie suddenly felt something against her hand. Damp feathers, meat loose against the bone. She screamed, but the old woman held her fast in a clutch of putrefaction.

'Look.'

'I can't!'

'Ya must!'

Warm on cold. A beak smooth as ivory. She guided Abbie's finger like a lover to the emptiness that had once harboured the sea and the sky. The gull's eye, picked clean, met hers.

'Make a wish.'

She tried to pull back.

'Ya mother says.'

'Leave her alone. She's dead!'

'Now!'

And Abbie's grief and battered dreams flowed like the neap tide that heaps and spreads itself, flooding and drowning the waiting land.

'Tha's better.' Lilith Leakes smiled in a black line as the cadaver rejoined the others. 'But tha's not the end of it. There's the history.'

'My history?' Abbie wiped her eyes with her cuff.

'No, Black Fen. The worst of all.' She scooped her grey-grass hair back into a rough knot, changing her face into little more than a skull. 'Ya got a few moments?'

Out of habit, Abbie checked her watch.

'I'm late already.'

'Ya need to know, but better make it soon. Afore I'm taken off in a bag.'

The urgency took Abbie aback. This was all too fast and unexpected from someone who was still a total stranger, and who'd already given her a fright. Yet there was information she needed, which obviously this old crone could provide . . .

'Well then?' Lilith Leakes persisted.

'What about Wednesday?'

'Suit ya'sen.' The hermit wrapped her filthy coat around her and gathered up her salvage. 'Evenings is best mind. I'm settled in by then. Ya know where I live?'

'Yes. Just past the Whiplash. Mrs Clapman told me.'

Lilith Leakes gave a dismissive shrug. 'Never 'eard of her. Still, I don't doubt some folks round here know more about me than I do mesen. Now, I do find tha' diverting.'

Abbie was aware of the seconds eroding further into the afternoon, but she still had questions to ask.

'Do you know a little girl called Rosie Quinn by any chance?'

The other woman stopped and stared so hard that Abbie had to look away.

'Please, it's very important.'

'I do and I don't.' She finally closed up the bag. 'Why ya asking?'

'She needs help.'

'My need's greater than hers.'

'But you gave her some old dolls. Why?'

The old woman sucked in her cheeks and spat out a bolus of phlegm. 'I'll tell ya when I sees ya next. And the rest. I'm weary now.'

Abbie took a calculated risk. 'Will that include Martha Robinson?'

The old woman jabbed a blood-smeared finger at her sleeve. 'I never talk o' the Devil away from my hearth, nor should ya, if ya'n got a whit o' sense.'

Then Lilith Leakes, spinster of the parish and last in the line of land reclaimers, walked away, bent low against the clearing sky, while her new acquaintance watched till she'd disappeared.

Pulling her suit jacket tight about her, Abbie wondered if the faint sound coming in from the sea was scavenging birds or the beginnings of that same terrible laughter.

Strangely emboldened by the hermit's words, she reached the forest of nettle and dock that bedded the north wall of Goosefoot Cottage and smothered the derelict barn once used for rearing geese. A trampled path led to the lean-to, which must have been the original earth closet.

Forbiddingly dark and overgrown, she'd never investigated it, and now wasn't the moment.

Abbie looked up. The sash window she'd photographed was shut. She still had a key, but not much time. She let herself in, praying with every breath that if Martha Robinson was connected to the place she wouldn't show herself.

It all seemed the same inside except for two Coke cans that lay on the table among a scattering of cigarette butts. However, something was happening overhead.

Her heart pounding, Abbie listened to the bed creaking on the boards, then crept upstairs, holding her breath. She pressed her face close to the bedroom door, whose ill-fitting panels gave her a narrow view. Her mouth fell open.

These weren't dolls, but children. Boys on top, with bare buttocks rocking in expert rhythm. In a split second she recognized them, the nearest pair being Emma Mason and Charlie Hunter, whispering and giggling, totally absorbed in their own sordid little world.

When Abbie finally reached the development, one of the brickies was waiting by the Show Home door. Small and wiry, his face had weathered into a mesh of lines like the marsh at World's End, he looked troubled.

'Can you spare a mo?'

'Sure, Greg.' Abbie went through to the kitchen and scrubbed off Lilith Leakes's filth. 'Sit down.'

'You see, it's like this.' He began clicking his finger joints. 'Nothing's ever gone right on that plot 2.'

'Go on.' She felt her stomach tighten.

'I've 'ad to work from the outside all the time, 'cos without the pre-casts in place, I can't put no weight on nothing, and there's no way the bloody stuff's setting. Looks like I'm two sarnies short of a bleedin' picnic . . .'

'That's not true.' Abbie tried to console him, all the time remembering her shoes.

'Anyways, I got three kids, bit of a mortgage, so I can't risk it. That house is something else, I'm telling you.'

'What about your mate Grant? What does he think?'

'Just told me to keep me 'ead down, like. But I can't.' Finally he took a deep breath, avoiding her eyes. ''E said 'e'd seen someone. A woman.'

Abbie picked up on his fear and felt again that murderous weight on her shoulders.

'What was she like?'

'Sort of pale, yellowy. Black clothes. She 'ad a kid with 'er. Carrying it, she was.'

'Girl or boy?'

'Boy, I think.'

O Jesus.

'Where was this exactly?'

'Inside the site of the 'ouse. On the concrete, walking round and round . . . No footprints neither.'

'Can you see if Grant's still there? It's urgent.' Her heart was thumping.

'I'll try.' The brickie ran out like a lurcher, treading air. Two minutes later and out of breath, he was back. 'Miss Parker?'

Abbie was already locking the door.

''Fraid 'e's done a runner. 'Parently 'e'd 'ad enough an' buggered off after lunch.'

December 1843

Abigail, Abigail, lady's maid. But I am the one serving her, *not the other way round like it should be. She's fatter than Mary was. Fatter than me in fact, with Uncle Kirton's red hair. Mercifully for her she just missed my birthday by a week, but that won't count for much. Not in my book at least.*

Nine

THE NEWCOMERS' SERVICE at St Mary Magdalene came and went, with more floral arrangements in place than people in pews, despite Quinn's apparent monopoly of the local press and notices on every lamp-post. He'd been as diligent as his faithful church dresser, Miss Lawson, to whom he was no less than a manifestation of the Divine. Her life was his, with these flowers being her proudest gift. She allowed no one else such a privilege.

So on this Sunday, as every other, seasonal blooms had been pushed and primped into every orifice of stone, marble and silver: the chubby angels' fists, the mouths of babes and sucklings . . . And gazing beyond this cornucopia, the Reverend Peter Quinn searched his congregation for any sign of the Holtbury girl who was now resident at the St George's Sails Hotel. And so preoccupied was he by her absence that the first four bars of 'O Happy Band of Pilgrims' started without him.

Abbie Parker, however, had other things on her mind. Not least that Simon Cresswell still hadn't replied to her last letter, still withheld his promises and carefully crossed kisses, things she needed now more than ever. Outside her bedroom window, three coal barges swayed end to end on the incoming tide. From somewhere nearby, a guard dog barked. She picked up her Barbour and went outside, where the sun found her face and seemed to gloat at her misery. As a further shield, she pulled up the collar.

She was now high up on Morpeth Bank, faced with the moribund salt marshes and the brackish sea sliding inland.

No wonder they call it World's End down there. Bloody well feels like it. She sensed again that utter loneliness. But maybe after all this was better than stewing in her room worrying too much, or going to visit her father. He'd changed into someone she barely knew. Someone for whom even routine was an adventure.

She ducked as a pair of black-headed gulls cruised close above then dived below the bank for garbage. She screwed up her eyes to follow them back into the sun, as a yacht sailed past against the tide. She listened as silt became silver water in the gulleys beyond the whispering grass, and her burdens actually seemed to lift as she followed the high track along before slithering down to the shelter of the bank – and to what Lilith Leakes had rejected.

Small bones, bubblewrap spawn and a faded playing card: the ace of spades.

'Could be lucky for some,' she thought, slipping it into her pocket. Then she saw what lay half buried in the mud.

Her Nikes sank to their tongues as she approached. There were Rosie's little wellingtons. She'd know them anywhere. Pink against the brown, one had keeled over, almost submerged now, but in the covering tide there was no trace of any footprints.

Abbie's stride lengthened. She seemed to be lifted up, as though weightless, then, like the picking snipes, she landed with nothing to grasp. The gulley widened beneath her, greedy for life. Any life.

'Help!' The wellingtons were gradually disappearing as the slough possessed her ankles, then her knees. The Barbour was weighing her down, welding her to the mud. Abbie screamed again, trying to find more solid ground, and at last began to move inch by inch towards a dune of dry grass.

She lay there panting, filling her lungs with warm fetid air, while half a mile away, on the highest part of the bank, the watcher lowered his binoculars and headed back to Black Fen.

Abbie phoned for help as soon as she reached Smithy Lane, keeping the booth door open with her foot as drying slabs of mud fell to the floor. She'd even found a lump of the stuff lodged in her ear.

After the third rejection of her coins, she gave up trying to contact Snutterwick police, swore at Holtbury's for still not having sent her mobile and dialled 999. Now anyone from anywhere would do. She looked over to the church and could see the gargoyle high up, its leering jaws silhouetted against the sky. She shook more scales of mud off her sleeves, then crossed the road to scour the rectory, a monolith of nineteenth-century brick veiled by trees.

Its narrow western wall reared up, fleshed out by dull green ivy which had crept round and almost covered the few windows at the front. There were no homely aerials or satellite dishes as on its neighbours in Smithy Lane. Just two crows on the chimney cowl and slates strewn below in disarray.

He's hardly into DIY, and what a miserable place to bring a child up, she thought, giving the old bell a hefty push. Its tired ring quickly petered out, so she pushed again. There was no response. She stood back to check all the windows, and suddenly one in particular caught her attention. It was a solitary skylight set low in the roof and, like an eye of the dead, it stared blankly at the sky.

Is that the Bat Room? she wondered, willing Rosie to appear. She wanted to investigate further, but she recoiled, the prospect of meeting Quinn again overruling all her other instincts. On this occasion altruism had become the feeble sibling of dread.

I can't. Sorry, Rosie, try and understand . . .

Abbie's eyes returned to the same window, where she could only imagine Rosie's face and her world of fear. The memory of that innocent child who'd so clung to her hand suddenly rendered her helpless and fresh tears filled her eyes.

Detective Inspector Mowbray of Snutterwick CID blocked out the early afternoon sun. He introduced WPC O'Halloran, and Sergeant Bryant, whose premature grey hair cancelled out what youthful looks still remained.

'You partial to mud baths then?' Mowbray joked as he led the way back towards the Rectory.

'You've got to try and find her!' Abbie called out, indicating the rectory. 'She's either in there or . . .' The words welled up in her throat. 'Or she's in trouble out on the marsh . . .'

'We'll give the house a go first. Sit in the car if you like. Might be needing you in a minute.'

'I'll stay here.' Her mascara had dried to dull stains down each cheek, tightening the skin. She got out a

muddied tissue and spat on it, until Julia O'Halloran
offered her a handkerchief and smiled in sympathy.

Mowbray came over, leaves from the rectory garden
stuck to his shoulders. 'No joy. All quiet, but info at the
church says the Reverend's got a Tiny Tots Service at
four o'clock. We could ask him then.'

'We can't wait that long. Two hours is two hours too
many.' Abbie looked tense.

Mowbray brushed himself off. 'Is Mrs Quinn usually
around on Sundays?' he asked.

'I'm not sure. There's no car and she's disabled,' said
WPC O'Halloran.

'Curiouser and curiouser. Right, let's go.' The DI
checked his watch. 'We'll just about beat the tide at this
rate.'

A straggle of onlookers had already gathered on the
corner by the council houses as the Sierra sped down
Walsoken Road, past the flags and the hotel and on to
Herringtoft. Then the marsh came into view.

'Down there!' She pointed, and when the car could
go no further, they got out and ran towards the encroaching sea, which was already encircling the furthest reedy
islets, licking the lines of junk. 'Now to the right!' Abbie
shouted, aware of a bird skull lying on the mud before
the water claimed it. 'That's where the wellingtons were.'

Too late. The current was now unstoppable.

'Leave it!' Mowbray bellowed. He'd seen a few corpses
float in before now after a day in the North Sea – not a
sight for the squeamish.

'Bloody graveyard!' In his haste to escape, Sergeant
Bryant left his shoes behind and saw them slide out of
sight.

Abbie surveyed the scene, while far away a ship's siren sounded.

'There's not a cat in hell's chance,' Bryant said bleakly.

WPC O'Halloran came panting up the slope as the big man wiped his brow. 'We'll just have to hope the kiddie's worked her way round to safety. If she's a light little thing, there's every chance . . .'

'She is,' Abbie said, and started a prayer, whispering Rosie's name over and over as though she might hear, her eyes moving from one restless eddy to the next. All the while the sea rendered everything the same as itself with no telling where people had been.

'We'll drop you off, then give Killjoy Cottage a knock and see if that artist chap Byers has seen anything,' Mowbray said.

He shook mud off his boots, then called HQ. No press enquiries yet and nothing so far to report. Then he assured Abbie he'd order a helicopter from Lippitt's Hill.

They dropped her off outside the hotel and, after she'd watched the Sierra disappear, she cleaned the mud from the front of the ace of spades, wondering why that miserably named cottage should be next on their agenda.

Inside the St George's Sails, Sheila Livingstone was cleaning the bar. A mix of Flash and air freshener hung in the empty air.

'What on earth . . .?'

For once Abbie wanted to hurry by. 'Not earth – marsh. Bloody place.'

'Look, I'm not even going to ask, but you go and get a decent bath. I'll put your clothes in the machine. Oh, and by the way,' the hotelier said, wringing out her cloth and starting on a pile of beer mats, 'you had a call. Really bad line though. It was from Germany.'

'Germany?' Abbie's heart quickened.

'Rheindahlen, I think that's what they said.'

They? Why not Simon himself? What was going on?

'Anything else?'

Abbie watched as Sheila moved on to the ashtrays, scooping out the debris with her finger.

'They said they'll try again tomorrow.'

'How kind.'

Sheila came over, but Abbie moved on up the stairs. 'Don't go getting upset. It'll be all right. You'll see.'

'No, it won't. I don't deserve anything decent.'

Sheila stared after her and Abbie turned to see her still waiting, as if she had something to say.

'Yes? What is it?'

'Nothing much. It's just that I've remembered who delivered that letter of yours . . . Been on my mind a while, that's all.'

Abbie gripped the banister, her breath on hold. 'Go on.'

'That nutty Lawson woman from the school – I'm sure of it. There was some do at the church when I'd just moved in . . . Well, anyhow, she was fussing and farting about with the precious flowers all the time.'

'So she knows Quinn well?' Abbie's heart was moving faster.

'Oh yes.' Sheila stepped back and went over to the bar. 'I'm surprised they let her loose in front of kids. No joking, someone really ought to give her a freebie makeover.' She was enjoying herself. 'God knows what happens to those eyebrows when it rains.'

Abbie made a poor attempt at a smile, but inside she was churning. Simon's lack of communication, the death threat and everything else were all mixed in a hideous incomprehensible mess.

We're seven upstairs now with two more yellowbellies from Fitting Fen and paying threepence a day which Moeder says keeps broth in the pot. They have horse hair to lie on while we have straw. My bed had rotted you see, being next to the pine end wall. While the lady's maid sucks on my buttons I dream of the rooms at Rievely where we collected a pie at Christmas. There were things the colour of Heaven from places just as far away. And ceilings so high we could stand without stooping. Maybe if I don't get to live there in this life I will in the next . . .

Ten

WHILE THE MONDAY bells of the retreat chimed a sonorous four o'clock for optional prayers over Crowland Fen and three elderly clergymen raked the grass at the far end of the lawn, the childless couple began their afternoon tea.

They sat on the semicircular patio that abutted the lounge of Haletoft House, but because of the shaded northerly aspect the once yellow brick under their feet was now a carpet of moss and algae.

Their robes of renewal were of the same green, several sizes too large and trailing over their hands.

'I'll be mother,' Peter Quinn announced, and poured from the pewter teapot before passing the full cup to his wife. She stared at the liquid spinning inside, reflecting the ancient elm that bowed and scraped overhead in the breeze.

'Be what you like. I don't care any more.' And for the first time in ten years of marriage she sounded as though she didn't.

'The trouble with you, Helen,' he said, keeping his voice low having made sure no one was in earshot, 'you expect me to keep up with all your little games and trickeries, and I confess I cannot.'

She swung her wheelchair round to face him, cut-glass eyes sharp in the pale oval of her face.

'What trickeries? What the fuck can I do, trapped in this bloody thing?'

He sipped his tea, letting his top lip linger on the rim to compose himself.

'But we know exactly why you're in there, don't we? And, as you know, the Good Lord sees everything.'

There was no way she could retaliate to his cruelty except by leaving her confirmation Pentateuch among the retreat's collection, in the hope someone some day might see what she'd written inside the front cover. The former point-to-point rider then stared down at her knees, which had once steered a ton of horseflesh round Levenham Fen every first Saturday of every winter month. Until she'd met *him*, the agrarian cleric. Until the fall. Now the joints looked pathetic, poking through the robe like little more than pebbles. Her thighs too lay wasted to bone. She ran both hands up and down, as though this might somehow energize them.

'Gehenna,' she said suddenly.

'Oh, stop overreacting, wife, for goodness' sake. Why has everything got to be such high drama?' Quinn's mouth had shrunk to an irritated line.

'That's all I've got left now, isn't it?' she wailed at his indifference, but he knew this prologue off by heart and, like the rest of his ministry, it was wearisome and irrelevant – an unnecessary burden. He took a forbidden watch from his pocket, glanced at it and swallowed his tea.

Suddenly a figure appeared scuttling towards them from behind the thatch of climbing roses. Brother Robert, rotund and worldly in off-white, his identification photograph dangling from his chest.

'Ah, forgive me, Reverend.' He glanced at Helen Quinn, then back at the house. 'You have a visitor.' It seemed more an accusation than information. 'Shall I ask him to leave or will you see him?'

Quinn was caught off guard. The contact was too early, too greedy. Nought out of ten for good manners, my friend. He pushed his empty cup and saucer away.

'I'm sorry you've been troubled,' he fawned. 'Yes, I'll see him.'

'Very well, he's in Visitor Reception.' The little administrator waddled off.

'I'll be along there now, thank you.'

'Who is it?' His wife searched his repulsive face for clues.

'God alone knows.' Quinn scraped back his chair. 'But I've a hunch it's either old Jeremiah for his session on the catechism or Marcus Wordlip for the Letters to the Corinthians.'

The lie was poor and he knew it. He'd not given private study for years. Besides, the whole point of clergy and their wives retreating to Haletoft was to be distanced and zealously protected from parish cares until equilibrium was restored.

He got up and leaned over her. The tea had made no difference to his breath.

'May I suggest, Mrs Quinn, that you go and wait in the bedroom?'

Every syllable, every nuance of his body language, spelt out *Get lost*. She watched as he strode away with a devilish purpose she could only guess at, and as she forced the wheels back towards the house, to finally leave her statement of guilt on the shelf, she felt her punishment was only just beginning.

The one shadeless bulb in Visitor Reception cast its unforgiving light on the caller, showing every crevice of his skin, every hair on his newly greased head. Like all visitors, he'd had the customary grilling and checking, and now looked the worse for wear.

'Can we talk somewhere else?' He kept looking round and Quinn picked up on this hesitancy with a frown.

'You're not going to let me down, I hope?' The Reverend opened the door and indicated the lounge down the corridor.

'No fear.'

But as he walked along behind the tall green figure, Philip Byers was greatly tempted to do a runner: either that or shit his pants before they got there. So this was the position they called 'between the Devil and the deep blue sea'. The cleric and the yardie to whom he still owed eight grand, and the rest. Byers felt sweat travel down between his shoulders.

The lounge was empty save for a cluster of vinyl chairs specially grouped for social interaction or the exchange of life histories.

'This'll do.' Quinn checked his wife had done his bidding, then chose the darkest corner, away from the French windows. He sat down opposite Byers and rolled back his sleeves to expose his white hands.

'Reverend Quinn, sir . . .' the artist began, unsure of the correct form of address, as he pulled out a piece of pocket-worn paper covered with jottings from a recent telephone call with him. 'I don't have to do this, you know. I haven't signed anything.'

Quinn edged forwards enough for a long hard finger to bore into the other's leg. 'I told you to burn that. Give it to me.'

Byers passed the note over, whereupon Quinn rolled it into a tight ball and put it in his mouth. 'Mr Byers,' he continued, having worked his Adam's apple up and down to try and swallow it, 'I think you labour under a misapprehension. This is strictly a business matter, not an affair of the heart. You have no choice.'

The painter of birds looked ill, and under his newly pressed clothes his whole frame trembled. OK, so he needed money to pay off Nelson Palmer, but not that much. Not enough to kill two people for it.

'I can't.'

Quinn's eyes hardened into his. His dead skin looked shocking close up.

'But you can and you will, or you'll find yourself fattening the fish in the Deeps of Lethe.'

Mention of that bottomless void off Three Fingers Beach sent a rush of terror through Byers, who was now hunting for his cigarettes.

'Not in here if you don't mind,' admonished Quinn. 'The less atttention we draw to ourselves the better, wouldn't you agree? Now –' he shuffled his chair closer, so that their legs were almost touching – 'you have a boat, correct?'

Byers nodded, feeling his bowels churn.

'And how far would you say it could travel without oars before –' he paused to choose the right words – 'going down?'

The other man worked his fingers like kindling wood,

cracking and splintering, while he felt the net closing in on the life he'd always dreamed of. A life of untroubled solitude.

'Depends on the tide. Six miles, give or take . . .'

'No give or take, I want *exactly*.'

'Seven, then. Heading north-east, but going out, mind.'

'Ah, as far as Lethe Island?' Quinn drew a map in the air.

'Yes.'

'Problem is, they'd be spotted. Think again.' Quinn leaned back, never for one moment letting his co-conspirator off his skewering gaze.

'Leave it to me.' Byers was desperate to get away, to blind Quinn with a science he barely knew himself. 'Main thing is, once I've got them nice and safe I can pick and choose. Sometimes, with a force five or more, the tide alters out towards Humber – kind of fans away from the Wenn and becomes a bit tricky.'

'Better and better.' Quinn smiled. 'And we make it sooner rather than later, don't we?'

'Course.'

'But don't hang on to them for more than half an hour or so. Killjoy's hardly up the Limpopo. And, by the way, watch out for rubbernecks.'

Byers stared at this man of God who could make even a feeble joke about the job in hand, and realized, with another turn of his insides, what he was up against.

'You'll need to bore some holes first,' Quinn said.

'That'll mean two hours maximum in the water.'

'Excellent.'

Byers fell silent. He knew he'd been a bloody fool ever to consider the proposal, but when Quinn had first phoned he was only ten minutes off the smack and hadn't been thinking straight. Now he was paying for it.

He got up, looking for the Gents, but Quinn restrained him.

'I'll decide when we're finished, Mr Byers, if you don't mind. Besides, there's just another small matter.' His eyes swivelled to the door and back. His voice was tense and low. 'The car? That is, if she decides to use it.'

'I've thought about that.'

'Good. Make it untraceable.'

'It will be.'

Quinn buried an arm in his robe pocket and withdrew a wallet held by a child's pony-tail scrunchie. He counted out a wad of tenners and pressed them into Byers's hand. 'Just in time for your next shot, eh?' His thin lips moved into a cold curve. 'The rest when it's done.'

'That's not fair.'

Quinn stood up, letting his hand penetrate deep to Byers's arm bone. 'You're in no position to argue. I'm depending on you, *mon ami*. Understood?'

The artist mimed a yes and, as soon as he was free, made for the door.

'One last detail, Byers.' Quinn caught up with him. 'When it's all tickety-boo, you phone me here. Remember, no one but you and my wife knows my whereabouts.'

'What about this lot? S'pose they start squealing.'

Quinn looked at him with disdain. 'These good people live by a different code. They've sworn on oath never to divulge who seeks their quietude here. To them, their temporary residents are sacrosanct and I'm afraid I had to lie about you.' He selected an Old Testament from the shelf. 'See no evil, hear no evil and the rest.' He waved it at Byers. 'As far as they're concerned, you're involved in Apocryphal research – books the Jews didn't think were genuine. Don't forget that.'

Byers grunted, then disappeared, passing Brother Robert and Brother Martin, who looked up from their Christian crossword.

He ran down the drive and, under the gaze of a curious Helen Quinn sitting by an upstairs window, crouched in the bushes to quickly and copiously relieve himself.

There are two mounds by the goose barn now and Moeder sits there plucking and crying when the sun allows. For every thirty she prepares, we get a half leg for the stew, but most of that is such thick yellow grease it's not enough. I have stopped going to Ma Tully's now as Moeder needs the extra wages, especially since Annie and Lazarus came out of her wound last May Day. One after the other like piglets and her holding on to me all pop-eyed like a sow . . .

Eleven

THE NEXT DAY at nine in the morning, in the Show
Home with both her panic button and her mobile
safely arrived, Abbie contacted Black Fen Primary School
to ask if Rosie had turned up at all but when the secretary
suggested she should speak to Miss Lawson, the deputy,
Abbie defiantly said no.

Then, angry because no one had phoned back yesterday as promised, she dialled Simon's unit at the Rheindahlen Barracks. The line was still poor and the answerphone
made her queries impossible, but she did leave her name
and the hotel number again. That was the best she could
do, apart from asking his parents for news, which would
have to be the absolute last resort. Cresswell Senior, in
particular, had never approved of his bright son taking up
with someone in the housing trade. It would have been
different if she'd gone for medicine or the Bar, but
Holtbury's – 'tat and more tat' – was hard for him to take.
Even his dental nurse wife and Simon's brother Matthew,
slumming it in Swansea, had more cred. No. She wouldn't
be contacting *them*, however desperate she felt.

So why that call from Germany? Maybe after the
Rambouillet talks his unit was out on secret manoeuvres.
Maybe there was an emergency somewhere, although
there'd been nothing on the news. Or was she now

merely an embarrassment to him? Abbie reorganized
the Holtbury files on heating and lighting, then tried
the Europe Rapid Reaction Corps' headquarters again,
where finally someone answered. Someone in a hurry.
A woman.

'I have passed your message on, but we won't be able
to call you back again. The 1 Signals Brigade is on alert.
That's all I can say now.'

Abbie pressed the receiver closer to her ear. 'Where is
he now? Why can't I speak to him?' she almost shouted.

'It's a bit delicate at the moment . . .' The woman's
excuses began to fade.

'Hello?' Abbie stared at the phone. 'Hello?'

But half of Europe lay between and if it weren't for
his photo in her wallet he'd be little more than a fudge
of memory to her beyond land and water.

Peering from beneath the edge of the Austrian blinds,
she could see that the view outside had changed. Great
breeze-block ziggurats lay alongside plot 2 and a mixer
was droning continuously. Three more men had now
joined Greg Pitt's team. At least something was going
right in this shitty world. Now it was time to see if
Mowbray had done what he promised and checked out
Killjoy Cottage.

Abbie locked up the Show Home and left the site
without drawing attention to herself, praying that Vallender wouldn't be phoning up for his progress check. Her
Polo crossed the Wenn by Midden Bridge and began
ploughing along Sedge Dyke towards Roman Road.
Farms and plots ended behind the continuation of Morpeth Bank – the bleaker end, with no trees, nothing
except a few spotted cows and the stub of a deserted
lighthouse. Boarded up and mildewed, its warning light

had been dead for thirty years, and a trail of late wilted
daffodils led to the door.

The moment she got out, the wind teased her hair
into a mad shadow. As she knocked at the lighthouse
door it whipped across her mouth while she shouted
Rosie's name. There was nothing to peer through. Salt
had permeated everywhere: the rendering, the rotting
sills, her lips. Salt and silence.

Abbie headed back to the car. When it came to Rosie,
there was something about being away from the gloomy
rectory that restored her courage and dispelled the shame
she'd felt there for not doing more.

The car rumbled along until the track behind the
lighthouse dwindled to mud, carved into deep ruts by
dog walkers' Jeeps. She parked up on the driest ridge she
could find and stuffed her camera in her pocket.

Stones coarsened under her feet and soft weeds bil-
lowed from either side. A short cut over the Bleakwold
end brought the shack into view, and a curl of smoke
from the only chimney moved on the breeze, bringing
smells of a recent fish catch.

Someone's snug, Abbie thought.

She drew closer and saw how the gravelly plot was
overgrown with sea rocket and sand spurrey, how curtains
at the windows had been crudely drawn shut. There were
no telephone cables, she noticed, but if this had been
designated an area of Outstanding Natural Beauty they
were probably underground.

Abbie knocked and looked around. A small tug was
heading noiselessly towards the river mouth, gulls following, while a rowing boat bobbed in its mooring below a
patch of land at the side. She heard music being turned

down and a man's voice as though talking to a dog. The door inched open.

'Yes. What is it?'

'Sorry to trouble you, Mr Byers,' Abbie began sweetly, 'because I know the police may well have been already—'

'The police?' The man tried to shut her out.

'Don't, please. There's obviously been some mistake. I just want to ask you something. It's urgent.'

He came out into the daylight, his face pockmarked by a different sun, with nicotine yellowing his hair. Abbie sniffed. His smell was like Lilith Leakes's and she noticed that his pupils were dilated. She was looking at a smack-head.

'Have you seen a little girl about? She's only seven . . . blonde, big fringe, like so.' Abbie drew an imaginary line below her eyebrows.

'You her mother?' Byers asked.

She was thrown for a moment. 'No. But I do care about her.'

'Your name?' The artist was getting nervous.

'Abbie Parker.' There was no point in lying about that any more.

The owner of Killjoy Cottage gulped inwardly. So here she was, the word made flesh, and such a pretty thing too, just like the other one. But he pulled himself together, then shook his head.

Abbie pointed over to Three Fingers Beach, where ochres and browns merged with the sea. 'It's possible she was running away from home.'

'Can't say I've noticed anything round here. I work indoors mostly.' He suddenly turned to face her. An irregular portcullis of teeth caught the sun. 'OK, so what's this kid's name then?' Byers pulled out a Rizla from its packet, filled it dextrously with tobacco and licked down the edge.

Abbie took a deep breath and decided to trust him. 'Rosie. Rosie Quinn.' The silence stirred with distant sounds. The North Sea on the move, inland. 'She's a pupil at Black Fen Primary School.'

'Oh, I remember her now.' Byers put all his effort into the performance. 'I gave a talk there last Christmas, showed the kids my work. You know the sort of thing, birds etc. Then they had to draw some themselves.' He lit the roll-up and smoke trailed into his hair.

'What were hers like?'

'Very strange, I'd say. Not birds at all.'

There wasn't time to ask more. All Abbie could think of was the killing tide, and a little girl trying to survive . . .

'You've got to help me,' she begged.

His eyes switched to the horizon. 'Come to think of it, I did see some kids.' He sucked the end of his roll-up into a glow. 'Just before the tide came in. Last week some time . . .'

'When?' Abbie demanded.

'Can't really say. To me one day's like the rest round here. They seemed to be playing though.' The artist found her intense gaze disturbing and, although he had always had a soft spot for a good-looker, she was making things difficult. He was losing his nerve, missing his chance . . .

'Did you see anyone being chased?' Abbie touched his arm.

'They were running about. You know how kids are on a beach.'

'Go on.'

'I remember thinking, Be careful, but I've got a show coming up in June and half what's in the bloody catalogue hasn't been painted yet.'

'Now look, Mr Byers,' Abbie said, her Show Home voice taking over, 'you're an artist. Were these children boys or girls, or both?'

'Girls, I'd say, but you try looking from here.' Hoping to sound normal, not flustered by his failure.

'You see, she had pink wellingtons, bright, fluorescent ones.'

Byers blew his smoke west as a cloud passed over. 'For fuck's sake,' he said suddenly, 'what d'you think I am? A bloody telescope?' He began to ease the door shut. That was her ration, like it or lump it. Next time he wouldn't be deflected. Next time he'd be ready.

She walked back to the car over the gravel, deep in thought. He was an accomplished liar all right, she could tell. And he was definitely on something. She'd been mad to trust him, but what else could she do? And as Killjoy Cottage grew small behind her against the sea, and the artist and his model resumed their work, she reached her car with increasing panic.

Lazarus is the runt of us all because his blood's the wrong colour and he falls over at the smallest thing. So even though he's had four winters he can only crawl to pick up the little stones I leave behind. Sometimes he sings to himself, 'Matthew, Mark and Luke and John', which Moeder taught to all of us. But one night the Devil's Mouth whispered to me that he'd bring everyone bad luck with those words — that God had made a terrible mistake with him when he and Annie shared Moeder's insides, and for this we would have to pay . . .

Twelve

As soon as she'd reopened the Show Home just after the mid-morning tea break, Abbie phoned Snutterwick police station to tell them her suspicions about Byers, but the desk sergeant said that Mowbray was off sick and O'Halloran was on a day's course at Hendon. She then tried Social Services, where a rude trainee said their Child Welfare team were in conference. Feeling empty and dispirited she doodled Rosie's face on the site plan, then rang the school again. The answerphone took most of her rushed and desperate enquiry, but cut her off before she'd finished.

'Damn.' Abbie got up and slung her jacket over her shoulder. So far there'd been no calls and no visitors to the site. She could sneak out to Amy Buckley at Canal Farm and be back in half an hour. Sod it, she had to talk to someone reliable and truthful, and she hoped Sheila's opinion of the farmer's wife was right. If Vallender were to ring, there was always the answerphone.

Abbie felt hungry the moment she stepped over the collie's sleeping body and into the farm kitchen, for unlike at St George's Sails something good was in the oven, and a batch of scones lay still warm on the table.

'He's no guard, I'm afraid.' Amy Buckley's country

face looked at the dog affectionately as she peeled her apron off over her shoulders and laid it on a chair. 'Not that we need one round here. Things are usually pretty quiet.' She opened the lounge door and immediately furniture polish and a sickly floral smell replaced the fragrance of baking. Mrs Buckley had obviously just applied air freshener. Abbie sneezed.

'Bless you.'

Abbie smiled. In the current climate, any blessing was welcome.

The room was dominated by heavy rustic furniture, part heirloom, part auction, and all of it kept in the immaculate order of the childless, with Royal Doulton and Worcester pieces crammed into a bay-fronted cabinet. Abbie noticed, among the figurines and gravy boats, three bisque porcelain angels hanging on fine threads, twisting slightly in the sealed air. She wanted to ask about their origins, but the two women were as yet strangers, unsure who would be first to plunge into the depths of chintz.

The carpet on which they stalled was thick-piled and covered in leaves and swirls, something unheard of in the Holtbury Prestige Homes range, where thin and plain had been laid in haste, already rucking up by the walls.

'So you're Abbie Parker.' Amy Buckley's curious but kindly eyes took everything in. 'I've heard a bit about you and that new development. Look, do sit down.' She finally pointed to an armchair.

Abbie sank below its antimacassar and matching arm sleeves, wondering what the woman meant. She could see the hedgeless fields stretch away towards Morpeth Bank. Without a wind, the black poplars stood firm as though guarding all its secrets.

'We've got a few teething problems just at the moment. Nothing that can't be sorted out,' Abbie volunteered.

'Well, God moves in mysterious ways,' the country-woman said with surprising feeling, and Abbie was tempted to tell her more. But not yet. One day, perhaps, when she'd sold a few more houses.

Amy Buckley picked up a gilt tray with ornamental handles. 'Would you like a cup of coffee? Or I do a mean hot chocolate, as Martin says.'

'Martin?'

'Yes, Martin Silver. He teaches at Black Fen. Still on probation, though.'

Abbie recalled the seabird tie, the sandals.

'I've only got a few minutes, thanks.'

The farmer's wife seemed disappointed, and Abbie realized from her lived-in clothes and cardigan buttoned tight over her breasts that here was someone who'd let herself go, who lived vicariously through whoever came her way, turning like a sunflower towards each encounter. And the young teacher was clearly the son she'd never had.

'Well, there'll be a next time I'm sure.'

Abbie leaned forward. 'Look, Mrs Buckley. I need to ask you some things and I'm not sure where to start.'

'About Martin, you mean?'

'No, about Lilith Leakes.'

The other woman stared, then frowned.

'May I ask why?'

'I'm supposed to be visiting her tomorrow evening. Apart from what she's going to tell me about Black Fen, I need to find out, for example, how did she come to know little Rosie Quinn so well?'

'Rosie? Oh, heavens.' Amy Buckley put the tray down again. 'I haven't the faintest idea.'

'It seems she's gone missing.'

'That's nothing new. She's always running off, that one. Always comes back too, so don't get alarmed.' She put a reassuring hand on Abbie's arm. 'I mean, if you lived in a place like that, with a couple of icebergs for parents, wouldn't you stay out all hours?' A mischievous gleam enlivened her face. 'I'm not saying it's right for a kiddie to be running around like that, but *everyone* knows her. She even comes here looking for bits of cake and the like.'

'There's no way she'd be at Clenchtoft, is there?' Abbie asked, trying to bring her back to the question. It was the first time she'd thought of that scenario and her stomach turned over.

'I doubt it, but what makes you say that?'

'Lilith Leakes gave her some strange old dolls.'

'Never.'

'She did. And told her never to change their names.'

Amy Buckley perched on the edge of her settee. She had whitened noticeably as Abbie spoke. 'Those dolls are *evil* and folks say that whoever possesses, or even touches, them, well, I don't know how to put this, but . . .' She stalled and Abbie's skin began to prickle, despite the warm room. 'We've all been around long enough to see what they've caused. I mean, there was Daniel Leakes's first wife, she lost her baby straight away.' Amy Buckley looked distressed for a moment. 'Then there's Miss Leakes herself.'

'Go on.'

'Folks thought she was expecting when she was well into her thirties, then all of a sudden it disappeared, so nobody was really sure. They're all dead anyhow,' she added, lowering her eyes.

You will all die . . .

Abbie saw the other woman's troubled eyes stray to the gap between the curtains.

'My God, that ties up with something Rosie said the other day.'

'Tell me.'

'That Lilith Leakes did have a baby and it was cursed.'

Amy Buckley got up and stood by the window, her face turned away from Abbie. In the silence that followed both women felt connected by more than fear. Amy Buckley turned round for their eyes to meet, as though this was her only lifeline in that whole haunted world, while the dog, who'd suddenly woken up, came to lie across his owner's feet.

'If you don't mind me saying so, Abbie, I don't think you should go to Clenchtoft. Are you listening?' Her voice had an urgency that took Abbie by surprise. 'And if you do come across the vicar's girl, make her promise not to see Miss Leakes again either, and to throw those dolls away. If you don't, *I* will.'

Abbie stared, disconcerted by the woman's unexpected vehemence.

'I've done that already, at the cottage.'

'Which cottage?' Amy Buckley's eyebrows almost met her hair.

'Goosefoot.'

Her listener fell silent, then, 'You've not been staying there, have you?'

'No, of course not.'

'Thank goodness for that.'

'I was looking for Rosie, that's all.'

That seemed to satisfy her, but not quite. '*You* didn't touch those dolls, did you?'

'Only for a minute. They were so foul I had to chuck them away.'

'Well, you'd better say your prayers, girl.'

'Oh, come on.'

'They were Martha Robinson's once.'

'So?' But that name brought back all the old terror, the racing heart.

'Her sister Annie had them in the end and gave them to Lilith Leakes before she died. I know, because when I was last over there, some long while back now, I remarked on them. They were the ugliest creatures I'd ever seen.'

'Mary, Abigail and Lazarus?' Immediately Abbie clapped a hand over her mouth, but it was too late. She felt the blood leave her face.

Amy Buckley suddenly started. 'Don't say those names, I'm telling you, Abbie. Not ever again, please.' She laid a finger on Abbie's lips. It smelt of cake mix.

'I'm sorry. I'm sorry.'

'It's just that I don't want any bit of her in *this* place. Not now I've got some peace here.'

Now? Here? What did she mean by that? Abbie's mind was in turmoil.

'I never talk of the Devil away from my hearth, and neither should you.' Amy Buckley pursed her lips with finality.

This was the second person who'd said the same. If Martha Robinson couldn't be mentioned *in* or *out* of a house, where could she be? And if, as Abbie now realized,

the contamination from her wretched life went so deep
that it affected people's souls, where did that leave Kingfisher Rise, and, worse, Abbie herself?

'Are you sure you wouldn't like some coffee now?'

'No, thanks, I've really got to go.'

Abbie stood up, her legs unsteady. The woman, too,
looked as if she had more than enough to cope with. The
light in her eyes had changed, and Abbie knew that
somewhere, somehow, the grim black shadow had now
also touched Canal Farm. She held Amy Buckley's hand,
which suddenly felt cold.

'Thanks for seeing me.'

The woman nodded, as if preoccupied.

'Now promise me one thing,' she said, opening the
door for the warm day to blow in. 'Leave it all alone. Say
yes, Abbie.'

'Yes.'

So I carried the runt down to World's End, and like a proper little piglet he liked the mud and the reeds tickling him underneath. But he laughed too much and I took fright lest the noise of it should reach the wrong ears. So I kept my boot on his back and he never rose again which is just as well. His twin sissen Annie's been sent to a family in Sleaford to stop her crying. She took my dolls without asking and I will never forgive her. Would you?

Thirteen

It was Wednesday 12 May. Still no Rosie and still no Quinns. Before going to work, Abbie stood outside the church in a light drizzle, studying the new scripted notice pinned to the door, regretfully informing the flock that all services had been cancelled until further notice. Also that the Diocesan Bishop had been informed and the family were now off for a well-earned break.

Bullshit.

She looked at the writing again, her stomach somersaulting. It was definitely the same as in her letter. The same italics, all tails and curlicues in perfect balance.

Miss Lawson again.

Abbie went into the vestry, her stomach hollow, her ears tuned for Quinn and for an encore of that laughter. But, to her surprise, the six photographs and that strange warning verse had vanished. Abbie checked carefully among other items of parish news pinned on to boards and scattered along the one bench, but without success. She wondered if they might all have been stolen, or if the Church authorities had removed them. And, for some unknown reason, she also wondered about those two little girls whom Hemmings had posed alongside their mother.

'We know one was Harriet, so who was the other

one? And what about her boy? Where was he?' Abbie said to herself. 'Maybe, as she was pregnant, he was still inside.' Her own muscles made a small spasm, so quickly she barely noticed, but an odd sensation seemed to linger beneath her stomach. Not time-of-the-month twinges, this was different, and as she moved to the door, the feeling diminished.

So who then were Mary, Abigail and Lazarus? she puzzled. But, unlike her pains, this question wouldn't go away. Abbie opened her wallet and drew out her prints of Lilith Leakes. She stared at one showing the crone's skull face, the wormhole eyes and the blob of snot blocking one nostril.

'Who are they?' she asked. 'You've got to tell me.' But, before any answer, before she could put the thing away, a sudden fierce draught hit her hand. The photograph wavered, until she clenched her fingers firmly over it and stuffed it inside her jacket.

Abbie ran outside and kicked the door shut, breath heaving from her lungs. It was as though something had tried to wrench the picture from her, as though she was never meant to know the answers. Martha Robinson was raising the stakes all right. And where would it end? *Where?*

The drizzle was now rain falling vertically from a concrete sky and spewing down from the gargoyle's mouth on to her head. The hotel was too far to escape to, so Abbie took shelter round on the east side of the church, under an umbrella of yews. She remembered what Quinn had said about a small school in the chapel, and maybe, just maybe, there might be some clues . . .

The hinges had rusted on wood so bleached and brittle she had only to push hard with her fingertips, leaving the chapel door open for a quick exit if need be.

'So this was it.' Abbie stared at the rows of high-backed chairs that faced a life-sized marble figure of Mary Magdalene. But on closer inspection, this was no ordinary statue. Here stood a woman of shame, head bowed, with tears adorning each cheek, her hands clasped together in a gesture of humility. At her bare feet lay a plaque which named Samuel Scott of Rievely Hall, 1818–73, as the donor.

Abbie remembered he'd also been responsible for that hideous Whiplash crucifix. Quinn had referred to him as a benefactor, but the landowner must also have been something of a High Church religious freak, she thought, judging by his strange gifts to Black Fen.

In the far corner she spotted several old desks in shadow, covered by lace cloths. She ran her hand over their worn edges and probed the inkwells full of musty fluff, until she found something else. The skin on her hands begin to tingle, her heart moving faster. GR and HR: her finger traced the carvings' grooves. 'Harriet Robinson and . . .' She tried thinking of girls' names beginning with G, but fear of being caught made her leave this gloomy place of learning to see if, by some miracle, Rosie was back anywhere near the rectory.

Over the road, someone was calling a dog and another person was lifting milk bottles off the doorstep, as she crept through the graveyard, dark and dank, slippery with moss. Abbie skidded, regained her balance and looked towards the upper windows.

I'm sure there's someone up there.

And the longer she stared, the more she saw, like looking at the moon. But this was no fantasy. The white face staring out was real.

She gasped. Panic reached her stomach, despite the fact the little runaway was obviously still alive.

Suddenly there was a noise. She flung herself down and her face was slimed with wet leaves as a preaching voice drew nearer.

'Being admonished of the great indignation of God against sinners, I may rather be moved to earnest and *true* repentance; and may walk more warily in these dangerous days: fleeing from such vices, for which I affirm with my own mouth the curse of God to be due . . .'

Jesus, he's back.

It was Quinn himself, coming her way. He wore a robe of institutional green, his face looking gaunt, stripped like a dead willow. There was also something in his hand, something so heavy that it lowered his shoulder and gave him a limp, while the look in his eye told of a battle finally lost. He was carrying an axe.

She thought she was going to be sick. It was just him and her now with a bit of flimsy weed in between.

'For now is the axe put unto the root of the trees so that every tree that bringeth *not* good fruit is hewn down and cast into the fire.' His arms began to swing, first left then right, and curses echoed when the blade embedded. Root, sap, blood, it made no difference. 'It is a fearful thing to fall into the hands of the living God; he shall pour down rain upon the sinners, snares, fire.'

Her own prayer was different as her body stayed locked rigid, barely hidden.

The nightmare passed with a thresh of foliage, a stab of bark, the monologue fading as she raised her head.

Count three and run!

Lifted by angels, it seemed, she reached the road:

Smithy Lane, Canal Way, any way. It didn't matter any more. Nor to Helen Quinn, who stayed at her skylight post, feeling the clouds' dark freedom touch her dreams and turn them into a nightmare.

Despite my efforts, our fortunes have not improved. Uncle Kirton passed to a better life last month with a boil on his hand the size of a barnacle's egg and Rievely have moved the geese over to Sleeper's Farm. Mr Scott said my Moeder and Uncle Poynton were felons after the Beadle from Herringtoft had told him lies. So now I work turning peat at West Winch from dawn till day's end. Rievely Hall won't marl the ground like they've done for themselves, but it's good enough for Hemmings, who saw my first blood come down my legs and remarked upon it for everyone to hear. That should tell you the kind of man he is . . .

Fourteen

DESPITE FEELING shaken after the encounter in the graveyard, Abbie did not leave the site till four. As Vallender's threatened progress check on sales hadn't so far materialized, she assumed that he'd had other matters on his mind.

Having had no breakfast, no elevenses, no lunch, she found herself in the lavatorial Burger King in Snutterwick, staring at a milkshake. She left it untouched, weighed down by too many anxieties. Was it really Rosie's face in that window at the Rectory? If not, who else could it have been? Why had her crazy father reappeared with his guilty ranting and that axe when he was supposed to be having a rest somewhere? And, as she noticed a couple nearby sharing an ice-cream sundae, where, for God's sake, was Simon?

Suddenly she was aware of people outside. She recognized Charlie Hunter and a woman she presumed was his mother, carrying a W H Smith bag full of something large. He was pointing openly at her and looked just about to stick out his tongue when Abbie got up to leave.

As she stepped outside, he prodded her. 'Hey, I saw you at the open evening, remember?' But Abbie couldn't smile. His antics at the cottage were still all too clear. Instead she crossed to the island and heard him snigger.

'Nice little bum, that.' He imitated her walk for a few paces before a smack and tears.

''Fraid the DI's out of town this afternoon.' Sergeant French's florid face stayed focused on the sports section of the *Snutterwick Echo* even though Abbie stood directly in front of him.

'What about Sergeant Bryant then?' She'd remembered his name.

'He's out as well.'

'And WPC O'Halloran?' Despair in her voice.

'Off on a call.'

'Look, I just want someone to go and check on the Reverend Peter Quinn.' The word reverend now sounded grotesque. 'He's going mad. I saw him yesterday waving a huge axe around.'

'Where?'

'By the rectory where he lives. Black Fen.' She ached for some understanding response, but his only interest seemed to be in the sports pages.

'Black Fen, eh? No peace for the wicked.' He finally folded the newspaper.

'I'm telling you, it's true.'

'Hold on, hold on. You can't go shouting things like that all over the place. My niece attends one of his meetings for young mums, and he's done a helluva lot for that community. Pity is, some never appreciate it.' Two eyes homed in on Abbie as though she inhabited a pickling jar.

'Your name please?'

Abbie relented, then leaned towards him. 'Why can't you just take my word for it? Things are happening there. It's getting dangerous.'

'Your address?'

Abbie gave the hotel's details, and he smirked as he wrote. 'Not exactly the Hilton, is it?'

Abbie coloured. 'I've actually had more advice and support from Mrs Livingstone there than from anyone in our wonderful police service.'

'I see.' He was writing that down as well.

'And why hasn't anyone called on that so-called artist Byers at Killjoy Cottage?' she continued. 'I'm sure he knows something about where little Rosie Quinn might be.'

'Rosie Quinn?' The sergeant looked surprised. 'What's she been up to now?'

But Abbie refused to be side-tracked. 'Didn't you know DI Mowbray and the rest were out looking for her?'

'No. Not a whisper.' His eyes glanced sideways at the newspaper.

O Jesus.

'Well, if nothing's done soon, I shall have to inform Social Services.' Abbie's tone hardened, her face unusually stern. 'Do you want a body? Is that it?'

'We have to be careful. We need evidence, not hearsay.'

She snapped open her bag and pulled out the still-perfumed envelope containing the death threat. 'OK, so what would you call this? Hearsay as well?' She passed the item over.

Snail-pace lips moved on the written words before he turned the letter over in his flabby hands.

'Mmm, this sort of thing's always tricky . . .'

'Why?'

'Some nutters even send them to themselves.'

'Look here, I've been threatened. Please read it again.'

The desk phone rang.

''Scuse me.' Then, after a check of his watch and a grunt, he was hers again. He pushed the letter back towards her. 'You're on dodgy ground with this, I'm telling you.'

'I know it's from Quinn and that Miss Lawson, from the school there. She's his runner, not that it looks as if she could walk more than a yard.'

The duty sergeant stared. 'May I inform you, my uncle's her mother's cousin.'

'I don't care if he's the King of Spain. This is serious! How would *you* feel if your wife or daughter had received this?'

The phone rang a second time and French picked it up, clearly glad of a diversion, but before he'd even begun to speak he was on his own again.

She took the roundabout out of Snutterwick, moving slowly together with what seemed to be the rest of the local population, in no mood for the visit that lay ahead.

But soon after the outlying cluster of villages, the road that stretched straight ahead was traffic-free. The Wenn bank sat close on the left, with nothing on the right save the occasional derelict hovel drowned by the wormless soil.

She thought of Clenchtoft, with Lilith Leakes waiting, and prayed there'd be no more dead birds about, or worse. Prayed too that there'd be a light on in the farmhouse. In her bag lay a notebook with questions already listed and the Polaroid camera with a new film, just in case.

Also the death threat she wanted the old woman to see.

Lilith was the clue to it all, Abbie knew that. Lilith Leakes *was* Black Fen.

As the Polo approached the Whiplash Cross, Abbie glanced back at the school and the church tower behind it. She circled the small concrete island on which stood a bronze crucifix now turned green with salt, then slowed at the sign for Clenchtoft.

She parked on a derelict corner of land. An abandoned tractor lay rusting into the ground, surrounded by trash. The lane itself was a minefield of potholes overgrown by shoulder-high nettles, with at the other end, in shadow, a cluster of police cars winking.

Piling bricks is the easiest labour, but he still won't allow me gloves. Some say I have the strength of four men and that God fitted me up better than any other girl in the gang, but they all still put their hands out when it comes to the sixpence. I've seen the look in Mr Hemmings's eye when he catches me emptying myself. Once he put his hand there and said I had a pretty weasel under my skirt. I cannot tell Moeder. She's ill and not working at all now. She throws herself about calling my sissen's name, yellow as a canary, and yesterday fell to the floor in a fever. I cannot cry for my eyes are dry as a desert.

Fifteen

On the day after Ascension Day, the local papers had room only for Lilith Leakes and their fictions about her life, but the fortune-teller's face was her own revenge, haunting all the region's front pages and terrorizing small children to an early bed of nightmares.

Abbie had sent one of her Polaroid prints to the *Morpeth Record*, but then the Anglia Press Agency muscled in. She wanted neither recognition nor money, just her past to be set at ease with the present, and some sort of future to live for. Nevertheless, the sparse details of the murder, combined with dark, gloomy photographs of the farmhouse, were enough to leave her in a state of dread.

'Shocking business.' Sheila Livingstone held up a glass to the light before filling it with Emva Cream. 'Who'd want to do that to a poor old biddy on her own I wonder?'

'She didn't strike me as "a poor old biddy" exactly.' Abbie was sitting at the bar with her espresso, still wearing her work suit even though it was five-thirty and normally she'd have changed by now.

'Oh, you met her then?'

'That time I saw little Rosie wandering around out on the marsh.'

'Rosie who?'

'The vicar's daughter.'

'You never mentioned anything about that, or about meeting that Leakes woman.'

'I'd actually planned to see her again yesterday. I reckoned it could have been useful. She was going to give me a history lesson on Black Fen, and show me things, psychic stuff, you know.' Abbie couldn't bring herself to mention Martha Robinson, much as she wanted to. Sheila's job meant casual conversation with customers and the Kingfisher Rise project was in enough trouble already without more local gossip.

'Well it's a good job you weren't around when her killer turned up. Just imagine . . .'

Sheila finished her sherry. 'Oh, by the way,' she said suddenly brightening, 'I've just remembered something Amy Buckley once told me.'

'Yes?'

'Apparently that old girl took up with some young sailor. From Holland he was, I think. Very tall and fair anyhow. Quite different from her.'

Abbie looked thoughtful, wondering why the farmer's wife hadn't mentioned this.

'I bet she'll be telling the police a few things. They go back a long way, the Buckleys.'

'I know. I went to see her.'

'And?'

'I can't tell you everything right now, but it's all pretty weird. To be honest, I've not wanted to alarm you, and anyhow . . .'

'Anyhow what?' Sheila stared at her directly.

'You're not my mother, you know.'

'Oh, I see. So I'm supposed to stand by and watch

you getting paler and paler, like some waif and stray. Off your food, not getting enough kip . . .'

'I'll be all right.'

Sheila looked unconvinced, then began thumbing through the *Yellow Pages* and reached for the phone.

'What are you doing?'

'Getting some big bloody bolts for that front door. Better safe than sorry.'

Abbie watched her dial, then took the *Morpeth Record* upstairs, cut out anything about Lilith Leakes and filed it with her letters.

She stood and stared out at the view beyond, feeling empty as a widow. This waiting was cruel, another less dramatic kind of death.

The *Norfolk Princess* was gliding out to sea and its mournful echo penetrated the very walls as she then rummaged among her Polaroid prints. The one she wanted slipped out from the others without encouragement.

'Who got to you first?' Abbie asked the face that now looked more hideous than the remembered reality. 'Tell me.'

But, like the church gargoyle, vigilant yet mute for all time, Lilith Leakes stared back, with her jaw set in a knowing smile.

Uncle Poynton's cousin by marriage has come over from Flatsoken to take her to where she was born, which is twenty miles from Pappy. I saw the box rock the cart as they put her on even though she weighed less than a rabbit. Uncle Poynton sent word he'd be back, but Ben Robinson won't have him near me and warned he had a knife ready. The last thing Moeder said was always wed a sokeman. At least he'll have a plot to feed you from. But Goosefoot will do us now I have his mother's ring on my hand.

Sixteen

THE YOUNG MAN huddled in the corner of the sprinter train that had left Peterborough half an hour late. He was glad he'd paid the extra for a first-class seat from King's Cross, at least that way he'd avoided the noisy shitheads going back to Shitland after a night's clubbing in London. He'd seen enough of those in the past eight months. Rheindahlen was full of them.

Shitland? No, hell, that was a bit unfair. She'd called it Wringland, almost proudly he recalled.

'Wherever a patch could be found just above the influence of the tide or near enough to some main channel for the rush and swirl of the water to drain the island – there the villages grew . . .'

Good old Belloc, he thought, turning his head to allow the endless horizontals of reclaimed land to tear through his vision.

In the days when he could still be bothered, he'd looked that quote up, first thing, once she knew for sure she'd be working there. She, Abbie. His Abbie. A for Ambition, P for Persistence, and, just in case, he had all her letters in his jacket.

His neck hurt and his throat felt like a pit of drought earth, so when the snacks trolley jostled alongside he just said, 'Beer.'

'No beer. Sorry.' The woman in a funny kind of overall looked him up and down 'We've had too much trouble with that, but would sir like tea instead?'

Simon had only to fix her with his fierce blue eyes for her to hurry by in search of a more compliant customer.

He slumped back, thinking. He'd relied on Ben Curtis to phone Abbie from the Mess payphone, seeing as they'd wasted his mobile and kept him incommunicado in a state of limbo. But the engineer had gone AWOL just when he'd needed him most. Absent without a bloody conscience more like, and Simon wondered where he was now, so he could eventually get even.

He, the Land Rover Sales Executive's eldest son, had been a month without TV or any of the normal perks of army life. And after a final medical with a Rorschach to round it off, he had been deemed in need of early leave.

'To sort yourself out, my man,' his CO had said. 'Go see your family for a bit, Cresswell, keep off the Pig's Ear, then calm down till we're ready to use you.'

That was twelve hours ago and now, as low-slung farms and knots of cattle skimmed by, it all seemed another lifetime away. To cheer him up, the nurse on the rehab ward had said to watch out for the bulb fields. 'Lincolnshire's all lit up like some magical party table, mile after mile, and if it's not daffs it's tulips, tulips, tulips . . .' His geography classes had promised the same, and both had lied. There wasn't a single flower to be seen. It was as if the whole landscape out there beyond the murky glass was some old sepia footage – a bare geometry of soil and drain of such bleakness he shivered and pulled his leather jacket closer.

He'd lost nearly ten kilos. That's what misery does, it literally eats you alive, and she'd notice straight away.

She'd go on about it, because she liked things perfect in life, but she was all he had. His family, in fact, he knew that now, heading east across England not west to Dan y Parc. Same latitude, that was all.

Snutterwick was grim, the only ornamentation in its featureless streets were For Sale signs on every other house. Most were due for auction.

The taxi, a rough old Escort, picked him up at four thirty outside the two-screen cinema after four vodkas in the Cock and Ferret. He should have phoned from the pub, given her some notice, but the call box was jammed with a foreign coin. Besides, a certain shame held him back from trying to find another.

He'd changed. He'd had to, after doing what his father wanted, while his brother, who'd fucked up big time since leaving Christ's College in Brecon, was pissing around Swansea with a camera in his hand. Media Studies he called it, sad bastard. Simon let his head find a hold on the worn fabric and closed his eyes as the car crawled along the Fens.

He'd not eaten since the night before and the drink still swilled round his body, stirring his bruises from the latest brawl, turning his raw knuckles into an orchestration of pain.

'You from Black Fen then?' The driver pinned his gaze in the mirror. It seemed almost a threat.

'Nope.'

'Oh, I get it.' The grizzled man of the world smiled. 'You got a bit o' betty there, then, eh? Say no more. Nudge nudge, wink wink . . .'

The soldier edged to the front of his seat and leaned

forwards. 'Look, chum, just mind your own bloody business.'

'No need to get uppity with me, mate. Only trying to make conversation.'

'Well, fucking well don't.'

Suddenly the car stopped, its engine grinding in neutral.

'Right. Out! You can walk to the land of the zombies on your own.' The driver began revving. 'Now.'

Simon dragged his bag off the seat and slammed the door. He'd had enough of fights. Anyhow, this one didn't interest him. He watched as the cab reversed into a narrow gap above a canal then set off back to Snutterwick trailing its exhaust.

Land of the zombies? What the fuck did that mean?

And, even though the sky seemed high and liberating with its far horizon, those words lodged like maggots in his brain.

He tried thumbing a lift, but traffic was scarce, none of it even giving him a sideways glance. Maybe because he wasn't keeping to a very steady course, or more likely it was his bag, almost body-sized and black, a bad choice in the circumstances. He cursed that he'd got no map and therefore the wide water coursing alongside him had no name. His adolescent geography lay back in the mists of time, but as a kid he'd loved to label everything: to colour in the arable, the fallow, the uplands and plains with the hues of heaven and overlay contours in fine unerring line as might a composer setting out the stave.

This lot here was different – all sucked from the sea, but only on loan until Greenland began to melt. As different from Wales as it could be. He looked round to see a battered white Lada pulling up, its driver about his age, bespectacled and Brylcreemed. At least it was a lift. He chanced a smile. Better than footslogging to Abbie's place with daylight on the wane.

'Where are you heading?'

'Shitland.'

Martin Silver seemed amused. He leaned over and, ignoring all his landlady's warnings about giving lifts to strangers, pushed the door open.

'Join the club.'

I have a girl inside me, I know it and when I'm over at West Winch cleaning up the field I bind her tight with my shawl so I can bend. Yesterday I fell to sleep standing up and when I woke Hemmings's hand was on my belly. I put my hoe through his foot. No work for a month and a visit from the churchman Pinkton Downey, who says I must purge impurity from my own soul afore I bring another into this vile world . . .

Seventeen

SHEILA EMERGED FROM the kitchen with several clean tea towels and a tray of still-warm glasses that reflected her flushed cheeks. When she noticed the shadow behind the frosted inner door she stopped and set down her tray, trembling.

'Abbie, can you come down?'

Until the extra security was in she was never going to relax, not even with the bar closed while she blitzed the laundry and put two loads through the dishwasher.

'What's up?' Abbie was still in her work suit, but it was her shoeless feet Sheila saw first, coming down the stairs.

'Look, there's someone hanging round the door and I don't like it.'

Abbie had never seen her in a state before and it unnerved her into a strange calm.

'Well, whoever it is doesn't look tall enough for Quinn, if that's what you mean.'

But Sheila wasn't convinced. She snatched at the phone.

'Hang on, hang on.' Abbie tiptoed over and stood close to the glass. 'My God.'

Despite its opacity, she could still make out the familiar shape of the head.

'Who is it?' Sheila hung back, now holding a barbecue prong in readiness.

Slowly Abbie slid the bolt and unlocked the door. She registered the black leather jacket, jeans split at the knees and the boots bartered from another country.

'*Simon!*'

They collided like the sea against a breaker, all time and distance fused in the pressing of heart on heart. He held her close like she'd remembered all along, his mouth grazing from her cheek to her lips, filling her with his alcoholic breath.

She pulled away and stared. 'You've been drinking!'

Oh, bloody shit, why do you have to spoil it?

Then another voice interrupted. 'It's a good job one of us was sober.'

She swung round to see Martin Silver coming over, carrying the hold-all, which he dropped by Simon's feet. 'He's well pissed, I can tell you. Still, he's got to the right place.' He turned away and a rogue strand of greased hair was lifted from his parting by the wind.

'Thanks,' Abbie called after him, noticing Simon already standing at the bar gulping down a beer.

Sheila bolted the door. Then she watched as the word Cresswell struggled from the pen before switching on all the lights to celebrate her relief that it hadn't been the axe man after all.

Simon pushed his empty glass forward. 'Now then, I'll have something large and obliterating if you don't mind. I want to forget where I've been and where I'm bloody well going. Make it a double vodka, and the same for yourself.'

Sheila looked embarrassed.

'No, you don't.' Abbie pushed his glass away.

Suddenly he gripped her waist, his strength different from before, taut and dangerous, honed to kill. She could feel his body hardening, but it was too soon, too easy.

'Please yourself.' She extricated herself and made for the stairs. It took four minutes to hang up her suit for ironing and another two to leave the hotel by the back door.

It was raw, not like early May at all, but it suited her mood well enough. The late afternoon chill left the tears cold on her cheeks as she crossed Herringtoft Road and turned up along the track where, apart from the birds, it was totally private, and where she could think.

This wasn't the man she'd been longing for, the one she'd begged to come back. The soldier she'd last waved away after Christmas was someone else and now, like his very own bag, was going to be a dark burden in a place that already held too much darkness . . .

Abbie pushed open Ox Tye Gate. No unleashed dogs here, no motor-powered vehicles or machines, but instead a confused and frightened young woman as the world beyond slipped into nightfall. She walked on into the grey, against darkening grey, while the predator turned birdwatcher, who'd missed nothing, slunk below the ridge.

When Abbie got back to the hotel, she discovered Sheila had dispatched Simon off to bed temporarily in room 7, the one next to Abbie's. She heard his dreamless breathing even before opening his door, saw his face turned her way but blind like a baby's, his ear pink and crumpled as if he'd just rolled over.

The smell of drink grew stronger as she reached him, and his outstretched hand spasmed in an empty handshake as Abbie leaned over to kiss him.

*

As dawn lightened the curtains in Simon's room, Abbie woke alongside him and, pressing herself close to his still unfamiliar thinness, locked her toes around his heels, as if this simple act might conduct some small measure of her anxieties into his sleeping form.

There'd been no chance of any real communication since he'd arrived to find out what had changed him so much or, for her to tell her own story because, from the moment she'd slipped into the warm sheets beside him, those demons had dissipated like the early mist itself.

But now, with Simon also drowsily awake and the sounds of gulls gathering over some newly berthed vessel in the Wenn, Abbie began to share more worrying thoughts with him than whether or not Sheila might have heard their love-making or which of them was going to serve up breakfast in bed.

She recounted her meetings with the grim gang labourer, making Simon promise not to breathe a word of it to the hotel keeper or anyone else. Then she went on to describe how she'd met the hermit, her revolting hobby, her unnerving predictions, and little missing Rosie from the loveless home, victim of sexually precocious bullies. Of Byers, whom she wouldn't trust further than the end of Simon's bed. And the weird Avril Lawson at that useless school . . .

The woman's name prompted Abbie to go back to her own room and return with the scented letter.

'This came the very first day I was here.' She handed it over, and just one glance at the contents made Simon sit up with a start. 'Shelia reckons that Lawson woman delivered it here.' He stared at the words, mouthing them over and over again, a deepening frown pleating his forehead.

'Christ, Abs, what the *fuck's* going on?' He got out of bed to put the letter in his jacket pocket then slumped back next to her.

'How do I know? But I can't get the Snutterwick police to show any interest at all. It's like wading through bloody treacle. They don't want to know about that – or anything else. So, they turned up to look for Rosie – big deal. But that was a whole week ago . . . There's only Julia O'Halloran who's halfway decent but she's well outnumbered . . .'

A vein in Simon's neck pulsed his anger as Abbie's acount of the local force grew worse.

'Look, Abs,' he leaned towards her and cradled her in his arms, 'I'll do whatever it takes to help you, and I know I'm just one fucked-up dongo – you'd be too if you'd been over there – but I'll make it all up to you, I promise, any way I can.' His clear blue eyes burned into hers, his hands gripped her shoulders, his damaged knuckles like rows of craggy peaks. 'I'll chivvy social services about Rosie first thing tomorrow, and that's just for starters, OK?'

'Thanks,' she whispered, as the incoming tide slopped against the quay and the church bells from Smithy Lane struck eight.

My spelling's getting worse with me being so far now from school. But I try. On Sundays after the service the churchman makes me chant the Catechism and the Collect of the day, or else the Psalms of David. To combat Popery he says. What I don't tell him is it's all fairytales and the one I really listen to is the Devil's Mouth especially when Hemmings's name is mentioned. Ma Tully died the day Grace tore my weasel with her big head. Ben Robinson's seed comes easy, too easy, and I'm still hurting . . .

Eighteen

MONDAY MORNING and the site office was stifling. Magnolia walls glared bright with sun and yet the heating, on Vallender's orders, was already set at the winter level to create a selling ambience.

Abbie sat with her line manager's letter in one hand and a Seven-Up in the other, all thoughts of Simon and Rosie replaced by her news. Suddenly the foreman came in unannounced, his eyes enviously on her drink, his hair plastered to his forehead with sweat. He looked exhausted.

'That looks nice,' he said.

'Have one. Have them all, what the heck?' She passed him the Holtbury Prestige Homes headed sheet. 'You received one of these?'

'Can't say I have. God knows, I get enough bloody paper—'

'Read it, please.'

Droplets of sweat landed on the signature. 'This isn't fair, Miss Parker. He's blaming *you*.'

'I'm glad you've noticed it.' Her face burned with heat and indignation. 'I mean, just how bloody grateful do you have to be for having a job?'

'I don't rightly know what to say.' He passed his hard hat from one hand to the other.

'Well, I do, and I'm taking it right to the top.'

'Oh, Lord.'

'Just because I'm female and young, he thinks he can intimidate me. Well, I'm not having it.'

'Quite right, and you can tell him from me as well, we still can't do nothing with that Ripton. Nothing wrong with the mix either, according to the lab. It's exactly the same as we've used on all the others. To be honest, I've never come across anything like this in my whole life, and that's what I came to see you about.'

'Would you support me then, Mr Fidler? Because Rodney Vallender clearly doesn't believe me. Will you come to head office and tell them? Please.'

'Look, my life's complicated enough here.' He watched the forklift through the window. 'I've got commitments, two kids at college . . .'

She strode away from him, down the steps, past the din of mixers and drain layers, straight to her car and her mobile.

'Mr Vallender please, if he's there. It's urgent.'

'Yes, who is it?' But she knew from his voice he must have been expecting her.

'Miss Parker, Kingfisher Rise.'

'Ah.'

'I don't like being threatened.'

'You're not, believe me—'

'Mr Vallender, either I'm in or I'm out. I can't do my job properly not knowing—'

'I'm trying to be fair.'

'Fair?'

'Look, Kingfisher Rise is our only non-mover, so what *are* we to believe?'

'But I've told you straight what people have seen and felt here, and what happened to me.'

'You're just stalling, and Holtbury's aren't biting. Now, either you secure a deal by mid-June or we'll consider re-appointing. This is a warning from the management, which will mean it's in writing.'

Silence.

'Miss Parker?'

She drove too fast and didn't care as long as she faced the horizon. Over dirt, then grass as far as she could go – to the furthest end of Herringtoft Track and towards the smell of sea. She thought of Simon back at the hotel, probably still in bed, probably drinking himself senseless. She chucked her mobile down the slope of the bank, spread her arms to the paling sun and drew in great draughts of air.

Freedom – as the inventory of Show Home trivia streamed through her mind and died with the day. Stupid frilly fripperies, the most unlikely things in gold. 'The only gold some might ever have,' Vallender had once smirked, except there were still no takers. As she walked, she thought of all the more useful things she could do with her life. And one of them was probably still confined in that cold bare room, in the company of bats.

After half an hour, Abbie retraced her steps, reaching the spot where she'd left the car.

Except no car.

She checked again and again, pacing backwards and forwards along the track, dizzy in a wind that was bringing the first touch of rain and blurring the sound of an RAF bomb practice over to the west, near Mickleton. Then she looked down to where long grasses and bog pimpernels now clung to the slope, flattened and torn by recent tyres. Her precious Polo lay upturned at the edge of Grim's Canal. She tried to think, she tried to run, but her legs would not respond.

'Hello, there! Are you all right?'

She rubbed her eyes. It was Philip Byers with something under his arm. He dropped his sketching easel and cupped both hands round his mouth.

'Can you hear me?'

'Yes.'

'Just wait there. I'll come and give you a hand. Looks like your brake cable went. Lucky you weren't driving.'

The minutes extended to eternity after the artist had vanished. High above, vast cumulonimbus clouds were gathering grey before the serious rain and her sobs were lost among the scavenging birds.

'Here we are.' Tobacco and that other smell on his breath. 'Good job I was around. I never usually work outside, too many distractions for my kind of subject.'

Abbie spun round. He had a rope all right, but not for the car. His movements were slick, practised, as he pushed her to the ground, bound her wrists together tightly, then strapped one of her legs to his.

*Now Ben Robinson works with me out
on the loam at Breakwell. He's the best
they've ever had at singling out beet
and onions, but Scott has put up our
rent while the Reverend talks of greed
and mammon to my deaf ears.*

6 December 1854
    *Harriet's head showed first like she
was coming out of St Nicholas's chimney. She took all day and night and
who can blame her? If I had my turn
again I'd have slipped the cord round
my neck like a mooring knot and never
known all this . . .*

Nineteen

A T 6.20 PM AS the regional news downstairs was ending with yet more speculation on Lilith Leakes's murder, Simon was halfway through a 'snack' of meatballs and oven-ready potato cakes. The way Sheila kept looking at the curtains while clearing up a nearby table told him something was wrong.

'Where's Abbie?' His heavy eyes looked past her to the door. 'Isn't she back yet?'

'Not to worry.' Sheila carried the tray through into the kitchen. 'I expect it's work.'

'But she's usually in by five fifteen. She told me in her letters.' Besides, all the incidents and observations that Abbie had told him about on Sunday hadn't stopped preying on his mind.

'Well, all I know is, she went off quite chirpy this morning. More so than usual, I'd say. That's 'cos you're here, of course. Never missed supper, though. It's the only meal I can honestly say she ever bothered with.'

Simon blanched at the past tense and pushed his plate aside.

'Don't you want that?' She noticed how his belt was fastened on the tightest hole, how his jeans were loose around his legs.

'No time, sorry.'

His head was hurting differently now and the afternoon's drink still soured his mouth, but teeth cleaning could wait. He tried phoning the Show Home, only to hear Abbie's clipped professional tones on the answerphone, so five minutes later, with Sheila teetering along behind, he made his way to Kingfisher Rise.

The rain, turned now to drizzle, soaked her fluffy mules as she picked her way over the slippery rubble.

'Shit.'

No, Shitland.

He was shocked by the chaos around him. The site looked as though it was suffering, waiting to die.

Oh, Abbie.

He led Sheila up the access route to the only finished house and knew she was thinking the same. *You couldn't pay me to live here.*

In her letters Abbie had written that she had her office in the Show Home garage, and had made it out to be rather classy. Yet here it was, cheap and bloody nasty, in the middle of dereliction, with not a kingfisher in sight. Plenty of hideous PVC, though, plenty of crap. The one thing his father was right about. He peered inside before sliding back the double door.

So *this* was where Martha Robinson had come calling . . .

'Now that's odd,' Sheila said, stepping out of her mules and leaving them on the mat. 'She always had a thing about locking up. Worse than me, if you like. There's no alarm set either . . . That's not Abbie.'

'You're right. I know.' He saw her Holtbury notepad lying open and a name in block capitals underlined: VALLENDER ASAP.

Her bolshie boss?

Simon dialled the number and got an engaged signal. He slapped the receiver down, frowning.

'Something's up.' He rifled the drawers and located the panic button. 'I can feel it.' His trusted sixth sense was kicking in.

'There's no one out there to ask either.'

'No, they all bugger off on the dot apparently. Brrrr, it's bloody freezing.'

Sheila crossed her arms over her chest. Something had suddenly made her shiver and she made a move to go.

'Just hang on. I won't be a sec.'

Simon ran into the hall of the Show Home and up the stairs, searching for Abbie in all the rooms. His footsteps shook the whole fabric of the house and Sheila thought of cardboard.

'Nothing doing,' he muttered. 'Right, I'm going for a cruise round. Are you coming?'

Then he remembered he'd got no car. The bastards in Germany had even taken that away from him. 'Fuck it, fuck it.' Simon hovered over the phone again. 'Let's call the cops then. It's seven o'clock now.'

'No. Not just yet, eh?'

'It's what they're bloody paid for.'

'She wouldn't want any crisis getting back to her boss. Why not just have a look around, for the moment, like you said. She may have gone up to Goosefoot Cottage for something.'

'Oh no.'

'Anyway I'd better be getting back.' Sheila squeezed the surplus water out of her mules and returned them to her feet. 'And I'll get you something ready. You've got to eat – you're just skin and bone . . .'

Skin and bone. You will all die.

'I'm OK.' But he'd suddenly turned quite pale.

'A boy of your age should be tucking in.'

He watched her go till she was out of sight, then phoned the police. It seemed as if the sergeant he spoke to could barely be bothered to continue their conversation after explaining that Mowbray and team were out investigating an incident near Kilntoft.

'*I'll* make a bloody incident if you don't send someone over soon,' Simon shouted. 'Look, she's just disappeared. Do you want another Lilith Leakes on your hands?' Even as he'd said those words, he felt a shiver pass through him. 'So move your lazy arse.'

Simon then fiddled with the security alarm but to no avail, so he found some string and tied it round the door handle as he left. She'd be in yet more trouble if someone broke in, but Abbie was still nowhere to be seen. Despite the apparent normality of Walsoken Road and Smithy Lane, he sensed that in Black Fen he'd entered a kernel of evil. It was tangible and, even worse, after just twenty-four hours it was beginning to grip his psyche.

He saw lovers cuddling in the phone box, just like he and Abbie had done once, a woman walking her dog . . . This virtual reality wasn't real at all. What was real lay in his heart. And that was a growing fear.

Where the hell *was* she? His jog became a run, round the Whiplash crucifix, and, having asked directions for Goosefoot from a passing cyclist, he set off north again towards Herringtoft. His wet leather jacket felt heavy on his back as he tried the cottage, repelled the moment he went through the gate. It was empty and evil, its black panes daring him to defy it. He took a deep breath, heaved up a sash window and entered the darkness beyond.

It was haunted all right, and not just because of the piercing cold. There was a tangible presence, something which made his heart race faster, in a vortex of terrible energy that seemed to emanate from upstairs. He was an unwelcome intruder, that was obvious, just as Abbie must have been. So what insanity had made her spend even one night in the place? One minute was too bloody long.

Jesus. It's all my fault. I should have been here . . .

He went back and stood in the wilderness outside, unsure of his next move, trying to regain logic and reason. She may have just fancied a breath of air – it was a better option than most. As he faced the treacherous spread of World's End Marsh, the heavens opened.

Susannah Buckley has taken Grace for a month so I can suckle Harriet in peace. She's a barren wife and likes a young one around the house. She asked if she might keep her and I had to hold my fists tight. Grace is from my body not hers, even though the child looks like she's been nesting in marsh water too long.

1855

Hemmings is renting West Winch. No wife yet, but enough girls to take his weight. I see it for myself, and when Ben Robinson tried for work after a bellyful of ale, he told him I'd taken it all and nothing was spare.

So Ben Robinson thinks of nothing but Scotland where beef is plentiful and the wages double. The hossman from Snutterwick will take him as far as Grantham, and then another coach up to Leicester. He promises to send money every four weeks and by Michaelmas we'll be rich enough to buy there, away from the pox and the plague of this dwelling he says isn't fit for pigs.

Twenty

BYERS HAD HEARD of Lilith Leakes's murder and Quinn's brainstorm at the rectory from the mobile greengrocer, Solomon Crisp, who'd turned up at Killjoy while the artist was in the throes of vital preparations. By acting normally – purchasing a pack of potatoes, even offering his unwelcome caller the usual cigarette, Byers doubted that the silly old fool had suspected anything. Ever since then he had been expecting a routine call from those CID cretins. It made him nervous, without a doubt, but the rigor mortis that seemed to characterize the local officers of the law was some comfort to him given his dodgy situation. Anyhow, he asked himself, what the fuck was Quinn doing out of the retreat? And where would he be heading for next? Byers farted, but it was no answer.

For him, this assignment had happened just in time and, thank the God of the marsh or whoever, it was finally going to plan. Soon that nutter would be out of his hair. Meanwhile, he had to keep telling himself, it was just a job, and a month from now all would be forgotten.

The painter drew breath from his labours and lit another cigarette. This time, indoors, with the curtains sealed against the spasms of brightness, he'd turned day into night. Nice and private, cosy even.

The watercolour on the table would be all that remained, his parting shot. Wet on wet, flesh on flesh, tones blurred by swiftness: a Madonna and Angel of the twentieth century. Less Renaissance, more the clever amateur, and apart from a couple of stained-glass commissions last year, a new direction in subject matter.

Then he went out to check the skiff, his yellow oilskins lending him a bulk he didn't possesss. No name to the boat, no colour either, just the bruised remains of white. An artist's boat meant for all his earlier good intentions of working direct from life, but this time oarless and with no artist on board. Only models.

It lay moored below the so-called garden where the deep tide obliged along its walled bank, free of reeds and other risky impediments, until the mouth of Grim's Canal. More importantly, it was invisible from the shore, while beyond stood the bleached shack, fresh painted when he'd first had a pride in his place by the sea. When it had truly been his haven.

Soon, with Quinn's money safe in his pocket, he'd be off again. Somewhere the Reverend and Nelson Palmer wouldn't find him, hidden in a honeycomb of sunless streets among the Umbrian hills. Part of the gesso-on-wood world he'd marketed countless times to corporate barbarians who couldn't tell cobalt from cerulean, yet who'd desired these remnants of medieval Europe far more than they did their wives.

Then scarcity had become drought, with most of the treasures that he had identified, already freighted to the New World before their provenance could even be catalogued. So Speers and Granger Fine Art Auctioneers, with the best address in WC1, became just another bankruptcy statistic. Nothing for him any more, their

bachelor traveller. Days on the road, nights sweetening
and dealing, all now as transient as the mists over North
Sand. If he'd not picked up an abandoned *Observer* on
the train and seen Killjoy Cottage advertised for 'strictly
the self-possessed', his story might have ended in a bedsit
in Orsett Terrace, topped and tailed by the predators of
the great metropolis.

Byers secured the knot and checked the boat for leaks.
There was no way he was going to drill holes like he'd
been told to. It was bad enough what that cunt was
arranging, but he'd picked the wrong one to do his really
dirty work. This way at least the poor fuckers might
stand some chance. Byers felt light-headed. His hands
began to tremble and he saw black water rise up to meet
his eyes. Time for the next shot in the arm. Urgent,
meaning *now*. He went back into the kitchen and rolled
up his sleeve.

Afterwards, Byers synchronized his watch with the
clock above the fridge. One hour to darkness and to have
the cargo ready. Tugging up the jacket zip he nicked his
chin. Turning to face the sudden rain driving inland, he
gauged that in these conditions, without the holes, it
would take till midnight to get them well off his pitch.
Then his problem would be someone else's.

He heard a sudden noise, pushed open the door and
moved towards her.

'Clumsy girl.' He picked up the used tubes of colours
scattered over the floor, and retied her feet.

Abbie stared dizzily into the gloom, half seeing his
dusty stuffed birds with their beaded eyes as he made for
the whisky.

'Fancy a drink?' he taunted.

Sad chat-up line. Sick party. She lowered her head.

Where was Simon now? Where was anybody? And why the hell was she here, posing for some weird painting, then trussed up and gagged in rags? Christ, she was cold, and all she could hear were gulls on the chimney or fighting round the bins.

She was slumped against an old sofa, as still as the citizens of Pompeii, when suddenly a mobile chirruped from inside the man's pocket. Abbie strained to listen as what sounded like orders came thick and fast.

Byers was ready. 'Sure, it's all hunky-dory. Two birds in the hand, if you know what I mean. Get me? Get me?'

Two birds? What the hell's he talking about?

Now he was being taken down a peg and not enjoying it. 'Course I'm being thorough, as my good friend here can vouch.'

Christ, her eyes above the gag looked so much better when she was angry. He raised his glass in a toast just to set her off again.

'Everything's in hand. I *am* a perfectionist, remember. Yes, we're bang on target, so worry not ... indeed ... exactly, squire. Contact at ten o'clock. Will do.'

Byers kept on drinking though he was high as a kite, with the pupils blacking out his eyes and his movements becoming more erratic. He gathered up a length of ancient rope he'd found in the outhouse. Then, like some bizarre maypole dance, he encircled her until the pupa was ready, the practised knots secure.

'Right. Now for the other one.'

The artist was gradually getting things organized and when he returned with a little girl Abbie knew who was the angel in his painting. *Rosie!*

Paper wings rustled the stale air as the child flew towards her friend, but Byers got there first and pulled them apart. For a brief moment their faces touched, before he forced the little girl down for the binding. No gags for this one, oh no, for that would have blunted his pleasure. He had to admit it was always the same after speaking with Quinn: a little more evil had entered his psyche, made him a little bolder. And where, he asked himself, would it end? That was the frightening bit.

Abbie questioned Rosie with her eyes: what in hell's name had she been doing for almost a week?'

He caught the look. 'She just sort of wandered into my life, didn't you, angel?' Byers had slowed, humming as he worked.

Abbie's eyebrows questioned her further.

'He found me. I got lost.'

'That's quite correct. Ten out of ten. And I have to re-assure both you young ladies that I am not a pervert or a paedophile.'

His breath was pungent, too close, but Abbie wasn't deflected. Her lips rubbed on the filthy bit of curtain so her shout through its layers of cotton were enough to be heard. 'Quinn's put you up to this, hasn't he, the bastard. Why?'

'Watch your language, Miss Parker. We have an impressionable youngster in our midst.'

'What are you doing?' Abbie shrieked, louder this time. 'Why? Tell me!' But Byers ignored her, concentrating instead on making Rosie immobile. Rosie's eyes were huge with fear as he secured the rope ends.

'I'll tape your mouth as well if you don't belt up.'

So the various knots were tightened. The prisoners stared across at one another uncomprehending. For a split second Abbie imagined it was an old woman who looked back at her.

'Half an hour to go. Time for a bite of something, I reckon.'

Byers went out and left them on their own. On returning he silently picked up the little girl, carrying her outside on his shoulder. Abbie screamed inwardly. But a minute later she too was airborne.

Outside, the rain had eased, leaving a blackness unrelieved by stars. The water had risen and slopped around the little boat as Abbie was dumped in, head-first, next to Rosie. The craft was rocking and rolling, meeting and parting on the swell. The mooring rope strained taut.

Rosie whimpered, her wrappings already sodden, but Abbie couldn't even whisper that they were going to be all right. Byers pushed the boat away from the side with his boot. It turned in the current and, like a piece of flotsam, was carried out towards the killing grounds of Cortlever Low.

Abbie desperately kept working her jaw until gradually the gag slipped down from her mouth.

'Listen, Rosie,' her voice trembled with cold, 'you've got to help me. Did that man Mr Byers say anything to you before he got hold of me? I mean about who's made him do this to us, and why?'

Rosie shook her head. 'He just kept saying how it was nice to have some company. And he showed me how to mix up colours, things like that . . .'

'Think, Rosie,' Abbie persevered despite her dread that their boat might keel over at any moment. 'Was there some clue he may have dropped about all this?'

'No.' Then the child hesitated. 'But he did say that my very best friend in all the world would be staying with him too, very soon. And I knew he meant you.'

'Had you told him about me, then?'

'I don't remember. But you *are*, aren't you?' Rosie fixed Abbie with an imploring gaze, unaware of her companion's sudden and inexplicable unease.

'Oh Rosie, of course I am.' She watched, unable to comfort the little girl who was squeezing her huge eyes tight shut until tears fell on to her cheeks. 'Don't cry. Please don't cry. We'll be all right.'

'But I want my wellies and my dollies,' Rosie whimpered.

'I'll buy you some nice new ones, but,' Abbie's voice was sterner than she intended, 'if you ever see those dolls again, you mustn't touch them, or even say their names.'

'Why not?'

'Because they're bad. They'll hurt you.'

Then after a few moments' silence the little face turned to Abbie and softly began to sing.

'Matthew, Mark and Luke and John,
Bless the bed that I lie on . . .'

And when she'd finished, the seven-year-old told her new best friend all the terrible things that her father had made her do.

As Byers had predicted, their unchosen bed lulled this way and that in the sluggish tide of East Foxton. The north-easterly too had dropped, leaving only the wail of nesting birds on Lethe Island to accompany the reluctant voyagers' breathing.

Sometimes the hull was clasped by reeds, at other times stirred along in little surges, so that by dawn, as anticipated, it was clear of the wrinkled sand and heading out to sea. Abbie's exhausted eyes opened to an all-encompassing sky with sheaves of cloud edging in from the south – hypnotic in their slow animation, deleting her past and her future.

She turned to Rosie, whose face was as pale as an old shell. Her eyelids flickered on the last of a dream. But *this* was no dream. The boat had taken in water and they lay half buried in their open coffin.

'Rosie?' Abbie nudged her.

Two innocent eyes met hers, then closed again.

'We've got to pray. It's all we can do.'

'Prayers never work. They're for dummies.' And with that, both fell asleep.

Suddenly a shout. Something was drawing closer, belching steam above and causing a swell below. The skipper of the *Skeldyke Glory* and three other crew peered down from the deck.

'O Jesus!'

'They dead?'

'Can't rightly say from 'ere.'

'No, we're bloody not!'

One man crossed himself, another fetched a line. The rope thudded by her feet, followed by a fisherman causing more water to slop over the side.

'Take her first, *please*,' Abbie implored, now fully awake. 'We're sinking.'

'Quick, man!' an urgent cry from above.

Their saviour passed one of them then the other to the rail.

'Who done this?' There was fish stink on his fingers as he unravelled the shrouds. 'Never seen this boat before.' Black eyes were fixed on hers, a flicker of suspicion round his mouth. 'You two bin playing some kind of game?'

Abbie's expression said it all.

'Right,' he said to his mate, 'you look after our friend here, I'll see to the little 'un.'

Abbie reared up, clutching her chest.

'Look, lady, we've seen plenty in the buff on our travels. You need to get out of this stuff, and quick . . .'

'I've radioed the Coastguard. They'll have rugs.' The skipper glanced up at the sky, his brows meeting across his nose. 'There's one mother of a storm over there, so get movin'!' He squatted down next to a still-sleeping Rosie as the nets were compressed and secured. 'She yours?'

'No, I look after her.'

'Who are you then? And who's she anyway?' Not unkindly.

'My name's Abbie. She's Rosie.'

Joe Liles stared at them. His face resembled a walnut with bright pinpricks for eyes and a mouth shrivelled by salt air. 'If we hadn't found you in time, God only knows. This is the worst bit of water I've ever come across. Only a few days ago two kiddies got into trouble just off North Sand.' A siren interrupted as a launch swerved in alongside and he stood up to greet the rescue party.

Abbie noticed the stretcher. 'I really don't need that. I'm OK.'

'Expert, are we?' Someone large dressed in orange took her head, while another raised her feet. In the background a radio crackled incessantly as though all the world was marooned out on the sea that day.

'Thanks,' Abbie called back, from safety, to the small fishing crew.

'Any time. All the best.'

Any time? I don't think so . . .

But soon their rescuers were out of sight, lost on the heaving tide.

Having decided that no urgent medical intervention was needed for the return journey, the crew member then pushed Rosie's damp fringe out of her eyes and turned to Abbie. 'Now tell us what happened, if you can.'

And, as the *Foxton Flyer* skimmed over the north Norfolk coast away from the gathering storm, the cleric's daughter finally opened her eyes from the depths of an unbidden nightmare, and her sudden scream sent the gulls back into the sky.

By Michaelmas we were all worse off and I wrote him that the Workhouse in Outwold was waiting. That the Beadle's been round again asking questions and knows from Susannah Buckley I've never in my life been deaf. Jealous folk now say Ben Robinson must be flitting, but I know the farm in Kircudbright is prospering well enough and he's saving with a co-operative with a little added each month. That's no good to me and his daughters who have to go bird scaring and following the dibble. Grace's hands are in a worse state than mine so I rub in goose fat and bind them up at night just like the ladies at Rievely, and tell Hemmings to leave her off stone picking for a while. He laughs in my face and I curse him again most sincerely.

Twenty-one

DETECTIVE INSPECTOR MOWBRAY'S huge thighs, close by, were the first thing Abbie saw when she awoke on that Tuesday morning in hospital.

'Lucky to be alive, I'd say.' He planted himself in a chair on the opposite side of the bed to Sheila and Simon, who'd been waiting anxiously for the patient to stir.

'No thanks to you or that dozy git of a desk sergeant!' The soldier glowered.

Shock and anger had paled him save for a wild red patch on each cheek, and Sheila only just noticed that his socks didn't match. Mowbray ignored him and got out his notepad.

'Simon?' Abbie whispered.

He bent over and kissed her, a wad of spearmint tucked in his cheek. He stroked her hair, her face, the bandaged wrists, then kissed her a second time. 'Christ, I thought I'd never see you again.' Then he turned to the Detective Inspector. 'So which evil bastard stitched all this up then? Someone who obviously wanted Abbie and Rosie dead.'

That last word hit the air like a bullet and caused the person in the next bed to stop eating.

'Because that's what it was — attempted bloody murder.'

'And that's why I'm here,' Mowbray said evenly.

Sheila placed an African violet on the locker nearby as Simon gave him another withering look.

Suddenly Abbie's eyes widened. She sat up in the bed. 'Where's Rosie?'

'Don't you worry your head about her now,' Mowbray said. 'She's gone where all children need to go – back with her mother and father. Apparently all's returned to normal.'

Abbie felt faint with an emptiness that was nothing to do with hunger.

'We'll look after her,' Simon whispered. 'I phoned social services yesterday, at nine. Funny how a solicitor's name gets things moving.'

'But you don't know any solicitors here' Abbie whispered.

'I do now, and Sleepy Hollow's holding a case conference about Rosie tomorrow.'

'Good for you,' Sheila murmured. ''Bout time as well.'

'Can I be privy to the conversation?' Mowbray cocked his big head. 'All this cosy subterfuge gets us nowhere. We need hard facts.' He produced a small pencil, which his hand immediately devoured. 'I've got quite a bit from what you already told the nurse, but there's something else I need to clear up.'

'What?' Simon challenged, but Mowbray ignored him.

'I know you're no bird-watcher, Miss Parker, so what were you doing out there on your own? Could it be you were snooping on people?' He pulled at the hairs inside a nostril.

Simon sprang to his feet. 'Bloody cheek.'

'Well, Byers could claim she was trespassing – when we find him, that is.'

'Shit, I don't believe this.' Simon buried his head in his hands.

'Property owners do have rights . . .'

'You don't have to say anything, Abbie.' Sheila's neck was noticeably reddening.

'I'm simply trying to establish the facts,' Mowbray said.

'I was way over on the other side, nowhere near his place!' Abbie shouted. 'If you must know, I was feeling totally pissed off.'

For a fleeting second, Simon felt that old shame clinging like an unwelcome guest. 'With me?'

'Course not.'

But the rest of what happened was a blur, like the crawling mist that was now denying the fens proper daylight.

'I see, pissed off.' Mowbray made it sound ridiculous as he wrote it down.

Simon snorted his derision.

Then she remembered something else. 'The car? Where's my car?'

Mowbray looked up.

'So you didn't walk there? What make?'

'Polo, silver metallic.' She'd loved it, worked bloody hard for it. Her home on wheels with the spare Ray-Bans, spare shoes and the UK road map Simon had bought her . . .

The DI shook his head. 'There's been no vehicle like that reported. You sure?'

She looked both flushed and dead beat. 'Look, I parked it at the end of Herringtoft. Next thing, when I got back it was down by some shitty little canal, for God's sake . . .'

Simon stayed close to her, breathing into her hair, like he always used to. It felt good, as if some sort of life was returning. 'That cunt Byers has nicked it, I bet,' Simon murmured. 'Hasn't anyone thought to go and take a look?'

'We'll check again, but we need to keep a bit quiet on all this for the time being. No use Byers or anyone else getting wind that you've shown up again. If he thinks you two have had it, there's a chance he'll get sloppy.'

Mowbray got up, avoiding eye contact. 'So let's play the game, shall we?'

'It's not us who need to do that,' Simon said.

'What d'you mean?'

'I mean that most of the public services round here seem to be as bent as bloody corkscrews.' Abbie's words, on Sunday, and now was the best time to repeat them.

The DI turned puce but Simon stood his ground.

'You never did go and see Byers, did you? Absolutely nothing's been done to help little Rosie, except that once, when her wellingtons turned up, and that's only because you thought a bad smell might follow you around.' Simon refilled his lungs. 'From what I've heard, that Black Fen Primary School is a bloody shambles, full of bullies and window-lickers, and now, thanks to your negligence, that little kid's in greater danger than ever.'

Mowbray's face resembled an aubergine as he paced around the bed. But Simon was in top gear and Abbie watched in amazement.

'We've got some poor old spinster who's been done in for no apparent reason, and my girlfriend here's been assaulted at work and had a death threat.'

Sheila gasped. So she was right all along, but that gave her no satisfaction. She looked at Abbie, then Simon. If he'd got half a brain cell, he'd want to take her away from here, as far away as possible. And Sheila was beginning to think she'd like to go too, as the breath of evil seemed to reach into even this sanitized environment.

'And what exactly do you mean by death threat?' Mowbray leaned forward.

Abbie and Sheila stared as Simon hunted in his jacket pockets and pulled that letter out, together with a can of Stella Artois, which he promptly hid again.

'This.'

'For God's sake, Abbie, why didn't you tell me?' Sheila said.

'Mmm.' Mowbray turned the page over, then brought it close to his face, wrinkling his fleshy nose.

'Your imaginative and proactive desk sergeant reckoned she'd written it to herself.' As Simon stroked her arm above the bandages he saw bruises on the undersides. 'Isn't that so helpful?' He felt the man's eyes boring through him.

'Was it you phoned him yesterday?'

'I did.'

'Well, he's regarding your intrusion as a nuisance call.'

'Good. Says it all.'

'What about that bloody letter?' Sheila demanded. 'That's much more to the point.'

'Look, I don't give a toss any more,' murmured Abbie, turning away.

'Don't say that.' Simon put his arms round her then fixed on the DI again. 'The situation here is fucking lethal. Quinn and that Lawson woman Abbie's told me about have put the frighteners on everyone, and I mean *everyone*. Now he may just have gone one step further . . .'

'All the more reason to just let it go, if you ask me.' Sheila reapplied lipstick without a mirror and pursed her lips.

'Which we don't.' Simon stood up. 'We're bloody well going to sort it out. Right, Abbie?'

'Yes,' she mumbled wearily.

But Sheila shook her head. Heroics were for story books, not for real people she had grown fond of. But the two of them were young and she could see the soldier's blood was boiling.

'So why aren't you out there looking for these perverts? Finding out who greased Byers's palm – because that's what it sounds like – and what's going to happen when whoever it is realizes Abbie and Rosie both survived. These two need police protection, not bloody excuses.'

'If I tell you we're understaffed, underfunded and—'

'All bloody related to each other, that's what I've heard as well.'

Mercifully a tea trolley rattled by. 'Strikes me it's corrupt and useless, your Grand Order of the Bogmarsh Freemasons or whatever.'

Mowbray wagged a finger. 'You be careful, my son, or I'll start taking a record of what you say. We have witnesses, don't forget.'

'Count me out,' Sheila muttered, trickling water on to the plant she had bought, for something to do. She'd spent her whole life avoiding hassle, keeping out of scrapes, but men were different: they seemed to need the clash of antlers, the fight to the death.

Abbie raised herself on her pillow.

'Detective Inspector,' she began reasonably, 'this is all missing the point. May I ask what *is* being done? *Now?*'

The man coughed, and sat down again. 'Fingerprints have already been taken and we've found several what can only be described as incriminating items—'

'Incriminating items?' Simon shouted. 'For fuck's sake!'

Sheila tittered. Mowbray shifted to the other buttock, too old and too tired to bother retaliating. 'We're in a cul-de-sac here. Our man has done a flit. We've got all airports and harbours on full alert. Scotland Yard is monitoring things. That's as much as we can do, till we get a sighting of Byers.'

But Abbie had slipped down again, her eyes closing as a nurse came over, checked her temperature and refilled the carafe as she urged the three of them to leave.

Simon watched anxiously. 'Look here,' he said, turning to Mowbray as they walked away, his voice softening, his fingers round the hidden Stella Artois, 'she and I have been under a hell of a lot of stress lately. Apart from all this, she's been threatened with losing her job and feels that the site's her personal responsibility, which is so bloody cruel. This whole place is like a graveyard of broken lives and nobody seems to give a shit.'

Mowbray checked each cuff in turn, avoiding the young man's troubled gaze.

'Why the hell do you think I've put in for early retirement?' he said quietly.

I laid a new brick floor at Goosefoot and stuffed old bedding in the holes beneath. We still get rats, but my bed and the cots that Buckley made are high enough to keep our feet from their jaws. Even when it's cold, the privy smells like Hell's tipped out all its dead, which reminds me that the Reverend Pinkton Downey was buried in Oxford on Sunday. His box had extra panels added for his greedy girth. More for the maggots, I'm thinking, and no loss to anyone . . .

Twenty-two

ABBIE TOOK THE Wednesday off work to recover. She'd begged Sheila and Simon to say nothing to anyone about what had happened in case Holtbury's took fright and found a replacement for her. As it was, she lay in her bedroom staring out at the Wenn and its strange waterborne world, hoping Sheila's call to Vallender had been convincing enough. Hoping Rosie was all right.

She heard the door open and shoeless feet padding across the floor. It was Simon carrying a tray in one hand and a bunch of something in the other. He looked better, even cheerful, as he laid the freesias on the sheet and hunted for a glass to put them in.

'Sorry I didn't bring anything for you in hospital yesterday. I just wanted to see you.'

'They're lovely.' Abbie smiled, but their smell was of the threatening letter, of death to come. And now everything had changed, even herself, changed for ever . . .

'So are you.' He angled the corner of a slice of toast towards her lips, acting like a real old mother. 'One for sorrow.'

She obliged and chewed.

'Two for joy.'

The same again.

'Three for a letter.'

Abbie took a chunk but didn't swallow.

'Four for a boy.'

She stopped.

'Go on.' Simon grinned. 'Like I said, four for a boy.'

'No.'

'Why not?'

'I don't want to think about that.' She spat out the unswallowed toast into the paper napkin. *Just me and my boy* . . . Every time she heard those words she would think only of what Grant Connell, the runaway pipe layer, had seen out on plot 2 and feel their grim ultra-sound touch her heart.

'Only kidding.'

'Good.' Abbie frisked his pockets with her eyes as he sat down. He couldn't be punished for ever. She knew why the drinking had started. If her father had pushed her into, say, chemistry or mathematics she'd have acted the same. 'Let's smell your breath.' She smiled and he pushed out his lips, blowing warm toasty air over her cheeks, then down her neck to her breasts . . .

'Did you really mean yes, we'd try and get to the bottom of things here, when you were in the hospital?' Simon asked afterwards, opening the curtains on to a dark lowering sky.

'But no more booze, promise?' She watched his taut slim back, his arms half the girth they used to be. 'Look at the state of you. You're still so thin.'

He turned and fixed his eyes on her as though in some inner turmoil. There was nothing to lose, a family to whom he was just a walking uniform, a job he loathed and would have to go back to, peopled by creatures from

the Dark Ages, but now, here she was, even more
beautiful than he ever remembered. And she needed him,
and perhaps Rosie Quinn needed him. That was enough.

'OK, I promise.'

'Good luck, you.'

He blew her a kiss, closed the door and dismissed the
stairs in three leaps.

He parked his newly hired Fiesta in the Disabled Drivers
section outside Snutterwick Social Services, then pushed
through the swing doors. A young woman was bending over a file. Her blonde head didn't look up. He
coughed.

'Be with you in a sec,' she said nonchalantly.

'You'd better. I need some answers about little Rosie
Quinn,' he began, but she persevered with her notes,
hoping he'd go away.

Her colleague had taken this man's previous call and,
as far as they were concerned, he was persona non grata.
Besides, she was used to aggressives and hysterics – they
came with the job.

'Hello? Mars to Earth?' he persisted, but she got up
to stroll over to a filing cabinet, as though the rest of the
day was hers.

She opened a drawer and extracted a green folder.

'Rosie Quinn. Q-U-I-N-N,' he spelt it out. 'The
vicar's daughter.'

'Ah. Are you Mr Cresswell then?'

If cows had blue eyes

'No, I'm Henry the bloody Eighth, and you, or
someone else, assured me on Monday morning that
there'd be a case conference today about her being
missing, God knows where . . .'

'I'm Miss Wright. That must have been Miss Tripp you spoke to.'

'I don't give a shit who it was—'

'Look, our EWO, Mr Werrington, has been following everything there. Rosie Quinn's not the only truant we have to deal with, you know.'

'She's not truanting, and don't go giving me any of that Children's Act crap either.' On his days in rehab the only information Simon had ingested lay in abandoned magazines or newspapers – the world's minutiae, learned by heart. Nothing had been wasted, every word a gold-mine. You never know.

'I'm sorry, Mr Cresswell, that attitude won't help. There are procedures to follow, as I'm sure you're aware.'

'Can't she go on the Children at Risk register?'

'Not immediately, no.'

'Well, I'm only giving you fair warning, my solicitor's getting interested, and then of course we have the press. They'll enjoy something like this.'

Cathy Wright kept her eye on him as she dialled her line manager. 'Better move on RQ6, Bob. Make it eleven o'clock. Fine. Will do.'

She turned to him. 'He says there's a phone box opposite the rectory. He'll meet you there. Is that convenient?'

'Thanks.'

'I hope you realize we might end up with egg on our faces. Kids are incredible fabricators, you know.'

'*I* never was. Anyhow, egg's better than shit.'

She closed the file and Simon blew his nose to celebrate. But outside the downpour had become a torrent, and he was forced to duck the puddles to reach his car.

His son Esmond Downey has come over from Marston, a scholar in Theology so folks say, and set for Mary Magdalene without a doubt. He writes his name in my prayer book and says it means grace and protection which is what God will give us through him, and on 2 August, the day Moeder died, he baptized the girls in the chapel. John and Susannah Buckley were in their best Godparents' clothes, and very smart they were too. I learned from her afterwards that my sissen Annie is set to marry Daniel Leakes. But when it suits me, Clenchtoft will kill her and her issue, that is my promise ... Still no money from Ben Robinson and Grace had sunstroke walking to West Winch so we lost five days' wages. Harriet is weeding until sunset and is too tired to sleep. We don't need to go to Hell, I say to myself. Hell is with us.

Twenty-three

THE REPLACEMENT PUNTO brought over from North Sand made Abbie feel like a learner driver all over again. She was also still tired after her ordeal and for two pins would have turned tail at the site entrance, but a couple of the men waved her a welcome which changed her mind.

The Show Home was still unlocked, a sackable offence, and her wariness at being there on her own became resentment against what – or who – had driven her into Byers's arms in the first place, endangering both her life and her job. But, by strange synchronicity, a handwritten envelope with the company logo lay on the mat. It was from Vallender, but like nothing else he'd ever sent, and she unfolded it to re-read at least half a dozen times.

His tone was formal and melancholy in turn. He was sorry about her recent 'flu and hoped she was feeling better. Realizing that she was doing her best in difficult circumstances, Holtbury's would extend her trial period until the end of August.

On the personal front, and in less careful script, he described how his wife, owner of a waxing clinic in Daventry, would be leaving the marital home after Whitsun. The letter had ended with a paragraph on his daughter, Gemma; because of his 'excessive mood swings'

Carol Vallender wouldn't be allowing him access. By this stage all punctuation had ceased, but that didn't matter, for his negotiator at Kingfisher Rise had the whole thing word-perfect by the time a new-model Fiesta powered on to the site. She put the letter in her case and watched Simon as he came up the drive.

It was strange him being here in the Show Home, her private space, but it neither took away her tension nor improved the atmosphere. She eased herself quickly out of his embrace, in case anyone outside should notice.

'I've finally got a result. They're meeting us at eleven,' he announced, then made a beeline for the fridge and hovered over the alcohol. 'Blood has come from the stone, *endlich*.'

'Great.' She reached over him and passed him a Lilt instead.

'Come on, Abbie, I've earned it.'

'Remember what you promised?'

Without an answer he sat down, thighs apart, in her seat, studying the plan in between slurps from the can. He bent his head lower; something had caught his eye. Something not quite right?

'Hey, Abs, look at this.' He was pointing at plot 2. 'Weird, man.'

She came over and brushed her palm over his shaved-stubble head. It felt nice, like her old velour school hat. Her eyes followed his finger. She froze. The whole block had been filled with red, thinner round the edges.

'Jesus.' He sniffed it. 'That's blood.'

Abbie screamed, scanning around instinctively for her sinister prospective client. It must have happened while she'd been outside on site, checking if there'd been any enquiries while she was away.

'It's her again! I know.'

'It's foul.' He got up and backed away, unsteady on his feet. Nothing usually frightened him. She hadn't called him standing stone for nothing, but this . . . 'Someone's got to see it.'

'How?'

'We'll go to Snutterwick cops. Make sure it's hand-delivered.'

'I can't.'

'Who'll notice your absence? There's hardly a stampede here.'

'Holtbury's might phone me, Vallender even.'

Simon turned. 'Him again?'

'Yes, him again.'

Simon looked out of the window. There was some activity over on plot 2, but nothing that seemed to be making any difference.

'You don't think one of them out there's been playing tricks, do you?'

'Don't be ridiculous.'

But it wasn't so far-fetched. She'd obviously left the office unlocked, so anyone could have got in. He saw her uncertainty, picked up the plan, making sure to keep it flat, and headed for the door. 'Shit, I forgot.' He stopped.

'Eleven o'clock?'

It was already 10.44.

With the site plan safe in the boot, they both waited outside the Smithy Lane phone box watching for any sign of a Social Services type of car turning off Walsoken Road.

Simon's Breitling showed 11.09. 'Come on, you wankers.' He began to pace around, feeling that same tension mount as when his unit went for War Strike briefings. Deadlines, rapid response, all to move things on, keep control . . .

'Give them another five minutes. The traffic might be bad out of Snutterwick,' Abbie said.

She watched the sky curdle to a yellow mist over the sea. The gulls too had drifted away, leaving an oppressive silence in their wake, until one of Quinn's teenage mothers with a squeaky pushchair gave Simon a flirty smile.

Simon looked after her, shaking his head. 'Makes me grateful,' he said when she'd gone.

'What for?' But she just wanted to hear him say it anyhow.

'You, of course.' He kissed her neck, then took her hand. 'Eleven-fifteen. Sod this for a game of bloody soldiers. Let's do something ourselves. You ready?'

Abbie nodded. You didn't need to be a member of MENSA to realize that Cathy Wright was taking the piss, and the mention of a case conference had just been a placebo. What really angered her was being taken for a dummy.

They crossed the road and stood by the rectory gateway. Whatever they had to do would be done openly, in full view.

'There it is.' Abbie strained to see that skylight window again, but the mulling mist gave nothing away.

She reached the front door before him, all her rage and frustration pressing the feeble bell, then bringing the knocker down again and again, brass on wood echoing in the dank afternoon, Simon's presence giving her hope and courage. Suddenly she smelt flowers, heard the swish of clothing as someone approached.

'This is intolerable behaviour!' the woman shrieked, as Simon gaped. He'd never seen anything so hideous, swathed in a fringed shawl, her face just visible behind the vast bouquet she carried.

'It's *her*. Avril Lawson,' Abbie whispered.

'And what are *you* doing here, you whore?'

Simon stepped in her way, every muscle tense, his fists ready, as Abbie kept up her noise on the door.

'That's my girlfriend you're referring to, so watch it! Now, if you don't mind, fuck off.'

Miss Lawson put her burden down: florist's blooms for the Mary Chapel, no expense spared. Abbie worked it out as at least thirty quid's worth.

'This is sacred ground,' the woman ranted. 'How dare you blaspheme!'

'Sacred, my arse.' Abbie stared into her enemy's black-rimmed eyes. 'Profane more like. The house of evil!'

'So go and play with yourself,' Simon was warming to the challenge. 'And, by the way, the police already know all about you.'

Abbie gaped at his daring.

'What do you mean?' The deputy head was now a different colour.

'Never you mind.' He tapped his nose. That had rattled the old bitch.

'I'll be reporting this abuse, and your intrusion, you'll see!'

'Yeah? Who's going to stop us?'

By now, a small crowd had gathered and only reluctantly allowed Miss Lawson to escape.

'You should hear what little Rosie Quinn told me,' Abbie shouted after her, suddenly enraged. 'Your precious Reverend is vile and depraved and his wife sits by and does nothing! And yes, we're both still alive, so there. They didn't manage to kill us.'

A collective gasp went up from the spectators, then silence as Simon turned to face them, deliberately choosing his words. Suddenly Sheila appeared, carrying two shopping bags. She took shelter behind him and put them down.

'If any of you lot want to help expose him,' Simon began, 'come over here. If not, go and do something more useful than just gawping.'

Abbie felt their disapproval. Saw that no one moved, until he walked towards them menacingly, then they began to disperse. She resumed banging the knocker with one hand, thumping on the door with the other, until he joined in, helping make thunder rise from the earth.

'Not much good for my business, this,' said Sheila, then put her mouth to the letter box and hollered. Not since her eventful marriage years had she made such a racket.

'Thanks, you're a brick.' Abbie patted her on the shoulder, then stepped back to scour the windows. 'Sshh. I'm sure I can hear something.'

'Probably just birds in the chimney.' Simon's ears were tuned to the inaudible, the way he'd been trained.

'No, no. It's more like footsteps.'

'Come on, the place is empty.' His eyes roamed over the whole miserable pile. 'But I'll go and check round the back,' he volunteered. 'You never know.'

'Be careful. He might have his axe.' Abbie then called out Rosie's name, telling her not to be afraid. She turned to Sheila. 'I'm sure the child's here on her own, scared to death, probably.'

The hotelier frowned. 'I don't think they'd risk that.

After all, she's pretty good at getting out. Anyhow, you don't know what you're dealing with.'

Abbie wasn't listening. 'I *know* she's in this house. I'm going to get Jason to try and crack the lock.'

'Who's Jason?' Simon reappeared, stained with lichen. He spat on his knuckles and wiped them on his jeans.

'He's a bloody good chippie who works on the site, that's all I know.'

'Bet you he'll not want to interfere.'

'He will if it's worth thirty quid.'

Simon followed her to the car, asking Sheila if she'd like a lift. The older woman declined.

Kingfisher Rise was deserted save for a few workmen's cars and two lads on bikes circling round, making drifts of gravel.

Simon climbed out. 'What are you two doing here?'

'Nuffink.'

'Off you go then,' said Abbie, making for the whine of a saw which seemed to come from plot 4.

Once her back was turned, one of the boys gave her a V sign. Simon charged them, but not fast enough.

'Rosie Quinn's mate! Rosie Quinn's mate!' they chanted, tearing away in a cloud of dust. It was then that Abbie realized who the boys were. Half of Black Fen Primary School's heavenly choir. Darren Greenhalgh and Charlie Hunter.

Simon watched them swerve along the Walsoken Road and out of sight. Abbie was already at the top end of the crescent, stepping over the debris in her best shoes. Jason Wright wiped his forehead. 'Little fuckers.' Then he noticed the state of her. 'You all right?'

'Not really. Jason, I need your help, now.' She got

out her purse. 'It's urgent. I want a lock picked at the rectory. It'll only take a minute. I'll give you £30.'

The joiner pondered, his hand exploring his stubble chin as if it was a stranger to him. Abbie sighed with impatience, looked to Simon for support.

'We've got to get a little girl to safety,' he explained.

'I ain't heard nothing 'bout any of this.'

'You wouldn't have. It's not common knowledge yet.'

'The rectory, you said? That's private property, innit?'

'Only the Church's,' said Abbie dismissively.

'Look, it's a bit dodgy for me at the moment. If I knew this job here was likely to be a cert. If I . . .'

Abbie didn't wait to hear his tale of woe, didn't pause to give him any reassurances, but dived back into her car, swearing at the whole of mankind.

'I'll do it myself then.'

'Just calm down,' Simon said, remembering the site plan still in the boot. 'Let's do this properly.'

'Properly? By the rules? Oh yes, and wait for kingdom come.'

'We'll be in deep shit if we cause any damage. Anyhow, we don't even know how Quinn's bloody mind's working.'

'I've got a good idea.'

'OK, but *we've* got to be cleverer than him – one step ahead.'

They paused by the church, where Zillah Watts, widow, of Breakwell Farm stood muffled up for the Arctic.

'Any sign of the Reverend or his family?' Simon asked her casually.

'You tell me. I've been hanging on and hanging on,' Mrs Watts complained. 'I was supposed to be checking the hymn books for repair, but everything's locked up. It's all very odd. We don't know when services will start up again. You couldn't run me home, could you? It's Breakwell Farm. Just turn up past the garden centre. Thank you very much.' The request was too sudden for Simon to refuse or make excuses, so he cleared his things off the back seat and let her in. As he drove off, Abbie, sitting next to him, looked back at the rectory windows in the gathering dusk. 'I won't be long, Rosie,' she whispered.

'Beg pardon?' said Zillah Watts from behind, smelling of camphor.

'Sorry, nothing.'

As the Fiesta reached the Walsoken Garden Centre and swung round into Swinefield Lane, Mrs Watts leaned forward in her seat.

'Things is getting bad here. I heard there's rum doings at that new building site an' all.'

Simon and Abbie exchanged glances. This one's yours, he winked.

'What d'you mean? Everything's fine,' Abbie countered.

'Well, you *would* say that. You're one of them, aren't you?'

Abbie felt impaled, willed Breakwell Farm to appear, *now*.

'Er . . . yes, but we've had no complaints so far. Quality homes, competitive prices, we're doing the locals here a big favour.' She hated every syllable, but, like a pioneer's stockade, the patter provided at least some defence.

The widow tucked her chin further into her collar 'I

expect they're off at that retreat again,' she said out of the blue.

'Who?'

'The Quinns, I mean.'

Simon crashed the gear and Mrs Watts let out a small cry at the suddenness of it, while Abbie caught her breath.

'Where's that then?' She tried to hide her curiosity.

'Goteland. It's a village on Crowland Fen. They've gone there a few times before now. It gives them a bit of peace from all us lot, I suppose.' But the woman didn't sound convinced.

Abbie thought quickly. This information could be useful. 'What happens to Rosie when they go away, or do they take her along as well?'

'Oh no, she goes over to Wisbech, with Mrs Quinn's parents.'

'Oh?' *Like hell she does.*

'Is that where Mrs Quinn comes from?'

'Yes. They used to own a smallholding. I think he had a permit to train horses once, and she used to ride some of them at point-to-points.'

Abbie thought of the wheelchair, those strong gripping hands. 'Is that where she met the vicar?'

''S right. He'd come over from somewhere west, I think. A real love match it was, did all their courting in Black Fen. Handsome young man then, as I remember.' She paused as Simon turned off Walsoken Road. 'And quite a few of the ladies started going back to church so they could clap eyes on him once a week . . .'

It was like some grotesque fairytale, but Mrs Watts seemed to enjoy the telling.

'So how did she, you know, end up in a wheelchair? Did she fall off her horse or something?'

Zillah Watts peered out over her collar like a pink sugar mouse fattened on the morsels of others' lives. 'Most folks like to think so, but I know different.'

'So what did happen?'

Simon gave Abbie a warning glance. Steady now, she told herself, we musn't scare off the goose with the golden egg . . .

'It was the stairs, you see,' Mrs Watts obliged. 'An accident by all accounts, but I don't think her own parents believed that . . . Mind you, they're getting on a bit – never come visiting like they used to. Still, they say families are like fish.'

Abbie looked round at her, puzzled.

'Don't take long to start stinking, see.' The passenger got her bag and gloves ready.

'That's a charming thought,' Simon said, slowing up at the Breakwell sign. He cranked up the handbrake and flicked the central locking to let the old girl out.

They both watched as she juggled with the gate latch while carrying her large vinyl handbag.

'Here, I'll do it.' Simon went to sort her out, saw the ruin ahead of him and felt sorry for this woman having to go back in there. When he got back to the car he said, 'Come on, let's make tracks. We're going somewhere nice when you've finished work.'

'What do you mean nice?'

'OK, quiet, then.'

Within five minutes they were once again opposite the church. Still no Cathy Wright or Angela Tripp . . . or Uncle Tom Cobbleigh. Time for action. Simon and Abbie again faced the rectory door.

'Rosie!' Abbie hissed through the letter box. 'It's me.'
Fear and cold seemed to numb all her limbs. She shivered
against Simon's body. 'Rosie!'

Simon's ear was pressed close by. 'You're right,' he
whispered. 'There *is* somebody in there.' He plunged his
hand into his pocket and produced a tiny spring, a
section of fuse wire and an elastic band. 'Best Boy Scout,
eh?' The spring slotted into the keyhole and became
almost lost. Nothing was connecting and his fingers
felt like lead. Then suddenly their silent prayers were
answered. The door gave way and eased open into the
darkness. 'Thank God.'

They were in the hall and from somewhere above,
amid the tapping of wood on wood, came someone's
moans of terror.

He found a switch and tried it. No lights. 'Fuck it.'

They groped towards the stairs. It was less dark now
and they could see better the shapes of old furniture:
dead men's chattels on a carpet threadbare and danger-
ously loose in places. On the first landing the tapping
grew more distinct.

Another flight, both hugging the wall, inhaling its
dampness, each step upwards bringing warmer air and an
amalgam of smells part human part wildlife.

The knocking was now quite plain. The cries clearer.

'Rosie, is that you?'

The banisters ended where the corridor became a
narrow passage and oak turned to stone, and where bats
flew free in the strangled air. This was where they found
her, and at that moment even four arms weren't enough
to hold her upright.

Someone has tattled to Esmond Downey that we are penniless, as he asked me to clean the church for a shilling a week. All the silver and brass and sometimes the window over the altar so I can see God's light better, he says. He is also teaching me to write again, which will no doubt be useful to my purpose. Often he takes my waist into his hands and keeps them there. His dairy skin has never seen the weather and his lips full as bladderwrack pull on my buttons till they're fit to bleed . . .

Twenty-four

THE BACON WAS like caviare, the eggs like oysters. Sheila Livingstone watched over her guests sitting on the scuffed red vinyl and smiled as the contents of their plates disappeared. Simon got up, kissed her on the cheek, then Rosie.

She was the cutest thing he'd ever come across and oddly she'd shown no fear towards him, a total stranger. In fact the opposite, and in turn he felt he'd known her for years. The grandchild his mother kept on about, the child he'd have with Abbie, one day, when all this was behind them, when Abbie was safe.

Sheila fetched her a packet of crisps and watched them going into her mouth whole.

'Are you Abbie's boyfriend?' Rosie asked him without a qualm.

Abbie and Simon exchanged glances.

'Sort of.'

'So do you play mummies and daddies?'

Silence followed as she crunched her way through the rest of the packet, then Simon got up.

'Places to go, people to see, sweetheart.' He held the car keys in his teeth as he retied his laces. 'See you later.'

'Bye.'

Sheila seemed unhappy. Abbie looked down at Rosie,

who was already half asleep. The child with no childhood, a fragment of crisp still on her chin.

'I'll put her in your room while you're at work, if you like,' Sheila suggested. 'There's some of Saffron's things she can have.' She'd never thrown her daughter's clothes out, and didn't understand how people could. Clothes were part of the memory, when there was precious little else.

'You've been amazing. Thanks.' Abbie stroked Rosie's hair. 'Keep her safe with you all the time, though, won't you? We can't take any chances.'

'Don't worry.'

Sheila started clearing up, but worries were settling thick and fast in her mind. What if Quinn should turn up looking for the child? What if someone else spotted her here and spilt the beans? She couldn't just close the place, couldn't afford to ... When Abbie had gone, she took off her apron and carried the sleeping child upstairs. And, as the clock chimed one Sheila locked the bedroom door.

During the afternoon, the rheumy mist lifted to reveal a clear hard sky, and Simon drove back from Snutterwick with his window down, smelling the earth and the water, letting the lingering smell of blood finally escape.

WPC O'Halloran had signed for receipt of the site plan with a frown. She'd assured him forensics would certainly look at it, but she couldn't promise anything immediately as it was more than likely some practical, if sick, joke. At least, like Abbie had said, she'd been responsive, treating him like a fellow human being, unlike that clown in Social Services who'd lied so badly in telling him that everyone else on the team was at a meeting in Cambridge when they should have been here in Black Fen.

One step forward, two steps back, useless to hope for anything else, but at least the CID were now *aware*.

Next stop, Abbie, then the hotel to check on Rosie. And then Goteland. He'd looked it up on the map already, decided to get a full tank of petrol and check the oil just in case. The word had an evil ring to it, but he felt like a nail drawn to a magnet. This whole business had that effect.

After work Abbie changed into jeans and a fleece top, while Simon finished his can of Coke and Sheila encouraged an Instant Whip into Rosie's mouth.

'We'll be two hours at the most, and back before nine anyhow.'

'Do try.' Sheila looked up. 'Best if you're here.' She didn't want to be left on her own with the child after dark, that was obvious.

Abbie looked at Simon. 'Do *I* have to go?' she asked.

'Look, take no notice of me, Abbie, I'm sorry,' Sheila broke in. 'I don't want to be a pain.'

'You're not, for God's sake. And cross my little heart we'll be quick.' Simon patted her arm.

Sheila managed a smile. He was a real charmer, and his was no *little* heart. She wiped Rosie's chin, then waved them away and turned the sign on the door to CLOSED.

In the chapel which is usually dark and quiet as the grave he says his sned is ready and have I ever seen one like it? I say the clay pipes along Slave's Drain are longer and straighter, whereupon he lifts my dress and causes me a deal of pain. Grace and Harriet sit in his school every Thursday. Numbers and the ways of the stars are what they talk about most and they are curious to know more all the time. Like Moeder said, education helps you clear the first hedge and I mean to set them a good example and practise spelling and punctuation.

Twenty-five

'HOLIDAY ROUTE. THAT'S a joke.' Simon turned the Fiesta into Drain Road, beyond the last dwellings of Black Fen. The yellow mist was moving inland with some urgency, hungry for land, any land – and souls, any souls . . . It was as if no sun had ever existed, that this opacity would be a prelude to everlasting night.

He'd always been susceptible to places – it was in his upbringing, forever watching the sky over Pen y Fan knowing that somewhere in the clouds, the air, the spirits of Rhiannon, Blodeuwedd and the rest of the Celtic host were waiting to be summoned.

'It's so creepy.' Abbie looked out over the nothing of Crowland Fen as he switched to dipped lights. 'You sure we're on the right road?' She put her hand on his thigh. It felt strong and hard. She was safe.

'No worries. But hey, see that sign?' He slowed up. 'Kilntoft. It's some massive fucking slaughterhouse. I looked it up.'

She shivered, remembering the blood on the site plan. When she'd tried phoning Vallender for a new one, some woman had said he was out of the office.

'What's the matter?'

His nose was practically against the windscreen, both hands now tight on the wheel.

'All those dead animals. The smell's getting into the car.'

No lights, just the darkening fens and the stench of death eking in through the radiator, round the windows, making her feel faint. He smelt it too and put his foot down, the road to the sea straight as a severing knife for the cloven-hooved, straight and clean – without mercy. In two minutes it had passed.

There were no signs, but the moment they entered the village, GOTELAND WELCOMES CAREFUL DRIVERS, they could hear the bells – gloomy things in the quietude, leading helpfully up Sinfold Lane. There wasn't a soul about. It was like a place of plague, no dogs, no walkers, and the few cars anchored in oil slicks outside the dingy cottages looked of another era.

Haletoft House was huge, seeming part of the yellowed mist, its dark mullioned windows like spinsters' eyes as the Fiesta parked in bushes at the end of the drive where the contents of Byers's gut still gave off a signal of fetid fear.

They held hands, the good-looking couple searching for their much-loved uncle. They were concerned, naturally, as he and his wife, Helen, had simply disappeared. It was the very least they could do to investigate, given the times we live in . . .

The chimes emanating from an adjoining tower seemed magnified not muffled by the mist which made any further rehearsal impossible. Simon gave her hand one last squeeze, then rang the bell by the solid front door. Abbie kept thinking of Rosie, hoping she was all right. It would be stupid to phone Sheila so soon, but she couldn't help worrying. Simon, meanwhile, kept trying for an answer.

'Come on, you old dossers, you can't be that bloody busy,' he shouted, unaware that everything he said was being taped in Brother Robert's little room.

The door opened with a rush of stale air.

'But we are, for our sins, we are.' The portly man in a stained white robe used the solid stump of his body to keep the callers out. He scrutinized them both over his wire-framed glasses, resting, for longer than she liked, on Abbie's breasts.

'Mr Quinn's my uncle,' she began, to divert him. 'We're really worried about where he and Aunt Helen might be. We were told to try here.'

Shit, she could act, Simon thought, wanting to thump this dirty little git in the smacker. Best leave it to Abbie then, whatever.

'And who gave you that information, may I ask?'

'Miss Lawson. She does the St Mary Magdalene Church flowers.'

A flicker of recognition touched the priest's face. He held the door open.

'You do know what we are here? I mean by that that we're a sanctuary for those called to the service of God, an inviolable place of respite.'

'She told me it was some kind of retreat, yes, and that he'd been here before.'

'I'm afraid Miss . . .'

'Longman, Stella.' It would do, second time lucky.

'And?' He eyed Simon with distrust.

'Jez. Jez Wheeler.'

Abbie tried to smother a smile.

'Bricklayer,' he elaborated. 'Black Fen.'

'Well, Miss Longman, I'm afraid we cannot divulge your uncle's whereabouts, even if we knew them.'

Simon edged closer. 'Look here. We've driven miles, and my girlfriend here is worried sick. What sort of Christian attitude is this, to deny her peace of mind?' He could see one or two green-robed figures haunting the corridor behind, but no one resembled Abbie's description of Quinn. 'There's also their little girl, who's with Aunt Helen's parents in Wisbech at the moment, but if her mum and dad don't show up soon, *they'll* be trying the police as well.'

Brother Robert moved closer. Small is menacing, Simon thought, despite the soft belly, the white chipolata fingers.

'Don't you threaten me, Mr Wheeler. I don't like your tone at all,' the fat man growled.

'Tell us if they're here then.'

Brother Robert looked around for support, but he was on his own. He assessed the young man's fighting hands and the eyes that cut through him like a fileting knife.

'They're not. If you don't believe me, I'll have to show you round.'

He waddled crossly through the length and breadth of that airless house. The conducted tour lasted quarter of an hour, down corridor after tiled corridor ending finally with the lounge, the most dismal room Abbie had ever seen. Although empty of people, it was full of fitted shelves stuffed with what looked like Bibles, prayer books, hymnals of all different shapes and sizes, some obviously very old.

With their obnoxious guide distracted by the sudden ringing of his office telephone, Abbie quickly told Simon about the prayer book which she'd seen at Goosefoot Cottage — something that had slipped her mind what with all the other recent distractions.

'It had the name Esmond Downey written on the flyleaf,' she added. 'Quinn made out he knew nothing about it, of course.'

'OK. We could see if it's here by any chance.' Simon's fingers trailed over the worn spines. Any volume he pulled out seemed to expire its own stale breath into his face. 'Could fetch quite a bit, some of these, you know,' he said, still keeping a watchful eye on the lounge door.

Abbie rebuked him abstractedly as she scanned the shelves for anything black, of similar size to that mysterious prayer book with those same worn corners. Suddenly she stopped, thinking she might have found it. But although this similar-looking Old Testament wasn't exactly what she was looking for, it nevertheless made her pulse quicken when she opened it.

'Hey, Si. Look at this.'

He came over, making sure his back wasn't vulnerable, as Abbie read from the flyleaf. ' "Helen Mary Quinn (née Perry), January 26th 1996. For my sins." For my sins,' she repeated. 'What's all *that* about, I wonder,' she asked herself, frowning, aware also of some extra pieces of paper folded inside the back cover.

'Proves hubby must have been here at some point. Wives don't come on their own, do they?'

'So what do we do now?'

'Let's take it,' Simon said. 'Might come in handy.' Then he heard footsteps along the corridor and he shoved the little book deep into his jacket pocket.

At that moment Brother Robert reappeared. His eyes switched from Abbie to Simon, who was pretending to view the garden.

'You've certainly got a terrific spot here.' Simon made

a show of peering out. In fact the view showed mist and more mist.

'I don't trust you two. Out, *now*,' the cleric snapped.

'Come on,' Abbie whispered anxiously. 'Rosie's waiting.'

'Accessory.' Simon made sure his parting shot was loud and clear as Brother Robert closed the door behind them. 'You'll enjoy hearing *that* in court.'

Heading back down the drive, and keeping to the gravel in the worsening light, they could see the Fiesta like a faint red stain against the leaves.

'That was a complete waste of fucking time,' Simon grumbled.

'No, it wasn't.'

'That little shit's a serial liar.' He reached for the door, then stopped. 'Hell, look at this. I locked it, I swear I did. This is crazy.'

He started to check his glove compartment, the map holders. Everything seemed in place, except for one thing. His hire form copy had gone – with his name on it, Lieutenant Simon Cresswell, address, St George's Sails Hotel. 'That's me stitched up then.'

Then suddenly they heard feet behind them, at least two pairs scuffling through the mist.

'Get in!' Simon yelled.

Central locking shut the intruders out: Brother Robert and a taller figure in green. 'It's Quinn!' Abbie screamed as the white hand slipped into his robe, then took aim.

The gunshot went to ground with a dull thud. For a moment the Fiesta hit bushes and veered out of control. Abbie gripped Simon's arm as the hatchback blundered along over a grass verge until their view cleared again.

Neither uttered a sound, while a broken sign for Oscarby End showed east not west, a gradient upwards past isolated farms, derelict Builders' Merchants and potato wholesalers, until the mist completely cleared.

The North Sea lay just below them, waiting with infinite patience, its calm unnerving. It spread to the left and right, as if marooning the settlement of caravans which clustered like larvae to the poor soil.

After he'd stopped the car, Simon leaned over and locked Abbie in his arms. She was sobbing with relief.

He studied the sky for any trace of the dying sun, but what lay above the remaining wisps of fog gave nothing away. Then Abbie saw him remove the car key.

'Where are you going?'

'Just a hunch. Won't be a minute.'

'Two minutes, no more. Promise?'

'I promise.'

Her watch showed 6.40, darkness in an hour. She shivered, watching him sprint towards a sign standing next to what had once been a five-bar gate.

SUN & FUN ALL YEAR ROUND, but half its letters had deteriorated.

Abbie watched him as he tried one caravan after the other. Some were boarded up with MDF, others with open windows trailed bits of curtain into the air. The salty atmosphere had exacted a high price, for they all looked pretty terminal, perched on their rusty axles and surrounded by junk. Who ever would want to hole up here, she wondered, checking her watch again. One minute to go.

There was a sudden rap on the glass. It was Simon.

'Christ, don't do that.'

'Come here, quick,' he said.

She followed him through the maze of caravans, their paintwork oozing black mildew, their names faded in the silence of decay: Restholme, Aysgarth, Downlea . . .

They stopped near a beige one, in slightly better repair than its neighbours, the grey nets at its windows speckled with dead flies.

'There, look.' He pointed at a wheelchair folded up near the caravan door. Abbie stared at it. It certainly looked familiar.

'Could be hers,' she admitted, anxiously checking that the woman's husband wasn't around.

'If it is hers, then someone's been careless.' Simon made a mental note of the wheelchair's make, Speedigrip, then ducked to the other side of the door, pressing his ear to the caravan's flimsy wall.

'You go back and sit in the driver's seat. Be ready to get the hell out of here.' He passed her the car keys.

'Simon, you're mad. Supposing someone's in there?' Her mind was screaming *No, no, no.*

'Don't be daft. We've just seen him up at the retreat. The fucker can't fly, can he?'

Abbie turned round as he began to fumble with the caravan door. Back in the car, she let the engine idle while her heart raced in her chest.

Come on, Simon. Come on . . .

The caravan was cold inside and felt unoccupied, without the usual residual smells of cooking or bodies in close proximity. But he wasn't alone. A figure sat motionless on one of the bunks, facing out to sea. It was a woman with fair greying hair, a face pale as chalcedony. Under her fingers lay a flowered boater which looked as though nesting birds had picked at it, sewn-on flowers straggling from its brim.

He noticed her withered legs, but pity wouldn't come. This was her all right. The wife, Rosie's mother.

Helen Quinn turned and fixed him with hard accusing eyes. 'Whoever you are, get out.'

Simon scanned the rest of the place but, apart from a pile of blankets on the opposite bunk, there was nothing to suggest anyone else was sharing the caravan with her. And, vulnerable as she was, like her daughter Rosie, she showed no fear. Perhaps she'd gone beyond all that.

A mother *sans* everything . . .

'Tell me what's this vicar of yours playing at?' Simon demanded.

Her mouth tightened, the eyes narrowed, grew darker. She clearly didn't enjoy his presence. 'He'll kill you if he finds you here.'

'He's already tried that, thanks. Just tell him from me the police are getting nice and close, that's all.' Simon stepped down on to the grass outside as Helen Quinn returned to her view – intently watching a powerboat trail a plume of spray in its wake. Someone's free, she thought longingly, aware of a draught from the door as it closed behind her.

'It's Martha Robinson you really want,' she suddenly shouted. 'The Devil's mistress!'

But her visitor was already halfway back to his car, hearing only its waiting engine throb in the damp air.

The Reverend Esmond Downey is giving me lists of words to learn by heart each week, and then tests me while he takes his pleasure. I confess what I do is wrong and God will see me, but men of this earth are weak, even men in God's service . . . On Thursdays at Goosefoot now we have a nice piece of chine and my money from him keeps fresh bread on the table so I cannot complain.

Twenty-six

THE FOG OVER Black Fen lay thick, unbroken, save for the sodium lights in Walsoken Road and the one security beam in Kingfisher Rise that laboured round its ruined kingdom. Nothing seemed to move or breathe under the weight of it. Even the three barges lined end to end on the Wenn lay still as coffins.

Sheila took longer than usual to answer the door, just to make quite sure. Relief flooded her face and she instantly forgot the evening's few lost takings. Simon glanced across at the bar, lifted Abbie's room key and went straight upstairs.

'It's been fine,' Sheila called after them. But it hadn't been. Every long minute clocked up on her slate souvenir from Betws-y-Coed had felt like an hour, every hour a lifetime. 'I looked in twice and she's probably still fast asleep.' Then Sheila helped herself to a sherry.

They both crept in on a scene of peace and calm. Sheila had bathed the child and picked the bits of bat shit out of her hair, which now spread shining over the pillow. A small pink hand lay cupped as if in anticipation. *Of what?* Abbie was suddenly overwhelmed by what they'd taken on. *Of love?* Yes, if she herself had anything to do with it, for Simon reckoned Helen Quinn looked like she'd rather given up on life.

'Poor little kid,' Abbie murmured, uncreasing the over-large nightdress to show a smiling Yogi bear right under Rosie's chin.

'She's beautiful,' Simon whispered, 'just like you.' Then he closed the door and kissed Abbie. 'Now am I allowed a drink?'

Sheila set out new tablemats for the occasion, then produced three oven-ready lasagnes and what was left of a tired salad.

'Brilliant, thanks,' Simon said, but his stomach really wanted the buzz of alcohol.

Abbie watched the second drink go down, then noticed Sheila hovering in the doorway.

'I've got to tell you both something,' she began. 'It's a bit tricky to explain really, but you ought to know.'

They both stared. Such announcements from her were rare, so something must be wrong.

'It's Rosie. You know when I bathed her, well, I found things . . .'

'Things?' Abbie felt her insides take a dive.

'She's bruised – you know, down there . . .'

Simon set his glass down. 'Shit. You sure?'

'Of course I am. I've been a mum, remember? It's not a normal injury, like she's done it on a slide or something.'

'I think I know what you're saying.' Abbie glanced towards the stairs. 'This ties up with what she told me in that bloody boat. This is what we're up against. This is the *evil* of the man, and why he wants us out of the way. We know too much.' She could see Simon tense with anger. Quinn had better watch out.

Having picked at their rubber lasagnes without much

interest, they both went to sit up at the bar, still preoccupied, while Sheila made coffee. Helen Quinn's Old Testament lay between them, with that yellowing church notepaper Abbie had noticed earlier spread out under their hands.

'Let's have a read then.' Simon's glass was again at his lips, his eyes starting on their journey of disbelief. 'Shit. It's by him . . . "I, the Reverend Peter Quinn, plead to my God, how do I answer this other voice that sits in my head? Those words of destruction whose origins must lie in a heart so vile as not to have been of your making . . . Do I shut my ears to it? But that, Lord, is like asking a cymbalist not to hear his own noise. Do I record it all as witness to my derangement? Or will the very nature of writing keep it in perpetuity? Tell me which road to take, I beg of you . . . Should I share these taunts and threats with some other in your service who can then lift this wickedness from me?"'

'"Some *other* in your service?"' Abbie repeated, frowning.

'Personal exorcism, that's what the fucker means.'

'Unless he's just trying to pass the buck.'

They stared at each other before studying the remaining sheets of paper, some of which had been folded for years, leaving a brown grid over the words. Each succeeding page seemed more intense, more desperate, with the wrestlings of a tortured soul against a greater unknown force laid bare, until, on Good Friday 1992 at three p.m. precisely, he'd scrawled over a whole page, 'My God, my God, why hast Thou forsaken me?'

'Maybe *that's* why he was heaving an axe around that day. He's all screwed up.'

'Better in than out, so they say.' Simon tried to make light of something that was terrifyingly obvious.

'It is a sort of confession.'

'Which is of course not practised in the Church of England.'

'And what about Helen Quinn's weird words here . . .' Abbie picked up the black book again and re-read the inscription. What *sins* do you think she means?'

'Being a neglectful mother, I bet.' Sheila said suddenly.

'Could be. Maybe there's more where that came from.' Simon was checking each page.

'I'm not going back to that place again, if that's what you're thinking.'

Sheila passed over the coffees and sat down with them at the bar, unusually silent.

'Fingerprints! Damn.' Simon suddenly looked at his fingertips. 'Mine'll be all over that book and those papers. Yours too.'

'What about everyone else at that retreat? They must have been gawped at at least a few times.' Abbie stared at her coffee. 'I doubt it, but maybe he deliberately left it out there to be found.'

'Maybe *she* did.'

Simon reached for the phone. 'Snutterwick CID please,' he said resting a leg on the bar stool.

Abbie watched him hard, willing him to stay there, not to disappear back to the business of war. Yet what did it matter? For Balkans say Black Fen. All equally shitty. All equally deadly.

'Haletoft House, Goteland. Yes, that's right.' Simon raised his voice into the receiver. 'And we also found his

wife alone in a caravan, a kind of beige colour. Sprite –
no reg number – at a place called Oscarby End. This
evening, yes, about seven o'clock.' Abbie waved the black
book to remind him. 'There's something else, two things
actually. Some pretty weird stuff hidden in this Old
Testament we found and . . . No, I've not had a few, do
you mind? I don't make things like this up . . . Who am
I speaking to? Sergeant French? Oh, not again.'

Simon looked despairingly over at Abbie and Sheila.
'Is WPC O'Halloran there? I left something with her . . .
No? Stupid of me to ask. Mowbray, then? Ah, right, he's
retired. Shit, of course, what else can one expect? I'll try
tomorrow, eleven-thirty. Give you time to come up with
something.' He slammed the phone down. 'Bunch of
wankers.'

He asked for another vodka and Sheila obliged without comment, then went over to their table and took the
remains of their meal back to the kitchen.

Unlike Abbie's, Simon's plate was almost empty –
fuelling his mission, she could tell.

'I'll wash up,' he offered, but she didn't want to lose
any more crockery.

When she came back she looked serious. 'I don't
know about all this other stuff here, but we need to
decide about Rosie – and quick. You do understand?'

Abbie nodded, resting a hand on hers as the souvenir
clock struck ten.

'Look, I've been thinking. I've got an uncle near here.
Graham Parker. He's an art historian and he's got a little
girl, Flora. She'll be six in August. They live in a village
just south of King's Lynn.'

'Very nice over that way. Is there a wife?' Sheila
tipped out another Marlboro, but forgot to light it.

'Yes, called Sue. She specializes in American Realism, something like that.' In fact it was his second time round and Abbie had not seen them since her mother's funeral.

'Well, that sounds useful.' Simon smiled.

'I think they might take Rosie, just for the time being.'

'Mmm.' Sheila frowned.

'What d'you mean?'

'I mean, do you really want to put your own family in danger?' asked Sheila. 'Wouldn't it be better if she went somewhere, you know, more official? A sort of refuge, like they have for battered wives.'

Silence fell between the three of them for a minute.

'She's got a point.' Simon studied his glass. 'But that's too risky. They could easily trace her.'

'Who could?' Abbie asked, disconcerted.

'The Family Protection Unit for starters. Never mind our local lunatic.'

'So what's the alternative?' Sheila was looking again at the stairs.

'There isn't one.'

The fog that sealed the hotel in with the rest of Black Fen had even penetrated the upper windows, leaving a film of mist hovering on the landing. Simon had reassured a nervous Sheila by double-checking all the ground-floor sash windows, and he now held Abbie's hand as they made for the bedroom. From behind its door came strange noises – burbling dream talk, then a whimpering little cry.

'Ssh.' Abbie gripped his arm. 'What on earth's she doing?'

'Only one way to find out.' Simon went first. The

room felt like ice, dark as a tomb, and Abbie could swear that the same smell of wet earth hung round the bed itself.

Rosie looked deathly white, her eyes wide open and unfocused, her lips quivering as she spoke.

'I'mtellingyouIneverbelieved*anything*thattoldwitchtold me about the dollies and what she said about having a baby so why don't you believe me? And why if you're so powerful like you say don't you tell my daddy to leave me alone and make Mummy stop him and Charlie Hunter and Emma Mason and Darren Greenhalgh and Cherry Pickering?'

'Rosie?' Abbie touched her hand. 'Who are you talking to?'

The child jerked upwards, her face shot with terror, her hair lank with sweat against her head. She began to sob as Abbie held her, her little body heaving. 'Try and tell us.'

But Rosie didn't need to say anything. Abbie already had a good idea who'd got there first.

Simon felt the radiator that had been set to Warm. It was as cold as marble and he shivered despite his clothes.

'Don't leave me alone. Please don't make me, like Mummy and Daddy,' Rosie called out suddenly.

'Of course we won't. You're staying with me tonight.' Abbie stroked out the tiny furrows in the child's forehead. 'Promise.'

The little girl calmed down, though she was still panting as if she'd been running away from some tormentor. She turned to watch Simon switch on the corridor light. He was nice – besides, she liked fair hair best.

Abbie knelt down beside the bed. 'Rosie, tell me who you saw. Was it a lady in a black coat and dress?' she asked gently.

'No, it wasn't like that.' The child seemed puzzled by her question.

'What then?'

'It was just a voice, really horrible – a loud voice.'

'Have you ever heard it before?' asked Simon, returning.

'No, but I know my daddy has.'

Simon and Abbie stared at each other and, even though the rest of the hotel was warm, Abbie felt her teeth jittery in her mouth.

Having her lieutenant beside her now seemed small comfort – the contagion had spread even here, to a little seven-year-old child, as if she hadn't experienced enough suffering already. Looking as serious as she could manage, she made Rosie promise not to say a word to Sheila about the voice.

Rosie would only be there for another day or two at the most, but if the hotelier received the minutest inkling of a malign presence here, they wouldn't have a roof over their heads.

'Promise me, Rosie, please.'

'OK. Now can I do a wee-wee?'

Abbie took her to the toilet, trying not to stare at the marks of violation at the tops of the child's thighs, even though a mother's instinct wanted to kill the man who'd done it. Then she tucked Rosie in again, on the window side of the bed, and began to undress.

Simon watched her taking off her fleece. Smooth skin, smooth hair – just looking would be his ration tonight. He touched her arm, blew her a kiss and went next door to his own cold bed.

For a while Abbie lay awake, listening to the rhythm of Rosie's breathing, calmer now, at one with the rising

tide and the nudge of vessels against the quayside's
wooden campshedding. She tried to weave a lifeline of
logic through her own sea of chaos. A doctor or nurse
ought to check this little girl over, but there was always
the same problem – she wasn't their child. They could
get done for abduction, but it wasn't them who mattered
here.

Later she checked her watch. It was 10.36. She crept
out of the room and downstairs to stale lasagne smells.
She lifted the bar phone and punched 192, angry with
herself for not having kept the number handy.

'Karen speaking, how can I help?'

'It's Dovenham, near King's Lynn. G. M. Parker.
Thanks.'

'I'm sorry, the number's ex-directory.'

'Since when? Oh, please, I'm his niece, Abbie Parker.
It's really urgent.'

'I'm afraid I'm not at liberty to . . .'

Shit, shit.

If she phoned her father, he'd want to know why she
was bothering them. He'd not even spoken to his brother
at the funeral, resenting the other man's cushy job in
Higher Education and his having a young wife happily
earning money and rearing a child at the same time.
Finally she dialled him. She could lie, like she'd always
done, and had a few convincing ones ready.

She listened to the phone ring, expecting the answer
machine, and as her ear tuned in to the continuing
silence, an echo grew that seemed to metamorphose into
a sickening hollow laugh . . . Abbie gripped the banisters,
her legs weak, her mouth dry with fear. Simon was no
distance away, Sheila also, but never in all her life had
Abbie felt so alone.

Back in the bedroom, she groped her way to the window, parted the curtains to let in some light and, on notepaper curled up like old ham, penned a brief note to Dovenham. The words lurching across the page, she begged Graham to phone her at work as soon as it arrived. Rosie had to be out of there without delay.

Abbie sealed the envelope with a parched tongue but forgot the postcode – what the hell. Then as she moved to stand up, she felt something under her fingers. Smaller than the Old Testament but with the same worn corners. Abbie let out a cry. Rosie woke up and turned to face her.

'Abbie, what's wrong?'

'I'm fine. You go back to sleep now.'

Rosie sighed as Abbie heaved up the old sash window just enough to stick her arm out. Enough to fling the Book of Common Prayer with a splat into the water below.

*Boxing Day 1861 and I am become a
widow on account of a herd of Angus.
Reuben Kingsley brought me the letter
two weeks after their hooves had trampled Ben Robinson into the next world.
The cold seals in my tears and the
hands of my daughters in mine. I tell
them their Pappy is away for a while,
but that while will never end . . .*

Twenty-seven

DESPITE THE CID's efforts at suppressing the North Sea abduction story, the Friday *Evening Echo*, with a circulation that spanned from Boston to King's Lynn, finally erupted into life with an account of the incident covering its first two pages. All the players except one were featured either in print or in photographs or in both, with two main questions being asked. Had anyone else been involved in the planning? And what possible motive could there have been for such a senseless and barbaric act?

A photo of Philip Byers standing alongside his work for the Foxhole Gallery in Stowton accompanied details of his parting from Speers and Granger Fine Art Auction-eers and some of his catalogue quotes on the beauty of medieval art. Speculation on his whereabouts was rele-gated to a mere paragraph.

In return for a generous cheque, the *Skeldyke Glory* skipper, who had a loft conversion to pay off, had given an embellished account of the rescue, while Mowbray, who boasted he'd done more than anyone in the force to try and apprehend the absent villain, was speaking from a new bungalow on the Isle of Wight. Abbie's short spell in hospital was also relayed, together with a one-liner on her post as sales negotiator at the Kingfisher Rise Development.

But it was little missing Rosie Quinn who dominated. Her face, taken from a recent school photograph provided by the head teacher, shone out like a sun, even in black and white, while underneath lay a heartfelt letter of thanks to all involved in her rescue, from her father and mother, ending with an urgent plea for any information on her current whereabouts.

'Damn that bungler,' growled the caravaner from his narrow bed high up on Oscarby End. 'He'll get nothing from me now.' It seemed that Byers hadn't made a single bore hole in the boat after all, or used an outgoing tide like he'd promised, so the troublemakers had survived. Both living to see another day – one day too many as far as he was concerned.

Restless and full of ire on his sliver of foam, Quinn felt for the Walther's barrel under his pillow. He'd tried to apply himself to thinking through alternatives, but his wife's presence had sabotaged any forward planning and more than once he'd been tempted to threaten her with the gun to get some peace. She'd carped on and on through all the hours of the night till he'd finally pushed her outside into the fog. And now in the clearer light of Saturday's dawn the secondary maggot in his apple sat outside in her wheeled contraption, the top of her stupid hat visible, still punishing him, he knew, driving him like that other voice to a point of no return.

Quinn sat up, tore yesterday's newspaper into angry fragments, then got up to scatter them outside into the wind. The woman in the wheelchair at the edge of the cliff watched unblinking as they circled upwards – like confetti, she thought, for the final and corrupt union of two evil minds.

New Year's Day 1862 and more bad news for us. A boy it is this time keeps my coat from closing and his kicking rucks against my ribs, so if I'm polishing the footrests in the pews I have to stand up quick for fear he is caught between my bones . . .

Twenty-eight

THE PALL OF suspicion descending after Lilith Leakes's murder had now settled over all the farms and smallholdings of Black Fen. This wasn't going to lift as easily as any early sea mist and its intensity had now become smothering, following Miss Parker's narrow escape with the vicar's daughter.

According to a police spokesperson interviewed on the local news, Lilith Leakes, in her eighty-third year, had possibly known her killer as there was no sign of forced entry, although no trace of any hospitality either. Nor of the old woman's head, but that grisly detail had been withheld from public knowledge. Instead, most of her grotesque collection from the marsh lay sealed in its place, in her pale old blood.

Last in a line of Lincolnshire drain builders, the female hermit had never married, although Zillah Watts seemed to remember gossip about some youthful seaman who'd called in at Clenchtoft whenever the *Koning Willem* was in. But that was years ago, and on one February day in 1954 the man from Zeeland vanished in a freak storm off the Texel coast, never to be more than a shadowy memory in that other land across the same sea. Just as to some Lilith Leakes had never been more than a loner to be avoided, eking out her strange days according to bird flight and the cast of the moon.

It emerged that her father, Thomas Leakes, had lost both his legs on the Somme, and had lain in mud for a week before burial near Thiepval – only half of him was ever found. His widow, Elizabeth, succumbed to fever the same day their daughter had turned from girl to woman, so would never see her only grandson take his first breath.

In those days, Lilith's mane of black hair was always loose to the waist, freed to the whims of the wind as she walked, straight as her stick, herding the heifers back and forth to the edge of Morpeth Bank. Dreaming under the sky by day, by night longing for love, until the next berthing on the Wenn. However, despite the hearsay which had grown like the bindweed at Goosefoot, no one now remembered any child, and apart from Gedney Stimpson, lodge keeper at Rievely Hall, who'd suddenly grown voluble just before his untimely death, no male companion either.

Now all was dissolved, and in that dissolving fear and helplessness gripped those still living in the shelter of the dyke. Statements taken were confused and unhelpful. Colonel Scott of Rievely was downright rude: he didn't want things raked up that might affect his business interests, and silenced his housekeeper with the threat of losing her job. On the other hand, Mrs Clapman, newsagent, revelled in it. After all, selling news was her lifeblood.

Zillah Watts's account was at odds with that of the Buckleys. The widow swore that Lilith Leakes had been taking opium since she was a girl and that was why her mind had turned. Amy Buckley argued that that was the

least of it but wouldn't be drawn any further. Wilfred
Dodds of Sleeper's Farm denounced the hermit as a
creeping sin on the land and the reason his turkeys had
turned cannibal. His neighbours disagreed, as they'd
thrived on the Fen and even ordered a spray of gladioli
to be left for her by Clenchtoft gate.

Nor was Kingfisher Rise itself exempt. Conjecture
had infiltrated the usual banter and job anxiety had
sprouted as another more sinister concern. The men
looked at each other differently now, their lunch and tea
breaks silent strained affairs. Twice the police had called
and twice gone away with nothing but dirty shoes.
Abbie decided it was still too early to mention Martha
Robinson to them – too early for that particular kiss of
death.

She arrived at work just as the early tea break was
starting. The men with mortgages were the most subdued. All of them local, except the brickies, muscled and
strong, she thought; more capable than Quinn of murder.
Normally someone would have waved a greeting, but
today they just wandered off and she felt a sudden
emptiness as she fumbled for the Show Home key.
Vallender, who'd been phoning every other day, had
suggested she take a week off after her ordeal, but she
still had things to prove. Still needed him to see she
could turn things round here.

Feeling something soft under her feet, she glanced
down. The same substance was smeared and stinking
round the door handle. Dog dirt or worse? Her stomach
heaved. A truck-load of pipes rumbled by. She yelled at
the driver to stop. He got out and loped over.

'Shit, man.'

'Precisely. Who's done this, do you know?'

'I do not, ma'am.' The tattoos on the Jamaican's arm moved with his muscles.

'Someone must have seen something!'

'Them kids 'ave been comin' in an' out again, but we're workin' up the far end most of the time.'

'Don't let anyone touch this. It's evidence.'

'Can't think who'd want to meself.' His lorry door slammed and the beat from his stereo throbbed like the only remaining heart in that tainted place.

He is the Reverend's flesh and blood that turns in my stomach, but when I begged his father to spare a widow like me some extra wages or give me something in advance for clothes and bedding after my confinement, this man of God called me a liar like all the Church family in Black Fen. 'So wild a country nurses up a race of people as wild as the fen itself,' he said, 'and you, Martha Robinson, are the worst of them.'

Twenty-nine

WITH SIMON GONE TO the police in Snutterwick to meet Mowbray's replacement, DI Stock, Abbie eventually left the Show Home and told the disgruntled foreman she'd be back within the hour.

The Monday mid-morning break had just ended and the population of Black Fen Primary School milled down the main corridor towards their classrooms, while in the distance the music teacher was closing the piano lid and gathering up his sheet music.

She followed signs for 'Office', knocked and walked in. It was a stuffy room made more claustrophobic by walls painted in tobacco-brown. On the desk, a printer buzzed intermittently. Abbie asked the secretary if she could see the head.

'She's at a Key Stage 1 meeting today.'

'Who *can* I see then?'

The woman, wearing an absurdly large spotted bow on her dress, looked up. 'We do prefer parents to make an appointment.'

'I'm not a parent and if I don't see *someone* right now I'll be making a formal complaint.'

'Wait here, please.' The secretary bustled to the door. Abbie heard her whispering, then little heels studding the lino.

'What can we do for you?'

Abbie stared. Avril Lawson was now in close-up and the black eyes glared recognition while the secretary subsided behind her computer.

'As you already know,' Abbie said, trying to control herself, 'I'm the local representative of the Holtbury Prestige Homes development off Walsoken Road. I've come to complain that some of your pupils are regularly creating a serious nuisance on our site.'

The painted eyebrows took flight as Abbie studied antirrhinum lips of pure vermilion.

'I'm sure our pupils are beyond reproach, Miss er . . .'

Whore, remember?

'You know my name very well.' Abbie heard the secretary's gasp.

'I've no idea what you mean, except that you're making a very serious allegation now.'

'About you or the kids in your charge?'

'Well, really. I don't have to stand here and—'

'Smell this.' Abbie unwrapped a pink tissue. The deputy head covered her nose.

'Anyhow, I now intend taking the matter further. The same set of bikes have been noticed several times and that's good enough for me. It was Charlie Hunter and Darren Greenhalgh the last time.' She resealed the tissue, dropped it in the waste bin, then pulled the door open. Frustration made her turn on a group of girls studying an announcement about an after-school disco. 'Can you let all your friends know that if any of them think it's funny doing damage in the new housing estate, then they should think again.' Six pairs of eyes looked round, but none she recognized. Big mistake? 'Sorry. It's the ones who call themselves the Gang I really want. Does anybody know where I can find them?'

The children looked at each other. One with big ears nudged the girl next to her. 'Tell her, Sammy. Go on.'

Her friend hesitated, but Abbie smiled encouragement.

'They're all away poorly. Some disease.'

'What do you mean, disease?'

Sammy Boyd cocked her head. 'Not sure 'xactly. Something like marylea . . .' A few girls giggled and they all began to drift away.

'*Nothing but malaria and the ague. And the worms all drowned . . .*'

'Do you mean malaria?'

'Yeah.' The child's bespectacled friend nodded. 'And they may have to close the school.'

'Yippee!'

'Cool.'

They left Abbie standing alone in a pool of dread, recalling Amy Buckley's warning, which had already made her fearful for Rosie.

Those dolls . . . Christ . . . They must have touched them, even possibly used their names. Abbie saw the sunlight disappear outside, taking her shadow, turning the floor almost black.

Simon? She had to tell him, had to tell someone. She left the Fiat askew on the gravel, didn't bother to lock it and headed for the hotel door.

The lounge bar was cool and dark, with the smell of washing from the kitchen. She could hear Sheila upstairs talking with Rosie.

A lone figure sat hunched on a bar stool, not bothering to look round at her. Three empty glasses were near his elbow, a fourth was at his mouth.

'Simon?' she ventured. 'I've got some odd news.'

'Oh yeah?' He almost ignored her.

'Those kids in the Gang, they've all caught malaria.' She'd planned to ask him what the symptoms were, whether it was contagious and how it could happen so suddenly. But the look he finally gave her stopped her in her tracks.

'And I've got bloody Kosovo.' He waved a letter headed B Signals.

'What?'

'We're going in, end of next week. Clinton's got itchy feet for when the bombing stops. Fuck it. Fuck it.' He finished his glass. 'I can't hack it any more. Can't the cunts *see* that? I just want to be here with you and Rosie. I want a life. Just think what some of my old mates from uni are doing now.' His fists clenched and unclenched. 'You can bet they're not crawling through fields full of bloody cow dung, or having to take a crap under some fucking peasant's nose ... If they were, they'd be off with Premature Voluntary Release at the drop of a piece of shit.'

Abbie felt hollow. Anything half decent, even a quarter decent, was always taken away from her, and his despair sounded like an echo already.

'Can't you make out you're still getting pissed out of your skull regularly?'

'What d'you think I'm doing now, for Chrissake? Anyhow, got to go and see a quack a week tomorrow. For a blood test, the works ...'

'Where?'

'London. St James's somewhere. All terribly stiff

upper, so Thank you, Mr Fucking Cresswell. Now I want another drink.'

Abbie saw Sheila standing at the top of the stairs and went up to join her. The woman, who'd heard everything, gave her a squeeze of the hand and a smile for encouragement. Abbie then went to find Rosie.

'What's the matter with Simon?' the little girl asked, looking up from the bedroom floor, her face smeared with Sheila's make-up.

'He's just feeling fed up.'

'Go and give him a kiss then.' The child beamed, and Abbie watched her painting her nails. ''Cos if you don't, I will.'

'I thought this'd keep her busy.' Sheila noted Abbie's stare. 'She's been at it since she got up.'

'That's nice.'

'I'm Barbie's sister.' The child blew the varnish on each finger, then frowned. 'Can I have a new dolly? A really pretty one this time, not like Mary, Lazarus and Abigail?'

'Stop that!' Abbie screamed and the nail varnish tipped over. 'What did I tell you? Never, *never* to repeat those names.'

'Sorry, Abbie.'

Abbie fetched some tissues and hastily blotted the worst, her heart thudding in her chest.

Sheila sat down on the bed, looking as if this was all beyond her. 'What's going on?' she mimed to Abbie with her lips.

'It's rude to whisper,' Rosie piped up. 'Mummy says.'

'She's quite right of course.'

Then, out of earshot in the corridor, Abbie told Sheila first what Mrs Buckley had said, then the latest news

about the school. Her friend shook her head. The para-
normal was beyond her – when you were dead, you were
dead, and no amount of speculation and folklore could
change that. Malaria, though, was something else.

'But we're not in the tropics here, for God's sake. I
mean, we don't get mosquitoes like that on the marsh
surely?' Sheila hunted for a cigarette, then realized her
packet was down in the bar.

'We used to. It was quite commonplace in the nine-
teenth century.'

'Really?'

'I'm deadly serious, Sheila.' Abbie looked it, too,
focusing her gaze again on Rosie for any unusual signs.
Then, reassured, she checked her watch and went back
downstairs. Sheila followed.

'I'd better be getting back to the site,' Abbie said,
going over to Simon. But he pulled away, scowling, and
drained his glass.

'I hope you're paying for those drinks,' Sheila said,
unimpressed.

He dug in his pocket, his wallet dropping to the floor.
It flopped open to show Abbie's face from her college
days in Leicester. She hardly recognized herself.

'Oh, come on, I'm sorry.' Sheila took an arm of each
and brought them together.

The kiss that followed was short and distracted. Then
Abbie left, closing the door behind her.

That kiss stayed on her lips all the way to the Show
Home and lingered like sunburn as she typed the same
letter to both the head teacher and the Director of
Education. Why wasn't this malaria outbreak public
knowledge? As sales negotiator she had a right to know,
on behalf of prospective purchasers. She would also have

to inform Holtbury's and they would want the problem of continual vandalism dealt with.

She doubted she'd get a response – it would be the same old story – but, after adding her signature, she felt better jamming the cap back on her pen. Then she faxed Vallender to confirm his booking at the St George's Sails for the second week in June.

The Show Home door stayed open now, whatever the weather, but no prospective purchasers came through it all afternoon.

Come on, Uncle Graham, phone me, for God's sake.

Finally the phone did ring. It was him, thank you, God, and sounding accommodating enough although doubtful. She let his educated vowels wash over her, the howevers, the maybes, until finally he agreed that maybe Flora would enjoy a new playmate.

Abbie stared out past the ruched curtains towards the skeleton of plot 2, grey and dismal under the forming rain. Grey in her heart too, as a sudden chill breeze lifted her papers off the site plan and on to the floor. She remembered Martha Robinson's ankles in their worn soiled boots and suddenly looked up, expecting to see her dark shape again.

Four o'clock: one hour to go. Time to ring the Bishop of Walsoken, something she'd been meaning to do for days. And then of course, there was Simon to consider.

He squeezed me as if I was a goose, to shut my gizzard. 'Like the ungodly, you are as chaff which the wind scattereth from the face of the earth. Not one living soul must see it, you Jezebel, or hear it once it leaves your sinful body. Remember the words of Revelation. "And I will kill her children with death."' His breath well nigh boiled my ear and I got to thinking that despite all I'd endured this was the moment I might die . . .

Thirty

TUESDAY'S NEWS OF a malaria outbreak and the school's sudden closure that same day, had leaked into the wider world, but to the man in the caravan, who'd spent since dawn the following day removing all his traces there, the only thing that mattered now was time. There was never enough of it, never enough . . .

Rechecking for hairs in the tinny plugholes, both his and hers, fingerprints on the few utensils. She hadn't done anything, of course, except lose her mind, and it had been no surprise to see her contraption gone when he'd first stepped outside. He wiped out the plywood wardrobe for the third time, in case fibres from clothes had got trapped on its rough inner edges.

The last time he'd been this thorough was years ago, cleaning out the milking parlour before the Marketing Board's inspections. But he'd enjoyed that, seeing all the chrome glisten under the lights, even though it left his hand skin rumpled like drowned flesh.

Long since then, other matters had taken over: the affairs of a divided soul shaped by the voice that had visited itself upon him, one who, without invitation, had lately told him he'd been careless and would soon be losing his life of freedom. Not your actual *life*, unlike me, it had said – but which is worse? – filling his head with a

tone so bleak and harsh it couldn't ever have been human
. . . But all the same, he listened and obeyed – as always.

He hauled his bird-watching gear from under the
bunk and applied the extra disguise of a small moustache.
He'd not shaved for a week, so the stubbled chin felt
suitably rugged under his fingers. Everything finished
now, with the semi-automatic once used for vermin by
his old farming hosts, the Baldwins, safe in his pocket.

He closed the door behind him and looked up to the
heavens out over the sea where indigo dominated the
shrill yellow of the sun to come. Dark and light, with
victory still to the dark, he thought, noticing her chair
wheels had left two depressions in the grass.

*Are you content now, whoever you are? Or will I never
satisfy you? Will your purgatory be mine to the end of my
days, your desires forging such a cage I can never leave? So
be it . . . So be it . . .*

Gulls followed his leaving, seeking detritus. They
hung overhead and, as if to empower himself, Quinn
sneaked his gun from inside the tweed and took one of
them, sending the rest screaming over the water. The
dead bird brought down with it a frill of blood, but he
didn't notice.

By noon he was expert in skirting the roads, ducking
alongside farms inland, moving south where there weren't
always walkways over the canals. By noon he'd travelled
fifteen miles when it was only seven by the crow's flight,
passing where he and his traitorous daughter would be
spending the night before getting a car from Boltings
auto auctions. It was a barn marooned in a sea of mangel
wurzels on Fitting Fen. It would do. At least until Plan
B . . .

By two-thirty p.m., Black Fen and his church were in

sight. The cleric unwrapped a Lion Bar, staring at a tourist map displayed behind dirty glass in the bus stop. Like just another visitor come to look at the plentiful birds in the area ... From the corner of his eye he spotted Avril Lawson waiting near the church. Now her purpose was almost over, she could wait till kingdom come. And one day he'd grant her that, but for now more pressing matters held sway.

'If you go against my wishes, there will be no more schooling for your children, no more work for any of you. I will attend to it personally.' Then Esmond Downey left me for dead under the Magdalene's statue, but as ever her head is bowed into her own sorrow so she sees nothing of me that I may receive consolation.

Thirty-one

'I'm sorry.' Abbie put her arm round Simon. She smelt of shower gel, her hair still damp. 'There's enough madness without us two falling out.'

He gripped his glass tighter, which showed how his knuckles' fighting wounds still hadn't fully healed. He kept his eyes fixed on the TV, where the runners for Wednesday's last race at Goodwood were being mounted in the paddock.

'Look, Si, we've got to take Rosie now. We'll talk it all through when I get back.'

She saw the other two coming downstairs and her arm slipped away. Rosie looked quite a different child in a white cardigan and corduroy dress. Socks with a border of daisies dazzled above each red shoe and she clutched the new brunette doll Simon had brought back from Snutterwick.

'Peaches an' cream.' Sheila proudly retied the little girl's bow, then started wiping the bar.

'Where are we going?' Rosie looked from one to the other.

'A holiday. Somewhere nice.'

'Is Sheila coming too?' Rosie asked expectantly.

'Yes, of course.'

*

The exile saw the rusted St George's Sails letters skewed haphazardly against the sky. Anyone with a sense of pride would have put that right, he thought, but not the slattern who'd taken over here. She was too busy interfering, like the rest of them.

Twenty yards and *omnia parata sunt*. Three cars in the forecourt, he observed, including the whore's Fiat, the sloth's Fiesta whose papers now lay in his pocket and the slattern's old wreck. Quinn stopped, holding his breath, anger pulsing at his neck, jerking at his heart. He didn't take kindly to being excluded, especially where his only daughter was involved.

'Can I sit in the front?' wheedled Rosie with imploring eyes, but Abbie wasn't going to risk her being spotted.

'You'll be much safer in the back, there's a good girl.'

Rosie sighed as Abbie handed her the new doll and the pink plastic handbag she'd bought her with a mirror inside its lid and little compartments for make-up.

'Abbie's right, darling. And it's not for long.' Sheila's relief at finally getting Rosie away from the hotel was obvious. She fetched her cigarettes off the bar as Abbie went over to Simon. She touched his shoulder but he flinched away.

'Please don't drink any more,' she tried. 'It won't help anyone in the end.'

'In the end is the beginning,' he muttered.

'OK, please yourself.'

'Why's Simon so cross?' asked Rosie as Abbie took her hand.

'Because *you're* going.'

'Say goodbye to us then.'

Rosie held up her new doll for him to kiss, but he

just continued staring at the screen, tears stinging his eyes. He blinked them away and only stole a look as they reached the door.

'I'll see you when I've had my holiday,' Rosie called back to him.

'Don't forget to close up after us, will you?' Sheila reminded him, for although she was glad to have a man in the place, she wasn't too sure about this particular keg on two legs. 'Remember, we're not open for anybody unfamiliar.'

Abbie turned, gave a small wave, then was gone.

He hated every cell in his body, every perversion of his stupid mind that was now letting what he loved most just slip away . . . Abbie, Rosie and Sheila were in danger and all he could do was keep his fucking hand on the bottle. OK, so he'd put a few pounds on his emaciated frame, done one or two useful things here, but Christ, when it was his turn to have his heart weighed against a feather, they wouldn't even be able to bloody well find it.

Simon slid off the bar stool and went to secure the door.

The little party emerged: the slattern, the whore, his own daughter clutching a few things, as they filled the white Fiat. No talking, no banter between them. He frowned at the realization they might be running away and felt for his gun, but thought better of it. It was too public here, too tricky.

He stood rigid and, so he thought, invisible, until he saw his daughter turn in her seat by the window and smile a goodbye in his direction.

A trawler somewhere out on the Deeps of Lethe sounded its arrival, like a death knell.

Abbie heard it too, and shivered, not letting Rosie see how the nightmare had returned to her. She'd probably never go near the sea again, in whatever lifetime she had left . . .

'Girls' day out, eh?' Sheila chuckled, turning her gemstone necklace to catch the last of the light. ''Bout time too an' all.'

Abbie overdid the choke and swore. She missed her previous car more than ever. Dredged up for examination from the mouth of Grim's Canal, it was now no more than a worthless shell coated by weeds and slime. This replacement railed against her handling and grumbled on into the afternoon.

1 March. I called in on my sissen Annie at Clenchtoft and smelt the ham and offal she was cooking from the gate which I swear made my child inside leap in hunger. If he cried I couldn't hear it because she stayed behind the door shouting that I'd killed my sissens and her twin so why should she help me? It is as well no other heeds her lies and I was tempted to bring an axe to her, but restrained myself being so near to time . . .

Thirty-two

SIMON SUDDENLY STOPPED at the door. He wasn't alone. Someone was already outside, a shape filling the whole frosted glass panel and pressing it open. He tried to turn the mortise, slide the new bolts, but this fucker was strong, just kept pushing his way in.

Shabby jacket, bird-watcher's hat and that weird moustache, but the eyes were the most terrifying of all. The eyes of a man possessed. So this was Quinn. At last. Abbie had been right about him.

Simon was ready, his mind gearing up over a body too full of booze. He lunged forward, gripped Quinn's gloved wrist like a steel vice as it was pulling out a handgun and cut off the blood supply. Quinn moaned as the gun spun to the floor and Simon booted it towards the bar. He then slugged his opponent below the belt, felt middle-aged parts collapse and reel in pain as the man lurched back out into the daylight, trampling his bird-watcher's hat underfoot.

'Come near any of us again, you crazy bastard and I'll finish you off,' he yelled, slamming the bolts and then picking up the weapon – a Walther with only five rounds left. Where the hell had he got that from, Simon wondered, as he ran upstairs to watch Quinn slink away up Walsoken Road, gripping his groin.

Simon's chest was tight as a drum, but Christ he felt
better, and this was just round one. He went into Abbie's
room, the bed neatly smoothed over, her clothes for
tomorrow already pressed and ready to wear. He smiled.
Funny, if Armageddon was due in half an hour, she'd get
out the bloody iron to prepare for it. He sat down in her
chair and saw himself in the dressing-table mirror.

You thick sod. Get that life before it fucking goes . . .

And for the first time in months, Simon Dafydd
Cresswell, lieutenant, junior to Captain Bernard Oliver,
1 Signals Brigade, realized he'd got things to be thankful
for.

Back in the bar and ignoring his unfinished beer, he
phoned Snutterwick CID again, asking for DI Stock,
who said he'd be round in twenty minutes.

Twenty minutes – a miracle. Mowbray's replacement was looking sharper every day. While he waited,
Simon paid the kitchen a visit. He'd got an idea. He
noticed the pans and griddles hardly used, the sheen
of newness everywhere. Sheila Livingstone had spent a
lot of money here recently and, thinking of the big
register, he admired her optimism. He opened the
fridge. It looked like supplies were running down. Just
low-fat this, low-fat that, nothing much to magic a meal
from, yet a stack of Bounty Bars filled the middle shelf,
together with little pink mousses and a clutch of mini
cheeses for Rosie . . .

Rosie?

He'd never said goodbye, not even looked at her.

*You shit, Cresswell. You shit, and you think you want
kids of your own!*

Hope returned with an investigation of the freezer,
and he worked out a menu – in celebration of what, he

wasn't quite sure, but *something* was needed. He then prowled round the hotel, from window to window, checking that creep hadn't fancied another thump in the nuts. From one he saw the unmarked car swing into the drive.

Unlocking the front door, Simon went out to greet the DI. The two men shook hands, both firm of physique, both combat-trained, that was for sure. The sun behind Stock's head lent a cherubic glaze to his already light hair.

'Well, Mr Cresswell, you *have* been keeping us busy.' It was neither praise nor accusation, simply a statement of fact while sharp brown eyes roamed from corner to corner, missing nothing. 'I'm glad, mind. This is all a very vexing business.'

Simon thought, he's not local. This DI was a northerner, probably Manchester.

'I was getting nowhere with Mowbray,' Simon began. 'Bloody nowhere.'

'Mmm. You've already said.'

Behind him another man, with a briefcase, got out of the Mondeo and came over.

'Someone's hat lying out there,' he said. 'Do I take a look?'

'Could be anybody's in this wind.' Stock ignored Simon's eyes and nodded yes to Etchells.

'He was bloody wearing it!' Simon almost yelled.

'So which way did he come from, this Quinn?' Stock loaded the name with such doubt, Simon felt his stomach grow tight.

'It *was* him. I already knew exactly what he looked like.'

'How come?'

'His bloody picture appeared in the local rag just after I got here . . .'

'So you'd never actually seen him – in the flesh.'

Dismantling had begun. *Don't let him do it to you.*

'But my girlfriend has and she . . .'

'Girlfriend?'

'Yes, Abbie Parker. She stays here.'

'Ah.'

Stock already knew all this of course, knew everything, but it made life more interesting to go one step at a time, keep people guessing. He gestured to the floor. 'Start with the usual, Mike.' He turned to Simon. 'Now what time exactly did he show, this vicar of ours?'

'Just after . . .' Simon changed tack. 'Just as the last race from Goodwood was starting.'

'You were going to say something else, I believe?'

Simon watched the door handle being dusted, then the mat slipped into a polythene bag. He stuttered. 'No, no, I wasn't.'

'By the way, where's Mrs Livingstone?'

'Cash and carry, I think.'

'Think?'

'Well, it's the only time she goes out. Anyway, I've not been here long. She doesn't tell me everything.'

'I see.'

'And your friend, Miss Parker?' Stock examined a beermat, then returned it to exactly the same spot.

'Said she needed new shoes.' All thoughts of a celebration meal turned to dust. He felt suddenly queasy.

'So it was just you and the Reverend here?'

'I told you that on the phone.'

'Of course.' Stock exchanged a smile with his colleague, who'd just discovered a dent in the floor. He studied it for a while but didn't pursue it. It could easily have been caused by a chair leg or a heel skid. Simon breathed a silent sigh of relief.

'So when does your leave finish?' Stock made 'leave' sound like a stretch in prison.

Simon wondered what the fuck it had to do with him, then realized he hadn't mentioned anything about his arrangements with the army.

'It's open-ended,' he lied. 'Till I'm sorted.'

Stock was now focusing on him intently. A body scan must be like this, Simon thought.

'Of course, you don't have to explain why.'

No, but if I don't you'll sniff it out somehow . . .

'Booze.' He found himself blushing.

'There's worse than that, Lieutenant, good God.' Stock smiled again at the third man, whose buttocks jutted out from under a table, and Simon wondered what he was being greased up for. 'Should think you're keen to get back to normal, aren't you?'

'Can't wait.'

Cunt!

'Queen and country, eh? Though what NATO thinks bombing our friend Slobodan will achieve I do not know. It'll only make matters far worse to my mind, and hey ho we'll have World War Three. Bloody Balkans here we come.'

Stock extracted a handkerchief and blew his nose loudly, leaving it red and shining.

'Where did you hit him?' He asked suddenly, out of the blue.

'The balls.'

Stock jotted that down, then glanced up. 'Self-defence you said earlier?'

'He had a gun. Looked like a Browning,' he lied.

'You didn't tell me that.' Mike Etchells stopped, made a mental note.

'Didn't I?'

'No.'

Time to start digging out. He was losing it. 'Christ, he took a pot shot at my car as we left that religious retreat. I phoned you about that.'

'Sure it wasn't something else you heard?'

Simon sighed frustration.

'Is that your car out there?' Stock pointed.

'Yes.'

'Take a look, Mike, while we're at it.'

'What are you going to do about him?' Simon yelled. 'The man's fucking mad. He could have killed me twice over now.' Blood darkened his neck. 'What about his wife and kid?'

'All hearsay, I'm afraid. No proof found of anything so far at Haletoft.'

'He nicked my car hire form. That's how he knew I was *here*. What about Oscarby End?'

'We're going there next.'

Mike Etchells came back. 'Nothing on the car.'

Simon could have hit them both. What did he have to do to convince them? Then he remembered something. 'Hang on.'

Two pairs of eyes followed him up the stairs. Stock kept his hand in his pocket in case. He knew all about army fall-out. Trouble was, too many of the poor fuckers who'd cracked tried to get jobs in the force, thinking they were God's gift . . . He noted the firm arse, legs a bit skinny but with good muscle definition.

Simon reappeared and passed him Helen Quinn's

Old Testament. 'Quinn's stuff's inside. Now you'll see
how bloody weird he is . . . There's also a snippet from
his wife in the front.'

'Bedtime reading then?' The DI glanced at the cover,
then slid it into his inside pocket.

'So what now?' Simon asked.

'You tell me.'

'Jesus!'

Stock relented. This one could turn awkward.

'Just keep your eyes open, tell the ladies to stay in
and get Mrs Livingstone to have her windows done. I
mean locks.'

'And what about me?' Stock looked him up and
down. 'You're a big boy now. You can take care of
yourself.'

I tell my sissen Annie, 'Out of the mouths of babes and sucklings hast thou, the Devil, ordained strength because of mine enemies . . .' and she trembles like a young alder in the sea wind for her ways have left her soul weak. I also tell her she's not seen the last of me leastways as she still keeps my dolls and treats them as hers . . .

Thirty-three

SOON THE LOCAL roads east widened to dual carriage-ways, Roman genius bisecting the flatlands without the hindrance of hills. Earth worked by women's hands and by children too wearied to sleep – born and buried in the soil without ceremony.

Suddenly, the outskirts of King's Lynn encroaching upon the Fens, and once over the Great Ouse Rosie sat up, restless with wonder. They stopped for flowers and sweets and, when they set off again, she kept her doll up against the glass so she could look out.

'Are we nearly there?'

'Not far now.'

'Is it near the sea?'

'Abbie'll know that one.'

But Abbie didn't answer.

Dovenham boasted five houses, a public telephone and a post box outside the Parkers' house. The smell of horses still hung in the early evening air, from the all-weather gallop at the end of the lane, and from the distant harbour the sound of seagulls filtered through the trees.

The Arbours lay invisible behind reconstituted-stone gateposts that held double iron gates. Sheila pushed the button and in her best voice announced their business.

The ironwork opened to a drive edged by the deeper darkness of pines.

Rosie craned forward, her golden head reflected in the glass. She'd abandoned the doll and instead gripped the seat. 'Where are we now?'

'End of the rainbow.' Sheila winked. 'Pot of gold.'

Rosie looking bemused, pressed her face against the window.

'There's a dear little girl here for you to play with.' Abbie said, paving the way.

'What's her name?'

'I've told her loads of times,' she whispered to Sheila. 'It's Flora.'

'That's what we put on bread at home.'

Sheila grinned, reapplying her perfume under each ear, but Abbie felt anxiety creeping in. What if it all went horribly wrong? What if Rosie ran away? There was a wild streak in her certainly, a recklessness that no one could control, but maybe that's what her father had done to her. Made his own child a fatalist.

'I don't want anyone to play with.' Rosie whined. 'Anyhow, I like boys best.'

'You just wait.' Abbie groaned inwardly. 'You'll have the time of your life.'

Trying to park, she squinted as a figure appeared from the porch and strode over towards them. He'd aged a lot, his eyes looking tired behind his glasses, and guilt made her more reticent than usual. He kissed Abbie immediately, then peered at her passengers.

'What have we got here, then?'

'This is Rosie and this is Sheila. They've both been really looking forward to meeting you.' The two of them got out, staring at the house and its grounds.

Graham Parker greeted them with a faint whiff of garlic, then lifted Rosie off the ground. 'Flora's asleep at the moment, she's been a bit under the weather, but you'll see her in the morning. Ah, and here's my wife Sue.'

'I thought you'd like these colours,' Abbie said handing her the bouquet. 'It's the least I can give you for helping us.'

She embraced the other young woman, feeling the brush of a downy cheek on hers. She clasped Sue's hand for a long moment, there being no need for words. Just to be safe here was enough. She noticed how her uncle's wife trailed a bare arm around the little girl's shoulders as they all walked towards the house.

'I can't thank you both enough.' Abbie began. 'The whole thing's been unbelievable.'

'I can imagine. Graham says we ought to call you Wonderwoman.' Her smile relaxed Abbie, as Rosie ran on ahead to explore her new home.

'It'll only be for a week or so, till I get things sorted out.'

'It's really no problem,' she said emphatically. 'I can easily pretend she's the first one I should have had.'

Sheila glanced at Abbie questioningly.

'Sue, not now, please.' Graham sighed.

But his niece remembered how his career progression to Head of the School of Critical Studies had always come first, over everything. So what did that comment mean? Had there been an abortion? A joint sacrifice?

'Rosie's quite an artist,' Abbie ventured, switching her thoughts. 'I'd be interested to see what you both make of her stuff.'

'Why's that?' Her uncle's wife and former student looked surprised, her top lip softened by blonde hairs.

'I think they're a bit odd – but then just remember her background.'

The smell of percolated coffee reached into the hall and Abbie realized she'd had almost nothing to eat or drink all day.

'Well, she can work alongside me, if she wants,' Sue said.

'That's wonderful. Look, can I ask you something? Would you mind keeping everything she does?'

'No problem.'

'They could help our case. So could the bruising.'

'What do you mean, bruising? Where?'

'You'll see when she has a bath. I'm afraid it's the father.' Abbie quickly lowered her voice as Rosie rejoined them.

For the first time Sue looked unsure. She led Rosie into the play room, where the others followed and stood as though marooned on the parquet floor. Rosie chose the one oriental-style rug and promptly sat cross-legged at its centre, which featured a dragon whose tail curled up over its back.

'Look, I'm in the middle of the world,' she said, grinning as her fingers worked over its soft raised pattern.

'Not the best, and certainly not from China, I'm afraid,' Graham said suddenly. 'That's what overpriced prep schools reduce you to.'

Sheila knelt down to give Rosie her doll. 'You've got no choice. Our local primary is appalling.'

Abbie thought of the poverty of Black Fen.

'We heard, on the news, it's closed,' Graham said.

'Not for long.' Abbie didn't want Rosie overhearing too much. She was also relieved that the Parkers obviously hadn't seen Rosie's photo and the Quinn's letter in Friday's *Evening Echo*.

'Coffee anyone?' called Sue from the kitchen, obviously making an effort, still perturbed.

Abbie looked at Sheila, who shook her head. 'We'd better be getting back, thanks,' she replied without enthusiasm, thinking of Simon slumped in the bar. 'Sheila here's got to be mein host for the evening rush.' Abbie bent to kiss the little girl's fringe. 'Be good won't you? I'll say hello on the phone tomorrow.'

'OK.' Rosie lay down on her stomach.

'Look, she's swimming.' Graham smiled as she wriggled her legs and arms in a very strange way indeed. 'Funny little creature.'

'What are you going to call your dolly?' Sue asked to divert the child as she set down the tray on a small table and handed her husband his mug.

After a long pause the seven-year-old, who was still spread-eagled over the dragon, mumbled into its mouth, 'She's a mummy doll, and her three baby dollies have gone, so she's going to be Martha.'

Abbie and Sheila reached Black Fen as dusk was beginning to fall, hiding the hatless daughterless poacher on his way to his chosen refuge in Fitting Fen.

Simon opened the door, kissed them both and watched with some pride their reactions to his labours. After Stock's visit, he'd almost not bothered, but he wasn't going to let some woofter cop screw him up.

'Candles, wow.' Sheila seemed mesmerized by the

neatly laid table and the smell of good food coming from the kitchen.

When they'd washed and changed, the party began.

'I should have said goodbye to Rosie myself.' Simon finished one orange juice and went for another. 'I feel a real shit about that now. I'll send her a note tomorrow.'

'Don't worry, she's fine.' Sheila was enjoying herself maybe too much, and looking more relaxed than they'd seen her for days. 'She settled in like a . . .' She searched for a simile, but gave up and helped herself to more casserole instead.

'A cat on the mat?'

But all Abbie could think of was Rosie's odd behaviour on the rug and her mention of Martha -- who had to be Martha Robinson. During the journey from Dovenham she'd worried non-stop that the child would be sent back to them by return.

'So what's all this really in aid of?' Sheila asked Simon, her mouth full, her eyes shining. No one had cooked for her in years.

'D'you really want to know?'

'Course. Be a devil.'

No, don't be. Not any more.

Abbie saw a shadow flit across his face. Something was up.

He backed down. 'Bit of a celebration, that's all.'

Sheila checked out her friend's engagement finger, while Abbie simply stared at him. If Sheila found Abbie difficult to keep up with, Simon was like Voyager 2.

'We had a visitor,' he blurted out.

They both studied him for the slightest clue, but he went for the pepper and took his time.

'Quinn no less.'

Two sets of knives and forks stopped frozen. Four eyes widened.

'You don't mean *here*?'

'In this very room.' He raised his glass. 'Here's to us and Rosie. Round one to Cresswell in the blue corner.' No one joined him in his toast, but the two women turned in their chairs towards the door as if the intruder was still standing there.

'I have to say he was not a pretty sight.'

'Oh, my God.' Sheila's napkin went to her mouth.

'I saw him off, no problem. Kneed him one, bull's-eye.' He dipped in his jacket pocket. 'They got his fucking hat and *I* got this.' The pistol lay flat on his palm.

Abbie gasped. 'Is that his?'

'Well, it's mine now. Looks like we'll need it.'

The festive meal disintegrated. Sheila pushed back her chair and left the room as if she wasn't coming back.

Abbie tried to keep her voice calm. 'When you say 'they', do you mean the police?'

He nodded. 'Came round quick as greased shit. Took prints etc. Oh, and that Bible thing.'

'Who came exactly?'

'DI Stock and his sidekick, Mike someone or other. Reckon they're both benders, mind. Had the feeling he was trying to get under my clothes, know what I mean?'

Sheila's door suddenly slammed upstairs, making the place vibrate from top to bottom.

Simon shrugged. His mother often did things like that and it didn't bother him as much as quieter forms of protest. It was his father who had the PhD in mental cruelty.

'Anyhow, Stock said she needs to install window locks.'

'For God's sake don't tell her that. It'd be the last bloody straw. Oh, Simon.'

'I didn't *ask* the fucker to come calling.'

'I know.'

'Good job you'd all gone . . . Christ, just think of it.'

'At least it's not you he wants.'

'Oh yeah? Having seen him, I personally don't think he's fussy.'

Abbie surveyed the table, the cloth he'd found, the unfolded napkins and unfinished food. 'Look, all that really matters now is us.'

'And Rosie.' Simon added.

'I meant her as well. We've got to survive.'

He watched her clear beautiful face fade like a sunless rainbow. He held her, felt her breasts against his shirt as both his hands moved round to her buttocks. Why he'd never even glanced at anyone else . . .

They went upstairs joined at the hip to her room, the further of the two away from Sheila's. On the bed – its under-sheet cool and smooth beneath him like her skin – the lovers were too engrossed in their healing passion to hear the peat worker's chilling laugh curdle into the room and blemish their muffled climax.

It wasn't until they'd gone down later to wash up, have coffee in the bar and switch on the late evening news that they learned Mr and Mrs Hunter of Bittern Avenue, Black Fen, had finally agreed to let the death of their only son from malaria, last Wednesday, be made public.

A gallows has come to Black Fen where Morpeth Bank meets Herringtoft. It was put together during the night, but the hammering of it like the Devil's anvil gave me no sleep, and now in the morning it is the first thing I see. Black and hungry against the sky . . .

Thirty-four

TRINITY SUNDAY DAWNED under a blanket of unrelenting rain that prevented anything living ascending from the sodden land. All wildfowl and foraging birds along the shore were grounded by the onslaught, squatting passively among the reeds.

Sheila Livingstone too was lying in, listening to the downpour, praying the guttering would hold, and the only thing she said to Abbie when she brought in her tray was how she was thinking of selling up.

Normally, Abbie would have tried to reason with her about her plans to give up the hotel, given her some time, but at ten it would be Charlie Hunter's funeral at Humberwell Crematorium. The first grown child since it opened six years ago, and whatever she'd seen him doing with Emma Mason, whatever he'd done to Rosie, he was still a kid.

Her instincts were to phone his parents and sympathize, then check on the rest of the Gang. But Simon had said no, he didn't want her being seen as a voyeur, even a witch like Lilith Leakes, and the firmness with which he'd said it was enough.

He was waiting for her outside Sheila's room and kissed her again, feeling that same yearning he'd felt every day in Germany. 'I love you, Abbie,' he murmured, his hand going to her blouse.

'I can't. Not today.'

Just being so close made his longing worse, but she looked past him to the grey veil of rain water that hid any view.

'I'm going to try phoning the Bishop of Walsoken again. We can't leave it any longer.'

'Please decipher.'

'An exorcism.'

He felt himself shrink, his desire for her suddenly a dream. 'That's going a bit far, isn't it?'

'I tried him the other day but his secretary said he was away and they're not that keen on doing them any more – too many nutters or whatever.'

'Too right.'

'But this is different. This woman –' she wouldn't say Martha Robinson's name, nor ever would again – 'this creature, has got to be stopped. Before anyone else here dies.' Abbie thought of Mr Mower and, for a fleeting terrible moment, of herself. She held on to Simon, feeling the blood leave her face.

'What's the matter, Abs? You look awful.' He stared at her, unnerved, as the automatic bells of St Mary Magdalene pealed out ten o'clock. She envisaged the flames beckoning the little boy's coffin, just as they had her own mother's. Felt the same devouring energy at that heart of darkness.

Simon then went to get another cup of tea. The boy's death had spooked her – badly – and he knew a hot drink wasn't going to make much difference, but . . .

Meanwhile Abbie had gone in to look at the pillow Rosie had slept on, saw the dent from her head, then studied the twist of hairs she'd left in the Noddy brush as a relic. She managed a smile as Simon returned and passed her a mug and a biscuit softened by neglect. Warm, safe, for the moment at least.

'So tell me,' he said, sitting down beside her, his arm protectively around her shoulders, 'there's something else, isn't there? Something you're not letting on about.'

Abbie nodded, then hesitated, not sure how to start. 'You see, there are these three dolls . . .'

Abigail, Mary, Lazarus . . . especially Abigail . . .

'Dolls?' His eyes narrowed.

'I've not had time to explain everything to you, there's been so much happening, but I first saw them at Goose-foot Cottage . . .'

And as the rain pocked the glass in huge orbs that distended and trailed down to the sills, she told him what little she knew of their history and their ruthless legacy that had meant the child had to die.

Simon sat with his head between his hands. OK, he was used to dreams and nightmares, and had always felt a Celtic intuition for things unseen, but this was so bizarre and grotesque – unlike any enemy he'd ever been trained to fight. And he felt powerless.

Then she suddenly abandoned her tea, got up to brush her hair.

'What are you doing now?'

'Going to make that call. Then I'm going out.'

'Where?'

'Clenchtoft.'

'Abbie, you're mad.'

'Well, I'll be in good company then.' She grabbed her Barbour, swerved past him and headed downstairs. She was outside and revving the Fiat before he could even warn Sheila she'd need to lock up the place in their absence.

'Stop, damn it!' He clung to the wing mirror and she unclicked the central locking for him to get in. 'Don't ever do that again – shutting me out like that.'

'I'm sorry.'

As Abbie stopped the car by the phone box, she noticed the school railings now carried notices printed in red about the continued closure. Someone had left a battered spray of flowers under the school sign. Even though it was Sunday and the rain was easing, there wasn't a child in sight anywhere near Walsoken Road or Smithy Lane. On Monday it would be the same. As she started dialling, she noticed Simon get out, post his note to Rosie and head towards the rectory, his jeans providing the only colour in the dank wilderness.

He still had the Walther and five rounds left. Five may be not enough, he thought, although he'd always come out top in target practice. This challenge was different, though, and the place looked worse than ever, with litter welded to the wetness along the path. Untouched pints of milk, creamed yellow in yesterday's sun, stood clustered by the gate.

Simon hurled them one by one at the garden wall and watched the streaks descend shroud-like over the dark brickwork.

The church, too, stood darkly glistening, as its gargoyle's glut of water battered the graves below. He read a message pinned on the vestry door. It was from the Very Reverend Basil Pierce, Bishop of Walsoken, apologizing to his flock for the second disruption that year and

comforting them with the news that the Reverend Derek
Jarrold, Rural Dean of North Sand, would now officiate
on alternate Sundays.

As Abbie introduced herself yet again to the same
bishop's secretary, Simon made a quick recce on the off
chance that Quinn might be hanging around. But everything was deathly still. Even the full-blown trees hung
limp, weighted by water. However, he noticed that the
bark on one of the ancient yews further down the path
seemed different from the rest and, as he drew closer, he
saw with a start what that axe had done. The hardwood
trunk had been almost severed with a single near-vertical
splice and gave off a sour, protesting smell as testimony
to the Reverend's terrible hidden strength.

Simon retraced his steps, making urgent plans from
connections almost too tenuous to be feasible, but which
nevertheless wouldn't go away. He recalled Abbie's
description of those weird photos in the vestry, particularly the one showing that faceless malignant figure in
black who was now determinedly making herself known.
And the more he dwelt on her, the possibility dawned
that the voice Rosie had heard at the hotel, and the evil
force her father had written about, might well be the
same. *Her.*

After he'd returned from London, he and Abbie
would visit the local record office. If no joy there, then
back to London. He remembered his A-level history.
From 1837 all births and deaths had to be registered, so
something somewhere, he convinced himself, was bound
to be written down in black and white. This had to be
worked through logically, not by jumping from one
fearful idea to the next. This deadly game had to be

sorted out before he went back to his regiment. *If* he
went back to his regiment . . .

He saw Abbie leave the phone box, her Barbour
spotted dark by new rain. She seemed worlds away. I'll
remember this, he said to himself, logging the sight of
her, thinking of posterity not death. She'd got more guts
in her little finger than some he'd worked with. But was
that going to be enough?

'Nothing doing,' she said bleakly, getting back into
the car.

'We could have another go on the way back.'

'I wish I'd hung on to my mobile. That was bloody
stupid of me to chuck it away.'

'They confiscated mine, for ordering my own bevvies.'
Simon rubbed his wet hair with her car duster. 'But
you'll need one after I've gone.'

She stared at him. *After you've gone . . . I knew it.*
That same hollowness returned as his blunder kept him
talking.

'You can get forty quid's worth of free calls, so you
can phone me every night.' He kissed her damp ear as
she reversed the Fiat, but his lips felt strangely cold.

Suddenly she spotted someone in the mirror. Someone in a long black raincoat with mascara-smudged
cheeks. The guardian of Quinn's place. The queen of his
sick heart.

'Shit, that's Avril Lawson. What's she doing there?'

Simon looked, then turned away. 'Ignore her. She's a
sad old cow.'

'How can I?'

And even though the wipers were swishing on full
speed, Abbie could see those crow eyes staring, the

predatory mouth fixed open. As she made her getaway, a huge pothole jarred the car's innards.

'C'mon.' Simon glanced back again. 'Let's chill.'

'I can't – and that's that.'

She'd mentioned the same deputy head in her letters to officialdom, but clearly letters were for losing and phone calls for forgetting. This whole place was a waste-land, and, like the tide's leavings, it was stagnant and murky. Which was why they were now already past Rievely Hall and negotiating the entrance to Clenchtoft Farm.

Simon stared at the mess, the dereliction, as they halted and Abbie changed into wellingtons, feeling a barrage of water on her back. They both stood for a moment listening – to every shadow, every battering of rain on the calf sheds, the creak of outer doors barely hinged. Quinn could be lurking anywhere here, but that was a risk they'd have to take.

Both crept under the police cordon, hardly daring to breathe, silent as the dead, invisible as the parasite army which bored into private darknesses. Nettles and bind-weed trampled to a slippery morass sent their feet splay-ing in different directions. A snag of barbed wire brought the only bright thing – blood from her arm, sweet and warm, pinking his teeth when he kissed it better. Every lower window had been boarded up. Abbie felt far too much a trespasser, so hesitated, but the old woman's words stayed in her head. Lilith had wanted her here, and the rain, as if colluding with her wishes, suddenly softened again to a drizzle.

'Thank God for that.' Simon swept the worst damp from his hair as he scoured the rear wall. Half brick, half timber, salted to grey, facing the sweep of Twelve Acre field to Leakes' Drain. There was one mesh window unboarded. They peered into its blackness before he started folding back the wires.

'Anyone here?' he called, checking Abbie was safely behind him. But only drips from the guttering replied as she gritted her teeth. No lights inside, just damp blackened walls crusted in mildew, some tiling and a ledge of stinking rags.

'Washroom, probably.' Abbie thought of the Willoughby's immaculate facilities and whispered, 'Jesus.'

'What's up?' Simon's voice seemed dismembered in the gloom.

'There's something here.'

At first she assumed it was a coat, until she felt a fabric landscape of seams and bodice buttons like Braille under her trembling fingers. Heavy and furred with rot, she could feel the dress tear under its own weight and knew she held another century in her hands.

'Hey, what the hell's this?'

Abbie frowned. She had touched something in the lining – not a prayer book, thank God, but bigger. Her fingers worked inside the smoother fabric and touched the book's cover.

'Let's take a look.'

Simon was still keeping watch, analysing every tiny sound of insect wildlife and the water invading the wreck of a house, boring in from the roof.

'That looks pretty old.'

'Maybe it's a diary.'

Abbie tried to make out what was inscribed on its frail pages but the drawings had faded, the light too dim. She plunged it into her pocket before grabbing his hand and creeping on into the kitchen.

Crockery shards rocked under their feet and a table corner poked her thigh as a sudden cold lapped her face. That smell again: of earth and rain so strong . . . She caught her breath.

'Simon!' she suddenly screamed, clinging to the oil-skin tablecloth, wishing she was under it, anywhere but here . . .

'What is it? Abbie?' He felt her shuddering, her fear burning against his body.

'It's her. Listen!'

'*See how the house of the Devil's dam has finally come to me. And mark how the rest will follow . . .*'

The voice Abbie dreaded more than anything filled the void, snaking into her clothes, into her head . . .

House of the Devil's dam? Which house for Christ's sake?

'Can't you hear?' she yelled at Simon.

He shook his head, watched Abbie's face in a trance of terror and felt utter helplessness. Martha Robinson seemed able to pick and choose: whom to torture, whom to spare. Although the labourer was invisible, when her clothes shuffled the debris of broken china, only Abbie heard it.

'If you've already got what you want, then why don't you leave me alone?' Abbie demanded.

Simon took her in his arms – it was all he could do.

'*What goes around, comes around, and there's no flames now from her hearth to keep me away . . .*'

'I don't understand.' Then Abbie remembered: 'I never talk o' the Devil away from my hearth, nor should ya . . .'

'*Wheels within wheels, you'll see.*' Martha Robinson's breath sucked in like the Wenn drawing the tide to its very heart. '*The appearance of the wheels and their work was like unto the colour of beryl; and they four had one likeness; and their appearance and their work was as it were a wheel in the middle of a wheel . . .*'

Abbie felt dizzy, spinning inside with the madness of it all. She tried to back away, but an ice pack seemed to cover her legs. Even Simon didn't even exist for her any more.

'*You hear me out, for there'll be times when you'll have need of me and I of you . . .*'

Now the voice possessed a grotesque gargling sound from deep in the throat as though its airway was strangled. Abbie remembered the black scarf, the yellow skin . . .

'That's not bloody true!'

But as before, she was overpowered by this hidden force as Martha continued in a more unsettling, confiding tone.

'*You see, I used to come here begging when I was wed. Have you ever had to do that? Have you?*'

'Tell her to go, Simon, *please.*'

But for the first time in his life he was speechless and utterly confused. Nothing had ever prepared him for this. Better to let the thing die out, he thought, holding Abbie tighter as the voice that spoke to her alone went on.

'*The worst was when my sissen took up with Daniel Leakes, who brought the drain down from Snake's Mouth. Well-off she was, but as God's blind I got nothing. She could see me and my girls from her window – us yellowbellies had the Goosefoot for four shillings a week. It wasn't worth a half of that but yet she had six beds for nothing.*' Martha Robinson seemed to sigh, suddenly weary. '*If*

Ben Robinson had been a sokeman with a plot of his own, like my Moeder had always said, we'd have had some rights, we'd never have come to this.'

Abbie was shivering dreadfully, trying to keep a grip on herself. 'It's not my fault.'

'We can all say that.'

'Look, because of you my job's all screwed up. The site's not selling any houses . . . What am I going to do? Tell me! Are you there?' she shouted, angry to have been so manipulated yet remain unheard. Her rage welled up, unstoppable, and Simon tried to drag her away.

'Come on, Abs.'

She wrenched herself free and battered the old tabletop.

'Damn you, Martha Robinson! Damn you!'

Simon's strength prevailed. He held the window wires peeled back for her but it was harder this time, as though something was holding them both to Lilith Leakes's last memories. Abbie ripped both sleeves wriggling harder to let the afternoon touch her face and Simon followed. Once free, they stood together in silence, letting her fear and frustration subside. Words completely deserted him for the moment.

It had stopped raining altogether and overhead a weak sun pierced the clouds as if drying her eyelids. Almost a blessing, Simon thought. God knows she needs it.

'Come on, Abs, let's get you back.'

'No. There's somewhere else we still need to look.'

Simon stared as she stumbled away from him, over rutted rivers of filth towards the barns. She was so courageous – how could he even think of leaving her? How? He secured his jacket and ran after her. These outbuildings lay on the eastern side, fallen in on themselves into fetid pools of dung, home to old car seats and rotting calf skins.

'What the fuck are we doing *now*?'

'I'm not sure. Lilith may have hidden something else here, you never know.'

She felt the book in her pocket.

'Jesus Christ!'

Simon covered his mouth, as he turned one of the skins over with his boot. The stench sent him reeling back, then falling on to something hard. His legs, scissoring with a life of their own, uncovered a shaft of wood. Not some random thing, more formed, and weightier than any piece of broken barn. And slender, almost womanly in shape. It was an axe, still serviceable – its killing end buried less than a hundred yards away from the house.

The rain makes those damned gallows even blacker, like a giant Testament with no pages bearing down on me. It's a terrible thing to see every day, but necessary according to mad Samuel Scott who has lost two servants to murder. They say William Pye of Kilntoft will hang next week for filling his father's mouth with chaff, so it's no farm he'll be taking on that's for sure.

Thirty-five

'QUINN HAD AN axe at the rectory, remember?'

'How can I forget?' Abbie couldn't let her eyes rest on any one thing for fear she'd miss the cleric's lurking shadow.

'We'd better tell that woofter cop.' Simon picked up on her nervousness.

'And I need to try phoning the bishop again.'

He took a stick of chewing gum from the glove compartment, then drove her car back to the phone box in Smithy Lane, legs still aching from the fall in the barn.

Damn! Some old geezer was already in there, taking his time. Probably talking to himself, Simon thought, taking Abbie's hand and feeling the pulse hammering in her wrist.

'Look, I'm going to tell the Doc I can't go back to Germany. Not after this.'

'Do what you like. I don't know what to say any more.' She felt as if that axe had severed her brain, splitting that terrible voice into separate echoes, the only ones she could hear.

'Abbie?' He took her shoulders, gently worked on them, let her lean against him vacant-eyed until the pensioner had finished phoning.

'I won't be a sec.' Simon leapt out. 'Keep thinking about something else, for God's sake.'

For God's sake? Why for God's sake? It's for the Devil's *sake . . .*

The Snutterwick CID line was engaged every time he tried. In the end he gave up and went for the bishop instead. Abbie had given him the number on a damp scrap of paper and watched from the car. He punched the code with some force, then drummed his fingers until a woman answered.

'Elisabeth Roux.' She wasn't going to make things easy.

'Is that the bishop's place?'

'You mean his office?' As if she had twenty plums in each cheek.

'Whatever.'

'To whom am I speaking?'

'Does it matter? We've got to see him urgently. My friend Miss Parker's been trying over and over again to get through . . .'

He studied Abbie in the Fiat, still looking dazed and pale, and his heart was hurting. All he wanted was to make everything better, but the mud of the Wash was slowly sucking him down.

'He *is* the diocesan bishop, you know.' Her condescension was undisguised. 'Six parishes and all far afield . . .'

'I don't bloody care if he's got six hundred fucking parishes.'

'So I'm afraid,' she said, ignoring his outburst, 'he's over at Humberwell for the next few days and can only deal with matters of supreme importance. If you'd like to leave a message— I'm only here until midday.'

'I'd like to leave a message all right.' Simon's fists tightened. 'Tell him we need to have an exorcism here in Black Fen. It's a matter of life and death. *Death* in bloody capital letters . . .'

He stopped mid-sentence. The cold bitch had cut him off. He listened hard, but instead of the normal tone in his ear came a sound he'd only heard in celluloid executions. He thought of the sudden scream of rope, the hollow drop from life to death.

Jesus Christ, what's going on?

He began shaking, for a moment losing his bearings. In his mind he saw a gaunt skeletal shape against the sky, like a blackened corpse, dead as driftwood, swinging in the wind. For a moment he stared at the receiver, then rammed it down – in the only exorcism he knew. A teenager with a pram was waiting outside, but soon moved off when she saw his glare.

He was in no mood now to speak to Stock or anyone, and as he walked back towards Abbie's expectant face he tried to cling to the rational order of things, yet deep down he knew that this evil presence would continue to sabotage any logic. To render him useless.

So why had Abbie seen the woman, heard her voice, her laugh, and not he? Maybe because the monster wanted something only Abbie could give her. That miserable plot of land for a start. And what else? He dared not think. Why then had that sound of execution just been for his ears? *She* was dishing out the Christmas crackers all right – or was he going mad?

Simon thought of his medical interview, less than forty-eight hours away, and knew he'd enough excuses for permanent sick leave and disability pay without having to invent anything. It was worth more than a thought.

'No joy with the plods or the bishop. Fucking useless.'
He shoved the driver's seat back and started the engine.

Abbie's face fell. 'This is what it's been like all along.
We'll just have to try an ordinary vicar. There's got to be
another church round here.' She tried recalling the site
promotional brochure, which included info on local
schools, doctors and vets. 'Hang on, that notice on the
vestry door said the Rural Dean of North Sand would be
holding a service here on alternate Sundays. Is that next
week, do you think?'

'We can't wait till then.'

'Right. So let's go to North Sand.'

Abbie checked her watch. 'What about Sheila?'

'We'll buy her some chocs. That'll cheer her up.'

The rain had turned to a drizzle by the time they reached
the end of Walsoken Road and entered Fitting Drove,
which curved eastwards beyond Leakes' Drain towards
Outwold. Simon thought again of Belloc – 'one does not
understand the Fens until one has seen that shore.' Like
Black Fen, this more northerly part was the same grey
blur of land and water.

A group of single-storey government buildings that
had never been rebuilt after the war, or converted into
anything lucrative, now stood like bad teeth against the
horizon.

'North Sand, four miles.' Abbie read the sign erected
beside what seemed the flattest, straightest road in Britain, cutting through Flatsoken and Fitting Fen, hemmed
in by unhedged quilts of cabbage and rape – the latter
sudden violent slabs of colour that made her blink. There
were occasionally barns fallen in on themselves, defeated
by the north wind. They stood as bleak punctuations to

the surrounding symmetry of big business. And one barn in particular sheltered a sleepless cleric listening to his own personal demon in its filthy darkness.

Simon wondered again about the sounds of the hanging he'd heard re-enacted through the phone line. Had that been a prison affair? Or was the gibbet somewhere else? Somewhere nearby even? And was it anything to do with Martha Robinson? He'd have to find out, for the memory of it wasn't going to leave him.

The village at least had a call box and he used it to try and contact Snutterwick CID again, while Abbie closed her eyes in exhaustion. He learned that Stock was in Wisbech investigating an incident of arson, so he told a tense WPC O'Halloran about the axe, watching his pound coin being reduced to ten pence far too quickly. She asked for his contact number again, said she'd pass his information on, hoped Abbie was all right. She was just reassuring him that everything was being done to find Rosie Quinn, when his money finally ran out.

Shit, fuck, shit.

Abbie was dozing, her face caught in struggling sun through the windscreen. Simon nudged her awake.

'I think we ought to have another look at that book thing you found.'

'Do we have to? Now?'

'Yes. We need to find out as much as we can.'

She withdrew it sleepily from her bag and passed it to him. He eased the hand-sewn pages apart as if it was some treasured family keepsake.

'It's titled 'Secrets by lilith annie leakes,' he noted. 'About the only thing that's legible.' As his head bent low over the grotesque maze of drawings and jottings, some smeared with animal blood long dried into the meanderings of the hermit's mind, Simon's frown deepened. 'She must have been on something. How can this sort of stuff be normal?' Each page revealed more depictions of innards, more wombs containing foetuses, until at the very end he came upon a baby's face dominated by two enormous eyes.

Abbie sat up to look at it too. It was truly spooky. Even though the sun warmed her skin, she felt some kind of chilly recognition pass through her.

'That's *her* child,' she said.

'Don't be daft.'

'That's why she wanted me to find this thing. Can't we keep it?'

Simon wrapped the book in his handkerchief and put it in her lap. 'No. There may be clues, but God knows what.' He thought for a moment. 'And when I get back on Monday, I'll check a parish record or two. Can you help me?'

'I've still got a job, you know.' But now that sounded bizarre.

'OK. Leave it to me.'

He idled the car along the village street of North Sand towards a general store whose drab front was cluttered by a stack of second-hand chairs and plants left over from the winter frosts. A rusty bell moved with the door.

Simon took a chance on a packet of Wagon Wheels and a carton of Quality Street. The woman in a none too clean apron seemed pleased to see him and asked where he was from.

'Black Fen,' he replied, and he might as well have uttered a curse, for the shopkeeper, suddenly silent, wrapped the chocolates quickly, almost threw his change at him and disappeared.

'She was a bit of an oddball in there,' Simon said, putting the purchases on the back seat.

'So would I be, living here. Just look at it.' At least Black Fen was crossed by other roads, turnings leading into turnings. This was just a single rat run, as proved by the clapped-out Bedford truck that screamed past them just then.

St Cecilia's loomed above the last of the brick cottages, another Norman tower, without its sister church's hideous gargoyle, but with gulls instead, arranged on its crenellations. The parish graveyard had been newly mowed and was home to a white Saanen goat pulling at the longer grass near the headstones with its bearded mouth. Simon wanted to stroke it, sheep and goats having always been part of his childhood at Dan y Parc, but no way was Abbie hanging round graves today, especially these tacky little cremation plots with their vinyl flowers.

'Maybe we'll find him in his rectory or vicarage, whatever they call it.' He wondered who the animal belonged to.

'We ought to try here first, though.'

She disengaged herself from him then moved on ahead. He followed her down the path between conifers and old graves that were part sunken, their body mounds cropped and marked by cloven hooves, their stones centuries old, lost to lichen, bearing inscriptions that could barely be made out, like 'Kirton Church, 1808–50', and, more clearly, 'Thomas Gloatby, 1800–1863. Drowned at Sea. Now at Rest.'

'Simon?' She was waving him on from the door.

Not waving, but drowning . . .

'Coming.' As he moved towards her the sound of a fugue, floating from inside the building, seemed for a second to lift him from the morass he was ensnared in.

Abbie went first through the vestry, which was cluttered with leaflets containing information about all sorts of things ranging from the Samaritans to visits to Oberammergau, then into the well-lit nave and an abundance of brass and gilt. The organist's playing died when she saw them hovering near the hymn books. This was practice time and all the locals knew better than to disturb it.

'Yes?' she called out. Meaning leave me alone, Bach is more important.

'Sorry to interrupt you, but where can we find the vicar?' asked Abbie.

The woman consulted her watch. She was tiny against the façade of pipes. 'He's usually here by now. Wait if you must.' Then she immediately struck a loud chord that made Simon jump out of his skin.

They chose a pew near the back and stared up at the window over the altar. A new work, obviously, judging by its simpler shapes and unlikely colours.

'That's St Cecilia.' A voice from behind made them whip round. 'Philip Byers, local chap, did the design, but we're not sure what to do now, after all that abduction business.'

Simon and Abbie exchanged a quick glance. Yes, she *would* tell him, now Byers had been mentioned.

'I'm Abbie Parker.'

Derek Jarrold lowered his gaze so he could observe her over the edge of his glasses. 'Oh, my dear. You were one of them. What can I say?' He looked embarrassed.

'Something to help us, I hope,' Simon said. 'Look, can we go somewhere private please?'

'Of course. Through here.'

Jarrold led the way into the sacristy, which was hung with cassocks and surplices and smelt of damp socks. He pulled out three wooden chairs and invited them to sit as the organ music changed to Buxtehude – sonorous and deep, matching their mood.

'What happened to Abbie and little Rosie was just part of it,' Simon started, then felt the sacrilegious lump of gun in his pocket. 'The trouble is knowing where to start.'

'We're pretty desperate,' Abbie said simply, and, looking at her, Jarrold believed her.

'If I can help, I will, but to be honest I've only half an hour before the choir arrives. Then that'll be that.'

Half an hour, thirty whole minutes. They wanted to cheer him, hug him, anything to thank him for being human. Simon nodded at Abbie to begin.

'When I first met Quinn, I mean the Reverend Quinn, at Black Fen, I was looking at some photos of nineteenth-century gang workers. He seemed to have heard stories of one of the women in particular, and of her girls, poor little things . . .'

'From 1862,' Simon added. 'Signed Gabriel Hemmings.'

Jarrold, who'd blinked at Quinn's name, frowned in attention. 'We had them for a month too,' he said. 'Despite Colonel Scott's objections.'

'Oh?'

'I had a rather forceful letter from him, requesting they be removed, even though they were only copies.'

'And did you?' Simon asked.

'It was taken out of my hands. One day they suddenly vanished. All very odd.'

'The ones at St Mary Magdalene weren't there for long either.' Abbie frowned. 'So how did you get hold of them in the first place?'

Jarrold scratched inside his dog collar. 'They were just sent anonymously. It was the same with the Reverend Quinn too, I believe. And yes, there was a note attached saying they *needed* to be seen.'

So someone else had suffered . . .

'Anyhow, it was just a bit of old history doing the rounds of the parishes, and good for showing the younger generation how lucky they are now . . .'

'Except for his daughter, Rosie,' Abbie said, with feeling.

'I have been praying for her.' Neither was impressed, he could tell. The younger man pinned him with his eyes.

'We think that Martha Robinson, the tallest figure in the photos, is currently on a mission – haunting Black Fen.' He checked with Abbie, who nodded encouragement. The dam had been breached. There was no holding back. 'It's as if she's seeking revenge . . .'

'Revenge?' The cleric looked bewildered.

'Yes, but we don't know what for.' Abbie continued. 'We also suspect her spirit's fixated on one of our plots at Kingfisher Rise, but will you promise not to breathe a word about that, please.' She leaned forward. 'I still work there, trying to sell new houses. It would be the kiss of death if that sort of news got out . . . But I'm worried sick something really terrible's going to happen unless she's driven away.'

'We can't wait,' Simon added simply. 'It's getting worse.'

'I see.'

'And there's *much* more going on, really weird things . . .'

The rural dean stared at his nails, his forehead bearing a deep frown. Did he believe her? Even *want* to believe her? 'Go on, please.'

'Well, for a start a prayer book keeps appearing, even though I've got rid of it every time. It has Esmond Downey written inside. Does that name mean anything to you?'

Jarrold scratched an eyebrow. Conversations like this were not that rare in this haunted part of the British Isles but, like the condemned men his grandfather had once counselled in the Scrubs, his hands were tied.

'I'm not local myself but yes, it certainly sounds familiar. I think the Downeys were once the incumbents at St Mary Magdalene. Father and son.'

Abbie held her breath. 'Do you know any more than that? I mean, are they buried there? Or even here?'

'Not here, that's for sure. Our radius extends for just twelve miles. Now I seem to remember that Oxford was significant somehow. In fact I'm sure of it.'

'Oxford's a big place.' Simon managed a smile.

'Indeed.'

'There's something else though.' Abbie decided to leave that particular cul-de-sac. 'Quinn's sent me a letter. Hate mail.'

'It's in the hands of the police now,' Simon added, 'though God knows what they've been doing with it.'

'And?' Jarrold was careful to ration his oxygen. He'd been there more times than he cared to remember. All he could safely do was make the right noises. As his wife always said, 'Think of a piggie in its straw, Derek, you've *got* to think of yourself.'

'The letter said, "You will all die . . ."'

'Oh, goodness,' Jarrold murmured, both eyebrows raised now.

'We think Quinn's being driven by something truly evil and powerful. We're not sure who or what it is, but at least we could start with Martha Robinson. We need your help, now.'

The rural dean got up and went over to the one small window. 'I can't afford to speak out of turn, you understand, but I am aware the Reverend Quinn *has* been struggling of late. I did hear about the axe incident, so I asked the bishop to intervene . . .'

'Yes?'

'Let's just say he's far too busy at present, so on this occasion it was best to draw a veil. Forgiveness, after all, is the cornerstone of our faith.'

Abbie looked over at Simon. This guy was decent enough, but they were getting nowhere. An all too familiar place for both of them . . .

'We did tell the police about that.' Simon said. 'And then we go and find an axe hidden, close to where Lilith Leakes was murdered.'

Jarrold turned round, powerlessness written all over his face.

'We also found his wife's Bible – well, just the first five books of the Old Testament.'

'Ah, the Pentateuch.'

'Whatever. At Haletoft House. Weird bloody place that.'

The rural dean's eyes grew large behind his spectacles. 'Haletoft, you say?'

'That's right. And as we were leaving he fired a shot at us. We know it was him. Anyhow, there's a big search on for him now.'

Simon the logician was losing the plot, but there was too much to tell and the minutes were ticking away.

'We found some notes he made in this Pentateuch,' Abbie went on, 'suggesting that some voice or other is getting to him. Something that's making him do things a normal vicar would never dream of. Surely we've *got* to have an exorcism, and Goosefoot Cottage would be the best place. Apparently she lived there, Martha Robinson.'

Jarrold looked uncertain. 'You've come to the right person, at least on paper. In this diocese, only I am allowed to perform them, but it's up to the bishop to authorize . . .'

'We've tried to get through twice.' Simon interrupted tetchily. 'No joy of course.'

'As I've just said, he's an extremely busy man . . .'

'Why don't you come and see for yourself!' Abbie interrupted. 'See how bad it's getting. I've heard horrible, cruel laughter and singing.' Her voice was rising and Simon took her hand.

'I also heard something else today,' he said quietly.

'What?' She stared.

'It was like the sound of someone being hanged.'

The vestry grew cold, the sunlight gone.

'You never told me, Si. When?'

'Just before we came here. In the phone box.'

Jarrold came and put a hand on their shoulders. 'You must believe me, I cannot interfere. We've just received a synod ruling that such cleansing is only to be carried out *in extremis*, that means where a life is in mortal danger.' He saw their expressions change but he hadn't finished. 'It was a majority decision that this ritual can achieve more harm than good. Often those who've been cleansed become suicidal, you see. If what you say is true and the Reverend Quinn presented himself for our help, then that would be a different matter.'

'A little lad from Black Fen Primary School, Charlie Hunter, he's dead because of all this.'

'Malaria,' Abbie added.

'Malaria?' Jarrold said slowly. 'Now that is strange. I didn't know that.'

'It was on the local news.'

'Oh?'

'And three other kids have come down with it as well. They all touched Martha Robinson's dolls, which were left in the cottage she used to live in.'

Looking perturbed, the rural dean sat down again. 'Dolls, you say?' He removed his spectacles and rubbed each lens with the corner of a nearby cassock, weariness showing in his eyes. 'We did have a number of parishioners out there who succumbed to that disease, but that was long ago. It's unheard of now, surely?'

'Exactly, so do we have to beg you?'

Simon's voice was hard in the silence as Jarrold fought with his own conscience. He was tired, too many needs, too many problems and too little support from his episcopal line manager. In three months he'd be out of it all – he'd promised his wife that. Yet as he studied them, he saw here two perfectly normal young people looking burdened beyond their years. He knew all about telepathy, autosuggestion and hysteria, his interest in Jung and Guirdham a specialist in regression, had begun even before his ordination, and he'd always made his own decisions irrespective of his place in the hierarchy. But now, as ever, he was helpless in consequence of the Synod's proclamation.

He clearly remembered those bleak memorials from Hemmings's camera and had to confess he too had found them disturbing, and not just from a sociological viewpoint. That tall figure *had* possessed a definite presence. A few parishioners had even remarked on it, while his old cleaner swore that some relative of the mystery woman was interred here at St Cecilia's, lucky to have had a Christian burial given all the family's sins . . .

'I promise you both I'll consult with my bishop tonight, but I don't hold out much hope. The climate in the Church has changed, I'm afraid.'

Abbie's hand tightened in Simon's. 'You *must* make him listen.'

Jarrold checked his watch, stood up and held the door open for them, his eyes following their silhouettes towards the daylight.

'I will try,' he called after them. 'Oh, just one thing . . .'

'Yes?'

'Mrs Jimson, our church cleaner over at Spittle Cottage, might be worth a visit.'

'Why's that?'

'It's best if you go and see her.'

Abbie felt hollow as she walked down towards the car. The sun warmed her arms but left her inwardly untouched. There was no help here either, she sensed that. No one to keep death away.

Simon started to follow her but stopped by Thomas Gloatby's gravestone. 'Were there ever hangings round here?' he asked before the cleric disappeared.

'Lord, yes. The last one was, let me see, 1865.'

'What happened to the bodies afterwards?'

Jarrold was torn between the imminent arrival of the choir and this obviously anxious stranger. 'Rumour has it that an old lugger would turn up after dark and take them out to sea.' He paused. 'They were the bad times then, what I call the dark side . . .'

Jesus wept.

'So where did the hangings take place?'

'Again, facts get lost in the mists of time, but I did hear once there was one site near Goteland and another in Black Fen.'

'Black Fen?' Simon swallowed.

'On Morpeth Bank, I think.'

Simon didn't wait to hear any more. That was enough and he had to go.

As the rural dean watched him leave, he offered up a prayer – for them both to know some kind of peace . . . But Simon wasn't after prayers now. He was dying for a fag or a drink, or both. The Fiat was where he wanted to be at that moment. But Abbie musn't know. She was upset enough, so he put on a brave face.

'Hi.' He planted a kiss on her unresponsive cheek.

'He knew what we were on about, all right. Why can't people here ever move off bloody square one?'

Simon kissed her again, then stroked the fourth finger of her left hand. 'There'll be something on this when it's all over, that's a promise.'

He saw her green eyes set with fear, her lips begin to quiver. 'I should have told you earlier, but I couldn't. I touched those dolls too. You know, when I rearranged them, made them respectable . . . and I've spoken their names. I'm sorry, Si, if only I'd known . . .' She stood there bowed, numb, as if waiting for the thud of hoofbeats and the headless coachman to gallop by.

'Come on, Abs. It must all be old wives' tales. That Mrs Buckley's just muck-spreading with words.' But he didn't really believe that, not for one minute, and Abbie's sudden look of disdain cut him short.

As a cluster of clouds darkened and lowered above them, Simon saw a boat butting against the tide, moving out to the Deeps of Lethe . . . He started the engine, pulled himself together. 'I'm bloody Hank Marvin! Shall we try and grab some lunch somewhere? Or d'you want to go and see that Mrs Jimson first?'

'No. It'll just be a snippet here, a snippet there, more time wasted. I want to find out properly about Martha Robinson and her dolls – who they represented, what's their story.'

'Like I said then, just keep Monday afternoon free.' He reached for the Wagon Wheels, hot and melting.

William Pye has croaked his last, beaten by the rope. Gloatby, the Hangman, let him speak too long and at the end all the drunks from The Sails were hollering for him to go to Gehenna and stay there. Then they got tar brushes, dripping to the soil like bad blood and made a blackamoor of him. To my way of thinking, this was worse than any Hell, real or imagined.

Thirty-six

WHEN THEY GOT back to the hotel, Sheila was still in her dressing gown. She perked up only marginally when Simon handed her the chocs, which were now in need of the fridge. She pointed to the phone.

'Abbie, your uncle rang. Said no need to call back.'

'I must. Is everything all right there?'

'Think so.'

Abbie dialled, spoke for a while, then her face relaxed into a smile as Graham passed her over to Rosie. The little girl told her all about playing with Flora and the den they'd made in the garden, how she liked baking coconut macaroons and how Sue had made another dress for her new dolly.

'Thank God for that at least,' Abbie said afterwards, sighing, then put her arms round Sheila's shoulders. 'And thank you as well. I'm really sorry about all this. We both are.' She looked at Simon's back. He was pouring himself a pint.

'Course, but we're winning,' he replied absently, before the contents of his glass went down in one draught. He then went for a second. Something else was seriously on his mind.

'That's £3.60, before you forget,' Sheila said, directing

her cigarette smoke upwards. Simon suddenly made a show of slapping some coins down on the bar, then made for the door. Abbie saw his fixed expression, car keys ready.

'Si, where are you going?'

'Where do you bloody think?'

No one could answer that one, and when the door banged shut, whether slammed by him or the wind, Sheila leaned towards Abbie.

'When's his medical interview?'

'Tomorrow. Why?'

Sheila killed her dimp and lit another. There's no more room in the ashtray, Abbie thought, musing on the probable colour of Sheila's lungs.

'Well, there we are.'

'There we are what?'

''S why he's ratty. Doesn't know if he wants to go back out there or stay here with you.'

'Yes, he does. He's going to explain to them what we're up against here, try for compassionate leave . . .'

Sheila inhaled, then let the smoke out again, loaded with her opinion. 'I wouldn't bank on it, Abbie. He's a born fighter, whatever he says about his dad pushing him into it.'

'Then why's he drinking so much?'

'He won't stop that, it's in his make-up. No, he probably couldn't cope with all the waiting around. Will they? Won't they? I mean, that war's been going on for months and now he's obsessively watching the news. I've seen him at it when you're out at work. I'd say he was keen to get on with it. Look at his fists, for God's sake, Abbie. You don't get them in that state working in a bloody hairdresser's, do you? If you want my advice, I think you ought to get out of this place, get on with your life. You've done your bit, God knows.'

Abbie stared at her.

'I'm only playing Devil's advocate,' Sheila continued, getting up and shuffling towards the stairs. 'But don't forget, I have been around a few more years than you.' Suddenly she stopped, bent down and picked up something off the top step. 'Hey, have you started saying your prayers or something?' she asked.

Abbie didn't want to recognize what Sheila was holding.

'Esmond P. Downey?' Sheila sniffed the pages. 'Is this some very ancient flame of yours, then?'

Abbie snatched the prayer book off her and went to find string in the kitchen. She then went out of the hotel and up to the top of Herringtoft, where she found a stone of the right weight. This she pressed into the leather sides, bound them tightly together with the string and tossed the whole thing into the Wenn as far as it would go.

Sheila's words repeated in her head like a metronome as she kept walking, occasionally checking to make sure that Quinn was not around. Sunlight and shadow met her face in turn, as tears filled her eyes. They blurred the track before her, still slush mud in parts, and her Nikes skidded deep into each little treachery. With each slide came more pain, more doubt.

Abbie hadn't planned to wander far, hadn't planned anything in fact, until she saw ahead of her a figure moving backwards and forwards, occasionally bending as though searching for something lost along Morpeth Bank. She squinted at the blue jeans, black jacket, hair a gold crop in the sun. Simon? What on earth was he doing there? She wasn't sure whether to leave before he spotted her, but curiosity drove her on.

'Can I help you?'

He whipped round, lost for words, and saw her pallor, her hair wild, almost red in the light of sunset.

'Four eyes are better than two, whatever you're looking for.' Abbie continued. But she knew she wasn't wanted here. Something was on his mind.

'I'll be back soon. You go home,' he said.

'You told *me* not to leave *you*, remember?'

'I know I did, but this is different.' His gaze trailed from the Herringtoft end to where the bank met Slave's Drain.

'How different?' She pulled stray hairs away from her face. 'Tell me.'

'No, it doesn't matter.'

'I let on about the dolls, when I could have kept that secret.'

'Abbie, don't.'

'I'm not going till you say what you're doing here.'

He looked fed up. This was the one thing he had to sort out alone, if only to spare her. 'P for Persistence – I've got to hand it to you.' He was still eyeing the ground in front of him.

'Too right.' She went up close and pulled him to her, her tongue in his ear, then in his mouth. A slow deep kiss, sinking one into the other ... sinking ... sinking ...

Simon pulled away, wiped his lips with his sleeve and, in that instant, Abbie saw a future without him. That was a sign, what more did she want?

She made for the nearby poplars whispering their secrets, then over Hicks's land, leaving perfect footprints

where once the shrieks and catcalls of a hungry crowd
had poisoned the air – and where Quinn lay sheltering
only yards away in Ten Barn field.

Simon barely noticed her departure. He was too busy
pacing the same stretch again and again, pausing to lift
stones, pull at weeds, then go back to the same spot
where his hunch was nagging him. Here, at the join
with Herringtoft, lay an oblong composed of four slightly
sunken hollows filled with sludge from the recent rain.

He began to dredge the stuff away, oblivious of the
little flints scagging his skin. Deeper and deeper, up to
the wrist now, with obsession his only tool. Suddenly,
delving in one of the holes, he could go no further. Using
a wad of fescue grass, he cleaned mud away from what
seemed to be the remains of a wooden stump. Old,
sodden, but oak nevertheless. He did the same with the
next one. There had previously been four squared timbers
here: four upright props. *So, Morpeth Bank, alias Murder
Path.* He knew that now . . . This had been the gibbet all
right, with its drop going God knows where.

He sat back on his haunches, not satisfied at all, but
rather plunged into a memory that had never been his:
the sounds of hatred and hubbub, the stink of fear. And
further away, along the bank, a pale horse waiting under
a black sky . . .

Christ, there but for the Grace of God . . .

Simon sprang to his feet, sensing the mass of sea
cloud draw inland and settle overhead. He hauled up his
collar, leaving clay smears on his best jacket and, while
the skies emptied their dolour over Black Fen, he charged
back to the hotel, stopping only at the roadside to let the
police cars, speeding away from Clenchtoft, drench him
with spray.

I can scarce recount that day full of a gale that snatched my hair and blew the tide in along the drains, chop chop, and rising as close to flooding as I've ever seen. I have told all those who enquire that it's an affliction of the bowel that has caused me to swell like a Christmas goose. Susannah Buckley thinks arrowroot and fennel will cure it, and last week she brought over a good supply.

Thirty-seven

WHILE SHEILA LAY in bed finishing off her carton of Quality Street, debating whether or not to get a valuer round to view the hotel, Abbie opened up her Show Home office after the Spring Bank Holiday with more trepidation than usual. No one was currently working down her end of the construction site and plot 2 stood swathed in black polythene held between the fittings and first blocks, yet billowing out on the wind like grim multiples of Martha Robinson's shadow.

Simon had gone to London. She checked her watch. In an hour he'd be there, making his own decisions. He'd left a note, *I love you*, on her pillow, and she stared at it now, until suddenly the phone rang and broke her reverie.

Derek Jarrold sounded different, subdued. No point in even listening to the inevitable, Abbie thought.

'I've done my best,' he began.

'But the bishop said no?'

'I'm afraid that's the situation.'

She wasn't even going to thank him for trying, it had gone beyond that.

'I'm sorry, really I am,' he went on. 'As I explained to you, it is out of my control, but I really must say something. It's been on my conscience since I met you both.'

She waited, eyes fixed on Simon's note.

'Get out of Black Fen now, Miss Parker, while you can – you and that nice young man of yours. If you were my family . . . well, you know what I mean.'

She put the phone down gently, leaving the man of God to his ineffectual calling, and just as she was unfolding the new site plan Vallender had sent, she noticed a police car cruise through the gates.

A tall figure in smart-casual dress got out and stood surveying the site before heading her way. He waited, obviously courtesy his middle name, while Abbie opened the door, rehearsing what not to say.

'Detective Superintendent Aldreth, Snutterwick CID.' His handshake was firm as he smiled. 'Well, this seems a pleasant enough spot here.'

'This isn't the biggest house in our range,' Abbie began. 'The Ripton's really spacious . . .'

You sound pathetic girl, you know that?

'I'm sure,' he acknowledged, while perching all six foot five of himself on a client chair. 'Look, Miss Parker, in case you're wondering, I've come to be of assistance.'

'Thanks.' Unsure of his meaning, she offered to repay this unexpected thoughtfulness with a passable cup of tea.

'So how's it all going at Kingfisher Rise?' He was eyeing the plan when she returned. No yellow dots signifying exchange of contract or red ones for completion – even a simpleton could see there was nothing doing here. She gave him the best mug.

'Fine, but as that plan's new, I've not had time to update it.'

'Ah.'

'You people have got the old one with the blood on it, remember?' she challenged.

'Of course.' He accurately measured half a teaspoon of sugar. 'What made you think it was blood?'

Abbie watched him take several small sips. Nothing in excess with this one. She had better be on her guard.

'We've had quite a few kids up here from Black Fen Primary School, messing about, doing damage. This door's not always locked if I'm showing other plots to clients. Oh, and the builders, I thought it might be one of them fooling around, but it's so unlikely.'

He was looking at her in a way she couldn't fathom, then he put his mug down. 'You've had other trouble here, haven't you?'

'No. Why?'

'Let's just say we know you have and leave it at that, eh? You see, I'm not sure what we can do about things – how shall I say? – of the mind, but we are examining the item you gave us all the same.'

Abbie resisted any urge to argue and bit her lip. She felt herself colouring from the neck up as she glanced at the unmarked plan and plot 2, looking normal at least on paper, and realized her trial period for selling any of it was slipping away. But the site still deserved a chance and Martha Robinson wasn't going to screw it all up.

'Does the name Grant Connell ring any bells?' Aldreth asked, catching her off guard.

Oh no . . .

Abbie stalled. Aldreth was staring at her again, as though he could see into her mind.

'He was a mixer. Only here for three months, though. Some of the other blokes reckoned he'd be a bit of a problem.'

'Oh?'

'They said he often used to come in drunk, especially on Monday mornings.'

The lie was complex, the hole ever deeper. By way of ending the matter Aldreth finished his tea and drew a slim notebook from his pocket.

'It's a common enough occurrence round here from what I gather.' He glanced up, meaning Simon of course, but giving her no time to react. 'Well, if you need us again, Miss Parker, don't hesitate.' He settled back against the flimsy chair. 'Now, I felt it better to update you in person rather than down a phone. We have had some developments.'

'Good. About my letter?'

'Letter?'

'Yes. I had one from Quinn, delivered, I think, by his sidekick, Avril Lawson. It contained a threat.' She took a sharp breath, '*You will all die*. My boyfriend gave it to DI Mowbray when I was recovering in hospital.'

'Oh?' Aldreth's frown deepened. 'Nothing's come through on it, I'm afraid. Mowbray's now ex-directory and incommunicado.'

'What? But it's vital evidence, surely?'

'I quite understand and I'll investigate it personally. A letter, you say?' Aldreth seemed momentarily disconcerted.

'Yes. And then what he said to the newspapers about catching Byers. Bloody cheek.'

He made another note, then looked up. 'Can't think what made him do that. Bit out of character, I'd say. However, my news now.' He ventured a smile.

Still seething, she poured him more tea, trying to

work him out, but he'd already stirred the bigger water leaving its surface occluded by mud.

'Thanks to yours and Mr Cresswell's help we've matched the fingerprints on the handle of the axe found at Clenchtoft Farm with those the intruder left at the St George's Sails, and as a result we do need to call our Reverend friend in for questioning.'

At last.

New fear spasmed through Abbie's body. She clutched the site plan, crumpling its orderly folds.

'I must warn you he's probably hanging around here, with a desire for vengeance now, and most likely in disguise.' He drank his tea contemplatively, his mind with the Eurocopter now covering North Sand, searching for the Quinns and their daughter.

'Why would he have hidden it at Clenchtoft? Unless . . .' Abbie faltered, feeling numb. 'Oh, my God. Do you think *he* killed her?'

'Until our full findings on Miss Leakes's injuries come through, I can't comment on that. It's not cut and dried by any means.' *Cut and dried. Not a clever choice of words. Be careful, Colin Aldreth.*

'Injuries? But the papers said she was hit on the head.'

'Again no comment. Now, whether his missing wife and child are with him is another matter.'

Abbie tried to keep her face a mask. This police officer was very, very clever.

'As you know, we pressed Haletoft House and finally they talked. Yes, the Reverend and Mrs Quinn were there, but after a week they managed to do a midnight flit, though you'd think a wheelchair would be spotted. No car, you see.'

'We saw that wheelchair later at Oscarby End,

though. I'm sure it was hers. They could have got a lift there.'

'Private vehicles aren't allowed at the retreat. Residents must come and go by taxi. But this aside, it's the child's absence that's worrying. She's not with Mrs Quinn's elderly parents in Wisbech. Mind you, they can barely look after themselves, never mind a young child. So there's been no sighting since she was returned home after – how shall I say? – the boat at sea business.'

The boat at sea business? Is that the best he can do?

'I just hope she's safe.' Abbie sounded suitably concerned.

'So do we.' Aldreth leaned closer, his face hardening. 'I ought to tell you that our Family Protection Unit is now fully involved, so any failure to disclose her whereabouts will be strictly an official matter.' His clear grey eyes bored into her, and she knew that one word from her out of turn might ruin everything. 'You also ought to be aware that Social Services are very upset by your boyfriend's allegations. I think, with hindsight, you'll both see they've done everything they legally can.'

Abbie's mouth fell open in surprise. Again she stopped herself.

He got up and straightened out his creases. 'Thank you for the tea.' He was courtesy itself once more.

Abbie watched him go, knowing there were more traps out for her than in the fields of Black Fen. The moment he was gone, she set the security alarm and locked up. She told a pipe layer on plot 12 that she'd be back in half an hour, then as the sky turned black she hurtled back to the hotel to warn Sheila and to clear away any traces of Rosie.

There is but one candle lit in West Winch Farm. Hemmings fears the dark just as I fear what I do next, and it is as if the wind's roar is born in his mouth as he sleeps. I use Uncle Poynton's spade, which he left for me at Goosefoot, to take up the boards in the beet barn corner. The smell stops my breath. It's as if the whole world has rotted in that spot. What a cursed place, and ever it shall be . . .

Thirty-eight

THE LETTER CAME by second post and seemed like some bottled message from a long-ago sea. Tense and nervy after deleting Rosie's presence at the hotel, Abbie'd opened the delicate airmail, wondering who on earth she knew in Pisa, but the first words explained it all.

Dear Miss Parker

I've just received a copy of the *Morpeth Record* from one of my London contacts and had to write to express my relief that you and the delightful Miss Quinn survived your trials in the North Sea. She is indeed fortunate to have such a friend as you.

My conscience has given me little sleep since that day, even though I have finally settled here in Paradise. I most sincerely hope that all the tribulations of that doleful patch of flatland will soon be resolved, but they cannot be unless Quinn is brought to justice.

In the University of Life I have met many whom I wouldn't hesitate to call the Devil's spawn, but believe it, he is high up there in the hierarchy and for the rest of my life I'll regret getting involved with him for nothing other than monetary gain.

Sure, I myself have got my own problems, certain weaknesses of the flesh of which you're now probably aware, but none I cannot solve. He, on the other hand, is evil incarnate. Who else would put his own daughter at the mercy of the waves? Or even yourself, an innocent young woman with the rest of her life ahead of her? Every Sunday since then, I have been to Confession. I told the priest at least I didn't make those holes in the boat as Quinn had ordered, so there is still some hope for my soul, he maintains.

I will end hereby urging you to leave Black Fen immediately and take that poor child with you if you can. Knowing what I know of him, I dare not think of what he will now descend to . . .

Finally, I hope you will find a mite of forgiveness in your heart for my actions.

Yours,
Philip Byers

P.S. The painting is yours if they don't destroy it. I must say, I was rather pleased with my rendering of your little friend's beautiful eyes . . .

As thunder bellowed in the skies and a sudden downpour lashed the Show Home windows, Abbie stared at the letter, her hand shaking. So she was right after all: Quinn had paid him for the attempt on her life, and the weakling had succumbed.

She re-read it twice, three times, lingering over his warning. Those words, even more than Jarrold's, struck fear into her heart, but the rest, the pseudo-religious tone and the remorse, didn't tie up with what she remembered of him. His cold urgency, the nicotine teeth – it was as if Quinn had cloned him to his own soul.

She'd forgotten the painting. It was true he'd made Rosie seem luminously innocent, straight from heaven. But did Abbie want to possess it? She didn't know.

She looked out at the soaked disorder of the building site and the heavy rain still falling. So it now took a class A junkie to give her some hope, to keep her going.

She is indeed fortunate to have such a friend as you . . .

'Thank you, Mr Byers, and that's exactly why I'm going to stay here. I'm bloody well not giving up.' Then, to be doing something positive, she dialled the police. 'WPC O'Halloran please.' The only one she could trust. The only one who hadn't made her and Simon feel like criminals. It was the policewoman's smile that had done it, but her voice when she answered, was deadly serious. Abbie frowned. 'Is anything wrong?'

Rosie? Simon? Sheila? Everyone she loved passed through her mind like a wind-blown current.

'Yes.' The WPC paused. 'We've just learned that little Emma Mason has died. She was the same age as my niece.'

'Oh, Jesus.' Her heart again, hurting, hurting . . .

'She was in IC for three days at Humberwell Hospital and then . . .' O'Halloran tailed away.

'Look, we've got to talk somewhere, please.' Abbie tried to keep her voice calm. 'I've had a letter from Byers and there are other things you need to know.'

'Can you get here for one o'clock. I don't take lunch breaks any more.' The WPC obviously didn't want to be overheard.

'I won't be bumping into the Detective Superintendent, will I?'

'Don't worry. He's out all day.'

'Thanks. I'll be there.'

Abbie spotted the yellow-caped foreman standing near plot 2 with a clipboard. She told him she had urgent business and, ignoring his worsening expression, she sped out of the sodden site. As she drove to Snutterwick through the lashing rain, she realized that her job was even more at risk if Holtbury's found out how much time she was spending away from her duties. But she had no choice. No choice at all.

My little Walter seems to know what place he is doomed for. He clings so tight to my shawl for fear of being parted from me. It's dark, so dark, and the wind moans through the latch of the barn door. The Devil has followed me . . . But what else is there? Walter isn't baptized so what will become of him I dare not imagine, but I know beyond all doubt that one day I shall have this child again . . . His fingers claw my neck and make such a wound on my cheek, I feel warm blood escape and touch him as I dig the hole to fit, thinking not to make it too small, that a little air might surround him . . .

Thirty-nine

WHILE ABBIE WAS sitting with WPC O'Halloran in Snutterwick police station's canteen, Lieutenant Simon Cresswell faced Dr Severus Farjeon for the second session of his assessment.

The former Gulf War veteran had spent since mid-morning briskly dealing with things medical. Blood test, eyes and hearing test, coordination routines and giving advice on a potential ingrowing toenail. Now it was one o'clock and while he retired for a sandwich and a glass of goat's milk, his patient was expected to complete a questionnaire, a lengthy psychometric exercise and write a page on self-perception.

This routine was Farjeon's speciality. The gilt on the gingerbread. Not that he pretended to be another Freud, Adler or even a Dr Rivers, but to him the mind of a man who could offer his life for an impersonal cause was a source of endless fascination.

'So how are we doing?' He stood at Simon's shoulder, a crumb lodged in his moustache.

'These questions are a bit near the bone, aren't they, sir?' Ticking and crossing the sheet, Simon had reached one on masturbation and frequency of intercourse.

'Precisely. What use is anything else?'

Simon put his pencil down. 'I can't do it, sir. This

stuff's none of anybody else's bloody business. It's nothing to do with drinking.'

Farjeon removed the offending sheet, put another in its place. 'We'll come back to that later. Try this.'

Erotic fantasies. Daydreams. Nightmares.

Simon hesitated as the doctor wandered over to his VDU and tapped the keys, logging in details of yesterday's other misfits.

For Simon, Erotic Fantasies began with the splayed thighs revealed in top-shelf mags smuggled into Christ's College, then the bursar's daughter, whose denim shorts curved halfway up her buttocks . . . But Abbie? No, it wasn't like that. Not now, anyway. He stopped, looked up and saw pigeons cruising to the guttering. He squinted to pretend they were gulls flown in from the sea . . .

'Keep at it, Cresswell,' the doctor said, inserting another floppy disk, 'and if you need to relieve yourself, you know where to go.'

Simon stared at him with scorn. '*Your brains are in your balls, remember that, you lot. It'll probably save your life.*' First thing the staff sergeant had said, and now it was more of the same. Farjeon was a prick on legs, just like the rest of them. He scarred through what he'd written with his pencil, blacker and blacker, till the paper tore like a wound.

'Now we don't need that, do we?' The doctor checked his watch. 'I've got another customer in twenty minutes. If you don't finish today, you'll be back for the rest tomorrow. Got a gap at two then. So take your pick.' He threw him a fresh pencil. It skittered away under the table and the lieutenant retrieved it, fists still clenched.

His writing was now erratic. Daydreams . . . were daydreams, nothing else. Nightmares? He lowered his

head, cupping both ears in his hands. He'd always had a
habit of doing that and once at school the whole GCSE
Religious Studies exam was spent listening to the pumping of his fear, listening to the sea off Oxwich Bay,
imagining drowning all over again . . .

But now he felt again those hand-span stumps on
Morpeth Bank, the viscous mud, the storm above luring
the waves towards the Wenn like huge dark tongues
lolling . . .

Farjeon's tap-tap-tapping of his computer in the corner was the rain hitting the gibbet and its broken burden
. . . sky and sea a dark vastness as the body is cut down.

*He feels the weight of it almost wrench his shoulder from
its socket . . . down, down to the lugger's slippery deck – the
blind vessel always waiting, lurching on the tide . . . Three
others from yesterday's harvest lie there, rolling back and
fore. But this one, a woman, taller than them all, keeps
them firm, stops the smell of corpses from leaving . . . And
now into the swell, defeated by the rush of water, they pass
into the thickness of sin, the numbness of another death. All
breathing gone, stopped up . . . stopped up . . .*

But Severus Farjeon, with a backlog of incomplete
files threatening his afternoon golf, continued typing even
though the young lieutenant had rolled to the floor,
clasping his throat.

I comfort him as I lay him into the ground, his head to one side so he cannot see me. His lids are closed against the earth and soon his little noises stop, so there's only my breathing left. My grief. When the boards are down again, all is done. My heart is broken. Woe betide anyone who from this night opens the prayer book Esmond Downey gave me, and may the power of darkness strike this place now and in the life to come . . .

Forty

'THE CUNT JUST let me lie there on the floor. I could have become another embarrassing statistic.'

Simon sprawled along the Fiesta's back seat while Abbie dealt with the traffic through Leytonstone in yet another unfamiliar car. She saw his clothes creased, his best jacket still blurred with Morpeth Bank mud that wouldn't go away.

'They could have kept you in a bit longer,' she grumbled. His phone call to the Show Home during the storm had scared her, he'd sounded so dazed and disoriented. No way could he have made it back on the train alone.

'So you just blacked out?'

A woman with an aggressive pushchair made Abbie stop at a zebra.

'That's what the quack said, but I don't remember.'

'When will they let you know? I mean about going back.'

'Said it could be very short notice. Depends.'

'On your report?'

'That and what Oliver's got to say.'

'Oh.'

'You sound well pee'd off and all,' he said.

She glanced at him in the mirror. 'Well, Fidler made a big song and dance about me leaving the site yet again. But it's not as if we've got a crush of buyers at the gates. D'you know, he's like some leaking bloody tap – one big drip. Anyhow, that's not all.'

'No?'

'For starters, Sheila's definitely getting a valuer in.'

'I'll have to get her some more chocs.'

'Be serious, Si. There's worse.'

'What?'

'O'Halloran reckons Mowbray's lost my letter from Quinn.'

Simon reared up and grabbed the back of her seat. 'You're kidding,' Then he slumped back. 'That fucking says it all.'

'Or else he's kept it.'

'Can't cope with that one. Sorry.' Then his heavy eyelids won and seconds later he was asleep.

They reached Black Fen at four-thirty. Thinking Walsoken Road might be under water, Abbie drove the long way round to the hotel, past the empty garden centre which was home to a few weary-looking saplings and stacks of cheap compost. Although the primary school was shut for the foreseeable future, several more bunches of flowers lay flattened by the rain near the gate. The dark undecorated windows gave the place a palpable air of sadness.

Suddenly a roar from above woke Simon up. Abbie opened her window, slowing the car.

'Christ, what's going on?' He peered out as a helicopter appeared below the clouds, spinning towards the sea and losing height. No lights, no signal of any kind, then just silence. A long empty nothingness as it plunged into the tide heaping towards the Deeps of Lethe.

They arrived at the St George's Sails without speaking.

Before all this, they'd have fooled around a bit, probably ended up in bed or on the floor, anywhere. But somehow physical desire had suddenly been plucked out of them, just like the broilers' talons over at Gosdyke – eventually to be gutted, like an edible shell for someone's dinner.

Instead, Abbie tidied the contents of her bag, cleaned her shoes and tackled the ironing. She collapsed the ironing board and checked her spare suit was ready for tomorrow.

'Hey, what's happened to Rosie's little desk and chair?' Simon returned from the shower, his skin pinkly soft, touchable.

'I've hidden them and her colouring books. Somebody called Detective Superintendent Aldreth turned up out of the blue at the site this morning and I wasn't taking any chances. Don't be fooled, he's a wolf in Pringle clothing.' She left him then and went downstairs for the 5.20pm Channel 5 news update on TV.

The Eurocopter crash came first. As the presenter was employing every dramatic trick in the book, Simon brought over two coffees oscillating in their mugs. He still wasn't 100 per cent sure of terra firma as he sat to watch the retrieval of its wreckage which had plunged into the deepest part of the sea with an eerie sense of *déjà vu*. Its four crew, all from Suffolk, had disappeared.

'Shit.'

On the screen the North Sea loomed unsated, its tide now powering inland. He turned away as, with a downturn to her voice, the newscaster spoke of the search for survivors recommencing at dawn. The coincidence of it all seemed too much and neither spoke, but when the scene moved to the small crowd of onlookers who'd gathered at Seal Point, Simon edged closer and took her hand.

'Do you see what I see?'

Abbie crouched by the television. Among the curious locals hooded up against the weather, the eyes of one man in particular were unforgettable – they were like those of a wall-eyed horse, full of white, cast on them both. It was Quinn, they knew it. He must be less than a mile away.

'Turn it off,' Abbie whispered, and in the quiet of the lounge bar, with just their thoughts welling and merging like the sea beyond, the phone began its sonic bombardment. The call was from Uncle Graham, sounding concerned that Rosie was spending a lot of time with Flora talking strangely to her new doll, Martha, about three other dolls she used to play with which had been lost. He wondered if this Martha was safe to have around, especially with Flora being so impressionable. With nerves fluttering in her stomach, Abbie said of course it was. Rosie was just a very imaginative child, that was all.

Her uncle then innocently relayed how Rosie'd described these three missing dolls down to the last detail, and with them being Victorian, he supposed, they could be quite valuable if they were ever found. Especially Abigail with the china head. Flora had asked him if Abbie's name meant the same.

Her heart plummeted. How could she think of everything – every shitty little facet of this whole business?

Oh, please God, not Flora as well . . .

Simon said goodbye to Graham for her, glad that Sheila was taking so long at the hairdresser's, but the moment he'd replaced the receiver, the phone rang again.

'Can I speak to Miss Parker please? It's important.' Although the caller seemed a long way off, his wheezing was all too audible.

'It's some heavy breather,' Simon whispered.

'Thanks,' she said drily. 'That's all I need.'

'I've been meaning to call for some time,' the man said to her.

'How did you get hold of my name?'

'The housekeeper at Rievely Hall gave it to me.'

Abbie looked at Simon, puzzled for a moment. 'Rievely Hall? I don't know anyone there.' She saw Simon shrug. 'Anyway, how can I help you?'

'I believe I can help *you*.'

Not a pervert, please not now . . .

'Who's calling?'

'I'm Ernest Stimpson. Gedney Stimpson's nephew.'

'Gedney Stimpson?' The name meant nothing until she remembered her first day in Black Fen. 'His grave is at St Mary Magdalene, with a Bible on it.'

'That's right.'

The old man seemed pleased she'd noticed. 'A good sort he was, my uncle, but terrible the way he went. Enough to make anyone lose their faith.' His voice wavered. 'Our family never got over it, you know . . .'

'Please tell me more.'

Simon pressed closer as the tale unfolded.

'Well, he started to work at Rievely Hall for old William Scott and his wife, just after the end of the war. They wouldn't have got back on their feet nearly so quickly if he hadn't had six pairs of hands on him . . .'

'So what happened? And what's it got to do with me?'

Ernest Stimpson took a deep breath. 'My uncle never married. He was always an independent sort, but I think he had women friends, mind. He used to say he liked a nice pair of legs, and I think that's why he used to go a-calling over at Clenchtoft.'

'Clenchtoft?' Abbie almost choked on the word.

'Yes. He used to say what a looker she was. Real handsome, by all accounts, but there were some rum goings-on at her farm, from what he said.'

'Such as?'

'She used to grow special poppies, proper greenfingers, he'd say, and she smoked a pipe of some sort, regular like.'

'Opium, you mean?'

'So he said, and she'd be out some nights under the stars without a stitch on, carrying those cut-up birds of hers . . . But she made him swear never to mention none of it to anyone, and certainly not a whisper of her being some kind of witch, communing with spirits and all . . . Look, Miss Parker,' he went on, 'my health's going downhill fast if you want the truth. I don't need extra worries. Not now. Anyhow, I was getting round to those dolls.'

'Dolls,' Abbie repeated, looking at Simon, then pinned her ear to the receiver. She was aware that Sheila had just come in, her hair re-shaped from the dryer.

'They weren't just any old toys, you know.'

'In what way?'

'My uncle said she was given them by her grandfather's first wife, Annie Church.'

Abbie scribbled the name on an empty page in the hotel register.

'The one who lost a baby just after it was born?' Abbie now recalled Amy Buckley's words.

'Yes. She was Martha Robinson's younger sister.'

'Annie, you said?'

Not Mary, Abigail or Lazarus . . .

'That's right. But there were others, too. I can't say them aloud, except one is the same as our Lord's mother, the other a maid and the last was a man raised up from the dead. He was Annie's twin.'

A strange silence fell between them. Sheila mystified, disappeared into the kitchen, trailing a scent of setting spray.

'All with the surname Church?'

'Correct.'

'And all living at Goosefoot Cottage?'

'So I believe.'

Abbie thought back to that one-up, one-down. It must have been a *crowded* hell.

'So Robinson was her *married* name?'

''S right.'

Suddenly Stimpson inhaled deeply. It sounded hard work. 'It was Annie who named the dolls after her brother and sisters, so they wouldn't be forgotten.'

'Why forgotten? What happened to them?' She glanced at Simon.

'Just disappeared. No one ever knew where or why.'

Jesus.

'When I retired I started to follow things up, but my hip's not been too good and I can't get about like I used to. Trouble is . . .' He hesitated.

'Go on.'

'There's no record of them at all. Not a bloody sausage.'

'Are you sure?'

'As sure as God's in his heaven. Now, I'd best be going.'

'But Mr Stimpson . . .' She tried to keep him talking, but to no avail. When she realized he'd definitely gone, she dialed 1471, her fingers trembling.

'You were called today at 18.29. The caller withheld their number.'

I cannot sleep since, but watch the moon's eye through the clouds, and listen to Grace and Harriet's breath rising, falling, as alive as my Walter is dead. The Devil's Mouth has given me words for the churchman, and these I say over and over again in the hope he will soon be the same . . .

Forty-one

ON THAT FIRST Wednesday in June, the sea fret still hung over the marsh beyond Crowland Fen, trapping the Paternoster which rose from the lone figure seated some twenty yards adrift of safety.

'Give us this day our daily bread. And forgive us our trespasses, as we forgive them that trespass against us . . .'

Helen Quinn didn't finish. She couldn't. The cold silt was holding her fast, too near the mud lumps scored by sodden gulleys. Too near land solid enough to take her pursuer's weight . . .

Her wheels were sinking, spoiling her plan to reach water in the shortest time possible. She twisted herself out of the seat and gripped the handles. She tried to push it, even to turn the thing over, get it nearer the sea, but her dead legs couldn't find a hold. She looked round. Saw the familiar silhouette begin to work its way down, through the reed banks and the tufted islands, and as he drew closer she fancied she saw horns. Or was it merely hair protruding above each ear?

Her breath came in short harsh gasps. There was only one way to escape. She lay down and began a leaden crawl away from him, her arms dipping and heaving into the slough with each stroke, her boater finally leaving her head.

He was shouting something, the usual rage, the same

obscenities as when he'd locked her up in the bat room, but her patient strokes took her further away to where the sea had thinned the mire and she could move more freely, albeit still dragging both legs behind. He wouldn't risk it now, not with what he had left to do, and as the water lapped against her limbs, bearing her out towards the Humber, a smile formed on her lips as she finished the prayer.

Forgiveness? That was ripe: a nice solid word for those never moved to exercise it. She recalled his sermons, elaborating on that word as an oyster brings a pearl from a grain of sand. And the fools had believed him, every last one, especially his flower arranger, with her adoration, her pestering late-night phone calls.

The swimmer felt strangely light, no longer burdened by the twin yokes of guilt and obligation. The outgoing tide was obliging, with murmurings of half-forgotten names: those whom her life had touched, those whom her life itself had made . . .

As she slowed, anchored now by the weight of her useless appendages, Helen Quinn saw again her first-born centred in the hospital scan, swimming for his life, as she was now doing, her waters contoured like the waters of the world. Kicking up her insides – Ross Joseph. Taken before he could even cry, by a shadow unknown in medical terms, a rogue spirit from the cleric's world of darkness. But she knew whose it was. Martha Robinson. Murderer. And for the one who came next, Rosie was the closest name to his she could find.

Rosie . . . For all my sins . . .

The missing child's mother stopped swimming, letting the pull of the North Sea draw her deeper into the early mist, weightless now she was clear of the third finger of Three Fingers Beach. On her own – the Devil nowhere. But while a helicopter somewhere further east began its second day's search, she heard an echoing laugh follow her – down, down, until she opened her mouth for the last amen . . .

That churchman has betrayed me, and the sky is spread so dark across Black Fen, even the birds have flown south for the light. The silence brings a sudden beating on my door. Four men, black as the Morpeth poplar: old Samuel Scott and Arthur Scott, Coates the Beadle, who'd all prospered with the Enclosures, and a sergeant from North Sand.

Forty-two

'So in all she had three sisters and a brother...' Abbie said more to herself than anyone as she and Simon left the St George's Sails for Snutterwick.

'We need to find out when they were born, when they died. And her as well.'

'Supposing, like Stimpson said, there's no record?' Abbie adjusted her Holtbury badge so it wasn't tilting. A Swedish couple called Martinsen had written expressing interest in visiting the site mid-morning and she had to get back there to lean on them while they were still warm.

'He may not have looked in the right place, so come on.'

'I've only got two hours.' Abbie complained, angry with herself that when she most needed it all her assertiveness training seemed to go out of the window.

'We'll do it.'

The Fiesta was hot inside, even though it was just nine. The sun, already high in the uninterrupted blue, lent an awesome clarity to the rape and cabbage fields sprung suddenly from brown along the Snutterwick Road. Just past Dydle Drove a group of masked protesters stood by a gate, their placards streaked by past rain: BAN GM CROPS. YOUR GUT, NOT OURS.

Abbie avoided their eyes. She'd seen enough hideous things to last a lifetime.

'They're wasting their time. No one can stop it now.' Simon stamped down on the accelerator, feeling his gun safe in his inside pocket, but the jacket Abbie had cleaned to perfection now felt like a sweat trap.

She stared out at the flatness, a renewed sense of foreboding filling her thoughts. 'I should have asked Quinn more about Martha Robinson when I first met him,' she said.

'Oh yeah? Mr Normal – not.' He was hitting eighty now through Close Flatton, his golden-stubbled chin jutting towards finding answers, the missing pieces.

A trailer marked 'Horses', a cement lorry and not much else as the miles diminished, except for a burnt-out Golf Gti upturned above the Wenn.

'Poor sod,' Simon said, keeping up the speed as Snutterwick's council houses straggled into view. 'He must have been doing a fair whack.'

'Just listen to Mr Pot.'

'What d'you mean?'

'I mean, we're all black, aren't we?'

A book sale was in progress at the record office and the one full-time administrator and purveyor of serious BO waved Simon and Abbie down a corridor signed 'Parish Records' past notices of a classical guitar concert and Workers' Educational Association classes. A huge and dusty plastic fern brushed Abbie's face as she passed.

'We've had a few in already researching Black Fen,' the woman announced, shepherding them along until they reached a room whose open door revealed wall-to-wall files. 'I hear there's been quite a bit going on over there, what with that helicopter crash and all. Time was when nobody ever showed much interest in the place.'

'Who's been here?' Simon's eyes were unflinching.

For a moment the woman looked puzzled by the question. 'Ah, I see. Well, there was a nice woman in a wheelchair, forgotten her name now, then a Mrs Buckley.'

'*Amy* Buckley?' Abbie asked in surprise.

'She didn't say, and, ah yes, a Mr Stimpson – very persistent he was.' Simon was thinking the same about her body smell. 'Some people never take no for an answer, though.' She pulled her jumper away from her armpits.

'I suppose not, if they're desperate,' replied Simon, trying not to breathe in. 'So what were *they* after?'

The administrator looked at him over her glasses. 'Someone called Martha Robinson, I think.'

Abbie felt her heart skip. Simon, too, fell silent.

'Mind you, they didn't seem to have much success with her.'

'So exactly how do we access these records? Are they on microfiche?' Abbie asked, anxious to make a start and then get back to work.

'That's right, and you view in here.' She led the way into a small side room overlooking the wheelie bins and rubbish bags from the adjoining school.

'Choose your church,' she said, pointing back at a shelf of large box files, 'and slot the fiche into here. It'll all light up and you can fiddle with the handle till you get the year you want, then Bob's your uncle.'

She left them sitting in front of the viewscreen with the St Mary Magdalene file alongside, and the moment she'd gone Simon reached over to open the sash window for some air, but it was wedged tight with paint. 'Damn.'

Abbie wrote the names they wanted on a piece of Holtbury notepaper. 'Look, I know what to do,' she said as she brought the glass plate down. It was slow but fascinating to watch original handwriting and the intricacies of local lives slide by, and now again the names she'd seen in the St Mary Magdalene graveyard came up: Grayling, Hickling, Ingoldsby . . .

'Too early.' Simon sighed as entries for 1838 scrolled by. 'Let's go for, say, 1842.'

'Hold on.' Abbie peered at the screen, but there were no Robinsons of any kind. No spinsters, no spouses, no infants of that name. 'There's nothing here. Come on, come on,' she urged, turning the handle. 'Please.' But the entries coming to life on the screen were all unknown to her.

'No wonder what's-his-face was so upset.' Simon got up and stretched. She saw his lean midriff, his muscles bulging the cotton T-shirt.

'But if parish records are for recognized baptisms, weddings and burials, then surely that would exclude all the free spirits – I mean those who didn't bother with the church. Or Romanies maybe . . .'

'True.'

'And Martha Robinson probably never went near the place, for whatever reason. And maybe, when she died, no one knew about it. She may have just gone off to live somewhere else, to another area altogether. After all, they were casual labour.' But that didn't tie in with the Goosefoot connection.

'So we could be hunting her for ever?'

'Could be.'

'Let me try Church, her maiden name.'

Abbie frowned at her watch, thinking of the Swedish couple. They'd be turning up at the Holtbury site in half an hour. She touched her badge: it felt pathetic now, and was still crooked.

'That doesn't seem to exist either.'

'Anything on Leakes or Scott?' Simon leaned over her. 'They were all ordinary parishioners, surely?'

Abbie started again, but the more she scanned the pages the more depressed she grew.

'Nope, not a single one.'

'Someone must have got the bloody wind up and altered the parish records way back, before they were microfiched.'

'So what do we do?' Abbie switched off the viewing machine.

'We'll try Gorrington.'

'What's at Gorrington?'

'A bit of luck, I hope.'

'Come on then. Might just get there before lunch.' Simon jogged towards the Fiesta, keys at the ready.

'I've *got* to get back,' Abbie protested. 'I can't leave the Martinsens just hanging around.'

'Jesus Christ, Abs, can't they wait?'

'You don't understand, do you?' She climbed into the boiling car, noticing with dismay one of her tights had laddered by the ankle. 'There's not been anyone else come through that door for yonks.'

'If they're really so keen, they'll leave a message and call again. We've got to do this – it's now or never.' He circled the Fiesta out of the car park, its wheels squealing at his determination.

Abbie watched the signs as strange-sounding hamlets came and went, buried in seas of fodder crops stretching away to the sky. She could envisage the foreman's ratty face and his impatient body language as the Martinsens turned up to inspect the site.

Simon manoeuvred a route through the one-way system and parked near the Wenn quayside, which was dotted with freshly painted capstans and litter bins for the summer crowds.

The town hall rose above an immaculately tended civic garden, accessed by a new ramp that had now replaced some of the steps. Abbie wondered if that same wheelchair had already been up here as they passed through a revolving door into a gloomy vestibule.

'Have you an appointment?' asked a young man in a tweed suit, who'd appeared from nowhere. Abbie noticed he wore a ring with an onyx and wondered idly who'd given it him.

'Yes.' Simon lied. 'Two weeks ago. Cresswell.'

'I'll go and check.'

Abbie looked at her soldier in amazement.

'Needs must.' He smiled as the man returned with a book.

'There's no record of that name in here. Sorry.'

Simon stepped forward and Abbie thought for a moment he was going to grab the other man's lapels, 'I don't know what your name is, but I did phone a fortnight ago. Now, who do I see to get proper attention?'

The young official looked round, perturbed, realizing

this one wasn't going to go away. Besides, the girl was looking upset and he was nothing if not a gentleman.

'OK. Follow me.'

He opened the door into a narrow room stacked with disk-storage boxes. At one end was a table set against the wall, at the other a line of computers.

'You'll have to sign in and list any indexes you've examined at the end. Strictly speaking, we don't allow the public into here, but' – he looked at Abbie again – 'we can make exceptions.'

'Indexes?'

Simon was too busy studying a CCTV positioned over his head.

'They're on hard-disk.' The young man smiled. He had the upper hand now. 'Everything's kept like that these days, and the Mormons are starting to collate all records country by country . . .'

'Mormons?' *Whatever bloody next.*

Another young man came in and made for the desk at the end. He was carrying a Marks & Spencer carrier bag and a mobile. He began eating a roll and not once did he look up.

'See him over there? He'll help you if you get stuck.' And tweed suit left them there, strangely disoriented, not knowing where to start.

Simon coughed and signalled for the trainee to leave his breakfast and attend to them. Abbie made a show of checking her watch.

'We haven't got all day, mate.' Simon pulled out two chairs by the VDU. 'We want all Black Fen records. Please.'

As the lad obliged, they soon realized he had no

knowledge of or interest in the area. It was just a name to him. But they needed him for the password.

They clicked on LOCAL SITES. The screen showed a map around the Wash divided into four, according to the main drains:

1. Humber,
2. Fitting,
3. Demon,
4. Lynn.

He clicked on 3, then stood up, oblivious of their reaction.

'Why Demon, for God's sake?' Abbie felt her pulse quicken.

'Wouldn't know.' He grinned. 'By the way, you can't print anything out. For observation only. If you want an index to take away, you've got to pay for it. Six quid a shout.' His little bit of power.

They concentrated, tense and silent, Abbie wondering about the visitors to the record office in Snutterwick. Why Amy Buckley? And that woman in a wheelchair must have been Helen Quinn.

From the DEMON section Simon selected 'Years beginning 1823'. He clicked first on BIRTHS.

'Let's look for any names we know: Leakes, Church, Robinson, Scott . . .' He moved the mouse from the first quarter of that year to the third. At this rate, it was going to take them another bloody century.

'We could try Search,' Abbie suggested impatiently.

'No. We might miss something.'

'OK. Judging by those old photos, if Martha Robinson was about twenty-eight in 1862, let's go for, say,

1834,' Abbie prompted, then held her breath as the cursor moved from surnames Blincowe to Dwering, Grayling and Hickling again and again. Nothing. Not even a Buckley, though they'd lived at Canal Farm since the Reformation.

He scrolled back to 1795 and on to 1808, then he stopped. 'Shit. Look at this.'

'Poynton Church. Born 2 October 1800. See FITTING.'

'Must be Fitting Fen.'

Simon trawled through a list of names from hearths long since lost to the sea, many vanishing in time, but Rievely Hall with its succession of Scotts for each generation was constant. They didn't have to worry about losing one or two kids, Abbie thought. They were the lucky ones . . .

'Here's some more Churches,' he said excitedly. '"Joshua Church. 4 March 1803" and "Kirton Church. 20 June 1808. See FITTING" again. Kirton's buried at St Cecilia's. I saw his grave there.'

'Clever you.' She was impatient. They'd hardly started all this and she had a house to sell. 'Try MARRIAGES.'

He scrolled up and down, assuming these men might have wed in their twenties. Only Joshua Church came up – married to Margaret Tapper, 8 October 1834.

'Looks like Kirton and Poynton were singles, unless they kept *stumm*,' he muttered. Another German word, she noticed, her nose almost on the screen, her eyes bleary. 'Hey, here's something else. "Annie Church to Daniel Leakes. St Margaret's. Kilntoft. 2 January. 1862."'

'Why not at St Mary Magdalene? He was local, surely?'

'Dunno.'

'Try BIRTHS again, and look for Leakes.' He sighed, but her tone gave him no choice. Something both Ernest Stimpson and Amy Buckley had said to her. There'd been a child.

The same names, half remembered, passed from top to bottom and bottom to top. Abbie prayed for one in particular to show . . .

'Stop!'

The trainee looked up in surprise.

'Here we go. "William Tapper Leakes. 3 July 1862. Clenchtoft Farm."' She felt her heart move faster. Some things weren't just fable but fact after all.

'Seems to have been a busy year for them.'

'Now go to DEATHS.'

'Look! Here he is again.'

'William Tapper Leakes. 4 July 1862.'

'Poor little sod. Only one day old.' He felt his skin begin to chill, as if death was breathing into his pores. 'It gets worse.'

Then suddenly that line slid from view and the next death moved up in its place.

'Shit.'

Abbie gasped while Simon pumped the mouse, but the name had gone.

He pushed back his chair. 'You try.' He looked round for someone to help, but the assistant was biting into another roll, salad cream oozing on to his chin. She finally accessed SEARCH, while Simon sat alongside in silence.

Martha Church. UNKNOWN.

Mary Church. UNKNOWN.

Abigail Church. UNKNOWN.

Lazarus Church. UNKNOWN.

'This is really crazy.' Abbie reached the end of the file with Zaznevic and Zdenov, foreigners who'd lived and died on the drains. Still no Robinson. Not a jot. Nothing on Hemmings, nothing on Downey either, the name in that prayer book. A blank on Stimpson too. His nephew's words were proving all too true, and the gaps remained stubbornly unfilled.

So, Abbie wondered to herself, what about 'my boy'? 'Just me and my boy . . .' She went over that first conversation in her head, remembering every syllable, every nuance of the woman's voice, knowing intuitively all this was a waste of time. That the deliberate deletions had already joined eternity.

Like sleepwalkers they went back through to the hall, leaving those strangers' names – those who'd been registered and given Christian burials, resting sweetly with the Lord.

'Yes?' The portly female clerk seemed irritated by their presence. She turned her back on them and began posting papers through a hatch in the wall.

'Something's wrong with your computer.' Simon tried to contain himself. 'We were looking at a name just now and it vanished. Half the stuff we need isn't on it anyhow and it should be.'

'What you see is what you get. Nothing to do with me,' said the woman, bending down to pick up a stray sheet of paper.

Abbie pulled on Simon's sleeve. He'd take on the world if it gave him grief.

'This is fucking typical,' he snarled at the clerk. 'No one here knows anything. No one wants to get involved. I bet if it was your kid dying of malaria you'd soon be pulling your fat finger out.'

'How dare you!' She turned around and walked away.

'I'll be reporting this cock-up, don't worry,' Simon shouted after her.

Abbie's heart sank. The Martinsens, her only clients on the planet, were probably right now waiting on the Show Home doormat with a mortgage offer already agreed.

The town hall fell quiet. They were now being totally ignored. Simon strode towards the exit then realized she wasn't with him. 'Abbie?'

But she'd felt impelled to return to the file room where suddenly one of the screensavers was changing from a gentle Milky Way of stars to something quite different. A cold moon was growing larger and larger, spliced by a wound that suddenly grew red till it became a face she recognized. Martha Robinson leered back at her. Abbie screamed, watching those lips move over the broken teeth, and that voice meant only for her snaked its way into her ears.

'Me and my boy have suffered enough, so leave us alone, you hear? Or do you want to end up like the Lady's Maid? . . . I'll not be warning you again . . .'

The strength of four men that I surely owe to the Devil returned and sent each to the four room corners, without a tooth left between them. Old Samuel Scott was taken away for dead, dribbling and scouring into his shoes with his son crippled at the knees, then when Coates had recovered, he and the wife beater from North Sand pinioned my hands. And before I could defend myself with words, the Beadle had tied a foul bandage round my mouth . . .

Forty-three

THE MOMENT SIMON dropped her back at the Holtbury site, Abbie tried to contact Mr and Mrs Martinsen on the number they'd given but without success.
The foreman grumbled that they were now off touring
East Anglia, looking at other housing developments, and
might or might not reappear.

She stared at the mess on plot 2 and the haphazard
pile of pipes strewn on the ground. The prospective
purchasers had evaporated, like everything else in her life,
into the mist of dreams, so that when Vallender phoned
to check on progress, she had to waffle, pretending that
the couple were still keen but were making further
enquiries about secondary schools.

After work, Abbie sat with Simon in the Sails' lounge
bar, where the sun beamed strange shadows of the
furniture on to the floor. They could hear Sheila hoover-
ing in a bedroom above, sounds like a lawn mower
drawing away, moving closer, dulling their thoughts. Two
mugs of coffee lay untouched.

The noise overhead suddenly stopped. Abbie and
Simon turned to look at the stairs, saw Sheila's new
mules and shaved legs. The hotel owner peered down,
surprised to see Abbie there.

'Everything all right?' she asked.

'So so.' Simon raised his hand to reassure her.

'Well, I've got some news.' She humped the vacuum down to the lower floor and clicked in its flex. 'I've decided I'm not selling. I'm going to give things a chance here – give this place a bloody good spring-clean for a start.'

'Brilliant,' Abbie said flatly.

'In fact, Mrs Turling's nephew'll be coming over in a minute to learn the ropes at the bar – to give me a break when I need it. But there'll be no more evening meals – except for you two of course.' She winked. 'It's too much hassle, so I'll just be doing B&B from now on.' She locked the understairs cupboard with finality and pocketed the key. 'I'm not letting the things going on round here drive me out. I've worked hard enough these past few years to get it all done up.'

As if on cue three fishermen from the *Wigtoft Star* came in and made for the fruit machine, bringing with them the smell of the sea.

Simon went over to the bar. 'Is it too early to sniff a bottle?'

Sheila smiled her consent. 'Have whatever on me.'

'Cheers.' He raised a double vodka.

'So are things moving on a bit?' Sheila asked. She eyed her new customers, trying to judge when they would move to the bar.

'Yes. Detective Superintendent Aldreth seems to be on the ball. In a different league from that wanker Mowbray, thank God.'

'Well, that's all right then. Ah. This must be Ricky.' A lad of about nineteen had just come in and made his way over to the bar. He smiled shyly at Simon and Abbie, then, after introductions, Sheila showed him where everything was. He'd worked the odd weekend in a pub before, so after only ten minutes she felt able to untie her apron and leave him to it.

She turned to the girl who seemed miles away. 'I was just wondering, Abbie, and don't jump down my throat . . .'

'What?'

'D'you fancy a walk later on? Just get some ozone into the lungs?'

'OK. I'll see how the land lies after I've done some paperwork.'

'Don't forget Quinn, for God's sake, Sheila,' Simon warned. 'He's getting bloody good at disguising himself. He even got here once, remember?'

'How can I forget, for Chrissake?' She looked over to the fishermen, eyeing them differently now, then stubbed out her dimp with a shaking hand. 'And what about Ricky over there? He ought to be put in the picture, surely?'

'Leave it to me.'

As the evening went on amid the hum of conversation, the lounge bar wall-lights were dimmed and the fruit machine winked to itself in the corner.

Upstairs, having finished a progress report for Vallender, Abbie opened her wallet again. The prints she'd kept of Lilith Leakes were inserted behind that of the child climbing into Goosefoot Cottage, and the one of Simon. As she extracted the first one, she recalled the faded flyleaf of *Secrets* and its grotesque inked drawings. Now in this pleasant room, the crone's face became suddenly a terrible reminder of the old woman's fate. But still she was all they had. The only one who really knew anything.

'I'm sorry, Lilith,' Abbie started, 'I did try to find you, believe me. Please help us. Please help those sick children. We don't know what to do any more . . .'

'Are you ready?'

Abbie jumped as Sheila stuck her head round the bedroom door.

'Sorry, did I give you a fright?'

'Just a bit.'

Sheila now resembled a post box, dressed in red PVC with lipstick to match, and was so busy studying Abbie's immaculate white trainers that she didn't notice her friend frantically trying to close the wallet.

'You're not wearing those, surely? Could be shitty underfoot.'

'I chucked my wellies out.' She didn't add, because they'd trodden in Clenchtoft's filth.

'Oh?' Sheila looked puzzled. 'I'll see what I can find.' She returned holding a pair of gardening shoes. 'My ma's,' she explained with some pride.

Abbie eyed the brown rubber slugs reluctantly, but put them on. Being far too big, they sighed noticeably with every step.

'Just the thing to pull the blokes, eh?' Sheila laughed, unlocking her old Cortina complete with its nodding dog and ancient toffees melted in their wrappers. 'Just look at the state of this thing!'

'At least it's yours. I'm still waiting for the insurance to cough up to replace mine,' Abbie muttered ruefully as road spray hid the sight of Slave's Dyke being pumped for the third time this year, and the blur of Buckley's farm.

'I've never even been up here before.' Sheila manoeuvred into a lay-by below Morpeth Bank and left the car in gear. 'It's quicker to get to the sea this way, so I've heard.'

'I don't want to go near it ever again,' Abbie protested, feeling out of control.

'You sound just like my Saffron when she was a kid. Can't blame you, I suppose, after everything.'

'I'll be OK,' Abbie said, quietly fastening her hood. 'Bit of a sad really, I am.'

'No, you're not.'

As they linked arms, Abbie laughed and then they both collapsed into giggles under the reddening sky.

After a moment Sheila pulled away. 'See who's first to that gate.'

'That's not fair!' Abbie saw the other woman had snatched a head start, careering down the slope through dull flattened grass towards the last stretch of land. Then Abbie did what Rosie had done. She left the borrowed shoes behind and sprinted easily past her rival to the target.

'I got a stitch!' Sheila grimaced.

'Go on, pull the other one.'

They sat down breathless and looked over to the mud, wrinkled grey like elephant skin as far as the eye could see. An open grave of infinitesimal bleakness – of less than perfect peace with the rush and drag of tides, the giving and taking of gifts.

Sheila pulled out her Marlboros and turned away from the sea to light up.

'Hey, what's that over there?' Abbie shouted. 'D'you think it's something from that helicopter?'

'Oh, shit.' Smoke eased from Sheila's mouth.

'Look there!' Abbie pointed, her eyes losing their focus. Forgetting she was wearing only socks, forgetting her fear, she yelled, 'Come on.'

'I'm not barking enough to go out walking on that stuff,' Sheila said, looking at the marsh ahead.

'And you think I am? Thanks.' Abbie edged her way down to where the sea leached through into the land, carrying the shoreline silt back to its origins. Soft and dangerous. She was close now. Close enough to see that what had caught her eye was a kind of hat. A boater brimming with seaweed. 'My God.' She searched for a stick, anything to pull it in. The first chosen reed snapped, so she tore at another, cutting her fingers in the process. She eased in the catch. Its top had been partially nibbled away, the freesias now no more than shredded rags. Abbie let the mud drip free of it, her heart racing. 'I remember this. It's Helen Quinn's.'

'Oh, Lord above. All I wanted was a bit of bloody fresh air.' Sheila's dimp hit the grass and died as her companion looked over to Three Fingers Beach for any signs of tyre tracks.

'Where d'you think this came from then?'

'God knows. It might have blown off her head somewhere.'

'She wouldn't have come out here in a wheelchair.'

'Maybe she was brought here.'

Abbie froze, the boater a dead weight in her hand.

'C'mon. Let's get cracking. Find something to put it in,' Sheila instructed, but her friend was scanning every nuance of bank and ditch for the woman's partner in life, and death. The Reverend Peter Quinn.

And as Sheila guided her back to the path, cradling the wreck in her mac, Abbie thought of nothing else but the web of evil now cast low and smothering over Black Fen.

I gnawed through the rag and begged to take Grace and Harriet with me to the prison, but the beadle said one evil mouth was enough to be feeding and they were to go to the workhouse at Gosdyke and be kept as cheaply as possible. I couldn't even give them a piece of bread or a kiss farewell, and left Harriet undressed and shivering. Their poor frightened faces will be a scar on my heart for ever . . . When I also begged to know where little Walter had gone, he spoke of a newly dug pit inside the prison walls for more unholy bastards and other foul waste . . . But when they think I am finished and gone, I will return him to his place of rest and dig so deep, so deep he will never be disturbed again . . .

Forty-four

NEXT DAY THE phone was ringing as Abbie turned her key in the Show Home lock and disabled the alarm. She prayed it was Simon with his medical results, but no, it was Vallender.

'All this stuff about a mad axeman vicar and his missing wife is the last bloody straw.' His voice reverberated into her head. 'We've been busting a gut selling Black Fen as a haven, not as a nest of bloody vipers.'

'I know. And so have I.'

'Can't you see, every paragraph in the press means an extra nail in our coffin?'

'I've said nothing, Mr Vallender. In fact my loyalty to Holtbury's almost cost me my life.'

'Look, Miss Parker, I'm not interested in fairytales. If I told you how much was already tied up in this site, you'd be on Prozac, like me.'

Abbie sat down, alarmed at his tone. 'You not too good then?' she asked.

'God damn awful if you must know.'

'I'm sorry.'

'The board hauled me in yesterday. I felt like some sodding rat in a trap. Holtbury Junior's a complete motherfucker . . .'

Abbie's mouth fell open. This did not sound like her boss talking. Something was obviously very wrong.

'In what way?'

'In every bloody way. They says they could make me personally liable, whatever that means.'

Abbie paused. It all sounded so familiar – now it was his turn. Sympathy and rejoicing jockeyed for position. She took the middle road.

'What about when things slowed up three years ago? Were you on the carpet then?'

'In Bristol? No. Anyway, that's history. We soon got into gazumping mode, with standard personal contracts, lock-out and loyalty clauses, pre-contract deposits, and business is still looking good ... We've responded by putting more properties in top locations on the market ... This was to be our flagship site, east of the A1 ...'

As his job-speak faltered into a sigh, she could imagine him sitting there, and despite the humiliation, the bullying, she felt no victory whatsoever. If he went down, so be it. Time was when she'd have clung to his side as he did so ...

'For a start, Shanks, your surveyor, should answer a few questions,' she said.

'What d'you mean?'

'The ground itself's not right, which anyone with half a brain cell could have found out. Apparently the farm it was built on didn't make half a century ...'

'He was just instructed to get on with it. Three other firms were interested then.'

'So *they* say.'

'It's too late anyway. The board is threatening to auction the lot, unfinished.'

A desperate silence fell between them.

'Are you still coming over Mr Vallender?' Abbie finally asked.

'Sure, from the tenth to the fifteenth.' And it sounded like he was smiling.

'Things may be better by then.'

'Here's hoping.'

The receiver was down for half a second before the phone rang again. It was Simon breaking in the new mobile he'd bought her, sounding far away and seriously pissed off.

'I've been thinking. We're not getting anywhere,' he said.

'We're not meant to.'

'I think we ought to go and see old Scott at Rievely Hall some time. His lot seem to have been heavily involved.'

'Fine by me.' She kept her eyes on plot 2 opposite, aware of the wind picking up and a sudden draught through the open window stirring the papers on her desk. 'I'd like to meet that housekeeper too. When?'

'I want to pester the planning department in Snutterwick first. I'll find out what they know about the site. See you later, after work, OK?'

'Fine.'

'Love you, Abbie.' Then he was gone.

Abbie stared at the phone, her mind in turmoil. She shut the window and then went to make some coffee, aware more than ever of the north-easterly wind powering against the flimsy walls, as though at any moment the Willoughby would fold into the ground like the fraud it was. And back in the site office, still clutching the warm mug, she noticed the noise was strengthening into a roar, as though not of the natural world.

Her instinct was to run and hide, but something stopped her. For above this deeply menacing sound came the cackle of laughter, so harsh, so cruel, her whole body shuddered into rigidity.

'*Dave, Greg, anyone . . . For God's sake!*'

But the site outside was deserted except for the polythene on plot 2. Its crazy dervish dance grew and grew to lash the Show Home door with wild shadows before subsiding into clothes she recognized with terror.

'*What's she been saying 'bout me, that witch Leakes?*' Martha Robinson's shawl blew like a sail round her face. A shroud covering a skull whose hollow eyes roamed over Abbie's whole body, before settling on her stomach.

'What do you want?' Abbie was faint with fear.

'*The book.*'

'What book? What d'you mean?'

Abbie tried to reach for the phone, then the panic button, but her arm was numb.

She played for time, willing desperately for one of the joiners on the site to come into the office.

'*The one you stole from Clenchtoft. I should have taken it off you while I could.*'

'So why mustn't we see it? What have you got to hide?'

'*Where is it?*' The woman moved closer, her hands stretched in anticipation, rope burns brown round each wrist.

'I haven't got it. I gave it to the police.' Abbie ducked before wrenching the door open and charging outside. She just missed the wheels of a passing fork lift and its brakes groaned as it lurched to a halt.

'What the fuck?' The driver's voice came down from

above her. 'You were nearly a gonner, Abbie, d'you know that? What's goin' on 'ere?'

'In there. She's in there, again!' Her voice was hoarse with terror, her entire being stiff as though dead.

It didn't matter any more who knew. Vallender's phone call had changed all that. Instead of fighting to save Holtbury's investment, she had to save herself.

John Wilkes slid from the cab and was almost blown along to the open door. He removed his helmet and sniffed.

'Christ, it smells like a bloody grave in 'ere.' His bulk completely filled the hallway designed for pygmies as he tried all the rooms in turn, while Abbie stood shaking outside the front door. Martha Robinson was no longer passive – she would use her strength in any way, even for murder. Abbie knew it now.

'Can't see nothing,' he said, his forehead moist with sweat. This was all beyond his comprehension. 'Look, me and that lot out there don't even know if we've got jobs next month, what with all the daft rumours flying about. We don't need this sort of thing as well.'

'Tell *her* that!'

'Well, I'll keep an eye out, do me best,' he said without conviction, replacing his helmet. 'Why don't you come over and join us for a tea break sometimes? Bit of company'd do you good.'

'Thanks.'

She was deep in thought as the fork lift's engine drowned the bluster of the wind. He notched it into gear, then waved and moved on, passing the Ripton, plot 23, top of the range with Victorian conservatory. Rejected on 10 May by Mr and Mrs Richards from Taunton. Like all the rest now, undesired.

Abbie watched the muck from his wheels colour the air. No way was she ever going back into that office. She could use the phone in the foreman's cabin and occasionally send someone in to collect any faxes. It was as though this decision lifted a weight from her shoulders and her trembling stopped. She peered in through the glass. Everything seemed normal, back in its place, except for her desk. And as she looked harder, she gasped, for on top of it, next to the site plan, a small yellow weed, beginning to wither, lay on the prayer book.

All Fool's Day, and good news has reached me in my cell. The Church in Black Fen is without its priest. They say he went out with Shanks to fish for his supper and a wave took them just off Three Fingers Beach. The Devil knows I've tried hard enough for this change of fortune, and it's Him I thank . . .

Forty-five

THE WEDNESDAY MORNING news from Radio Humberside that Helen Quinn's wheelchair had been dredged up where Three Fingers Beach meets North Sand caught most of the local population unawares. It came a poor third to a Harrier crash on Bickling Fen and a house fire in Etterton, but slowly, like the sea which had upturned the wheelchair, toyed with it and borne it to rest inland, the implications gradually dawned.

To Abbie Parker it compounded her underlying dread. If its discovery really did mean Helen Quinn had died, who would be next? And what about poor Rosie? There was little anyone could do until the woman's death was confirmed, and when an alarmed Uncle Graham phoned she'd managed to calm him down. Even WPC O'Halloran seemed to know nothing except that another helicopter had already been sent for, and to allay Abbie's fears, the young policewoman suggested this latest flotsam, like the boater, might represent something completely innocent. 'It may just have been dumped, that's all. Maybe she's got a new one, or she was caught out by the tide and is waiting to be rescued somewhere ...'

Abbie had wanted to shake O'Halloran into the same sort of terror she herself was experiencing, to tell her that she wasn't a moron, but the policewoman's optimism was set fast. She was above it all, detached and objective as duty demanded.

After work, while waiting for Simon to turn up so that they could go to Rievely Hall, Abbie sat at one of the bistro tables set up daily outside the hotel. She was depressed despite the sound of All Saints on her Walkman, a glass of Vodka to hand, and the last of the sun on her face. She'd just opened Rosie's latest letter to her that had arrived while she was out. But this was no ordinary letter. The small written section was framed by detailed drawings of genitalia, interwoven with several childish faces all violently coloured in.

Abbie peeled off her headphones and folded the letter quickly as Sheila joined her, blowing smoke.

'You heard the news? It's bloody unreal.'

'I think Helen Quinn killed herself.'

'Christ.' As the hotel owner dragged a chair into the late sun and crossed her white legs, Abbie noticed their crop of dark stubble. Her own needed doing too but that was the least of her problems. Sheila stared at Abbie, inhaling. 'Look I don't want to be personal, Abbie, but you're not unwell, are you? You look so pale and your weight's really gone down.'

The young woman gave her a glance. 'No.'

'So what's up then?'

There was too much to say and she didn't want to scare Sheila into thinking about selling up again, so she diverted her on to concern for Simon. 'I'm worried about him having to go back to the army. Stupid really. That's his job.' She passed over Rosie's handiwork. 'What do you make of this?'

Sheila's frown deepened as she studied it.

'Those faces are the kids in that gang.' Abbie explained.

'Hey, I meant to tell you.' Sheila looked up. 'There's another child fallen seriously ill. Cherry someone. Black Fen Primary School again.'

Abbie's heart sank. 'Cherry Pickering?'

'That's it. Might hear about it on the news later.' Sheila then returned to the drawings. 'How on earth could a seven-year-old do this sort of thing?'

'How could *anyone*?'

'The little monkey must have sealed it up in the envelope before anyone saw, that's all I can say.'

'This just backs up what she told me earlier in that boat. What we've seen for ourselves, for God's sake. *This* is evidence.' Abbie slotted it back into her wallet, next to the photographs she'd taken out on the marsh.

'I'm seriously worried about her.'

'Join the club.' Abbie really wanted to spell it out to Sheila how much danger they were all in should Quinn decide to reappear, or if that malevolence in a black-clothed woman's form kept up her role as the Grim Reaper. 'That's why Sue and Uncle Graham have got to hang on to Rosie for a bit longer. Then I'll see if I can get her made a ward of court – maybe even get adoption proceedings off the ground.'

'That'll take time and money. Besides,' Sheila added peering at her friend, 'd'you really want to take on all her problems?'

'I'm shit scared by it all if you must know.'

'I believe you.' Sheila pocketed her cigarettes as Abbie finished her vodka and set down the glass.

'We musn't be tempted to tell the police. They're not on our side. Not yet anyway.'

'What *do* they need to convince them? Body bags?'

Abbie stood up. Her calves striped by the cane chair.

'Where are you off to?' Sheila asked.

'Places to go. People to see. If Simon gets back, can you tell him I've gone to Nest Cottage? It's down Walsoken Road on the right, just before that Whiplash thing. Thanks.'

'OK. Best of luck whatever.' Sheila turned to scrutinize one of her rare regulars on his way in. Then she scribbled the name of the cottage on an old beer mat and frowned again. She wasn't happy. Not at all.

Susannah Buckley tells me that the very same evening, one of the doxies at West Winch saw Hemmings took ill after a kidney pie and lie by the hearth drowned in his own vomit with his breeches filled up like bags of blood. How much is made up I do not know, but again I give thanks even though I too can feel Death's fingers beckoning . . .

Forty-six

THE DWELLING MATCHED its name, set back off the road and nestling as it did in the long shadow of Rievely Hall between two giant magnolias. Carbuncled by gables and chimneys, this additional dwelling to the main Regency house attracted more than a passing glance from those interested in the idiosyncrasies of local vernacular style. After Gedney Stimpson's demise in 1968 Nest Cottage, formerly the Lodge, was leased to the young Avril Lawson at the start of her teaching career. The date of its construction – 1835 – was set under a scalloped eave.

A path of diamond tiles shone in the evening light, edged by perennials, pretty as a postcard. But not quite, for all the curtains were drawn, giving the place a furtive air. Abbie tried to peer through the stained-glass panel after she'd rung the bell, despite the off-putting NO HAWKERS OR CIRCULARS notice, rusted round the supporting nails. She detected a shiver of movement in the hallway inside, and took a deep breath.

At first a strip of darkness beyond, then half a red mouth, a hand. The chain pulled taut.

'Hi, it's me again, Miss Lawson.' Abbie's confidence was forced and wafer thin. 'We need to talk.'

'I've no wish to speak to you again, young madam.

You've made enough mischief already.' Abbie caught sight of two girls on bikes short-cutting across the grass. She pushed a toe forwards.

'I don't really want to explain standing out here. It is rather public . . .'

'I'm busy.'

'Look, Miss Lawson, it's urgent.'

The chain's sharp release made her start as the door widened. She gasped at the apparition in front of her: Earth's crust make-up that fissured when the woman moved her face, lipstick smeared at random as if put on by a blind person. Yet that wasn't all: it was a nun in full habit who led her into a lighter room with two leaded windows overlooking a patch of garden where Rievely Hall cast a sharp shadow dividing the plot, and in the triangle of sunshine two thrushes were tugging at worms.

'Well, what is it?' The smell of incense lingered from somewhere as the deputy head fiddled with some flowers on a makeshift altar draped in Flemish lace. A pair of half-melted candles set in silver holders burned at each end.

'It's about the Quinns.'

The caricature nun spun round and Abbie wished she'd waited for Simon. She quickly assessed her method of exit if need be.

'What business are they of yours?'

'We've got to find Mr Quinn before he does any more harm.'

The older woman's face changed colour. Then she crossed herself. 'We?'

'You may be in danger yourself, Miss Lawson. Everyone knows you're his right-hand supporter at the church – and more.'

'Everyone is wrong.' Her expression widened the cracks around her mouth. She looked truly hideous.

'I don't think so.'

The nun turned to the window and gripped the ledge with mottled hands. Her shoulders heaved on a swell of spinsterly unhappiness. 'I told the police everything I could. About all the good he's done for the local people, how he's more than doubled the congregation here . . .'

Abbie watched her knuckles stretching her skin and decided to leave the matter of the letters till later.

'He's a troubled man, not an evil one,' the nun continued between clenched teeth. 'The evil is in this world around him, not *in* him.'

'So what's this voice he keeps hearing?'

'You be careful what you say.' Avril Lawson's wet eyes glared through the black mascara. 'People are too quick to judge, too ready to make mischief . . .' She paused. 'And just when he needs me more than ever, he's gone – taken himself away.' She wiped her mouth with her sleeve, leaving a vermilion smear on its grey. Abbie wanted to mention the axe, but once more this was not the time, now that Avril Lawson was in confession mode.

'So what about his wife?' Abbie asked innocently.

'I should say God rest her soul, but she was the worst sort of creature for him. Even before her accident . . .'

'Accident?'

'Oh yes. It was on 18 January, only this year. I'll never forget it. She'd been in at the school helping the class with raffia work and wanted to take the child home for lunch, but the little vixen had disappeared.'

'Rosie?' Yet Abbie was thinking of that other date in the Pentateuch. January 26 . . . Just shortly afterwards . . .

The nun's face hardened. 'Yes.'

'And?'

'That's when her mother fell downstairs.'

Suddenly Abbie was back in that dark maze of corridors, cold slippery floors, the stink of bats, and felt as if she too was falling . . .

'Where? In the rectory?'

'Good Lord, no. Up at Goosefoot.'

Abbie's hand covered her mouth.

'I always thought she was pushed, mind you. No one'll ever make me say any different.' The woman sniffed, the whites of her eyes yellowish and unhealthy. 'And *she* knew who did it all right.'

'But what was Helen Quinn doing there in the first place?'

'Looking for the child, of course.'

'So did one of the kids do it? One of the Gang?'

'I very much doubt it.' A disconcertingly knowing look came into her eyes. 'But they have their secrets, like the rest of us – even beyond the grave.' Her mouth tightened to a red wound. 'But I do know two of them wouldn't be dead now and the rest in danger if it wasn't for that child . . .'

'You really hate her, don't you?'

'Yes. She frightened them, that's for sure, by telling cruel lies about her father and showing them things they should *never* have seen . . .'

Abbie felt her stomach tighten, thinking of the dolls and the drawings again, the kids upstairs in the cottage weeks ago.

'What do you mean *things*?' Abbie ventured. 'Do you mean sex?'

Avril Lawson looked flustered. 'All I'm saying is, it's better she's away from here, wherever that may be. Don't be fooled by those pretty little plaits and her charming ways, because if I ever get my hands on her ... Now I think, Miss Parker, you know enough already and some words are best left unsaid. As you get older you may understand.' She pinched out the candles between her fingers as if to close matters.

'How dare you patronize me after what you and Quinn have been up to?'

Abbie felt her sudden rage, the draught of air as the false nun swept past. 'Is that how he likes to see you, his *mulier florum* or whatever, dressed like that?' she mocked, realizing she now had nothing to lose.

'Get out.'

The front door lay open behind her, but Abbie stood her ground.

'One more thing, Miss Lawson. If you do know where Quinn is, you have a duty to tell the police.'

The closing door pushed her away, with bolts quickly drawn, the chain once more in place.

'And if he's planning any more death threats, or following me around, he'll be past tense as well!' Abbie yelled, pounding on the glass and immediately feeling better.

A passing dog walker stopped to stare at the figure in the divided skirt striding down the path to her car, where a good-looking young man was waiting.

This prison on Scarewell Fen is new and the zealots say it needs filling. I have the number 32 on my chest, and before this week is out there will be a hundred of us. Drunks, debauchers, swindlers and takers of cattle — nothing near as wicked as what the man of the cloth did to me . . . but for death, the four conditions remain, and the police magistrate, Bickersley, could not once look me in the eye when he spoke of my little Walter and the black square of cloth met his head.

Forty-seven

'SHE'S MAD TOO,' Abbie said after she'd kissed him. 'Completely bonkers. All done up as a nun, if you please.'

'A Sister of Mercy, eh?' Simon saw the rash of colour on her face and felt her racing heart next to his jacket. She could be beyond him too. Sometimes.

'You shouldn't have gone there on your own.'

'I know. Sorry. Still, she did tell me something interesting.'

'OK. Spill.'

'She reckons Helen Quinn was *pushed* down the stairs.'

'Who by? Quinn?'

'She wouldn't say, but I'm sure she knows.'

Abbie let him into the car, idled up to the Whiplash crucifix and circled round it four times. Although her thoughts were in chaos, one kept coming to the surface. 'You don't think the old bat's hiding him in her house, do you?'

'Shit, I never thought of that.'

She drove past Nest Cottage again so they could catch a glimpse of the bedroom windows, but the magnolias' waxy burdens hid them from view.

Simon had other things on his mind, not least the awaited letter from St James's, and meanwhile things this end were getting no further forward. It was like an assault course of delays and half-truths, and just as bloody pointless. If it wasn't for little Rosie's predicament, and Abbie being too scared to return to the Show Home, he'd have felt inclined to phone his CO to say he was ready and willing to go back now.

'How did you get on with the planning office? Any joy?' she asked.

'Bloody closed, weren't they? In-service training or some crap like that.'

'Surprise, surprise.' She turned off Walsoken Road into Tithe Lane, which was still rutted, unmade. She could imagine what it had once been like in the days of carts and coaches and dresses edged in mud . . .

'OK. Next stop, the upper cruster, like we planned.'

Simon shifted over to the window. 'Didn't Gedney Stimpson work for that lot?' He pointed to Rievely Hall. It was built in the same red brick as the Sails but that was about the only similarity.

Abbie duly found the entrance, framed by balls on pillars, the usual gentry thing, announcing a huge weed-free drive. Its manicured edges led to portals obviously not part of the original front but a later neo-classical addition. On the first floor two upper windows still remained bricked in.

However, one thing marred the ambience of exclusivity and wealth: the smell of turkey shit wafting over from Sleeper's Farm. So strong was it that when Hanneke Schaap, the elderly housekeeper, answered the door, she avoided their eyes and kept her hand on her nose.

'Does the Colonel expect you?'

'Er . . . yes. It's Prince's Trust business,' Simon lied. 'We contacted him last week.'

Abbie stared in admiration. She'd never have thought of that one in a million years. He squeezed her hand as the eighty-year-old woman let them in.

'Wait a moment.' She flip-flopped away down to the end of the hall, and moments later sounded the bass notes of the nearby clock and the footsteps of its owner.

'Yes?' Colonel Horace Scott stood well over six feet tall, his back straight as a slat handle and cheek skin raw from a recent razor.

'We know you're busy and it is a bit late,' Abbie began in her most professional tone, 'but we need your help if you've got a moment.'

'Names, please?'

'Abbie Parker and Lieutenant Simon Cresswell.'

'Lieutenant, eh?' His eyebrows rose. 'Where?'

'Rheindahlen, sir.'

Abbie thought he was going to salute, but at least her ploy had broken the ice. The Colonel seemed content enough.

'Look, we're not really from the Prince's Trust. We're . . .'

'Coffee, Mevrouw Schaap!' Scott interrupted. 'The proper stuff if you please, not that dribble from the farmyard floor.' And when he had heard her bleated reply from an unseen kitchen, he ushered the two into his study, towards a chaise-longue and a captain's chair in worn velvet under prints of his father, William Scott, and his fat Norman wife, Octavie Hulot. There were no other portraits or photographs, and Abbie noticed the man's fingers were ringless.

The Colonel eyed Simon's jacket, still with the

Walther in hiding, then sat down opposite, close enough for them to see that his Adam's apple was scored by hyphens of blood, some still weeping on to his collar.

'Now it's my firm belief that we are here on this earth to help those in less fortunate circumstances, so,' he said, crossing long legs that ended in bright chestnut brogues, 'what can I do for you?'

Simon remembered Derek Jarrold and another promising start. He wasn't holding out much hope here either.

'Have you ever heard of a woman called Martha Robinson, from 1862 or thereabouts? Her photo was displayed in the church vestry not long ago . . .'

'She was one of Gabriel Hemmings's gang who worked around here at least some of the time,' Abbie added.

The old man's eyes hardened. His legs uncrossed, as if he was about to get up.

'We never speak of her here, and what's in the past should stay there. My grandfather, Samuel, was a noted benefactor and philanthropist, but there were those on Black Fen who to his mind were beyond redemption.'

'Why do you say that?'

'It has to be more than coincidence that anyone who ever crossed her met an appalling end.'

'Did Gedney Stimpson as well?'

Horace Scott fixed her with a stare, as if trying to gauge how much she knew. 'The man was foolishness personified. One should not speak ill of the dead, but he brought it upon himself.'

'So how did he die?'

'He was sucked into the mud after his skiff keeled over.'

Silence then. Simon's arm tightened on Abbie's as if she was driftwood floating in the sea, and he felt the same burning round his throat as on that day in London, his tongue dry and stiff.

'So why won't you tell us more about Martha Robinson?'

'Because I can't.' The eyes had changed. The man who'd faced the Huns in Falaise now saw a different enemy.

Suddenly there was a timid knock at the door. 'Excuse me.' The woman brought in a tray of three coffees already slopped into their saucers. Avoiding the visitors' curiosity, she hurriedly wiped underneath the Colonel's cup with the hem of her skirt and scuttled out.

'Poor Mrs Sheep.' Horace Scott ignored his drink. 'She's easily upset these days. Not had an easy life, you know. Still, I'll go to my maker knowing I gave her a decent roof over her head, even though she's been less than forthright with me of late.'

'Oh? In what way?'

'Let's just say she seems to have her own agenda.'

Abbie and Simon shared a glance, wondering what she'd done apart from getting Ernest Stimpson to telephone Abbie.

Simon coughed to change the subject. 'So what about the rest of the Robinsons? The ones who lived at Goosefoot?'

The Colonel sighed with impatience. 'I really have no idea. Black Fen was full of temporary workers at the time. A lot of Dutch and Prussians came over as well, and after a year or two they were never seen again. That's how it was then. A transitory population.' The Colonel stood up. 'Now you must excuse me, I have letters to write, even though, when you are my age, one's friends are as rare as corn in the desert.'

But Simon wasn't finished. 'There are no records of her on the parish database. Or of you for that matter.'

'I don't know what you're talking about. Now please . . .' He held the door open.

'Did your family own West Winch Farm, sir, where the new building site is?'

Annoyance kindled in the old man's eyes. 'No. It went to the Shanks during the Enclosures.'

They could tell he was fabricating. For some reason he didn't want to be associated with the place in any way. 'But Gabriel Hemmings worked for Rievely Hall, not for the Shanks . . .'

Colonel Scott looked agitated. He snatched up an envelope, then, having slotted some papers inside, ran his tongue along the flap and sealed it down. 'I really must ask you to leave now. I'm very busy.' His veneer of hospitality had melted away. Here was a man desperate to keep his family's secrets within his own walls. His eyes had become suddenly cold and glassy, like a lizard's.

The housekeeper was nowhere to be seen as he opened the front door on the turkey breeze and a tiny man hoeing in one of the far beds.

'My third complaint to the council about this smell is in the post.' The Colonel was suddenly behind them both, breaking Abbie's train of thought. 'We'll be getting that Sleeper's Farm back from the Dodds's one day, you'll see. All eighty acres of it. It's called reclamation, my friends.'

They left him surveying his kingdom, the sense of corruption and cover-up suddenly worse than anything coming from the Dodds's crowded crates.

'Grasping old git. He's got more sides than a bloody Rubik's cube.'

They returned to the car thwarted and angry.

'What did you make of that old girl?' he asked.

'I think she's scared out of her wits.'

'Me too.' Simon helped himself to a stick of chewing gum from the glove compartment. 'Now if we could either get hold of any old maps of the West Winch land or any initial Holtbury site plans, we can prove Scott's telling fibs.' Simon checked the time. 'Is there anything at the site?'

'The foreman might have something in that slummy dump of his.'

'OK. So we go take a look at them tomorrow.'

'He won't like that.'

'To be honest, I don't give a shit.'

The following morning found the man in question working at the top end of the Kingfisher Rise site, supervising decorative roof tiles that had slipped from the Ripton into its guttering, leaving unsightly gaps.

'He's safely up a ladder. Great.' She led the way into the man's den, wrinkling her nose at the disorder. No way was she going to share this hole with him. She'd been mad to even think of it. Prehistoric coffee dregs, a heap of fetid work shoes and not a square centimetre of free space on his picnic table.

'It reminds me of your room at uni.' Abbie smiled at Simon, pulling open a filing cabinet stickered with memos. The seriousness of what they might find there made her hesitate. Maybe, she thought, some things were best left undisturbed. 'You do this one. I'll try over there.'

But Simon hadn't heard her. His mind was fixed on

the stumps on Morpeth Bank and their recent encounter with the secretive Colonel Scott.

'Widows' Drove, Piddle Drove and Turncoat Drove . . .' Abbie's fingers worked through the drawers, where chaos also reigned and nothing seemed relevant.

Simon's head, however, was bent over a sheet marked by mug rims, obviously much pored over once. 'I've got this plan here – apparently for only twelve houses.'

Abbie came over. She recognized just the left half of the existing crescent only, carved up into plots with oblongs for homes and separate squares for garages. The rest of the site was earmarked for 'Residential Landscaping', with a fountain, benches and ornamental trees sketched in. Now she understood.

'Look at the date – 15 January. They must have squeezed in some more houses at the last minute.'

'Very last minute, obviously.' He set it to one side to study the second folded document lying underneath, which was on older, more fragile paper. He tried to spread it over the rest of the paraphernalia on the table and froze as the last section unfolded. 'Look at this, Abs.'

'Oh no.'

She didn't need to get any closer. This time the smell was, if anything, stronger. She turned to press her head against his chest, and realized his heart had quickened. Under Simon's hand lay the ground-floor plan of Kingfisher Rise's nineteenth-century forebear. *West Winch Farm, property of Samuel Wiley Scott.* Scullery, store, parlour, smoke room etc. and outside it, in the pattern of waste pipes which straggled through the site of the old outbuildings, a trail of dried blood led to the current plot 2.

'What the hell do we do now?' Although Abbie glanced out of the filthy window for any sign of Martha Robinson, she knew she was here, inside, with them – watching. She sat down on the one available chair.

'You tell me.' Simon refolded the chart and slipped it inside his jacket. 'I'll get a photocopy made of this, then at least it can't be spirited away.' He was thinking of Mowbray and her scented letter – and how the current lot in Snutterwick CID didn't seem to be doing much better. 'Christ, I could do with a drink.'

Abbie stood up and fondled his earlobe. Soft and warm like baby skin ... baby skin. O God, no. She suddenly wanted to heave, to lose all the evil that had lodged in her deepest thoughts, and he held her until the foreman was seen climbing down his ladder.

'Look, I'm going to see that old girl at Rievely again,' Simon announced on their way back to the Show Home. 'I'm curious about her name for starters and Scott's innuendoes. I think she may know something. Will you be OK here? I'll only be half an hour.'

Before she could reply, Fidler was advancing, his face as ruddy as a Pink Lady apple.

'Those Martinsens phoned again,' he snapped. 'You'll be losing them unless you stick around and see them.'

'Thank you.'

She saw Simon tensing up and led him away to the site entrance. He paused by the Ripton, where the black polythene now lay subdued under even more bricks – where nothing was happening. If asked to describe the aftermath of a nuclear drop, this would be it for him. Where blocks and mortar were just messy heaps and abandoned window-frames skewed on their corners. He felt the plan in his pocket and had the urge to grab a spade and start digging, but there were yet more questions to ask, and still a ton of grief to come.

The sun had risen large over the North Sea and with its early strength burnt the wind into submission. It now powered into the Show Home office and, despite all the open windows and her reluctance to be there at all, Abbie was welded to her seat. She'd repositioned her desk yet again, and every other blink of her eye was towards the door for Martha Robinson's return.

Vallender had sent her a second panic button in a used Jiffy bag with a note that it was in case she mislaid the first one. He also confirmed his date of arrival. She hung the thing round her neck, but it was now more of a burden than a blessing in this heat, just like Avril Lawson's innuendoes about Rosie that wouldn't go away. Was she, this child's 'good friend', making the biggest mistake of her life by adding the Parker family to the trap?

Abbie trawled every morsel of memory: the small face so like Helen Quinn's, the wheaten hair and huge blue eyes, all declaring herself Innocent, Not Guilty. But something had changed. Dread had replaced honour, and death was its pay-off, so that when the phone suddenly rang she thought it was her uncle with bad news.

'Miss Parker?'

'Yes?'

'Olaf Martinsen here.'

Christ, Abbie. Get a grip . . .

'Hello. I'm really sorry I wasn't here to help you the other day. Where are you calling from?'

She heard him consult with his wife. 'Slaketon. Outside Harwich. We're just taking a look round here for a while, then we'll be back with you. We still have interest in the Ripton type of house, Miss Parker. We like the sound of its guest room en-suite very much, also the kitchen/breakfast room.'

Apologizing again, she tried to pin them down with a day and a time, but the Swede preferred 'to be flexible'. In other words, to muck her about.

The moment the call ended the phone rang again. This time it was Vallender, using her first name rather intimately.

Oh no, not now, please . . .

'I've just had a call back from the Martinsens,' she got in first, putting on her negotiator voice. 'You know, that Swedish couple.'

'Terrific.'

'They like the Ripton layout.' It was hard to pretend she hadn't heard his sarcasm, but still wondered why he wasn't chuffed at the news.

'Bloody bullshitters.'

'Pardon?'

'I've been in this game long enough to know the sort. They prefer Blackpool rock to building sites. Weekend wasters, don't trust 'em further than I can throw their bloody ice-cream cornets . . .'

'But it's Friday.' Abbie couldn't believe her ears. 'And anyhow I'm doing my best. You always said—'

'Yeah, yeah.'

'Mr Vallender, are you all right?'

'Not sure. You off now?' His tone seemed almost wistful.

'I've got shopping to do, one or two things.' Meaning Simon.

There was an uncomfortable pause.

'Look, I might be held up next Thursday. Need to sort out some paperwork for the wankers in HQ. Why I phoned, really.'

'That's fine. No problem.'

Abbie stared at the receiver, now sensing she had the upper hand in the uncertainty stakes, and a confusion of feelings that wouldn't leave her as she stood outside for a moment under a huge blue sky set fair for the weekend. She wondered how Simon was getting on at Rievely, when the phone trilled behind her.

'Detective Superintendent Aldreth here, Miss Parker. Sorry to intrude again.'

'Yes, what is it?'

'Nothing to get alarmed about, but we've had some useful news.'

Abbie sat down, fearing the worst.

'We've received some information which seems to link the Reverend Quinn with the Hereford area at some point in the past,' the mellow voice went on. 'It's a long shot, but seems to tie up with one or two things Miss Leakes wrote down.'

'Wrote down? They were just scribbles, surely?'

'I know what you mean, but we did get some help: a graphical psychologist and a specialist in drug-induced imagery who's over from the USA.'

'I see.' Experts she never knew existed.

'Funny thing is though, the day after they'd looked at *Secrets*, the thing vanished.'

'What?'

'From our strong box, no less. This sort of thing's never happened before.'

Abbie felt her heart pound in her chest. She remembered Martha Robinson at Clenchtoft, then recently at the Show Home. Her terrifying face again on the computer screen and all the missing names in the parish records. There seemed no limit to her ingenuity. A soul adrift, bent on revenge . . .

'Someone wanted it badly then.'

'In a logical world, yes.' Aldreth paused. 'So it's all a bit of a mystery one way and another.' He tried to make light of the disappearance, but she wasn't going to help him out. Why should she? Not after the fiasco with her threatening letter.

'You were saying about Quinn?' she reminded him.

'Ah yes. We're still investigating that Hereford connection, but more immediately, we're extremely concerned about his daughter.' His pause that followed seemed loaded and Abbie bit her lip, wondering where this was leading. 'Though the longer her absence goes on, the less optimistic we can be. Of course, Quinn may well be looking for her, in which case we must be extra vigilant.'

Relax, she told herself. If Aldreth had sussed what she'd done with Rosie, she'd know about it.

'Tell me more about the Reverend,' Abbie tried to divert him, and to her relief, it worked.

'Well, it seems our friend Quinn was connected with the Marches for some time,' Aldreth volunteered. 'Apparently he inherited a dairy farm from some people called Baldwin.'

'A farm?' Abbie saw the cleric's white hands and perfectly manicured nails. This didn't tie up at all. 'Are you sure?'

'As sure as we can be. They'd had some accident, many years ago now, though we're not sure of the circumstances, then the place passed to him.'

'What kind of accident?'

'Like I said, we don't know yet.'

Her heart was thumping again.

'By the way, a Miss Wright from Social Services told our FPU that you yourself had plans for Rosie Quinn. Is that correct?'

Abbie sighed for his benefit, but inwardly panic took over. 'Superintendent, I've got more than enough on my plate already. I can't worry about someone else's child. I've not seen her here for weeks.' How she loathed that stupid bitch Wright and her useless files, her pretence of caring – even her telephone manner.

Aldreth cleared his throat. Whether he believed Abbie or not was unclear. 'There's still no sign of her mother either. The hat and the wheelchair may just be red herrings. Still,' he added, 'be on your guard. If you notice anything suspicious, give us a ring on this number. You'll get through to me personally.' He recited his extension.

'Thanks.' Abbie's gaze rested on the door, just in case. Then she made a decision. It wasn't just the Reverend Jarrold who had to know. It was time to share things. 'There *is* something else. I was wondering . . .'

'Go on.'

'It's about that dead woman Martha Robinson. I'm bloody terrified of her if you must know.'

'Look, forget about that and try to get some rest.'

'She's actually *here* on the site. Not just when I'm alone either, though that's the worst. I'm telling you, I think *she* took that *Secrets* book from you.'

'Talk to me after the weekend. I must go now.' He was clearly getting impatient. And as he put the phone down, contemplating the tea-vending machine opposite, the latest news of Cherry Pickering slipped from his fax.

This sudden abandonment left Abbie with a debilitating desire for eternity, for herself and her mother, to confront this damaged soul called Martha Robinson in the afterlife and fight it out once and for all.

She felt the panic button cord tighten suddenly round her neck, forcing her carotid artery into frantic motion, her throat trying to swallow air repeatedly as if it would never do so again. She unwound the thing quickly, threw it on the desk, then tried to contact Simon's mobile.

His battery was down maybe. There was no response. She glanced through the window and caught her breath. Someone was coming into the site, and he didn't look Swedish either. For such a hot day, the mackintosh looked incongruous, the briefcase even more so, and the man's red-brown hair was gelled against his head.

Abbie moved to the door, letting one mock-Georgian pillar shield her from his direct view. He was heading her way, undistracted by any other activity on the housing development. And now she recognized the legs, the stride ... No time to phone Aldreth or anyone else. She realized she was dead meat.

Abbie shut the front door into the hall and scrambled up the stairs to Bedroom One, which had a clear view over the rest of the site. Now there was no sign of him. He must already be in the office below. Abbie stifled a cry and shut herself in the en-suite bathroom, where the lock moved stiffly into position as his steps met the bottom of the stairs.

'Jesus help me.' She huddled in the corner. There was

nowhere else for her to go as Quinn tried all the doors in turn, even the airing cupboard, and with each failure slammed them shut again with such ferocity that the house shook to its core.

Finally he pushed and pulled at the door which was her only defence, adding a stream of blasphemies to phrases from the Bible – like the last time she'd heard him, but worse, far worse. This was personal. He wanted Rosie, he wanted her best friend and that fucker with the shaved head who was helping them both.

Suddenly she heard another sound – someone yelling up from below. Abbie stood on the loo seat and opened the tiny frosted window just as the door lock was beginning to give and the plywood splintered into a foot-sized hole.

'Simon! Up here!' she screamed.

The door battering gave way to a scuffle, with finally the dull thuds of a body falling down the stairs. Abbie knelt down to peer through the gap Quinn's boot had made and, with a flood of relief, she recognized the top of Simon's head.

She undid the lock and crept out to watch as he kicked Quinn into standing at the foot of the stairs, then shoved him along the hall to her office, his gun giving the stumbling figure no chance to duck into the kitchen for one of the display knives.

Quinn turned briefly, recognizing his own weapon. He lunged, but the soldier was quick, well trained and nearly wrenched the intruder's arm out of its socket. He was tempted to shoot the man, but with only five rounds left and God knows where he could find any more, it was too risky. Worse was to try and tie the cunt up. That way he could get himself trashed, and lose the gun. *Shit, Cresswell, where are your bloody balls?*

Quinn staggered away from the house, his raincoat flapping like old sails, while Simon contacted Snutterwick CID and the trainee constable manning the desk. After describing the incident he wrapped his arms round Abbie, a united force for a few precious minutes. But he knew he'd let her down.

'I should have finished him off while I had the chance.'

'He could have had a knife for all you knew.'

'Look, next time, no ifs or buts, OK? That's a promise.'

Then he noticed her neck. 'What the hell's that?' His finger traced the reddened line round her throat. He'd once seen a failed suicide at Rheindahlen, sufficient reason to open another bottle under the bedcover. 'Go on, take a look.' His eyes different, frightened, he stood next to her by the cheap gilt mirror.

Abbie gasped. It was a horrible disfiguration and seemed to be growing darker even as she stared. She suddenly remembered the weal on Martha Robinson's cheek, that black rag tied around her neck . . .

Jesus.

'I think it's just from my panic button. The cord was getting tight, that's all.' But as she spoke, the line on her neck was widening, starting to bleed. Simon sensed her breath falter, saw her sway off balance. He grabbed her first as the choking started, the same as he'd experienced at his medical. Now it was her turn . . .

He punched 999 and his voice became hysterical. She was dying, his beautiful brave Abbie, and there wasn't a fucking soul around. Except something opposite, seen through the window's glare, a shadow, upright, carrying something round and round the half-finished plot 2. It turned just long enough for him to see its yellowed skull smile before disappearing.

*I have refused all food and sent away
the chaplain, and in my delirium see
nothing but the gallow's black bones
and the* Bridport Dagger *up on Morpeth Bank. Besides, Samuel Scott has
insisted on the resurrection of the Neck
Verse just for me, knowing full well I
will refuse to speak it. Its words are for
simpletons whose God has long been in
the Devil's pocket, which seems a less
cruel place for anyone to be . . .*

Forty-eight

'THERE'S NOTHING THAT a day in bed won't mend.' Dr Purbeck finished his check-up and took Simon to one side. 'See that nothing upsets her for the time being. She's had a nasty shock. Though her blood pressure was worrying when I first saw her, it's on an even keel now.' He folded his glasses into their case and went to the window, from where he could see Herringtoft Track rearing up at the back of the clinic garden. 'If you can both get away for a few days somewhere completely different . . .'

'Why do you say that? I mean completely different?'

Donald Purbeck avoided his eyes. 'Let's just say a change of scene would do her the world of good.' He rewound his watch, then helped Abbie off the couch. 'You're lucky to have such a sensible young man, Miss Parker. As I tell my own daughter, they hardly grow on trees.' A weak smile strained his mouth as he passed Simon her prescription. 'One each night before sleep will help no end.'

They were ushered out into the afternoon sun, Abbie still feeling dizzy but at least able to breathe and swallow again. The six gabled houses around 'Peace-holme' cast huge shadows into the road and from high up by the Wenn the bird-watcher with his new hat saw them pass from light to dark on their way back to the hotel.

Simon stayed close to her, occasionally staring at her neck. The marks had completely vanished by the time the ambulance arrived. There'd been nothing, not even a bruise to show for it all, and if the paramedics had thought they were just a couple of space cadets they'd disguised it well enough.

Simon wanted to tell her about his chat with Mrs Schaap and the episode with Farjeon, but now wasn't the time for that. And he knew with a heavy certainty his letter would come tomorrow.

'I know somewhere we could go for the weekend,' Abbie whispered as they neared the hotel. 'Aldreth said Quinn may have once owned a farm in Herefordshire, and another name, Baldwin, was mentioned. It seems they had it before him. We could at least have a sniff round. Ask a few questions. What d'you think?'

Simon's eyes bored into hers, reflecting the sky and more. His hand tightened on hers. 'For a start, I don't think we should be too far from Rosie. Anyway, Herefordshire's quite a big county . . . Where would we start?'

'I could get more details from the police.'

'No.'

Sheila helped put Abbie to bed while Simon phoned the foreman at the site, explaining that she was unwell after Quinn had come calling. Fidler sounded even more brassed off. There'd been cops all over the place, but the sniffer dog had refused to go near plot 2 and eventually had to be muzzled, then carried past it. Simon tried to get more information, but the miserable old fart put the phone down on him.

He then poured himself a double whisky. Things were getting worse. What would be next? He looked at the stairs then snatched up the phone. Aldreth's line was engaged, Stock and O'Halloran were out.

'Anybody, please, for God's sake.' His knuckles drummed on the bar top with frustration and when yet another new desk sergeant finally answered, Simon's request for full police protection came out all wrong: a jumble of anger and fear emerging instead. Better if he'd pissed into the wind, he realized. He gulped down the last of his drink and reached for another.

Sheila joined him on a bar stool, noticeably smarter and wearing shoes instead of slippers, her recent hairdo still intact. She set down a little pile of photographs of Lilith Leakes and began tearing them up, one by one, into tiny squares.

'Where did you get those from?' He stared at the old woman's gaping mouth, the hollowed eyes.

'On Abbie's dressing table. I don't want those bloody awful things in the place any more,' she said vehemently. The few drinkers by the door turned round to stare. 'There's enough weirdos around here without giving these house room. Anyhow, Abbie said I could get rid of them, so I think I ought to put the poor old girl to rest – scatter her on the water.'

She rose and went outside, walking the few yards up to Herringtoft Track, and stood watching as the fragments danced in the eddying tide and then disappeared. When she returned to the bar, Simon was on his third drink, with a tenner and a fiver by his elbow to appease her.

It looked like Sheila really was making a fresh start, beginning with the installation of high-tech burglar alarms in all the rooms and a security light outside. For Abbie and Simon only the supper menu had been revamped, swapping ready-made frozen meals for baked potatoes with different fillings and fresh salads, while breakfasts would now offer croissants and even kedgeree. She'd also advertised the hotel, like in the good old days, and arranged with a ship's captain to give her guests sunset excursions to East Foxton on request.

'Hi.' Abbie came over to join them, still pale and wobbly. She noticed Simon's glass, could tell he'd started drinking seriously again, but said nothing.

'I thought I told you to stay in bed, my girl,' Sheila chided.

'It's not much fun being up there on my own.'

Simon knew what she meant and kept his head down. Maybe tomorrow he would know the score.

Sheila fetched herself a coffee and switched on the bar TV. The local news included a report on the alarming increase in summer truancy in the Fens, and ended with some Cambridge statistician's paper on the shortfall in live male births around the Wash. Sheila lit up, frowning at the next news item. Cherry Pickering, a pupil at Black Fen Primary School, had just died in Peterborough General Hospital from malaria.

The lounge bar fell silent around her. Even the storemen from *The Valkyrie* stopped to listen as a Department of Health spokesperson struggled to allay public fears that an epidemic was on the way.

Sheila put out her cigarette and Simon pulled Abbie towards him. She was remembering the school Open evening and that bedroom in Goosefoot Cottage where

she'd last seen the child, while he could only think of
Quinn, and how he'd soon be sniffing around them again
after his Show Home humiliation. Even more hungry
and desperate.

The beatings don't trouble me, nor the turds they now put on my plate instead of vittles, but when they take my blood to see if it's any different from other women on Scarewell Fen, all my strength is drained away. Now it is time to recite this wretched verse which Moeder once taught me: 'Have mercy upon me, O God, according to Thy loving kindness; according unto the multitude of Thy tender mercies blot out my transgressions . . .' But to save my miserable life, I cannot say it.

Forty-nine

To any casual observer, work on the Kingfisher Rise development was proceeding normally, but the banging in of plot fencing disguised the real truth, known only to those within. That there'd not been even a whiff of any contract exchange, let alone any house sold.

Abbie had left Simon and the remains of his hangover standing outside the Sails to waylay the postman. He'd said if the report on his medical didn't come in the first post, he'd ring up that bastard in London himself. NATO was finalizing its ground force, the move into Kosovo imminent. Simon had looked grim, too preoccupied to wave goodbye, and the moment she reached the Show Home she had moved her desk as close to the door as possible, then gave him a call. It was Sheila who answered.

'He went out five minutes ago, while I was washing up.'

'Did he say where?'

'No. I just heard the car starting, that's all.'

Abbie could tell the other woman was nervous. Sheila had got used to Simon being there, like having a guard dog, only better, she claimed.

'Has the postman been yet?' Abbie's heart quickened waiting for Sheila's reply.

'Why? Are you expecting anything special?'

'Not me. Simon.'

'Oh.' A pause that lasted long enough to make Abbie feel sick.

'He's received a letter, hasn't he? Tell me.'

'You know what it's like. Prize Draw Finalist stuff, Barclaycard bumf . . .'

'Tell me.'

'I think so. Yes.'

Abbie slapped the phone down and was just about to sneak back to the hotel when it rang again.

Shit shit shit . . .

'Miss Parker? It's Anya Martinsen. We're on our way over.' Abbie tried to sound pleased.

'Where are you now?'

'Black Fen. Near the garden centre.'

'Great.' With tension raising her voice in pitch, she gave the woman fresh directions towards the site's turquoise flags. She was desperate to go and find Simon, but the inevitable was only seconds away.

Abbie stuffed her new panic button in the drawer – there were already enough turn-offs in the place without that being on show. She felt her neck reddening and her breath straining as she waited outside in the sun, checking her tights and fingering the stupid badge that kept slipping sideways . . .

A brown Volvo glided through the gates and in less than a minute Mr and Mrs Martinsen, wearing identical lemon-yellow tracksuits, were sniffing the air of Kingfisher Rise like hounds, while their three teenagers remained in the car, sounding the horn as they fought over music tapes.

Having got the preliminary greetings out of the way,

including a query about the local malaria problem, the couple began their tour of the site. Looking quietly keen and smelling of fabric conditioner, Mr Martinsen allowed his wife to walk in front, while Abbie followed, listening to their domestic dreams. No one had ever talked about the development in this way before, or even seen a shred of possibility in the place. She pinched herself furtively to make sure she wasn't hallucinating.

They announced that they'd want to build a sauna in the garden and were willing to pay extra for the installation of a Jacuzzi. For them the Ripton layout was just perfect. So yet again the three adults marched round the whole crescent, stopping now and then to consult the plan and to check out wind directions. As Abbie listened to their private ambitions, spoken in such perfect English, she wondered about Simon's letter and where on earth he had gone, and prayed that plot 2 would once more pass unnoticed. She'd even thought of changing its listing from Ripton to Willoughby or Somersham, but that might only cause further complications.

'A rock and a hard place,' she muttered too loudly.

'What is that?' Four aqua eyes met hers.

'Nothing, really. Let's take another look at plot 7, shall we? It's almost finished now and has lovely leaded windows, as you can see . . .'

'No, no, no. We must have the biggest garden possible,' Mr Martinsen insisted.

Abbie's stomach seized up as they held the plan against the Portakabin and pointed to plot 2. Olaf Martinsen checked its measurements again. It didn't take an exam pass in geometry to see he was right. The plot had the greatest depth of garden within its perimeter.

'This would be ideal for us.' Anya Martinsen beamed. 'We could be having our first Christmas in England . . .'

Abbie hung back in dread as they examined the early plumbing work in the roofless house, two blond heads kissing, hands touching buttocks then linking, united in their imaginings. 'Olaf's an oceanographer, you know,' his wife said suddenly. 'He's obsessed by tides and currents.'

'That's nice,' said Abbie, hearing a car coming in fast: a white Xantia with mud scuffs along its door sills. It was Vallender, two days early, and her heart stopped as he braked.

'Excuse me one moment,' she said to the couple, who were too absorbed to notice. God, he looked different. His suit creases were less than razor sharp now, and not just from the journey here, she could tell, while his dark hair curled over a shirt collar that had obviously lasted him a week. As the sales director kissed her on the cheek, two days' growth of beard and a reek of aftershave assaulted her senses, adding to her confusion. There was no ring on his finger.

'We've got the Martinsens here looking over the place again,' she whispered.

'So I see.' He yanked his case from the boot and slammed it shut.

'Cash buyers, I think,' Abbie added proudly.

'Good-oh.'

'Look where they are though.' The Swede was now taking photograhs of plot 2, arranging his wife in each shot, showing no concern at the untidy heap of breeze blocks or their still-dark mortar mix leaking on to the concrete floor.

'Like I said, what will be will be.'

Abbie followed him into the Willoughby, utterly bewildered.

'I'd better stick around with them,' she volunteered. 'Try and get them to put pen to paper before they go.'

The brickie, Greg Pitts, gave her the thumbs-up and a knowing smile, so she ventured back to the Scandinavians now standing in the kitchen/breakfast area.

'Your Mr Fidler was most helpful last time but he did not say what ceiling texture you use on the Ripton. Is it the same as over there?' Mrs Martinsen pointed to the Willoughby, where Vallender was pouring himself a courtesy whisky.

'My wife means Artex.'

'That's standard,' Abbie informed them, finding it hard to keep her tone professional. 'But obviously the swirls vary from property to property. We've been making a big effort recently to lose any dangly bits.'

'Good. We wish to avoid that if possible. We like things nice and smooth.'

'No problem. That can be arranged. I can also show you a selection of flooring finishes and of fitted-wardrobe styles. If you'd like to come over . . .'

They conferred and then made to move, attempting to shift one immaculate foot after the other, but the two pairs of spanking new trainers held fast. Abbie tried to help Mrs Martinsen forward but the woman merely fell on all fours. Her husband, powerless, bared his teeth.

'Help!' he called out. 'I'm sinking!'

'Hold on there! We're coming.' The foreman ran down the Portakabin steps while Handel Myers, the oldest in his team, grabbed planks and followed. The noise of fencing work suddenly stopped.

'Don't panic now,' Myers shouted, as the men laid the lengths of wood end to end and tightrope-walked to reach the stranded couple.

'Miss Parker, you should have checked with us first before allowing the public in here.' The foreman's disapproving camel profile was highlighted by the sun's glare.

'We're not the public. We're potential purchasers,' the still-immobile Mr Martinsen protested.

The foreman pulled a screwdriver from his pocket and gouged round the captive wife's hands and feet while she began to sob.

'Not set yet, the cement, see. Should never have stepped on it,' he admonished.

Abbie blushed. She suddenly hated him and his clumsy hands. Hated him for making her look a fool. 'I'm terribly sorry.'

She could see the couple's children clamouring inside the car as their mother managed to stand and shuffle towards the door-frame. Their father took longer to release, but with one giant step he was out of trouble. They scrutinized the uppers of their trainers in dismay, then saw the severed soles stranded like dried fish.

'Christ, it's set fast!' The old joiner prodded the surface with his rule. 'You were lucky.'

'We came here to buy a house, not to risk our lives.' The woman was still tearful.

'We'll have to go and sort out some kind of compensation for you. It's about time Holtbury's were put in the picture about this place.' Fidler gave Abbie a withering glance, then noticed the parked Citroën. 'Your boss here then?'

'I don't know,' she lied.

'Well, I'd like to have a word with him.' He led the

way to the Willoughby house, unique in its completeness, and, like Aldreth the policeman, both Swedes had to stoop to enter.

Abbie coughed in warning. Vallender looked dreadful. He glanced up, seemingly unable to stand as the four of them surrounded him.

'We have a problem – sir.' Fidler spread out his fingers. 'These good people are potential customers and have just ruined their footwear on plot 2. Can we make some sort of compensation now so they can replace them?'

'Ah, if only life were that simple.' The sales director leaned back in his chair, his eyes blearily unfocused. 'But from bitter experience I can tell you that it bloody isn't.' The smell of drink hung in the stifling room. Abbie tried to catch his eye, to elicit a correct response. When none was forthcoming, she wanted to crawl under the desk.

'Look here, I cannot drive a car like this!' Mr Martinsen lifted a foot to show his ruined sock under the top half of his trainer.

Abbie could bear this no longer. 'I'll go to the shop in Snutterwick now. What sizes are you?'

'Forty-one and forty-five,' was the icy response.

'Right, please sit down.' She brought in more chairs, which they gratefully took. 'It shouldn't take me more than half an hour. In the meantime, Mr Vallender, if you could show our clients some of these optional features so they can choose . . .' She pulled some catalogues from the cabinet, spread them out in front of him then made for her car.

The road at noon was clogged with market traffic. She took risks overtaking and dodged some lights on red

– anything to reduce the Martinsens' time with Vallender and lose for ever her only hope of a sale.

The dual carriageway proved worse, with high-sided trucks from the ports creating darkness either side of her. She switched on Radio 1. Nothing. No music, no chat, just strange faraway laughter that crowed its hatred into the car, freezing her hands to the wheel.

''Fraid they've legged it.' Vallender, still seated, smiled up at her when she returned at midday. His shirt collar was open, his tie askew.

Abbie threw down the shoeboxes and kicked them into the corner.

'It's OK for me to waste all my effort, isn't it? You could at least have kept them interested – even in another Ripton. I don't understand you. I had an August deadline from you, remember?' She glared at him uncomprehendingly, then noisily cleared away the cups, folded the site plan and held up his half-empty bottle.

'Did anyone see this?'

'I don't really care.'

She wanted to warn him that he was losing it, but couldn't. Too many things were going wrong. Things she didn't understand.

We've got to get something done about that woman. It's like she's following me, trying to make me go mental.

Vallender watched her every move, and the more he saw the more he liked. 'What's the matter with you?'

'You wouldn't understand.'

She thought of Simon, ready for anything and right behind her. Vallender, for all his glossy career moves and his trade spiel, didn't have a bloody clue. Abbie then noticed that George Fidler and the drain layers were all looking their way.

'I think you ought to show your face out there. We don't want him blabbing over your head.'

'Pond life.'

'What?'

'If they'd got a tenth of your oomph this whole bloody thing'd be up and running by now. As it is we have a major cock-up.'

Abbie stared. The flattery was alarming. 'They only need some encouragement. Once people see a few actual plots ready . . .' she persevered.

'What people? The men on the frigging moon?' He unscrewed the bottle cap again and swallowed.

'I know you've got problems at home, Mr Vallender, but this place is *your* job, *my* job. As you said, I've only got twelve weeks to turn things around . . .'

'Jobs, jobs . . . what the hell's the point? I had a wife and kid. A lovely kid.' His dark hair spiked out between his fingers. 'All gone now. All kaput.'

Abbie moved closer to him, sensing his loss would somehow one day be hers as inevitably as the tide heaping down the shipway to Black Fen.

'My dear wife thinks Gemma'd be better off with her as I'm obviously more married to fitted carpets and bloody gold taps . . .'

'I'm really sorry.'

'So am I. Now the CSA are sniffing about, so I'd be better off redundant.'

'It's not fair of her to keep Gemma from you. Daughters need their dads.' But she thought of Rosie and Quinn. Then her own father.

'In a year's time, my kid won't even know me.'

'Course she will.'

Vallender looked up with a deep blue gaze, an expression she'd never seen before. He hadn't come down here to check developments, to cancel materials for the next phase. He was there for her shoulder to cry on, and not so long ago she'd have given it willingly.

Suddenly his hand was on hers. 'I need you, Abbie Parker.' A draught blew some papers to the floor. She bent to pick them up, her eyes moving to the open door.

'No, you don't. You need to think about saving this place. You need to get a priest to exorcize it. God knows, I've been trying hard enough.'

'Holy Jesus!' His forehead banged the desk before a knock and a cough were heard from outside. Fidler gave the younger man a disdainful glance.

'*Heil, mein Führer,*' Vallender slurred. 'How goes it?'

'Bloody terrible, if you must know. I've come to say I've got an interview Wednesday week. Tunisia. Been waiting for the call all morning.'

'Ah, a Desert Rat no less,' Vallender snorted.

'Mr Vallender, please.' Abbie fetched her diary and tried to sound normal. 'That's fine, Mr Fidler. We'll get someone else to keep an eye on things out here.'

'Who are your referees?' Vallender asked.

The large man looked peeved. He'd expected at least some sign of regret or a thank-you.

'That's my affair.' He picked up his hard hat. 'You're all on a hiding to nothing with Kingfisher Rise. That's my opinion.'

Abbie remained silent till he'd gone. She heard Vallender get up from his chair, then felt two arms surround her, his breath burning her ears.

'Stay with me tonight.' He clung to her with the

strength of a drowning man holding on to the only thing
of worth in his sea of failure.

'I can't.'

'Yes you bloody can.'

Simon, what am I doing? Where the hell are you?

Then she turned to receive his kiss.

The St George's Sails Hotel smelt of cooked liver and
polish. Newly bought clusters of fake foliage cascaded
from the walls and a couple of pictures of Marilyn
Monroe hung in place of the Smitheyland Hunt.

The two Holtbury employees sat stiffly in the one
window seat. Their conversation was bland, yet all the
more painful. The Martinsens, Fidler's departure, the
Somersham bathroom tiles that were all faulty. Thank-
fully nothing about the kiss which had been probably the
best four seconds of Vallender's life – or the way her
body had felt against his . . .

Behind them on the tide, *The Happy Wanderer* dis-
charged its cargo of pallets to a chorus of shouts and
somewhere in the sky a helicopter again scanned the
shore.

Vallender had managed to comb his hair and
straighten his tie. His aftershave was nothing Abbie
recognized, but then she had other things on her mind.
Simon still hadn't come back and with each minute her
anxiety – and guilt – grew. To reassure her, Sheila had
phoned the two other pubs in Black Fen, her rivals when
she'd first moved in although now she was past caring.
Neither had seen anyone of the lieutenant's description.

Abbie turned to see Sheila coming over carrying a
familiar pink envelope and a bottle.

Rosie?

'This came second post.'

Abbie took it, frowning. Why did she always have to assume the worst? 'Thanks,' she said quietly as Sheila straightened the curtain behind her.

'By the way, Mr Vallender, if you want your shoes cleaned, just leave them out. Now, how's that for four-star service?'

'Spot on.' He glanced back at Abbie, who quickly pocketed Rosie's envelope.

Sheila set down the wine, a Burgundy, blood red in the shaft of early evening sun. Vallender stared at her purple nails, her red-light lipstick. A moment later and Abbie opened the letter under the table edge. Her face suddenly turned pale as she got up and ran out. Sheila followed her, twisting on her heels, leaving Vallender sitting on his own.

'Take a look at this,' Abbie whispered, spreading the hand-drawn comic strip out. This was no ordinary story in pictures but instead a grim sequence of stick people identified by names above their heads. Daddy was depicted penetrating Rosie with Mummy looking on. Then came Rosie herself, complete with speech bubble, telling the Gang what to do, Darren Greenhalgh, Cherry Pickering, Charlie Hunter and Emma Mason. Next, the three antique dolls, Mary, Abigail and Lazarus, drawn smaller, but posed the way Abbie had found them at Goosefoot Cottage. Then the final square, Rosie pushing her mother down the cottage stairs and 'this is wot I did' scrawled in big letters underneath.

For a whole minute neither woman spoke.

'I can't believe it. It's got to be a hoax. Someone else

has done this,' Abbie whispered. But the pseudo-nun and her story came to mind, everything tying up, and in that moment she was filled with an unutterable bleakness.

'She's just a little kid,' protested Sheila.

'We've said that before, remember?'

'So what are we going to do now?'

'Tell Uncle Graham and Sue. They've got Flora to think about.' Abbie felt a creeping numbness as evil's vapour seemed to billow closer.

'Come on, Abbie, you've done your best for her. Let it go now. It's too dangerous.' She glanced over at Vallender and then back to her friend. 'By the way, is he number two? Your reserve?'

Abbie mock glared and gave her a shove. 'No, he's my boss. I told you.'

Mrs Turling the Tuesday cleaner, speckled as a summer pudding, emerged from the kitchen, reminding Sheila that her nephew would be along by six to help out in the bar again. She then gathered up her bags and waved goodbye as Abbie dialled the Arbours and made nervous contact with Graham.

'Where are you both off to?' asked Vallender, pouring himself another glass from the bottle.

Sheila gave him her version of a seductive smile. 'We've got to go and pick up some stuff from the Cash and Carry. It's late night opening tonight.' She surprised herself by lying so convincingly. One arm was already in her jacket, the other flapping loose behind her. 'We should be back by eleven, but please lock up after Ricky's gone.' Sheila's lipstick was reapplied without a mirror, then she snapped her bag shut. 'There's a liver and bacon hotpot that just needs reheating, if you want it. Oh, and by the way, we don't know when Simon'll be getting back.'

'Who's Simon?' Vallender asked.

'Just one of my other guests.' But he likes a drop in the evening, so he might be the worse for wear.'

'That'll make two of us then.' Vallender stretched and yawned as Abbie and Sheila exchanged glances. 'Take care,' he said, and meant it as Ricky Turling duly arrived and refilled the espresso machine with coffee.

And, with its furry dice swinging dementedly, the Cortina lurched over the gravel and headed east, while Abbie's eyes scoured the Walsoken Road for any sign of Simon.

25 April 1862

A crowd of mostly women wait on the wet earth below the Bank. Worms, I call them. Black worms that this Fen's never had, until this day. Some have come by the Great Eastern, some by cart but most on foot, I can tell, and all for one purpose. I recognize Uncle Poynton. He's trying to reach me, shouting something till I hear it. He says he's my real Pappy then disappears before the crowd can take his ears off his head . . . So what am I to make of that?

Fifty

'ROSIE DOESN'T KNOW about her mother's disappearance yet, thank goodness.' Uncle Graham led Abbie and Sheila into the kitchen and pulled out three chairs. Herbs and onions hung from old curing hooks and something nutritious simmered on the stove.

'I'd leave telling her for the time being,' Abbie said, looking round for any sign of the child.

'OK, but it's very odd, that. She's never once mentioned either of her parents, and of course that makes Flora all the more curious.'

'It would do.' Sheila fumbled for a cigarette, then decided against it.

'Look, I think you ought to see this.' Abbie passed over the pink note. 'It came in the post today.'

The art historian turned it over in his hand. 'She must be nicking my stamps,' he said, then yelled, 'Susan!'

'I'll get her.' Abbie was already by the door.

'No, wait. We can't risk leaving the girls alone together . . .' He suddenly looked ten years older. 'D is for Devil, the cause of all woe . . . and the Devil has too many siblings . . .'

Abbie stared in astonishment. 'Where d'you get that from?'

'A collection of cautionary verse I saw in Lincoln once. Nineteenth-century, I think.'

'Hi.' Susan Parker appeared in a denim pinafore dress, with the two little girls alongside. 'I was just on my way downstairs. What's the matter?'

Rosie stared at Abbie and Sheila as though they were strangers. She looked plumper now, her eyes huge behind fun glasses embellished with a great hooked nose. She wore a green cardigan over a yellow dress the colour of buttercups and socks to match. Abbie wanted to hold her tight, to say she understood, but the child's letter was in full view. Rosie spotted it at once.

'Did you really push your mummy down the stairs?' Abbie whispered, but the child tore away from them and ran through the door, her screams echoing until the house fell suddenly silent.

'O Christ, that's done it.' Sheila murmured.

'Flora! Come here!' Graham shouted at his departing daughter, and the biddable child ran back to them.

Then Abbie moved. She walked through the house from light into darkness, where suddenly the shaded lawn became hooded shrub, still damp out of the late sun and littered with abandoned playthings scattered in mayhem. She saw Rosie's joke spectacles, like some grotesque souvenir, and ran on under the trees yelling until she was hoarse.

Here an old shed surrounded with nettles leaned rotting to the ground, there a new but uprooted 'For Sale' sign. She barely noticed these as she stormed through the thickening foliage.

'Abbie?' said a male voice.

She spun round, Quinn never far from her thoughts. But it was Uncle Graham pushing his way between dock and ivy, with fresh scratches on his cheek. 'Listen, we've got to let her go.'

'You can't! Not now! She's safe here.'

'Believe me, Abbie, it's for the best. Anyhow, I assumed that's why you're both here – to collect her.'

'We came to warn you, that was all.' Her voice faltered. 'What about her father? He'll kill her.'

'And us too, more than likely. You should have been straight with us.'

'I'm sorry. I had to give her a chance.' Abbie snapped a branch in two, loud enough to make birds nearby spray out of the trees. 'Whatever she's done, it isn't really her fault . . .'

'Quite frankly, that isn't my concern. I've got other things on my plate . . .'

Abbie listened to the undergrowth and its shadows. Wild things moving under the skin of humus . . .

'Actually, it's my job,' he continued. 'Come October, I'll be, as they so nicely put it, surplus to requirements.'

Abbie stared. 'That's impossible.' Jobs in higher education were for life. Unlike hers, of course.

'Student class numbers are right down. Too few takers in my subject. Not trendy, you see, at least not with the ones who want to play at being artists themselves . . .'

Abbie thought of her father, desperate to leave his insurance job, yet hanging on for a pension. She knew now he was the lucky one. At least he had a *choice*.

Suddenly her uncle picked up the 'For Sale' sign and flung it even deeper into the brambles. 'Damned thing was only up two days and we had people crawling all over the place. I couldn't take it.'

Abbie frowned. 'Did any of them see Rosie?'

But he wasn't listening. Tears stung behind his glasses, the worst scenario yet to unfold.

'D'you know, I decided I couldn't bear the thought of leaving here. After all it's where Flora was born and Sue adores it.' His voice trembled. 'Still, we'll see if we can manage here somehow. We get a year's grace with the mortgage . . . time to pay a few things off.'

'So Rosie was the last thing you needed. I'm sorry,' Abbie said. 'I was stuck in a corner too. I had to do something . . . O God, Uncle Graham, where d'you think she is now?'

'You should have warned us about that too.'

'What?'

'That she likes running away. We were worried sick Flora would follow her . . .'

Abbie felt her stomach turn to lead. She'd not helped anyone by her actions. In fact, all her clever planning had just created more problems.

'Last week, she was found alone up on the gallops,' her uncle continued in a solemn tone. 'One of the girls had the sense to bring her home. I keep saying thank God she didn't take her to the police instead. We'd all have been in it then. In the end I pretended Rosie was my niece, but I don't like having to lie, Abbie.'

'I know. I'm really sorry.'

His voice softened. 'Now don't worry too much. She'll come back. Rosie likes Sue's home cooking too much. At least we know some of the problems now, and I've got a few things off my chest.'

'Uncle Graham, just tell me something.'

'Go on,' he said wearily, feeling a tear warm his cheek.

'I know this sounds totally mad, but have you or Sue or even Flora heard any kind of strange laughing?'

'I don't know what you mean.'

'I mean back in the house or outside. Like a woman deranged.'

Graham Parker frowned. 'No. Nothing like that.'

They set off back to the house, where evening sunlight freckled the edge of the lawn.

Three figures stood grouped waiting by the porch. Sheila looked anxious, her cigarette smoke blue in the light, but Susan looked almost relieved. Abbie hurried towards them, leaving Uncle Graham behind. Her hair was everywhere, her suit scagged by thorns, with no sign of the Holtbury badge.

'I've got to phone the police and tell them she's gone.' She was panicking now.

'No, we've got to leave them out of this,' her uncle said firmly behind her. 'There's too much at stake for everyone.'

Abbie turned to face him, despair darkening her face. Another trap had been sprung, and she and Rosie were caught in it together.

*They've piled up what's left of my hair
and covered my scar with lime which
makes it feel as if a scythe is stuck deep
in my cheek, bringing Death closer.
Even the rain cannot help it, and I see
children watching as Gloatby binds my
hands to my sides – the hands that
have worked and changed the very
ground they're standing on. And for
what, I ask? Not for Grace or Harriet,
that's for sure. They have gained less
than nothing.*

Fifty-one

ABBIE AND SHEILA left Dovenham late, driving into a sudden storm that swilled rain across the roads and threw spray into the sky. Neither spoke and as their worries about Rosie grew, so the pink envelope became more crumpled in the hotelier's hand. Nearing Wednesday Bridge, the thunder's grumbling changed to a roar after each split of lightning and Sheila slowed the Cortina into second, careful not to let it stop. Petrol was down to a quarter full with not a garage in sight. She tried not to look at the gauge, instead trusting the old crate to get them back home with a private prayer and a surreptitious pat on the steering wheel.

No one was out in this awful weather, and as they passed through silent villages and hamlets set like tiny islands in the sea of fields, Abbie noticed upper-room lights being turned off. At least the inhabitants had a bed to count on.

Simon felt the storm too. Its beginnings teased his hair and the early ominous raindrops landed on his bare shoulders one by one, until he was wet all over. The wind picked up and the sky rolled itself into a sudden and premature darkness empty of birds. Yet he wasn't alone. *She* was with him, an icy shadow invisible yet magnetic, pulling him up towards the path above the poplars.

He was beyond shivering, his body so rigidified that the climb was painful, his legs like wooden struts. But *she* didn't care. Why should she? What difference did one more witness make?

His head felt like a punchball. Six whiskies at the Gull and Plough and the same again at the King of Tides had given new meaning to the word throb, and he'd then driven too. Christ, he'd actually managed to get from Sinfold to Black Fen without being stopped, but where were all his clothes and the gun? Where was the bloody car itself now? He'd forgotten, and it didn't matter, because that was his transport to Gatwick on Saturday. And Gatwick meant going back to Captain Oliver and the Signals Brigade. Then death in a lime pit somewhere, no brains, no stomach . . .

He reached the highest point of Morpeth Bank, the first sea defence built with the muscle of Europe. Only once, before the Great Exhibition, had the waters breached at the join with Herringtoft, delivering six inches of mud to Black Fen. So an anxious Hanneke Schaap had told him when Horace Scott had finally left her to attend to his pheasants. And that wasn't all . . .

Simon crawled naked on all fours, the rain now sluicing off his back, birching his buttocks, and still that presence clung like an incubus, driving him onwards blindly, recklessly, as if to deprive him of all his thoughts, all his memories. But certain images stayed obstinately fixed: Abbie, little Rosie, sometimes his mother, and then the woman he'd seen again at Rievely Hall . . .

The housekeeper had kept her head lowered as she'd spoken of her only son, born when she was in service in

Middelburg at the age of sixteen. He who'd loved the
drain builder's granddaughter more than his own young
life. Who'd not lived to see his own boy after the birth,
never held him close to keep him safe from the evil that
had forced Lilith Leakes to hand him over to strangers.
People who might easily now be dead.

'And the worms all drowned,' Mrs Schaap had said,
tremblingly quoting from a strange bloodstained note
received just after her son's death at sea, turning her grief
into a mission. But it was a mission, she'd told Simon
weeping openly, that, despite what little Gedney Stimpson had revealed, would never end . . . And that's why
she was given Abbie's name.

Simon stood up and stretched his arms out to that
same blackness, that same obliterating fury, prepared to
plead with Martha Robinson to leave Black Fen in peace.
But before he'd even started, he felt his throat seized, his
hands too, being pulled down and kept close against his
body. He twisted, spinning round and round on the
slopping mud to loosen this tightening, but his feet were
suddenly entrapped as a gruesome cackle reached his ears
and grew, as though bellows-fed, till he thought his mind
would burst.

He'd no hands to stop it, no voice to overlay it. There
was only one thing he could do. With a supreme effort,
he drew himself into a crouch and rolled down the slope,
out of the worst of the gusting rain, away from the
terrible sound that still lingered in his head. He was
among trees weighted down by water, relieving their
surplus on to the land in a vengeful collusion of power.
But at least he was free of that influence and for a few
seconds struggled to work out his bearings.

Suddenly, he felt movement from underneath him,

like that time he'd kipped out at Delphi and awoke to
find his sleeping bag full of ants. But this was something
different. His hand explored his body, then retracted as
he yelled out. He was slowly being covered by maggots.

Flicking at them was no good and in the dark he
could only feel them trailing towards the points of entry,
so he grabbbed a tuft of grass and rubbed at his exposed
skin in frantic frightened motion till it was sore.

Then he ran – smeared by grass stains, glistening with
slime – across Hick's land, somehow missing the squirrel
traps and the rabbit springs, until on the stroke of eleven,
as Quinn reached his Fiesta near Goosefoot, Simon ran
into the glare of the St George's Sails' security light and
hammered on the lounge bar window.

'What the fuck?' Vallender got up from the *Frank Skinner
Show* and peered outside. The temporary barman had
just left and a succession of beers throughout the evening
had mellowed the Holtbury sales director into intermittent sleep. His bleary eyes blinked at the bright naked
figure darting around in front of the hotel and his first
thought was Care in the Community – but this nutter
was calling Abbie and Sheila's names as if he knew them.

'Who the hell are you?' Vallender mouthed behind
the glass. Too many rugby club showers had left the male
body with no surprises for him, but this guy was risking
it. Anyone could have seen him and called the police.

'I'm Simon Cresswell – Abbie's partner. Let me in,
for fuck's sake.'

Partner? This lunatic?

Vallender went to the door, undid the bolts and
opened it on the chain. 'What's her surname?'

'Parker.'

'Where was she based before here?'

'Northampton. God damn you, my balls are dropping off.' Simon's fists were working on the wood.

'Who does she work for now then?'

'Frigging Holtbury's. Give us a break, will you?'

Vallender finally released the chain and stood staring as Simon bounded past him and up the stairs into his bedroom, leaving a trail of boozy breath. He had a good body, though, much better muscle definition than Vallender himself.

'Shit shit shit.' Simon remembered Quinn's gun in the glove compartment, still sitting inside the unlocked car. Vallender listened to the slam of the wardrobe door and the drawers as he found fresh clothes.

'Hey, mate,' the soldier shouted down the stairs. 'Can you do me a big favour?'

'Depends.'

'Where're Abbie and Sheila?'

'Late night shopping. So they said.'

'Look, there's a car I need to retrieve and it's not even mine.'

'Where?'

'Christ knows. Let me think for a minute.' He plunged his head into his hands. Then he remembered that shitty little cottage.

'Over by Goosefoot. Turn left out of here, then second right opposite the newsagents into Smithy Lane. It's at the far end – all on its own.'

Vallender frowned. He felt knackered and this man was clearly pissed out of his skull. Someone had to be there for when Abbie and the other woman got back from the Cash and Carry.

'Keys?' he asked reluctantly.

'I left them inside it.'

'What about your clothes? Do you normally drive round bare-arsed?'

But Simon was thinking of something else. 'There's also a gun in the glove compartment,' he said.

'A gun?' Vallender looked perturbed, but sensed the soldier's desperation.

'Yeah, a Walther, but mum's the word. OK?'

'Lock up after me then.'

Simon came down less quickly than his journey up. He held on to both banisters and Vallender noticed that beneath old jeans his feet were brown with dried mud.

'What the fuck have you been up to?' He drained his beer. 'You look like you've gone paddling in a sewer.'

'I have. Thanks, mate.'

Simon slid the bolts and listened as Vallender's footsteps receded. Then he sat down in the window seat, burying his head in his hands, not that it made any difference to the pumping in his skull. The sound of that woman's laughter had changed him somehow. Osmotically, she had hooked him in, needing him for some purpose he didn't dare think about. It was crunch time for him all right – not just here with Abbie, but in the only career he'd ever pursued. He prayed Vallender would find the gun.

St Mary Magdalene struck eleven-thirty and Simon checked his spare watch. The Breitel was worth ten times as much, so he hoped that this stranger would find it intact as well. He was wondering idly who the other man might be, and what had brought him here to the Sails, when suddenly he was aware of the Cortina in the drive.

*

Abbie stared at Simon's feet and hissed at him to go and wash before Sheila saw them on her newly cleaned carpet. The smell of drink was something else she noticed. He'd been at it big time, she could tell, following him up into his room.

'Where've you bloody been?' he asked her, sitting on the bed and almost keeling over.

'Where have *you* been,' she retorted. 'And where's your car?'

'My own business to the first question, and re the second, some bloke downstairs offered to fetch it for me.'

'Vallender?'

Simon started. 'That pig? Shit!'

Abbie sat down next to him, wrinkling her nose. He stank like a distillery, but she needed to know things. 'He's been acting OK lately. Got a few problems himself, which make me feel a bit sorry for him ... But never mind Mr Vallender, did you get your letter?'

'You? Feeling sorry for him?' Simon said, avoiding the question. 'I don't believe this. After the way he's constantly dumped on you.' He thumped back on the bed.

'Now are you going to tell me about your letter?'

'No.'

'Simon, I've got a right to know.'

He gave up the struggle to resist, leaned against her and blew hot brewer's air on her neck. '*Ja, Ich gehe.*'

There was no ensuing kiss, no further contact. If he was going back, Abbie thought, pulling away, best to let him get on with it. She was no longer any competition for his fighting instincts, or for his father's misplaced ambition. Not now. Not ever. But there was one thing that might make him change his mind.

'Rosie's disappeared.'

Simon sat up. 'Where, for God's sake?'

'I don't know. We went to see her after I got this.' She pulled out the envelope, now little more than damp tissue, with the child's letter stuck hopelessly inside. 'It shows what the Gang did together, obviously under her influence, and how she pushed her mother down the stairs . . .'

'O God.'

'And Uncle Graham's told me not to call the police.'

'I don't fucking believe it.' He'd heard too much. Above all, he craved another whisky. He got up and lurched to the door, and she didn't even try to stop him.

At least my Grace and Harriet will not know the way in which their mother leaves this earth. They both have the Yellow Fever and are not long for it themselves, according to Susannah Buckley who took quite a delight in telling me. A fine thing for a God-mother. In those days I believed in such comforts, but now Satan wills me to place a curse on her and all those at Canal Farm, all at Rievely, all at Black Fen . . .

Fifty-two

ABBIE HAD LISTENED to her clock all night. Normally its ticking lulled her to instant sleep, but her mind kept swimming with fear and foreboding as the northerly rain lashed the window. Simon's news and his bizarre appearance, Rosie's disappearance and Vallender still out there in the storm somewhere, and she herself too tired to respond . . .

At seven o'clock, by the time she'd showered and spruced up her badgeless suit for work that she wouldn't be doing, Vallender still hadn't showed. No message, nothing. Without any prompting, Simon sprinted round to Smithy Lane. He'd thought at first her boss might have nicked the car and done a bunk, even though his own Xantia was still parked at the hotel. After all, if the man had serious problems he might not have been thinking straight. But the moment he turned the corner by the phone box he knew something was badly wrong.

The red Fiesta was there all right, but inside it, in the driver's seat, Simon could see a shadow slumped over the wheel.

'Holy shit!' He pulled the door open, forgetting about disturbing evidence or that whoever was responsible might still be hanging around. His stomach heaved at the

amount of blood from the shoulder wound that had
darkened on the man's thigh.

'Vallender?' he whispered, glad not to have to use the
familiarity of his first name. 'You poor sod. I'm sorry.'

He tested for a pulse – it was weak but still going.
Simon pressed the car's horn, hoping someone in the
council houses some distance away would respond. But
he was on his own and it was all his bloody fault. He
next tried the call box nearby. OUT OF ORDER was
Sellotaped across it, and he cursed himself for leaving his
mobile back at the hotel. Then, miraculously, the newsagent's youngest son came by on his bike, delivering
papers.

'Go and call an ambulance!' Simon yelled at him.
'999!' The boy jettisoned his bag and pedalled back to
the shop standing upright.

Vallender was still alive – only just. Anyone less fit,
the ambulance crew confirmed, would have been a goner
by now. At one stage, Simon ran into the rectory garden
and threw up in the bushes. Meanwhile, DI Stock in a
green anorak and cords, had arrived and organized his
forensics expert and another detective to check out the
car.

'What kind of gun was it?' Simon asked innocently.

'Sorry. Can't reveal that yet. But I do have a theory,'
Stock said, watching as Etchells bent down to examine
the sills.

'It was Quinn – thinking it was me.'

'We're not discounting that, but in these cases sometimes all is not as it seems.'

'Oh, come on. He's on the bloody prowl.'

'He won't be the only one. We're starting a search at
nine by Snake's Mouth.'

Snake's Mouth? What a terrible name, Simon thought.
O Jesus. And guilt that was never far away spilled over
into a confession.

'Look, I was rat-arsed last night and when I got back
to the hotel I asked Vallender to go and collect my gear.
It was all in the car.'

Stock stared at him, contempt curling his top lip.
'And?'

'Quinn was probably lying in wait. After all, he knows
the car. He took a shot at it up at Haletoft, remember?
Trouble is, this time it was Vallender inside.'

'What gear do you mean exactly?'

'My watch, a Breitel, damn it, and my clothes.'

'So what were you wearing when you left the vehicle?'

Simon blushed as the two other men looked up.
'Birthday-suit job if you must know. You see, at the time
I didn't give a shit . . .'

'No, I don't see, and you'll need to come to Snutterwick on Saturday morning to make a statement. Your car
meanwhile will be taken away for examination.' Any trace
of earlier cordiality had gone. This was business – on his
terms.

'But I'm due to fly back to my unit that evening. I
was going to return it to Wisbech on Friday.' Simon kept
stubbing his boot against the car's tyre.

'Your problem mate. You set this one up.' Stock
checked the Fiesta's doors were locked, then radioed for
a recovery vehicle and told the other detective to stay put
until it arrived.

'It was the thought of leaving my girlfriend here that
did it.'

The excuse sounded sad, and Stock treated it as such,
getting into the police car without replying. He then

revved the engine, turned almost on two wheels and sped past Herringtoft.

Two stories broke on the local news that Saturday morning and, in the St George's Sails, Sheila stopped in her tracks with plates of breakfast balanced in both hands as the newsreader relayed information on the Vallender shooting and the continuing hunt for the Reverend Quinn.

The scene of the incident in Smithy Lane was followed by an artist's sketch of the vicar himself, without his clerical collar. Those hooded eyes sent a shiver up her back as the report continued: 'The police are anxious to trace the Reverend Peter Quinn of St Mary Magdalene Church in Black Fen in connection with this incident. They warn he could be armed and highly dangerous, so on no account should any member of the public try to apprehend him . . .'

'O God,' Sheila whispered to herself, but in blissful ignorance two hungry crew members from the *Winding Star* yacht were already helping themselves to the food as it landed on their table. She stared down at the two women, thinking that one of them could just as easily have been a man in disguise, but she didn't stay to find out.

Abbie hadn't yet eaten anything at all. Just the smell of cooking from the kitchen was enough to put her off, while an unspoken terror for Rosie's current plight hindered her normal thinking.

She waited until Simon had finished his toast, then drove him to Snutterwick through the rising mist. She was tense and silent while he concentrated on how to make his story more believable. When she finally dropped

SALLY SPEDDING

him off at the police station she suggested they meet up in Burger King at eleven o'clock. Then she got out her street map. This showed Snutterwick General Hospital to be on the edge of town, and when she arrived ten minutes later, was told by the nurse in Reception that Rodney Vallender was now out of intensive care and had spent a comfortable night in the recovery ward. He seemed peaceful and stable, his deep blue eyes open but unseeing. The staff nurse assumed Abbie was his girlfriend as he'd murmured her name twice in the ambulance. But no, Abbie'd put her straight, he had a wife and daughter, then gave them as much information as she knew herself, about his job at Holtbury's and what he was doing at the Sails in the first place.

She left him staring blankly after her, and before she reached the ward door she turned round to see him smile then turn his head away.

At ten past eleven, from her seat by the window of Burger King, she noticed Simon crossing the road towards her – his hair light gold in the misted sun, his body language spelling out purpose. Yet to her, on his day of leaving, he was little more than a mirage. Just another ghost coming to haunt her . . .

He kissed her cheek then led her towards the counter where the smell of frying beef was making her even more nauseous.

'Stock gave me a dressing down. Really enjoyed himself,' he said, checking out the colourful menu overhead.

'Clever you,' she said slowly. 'So that means you're still going to Germany?'

'Look, Abs, I'll be back in August. Then we can pick

up where we left off.' He tried taking her hand, but she pulled it away. Then one of the servers took their order. 'We should find out more about Lilith Leakes's son. At least I now know who the grandmother is . . .' He paid, then picked up the tray of two coffees and a quarterpounder and returned to the table.

Abbie shook her head as she followed him. This was no longer going to work.

'It'll be too late then. Don't you understand?' she said, sitting down next to him. Her eyes grew wild, her cheeks colouring, and if he was honest with his feelings, with what had happened to him up on the bank, and subsequently to Vallender, he knew she was right.

'You were a total pig to send him out on that errand last night. D'you know that?'

Simon put his forehead on the table and a couple nearby turned to stare.

'How was I supposed to know that cunt Quinn was going to be in that exact bloody spot? If I said sorry to you a million times, it wouldn't be enough.'

She looked at the tiny furrow between his brows, his anxious eyes.

'Do you think he'll be all right?'

'Who? Vallender?'

'Who else?'

'Course. He's a rugby wallah, isn't he?'

'But he'll need something to live for, won't he? Everybody does.'

Simon stopped drinking, his styrene cup in mid-air. 'So what does *that* mean?' He put it down slowly, watching her intently.

'Nothing. It's just he's had a rough deal recently.'

'No more than me.' He got out his wallet and

produced her photo. 'You don't know how many bloody times I've looked at this when there was nothing else to keep me going. And I mean nothing else. Stuck out in some godforsaken dump surrounded by either twats or control freaks . . .' He had raised his voice, unaware of the neighbouring shoppers' glances.

He moved closer to her, his knee touching hers, his arm a warm harness round her neck, but Abbie didn't respond. He put her picture away. 'Whatever, Abs, you've got to trust me.'

She got up and went to stand outside, letting the world drift by her unnoticed on the damp pavement. When he emerged, she followed him like an automaton to the car.

Later, she could hear him upstairs doing his packing with the bang-bang of anything that opened and shut. He'd always been noisy like that. In the past it had been a joke. Now it was a sick joke.

Abbie sat in the window seat she had shared with Vallender the previous day and looked out to where his Xantia still stood, dominating her Fiat. She found herself willing him to recover safely, and then what? She kept her eyes shut as if that might reveal to her some kind of future, but all she saw was a dark void – ready and waiting for the next time Martha Robinson chose to fill it . . .

Not so long ago she'd have gone out and scoured the flatlands, even swum the sea, until she'd found a trace of Rosie. But it was as if some things had now been torn out of her for ever: love, desire, the need for a child of her own, all lost to the forces of darkness, beyond her reach. Beyond anybody's reach.

She heard another drawer shut, another open. Simon was obviously doing a final check that nothing was being left behind. Why shouldn't he? The next time he turned up, she wouldn't be there. It was as simple as that.

Sheila brought over an ashtray and sat down. Abbie noticed the woman's hand trembling and gave her a smile which the hotelier rightly guessed was a piece of good acting.

'Don't worry about things now,' Abbie said. 'It'll all work out.'

'I hope not the way I'm thinking.' Sheila inhaled and kept the smoke in her mouth for longer than usual. 'People round here are getting cold feet. There's too many other pubs in the area for this one to matter much, what with those poor kids dying of malaria and a murderer on the loose.'

She turned to watch Simon drag his black bag down the stairs and leave it by the door. There it squatted symbolically, bulging with the evidence of his imminent desertion. The two women ignored him, because neither knew what to say, and after he'd written something in the Visitors' Book and left four twenty-pound notes on the bar, he went straight for the outside door, hefted the bag on his shoulder and left.

Abbie didn't even turn round to look. She couldn't. Just listened to the sound of tyres on the forecourt, the sudden lurch of gear, then the ensuing silence.

'Go and see what he's put in the book,' Sheila said, exhaling.

Abbie walked over and found the page. He'd written, 'I love you, Abs. Will you marry me?'

He also wills me to curse in His name
everyone whose eyes are on me this day,
and their issue. To curse those who
stole away my only playthings and those
who would use my own issue's resting
place for profit. This I gladly do . . .

Fifty-three

WHEN ABBIE ARRIVED at the Show Home on Monday morning, she found two bunches of flowers propped up against the door. She turned over the label on the first – a spray of pinks and matching gerberas, and saw the note 'RV, thanks for seeing me.' The second bunch from Simon, via Interflora, was composed of ten red, newly opened roses fleshed out by ferns. It too, had a card. 'Back soon. Simon. XXX.'

Abbie arranged them in separate pots at each end of her desk, then sat down between their different scents to collect her thoughts. Suddenly a small figure in black, with a large bag, appeared outside, as if from nowhere, and waited to be invited in. At first Abbie feared this was a shrunken Martha Robinson standing there and was ready to take flight, but she soon recognized the old housekeeper from Rievely Hall. Hanneke Schaap was in a state of considerable distress.

'Can I get you something?' Abbie pulled out a chair and chose to ignore company policy on making personal remarks. 'You don't look very well, if you'll forgive my saying so.'

'I'm not, thank you. But that is what fear does to me, Miss Parker. Yes, I would like a cup of tea if that is possible.'

'No problem.' Abbie moved quickly as though the hot drink might prove a matter of life and death, listening as her visitor pulled various papers from her bag. When she returned with a cup and saucer she gasped. Spread out on the desk were what appeared to be the same plate-camera photographs she'd seen displayed in the church: Martha Robinson and her girls.

'These are the originals which I found in the colonel's study, so rather precious,' Mrs Schaap began. 'I had copies made, you see . . .'

'And you sent them to the two local churches?' Abbie interrupted, unwilling to look again at the all-too-familiar figure who, as before, dominated the rest.

'Yes, I had to. I had to let people know . . . To warn them.' Her eyes brimmed with tears.

'What about that strange verse that was displayed with them here at the church?' Abbie asked. 'You know, D is for Devil the cause of all woe etcetera?'

The housekeeper frowned, her lips beginning to twitch as if she might cry at any moment. 'I have no idea. Oh, how awful, how awful . . .'

'You're very brave, Mrs Schaap.' Abbie looked out at Plot 2, though unable to focus on it. She didn't need to ask why, as sitting next to her was another poor soul seemingly frightened out of her wits. The woman could barely stop her cup from rattling.

'Tell me your side of things, if it'll help,' Abbie said, fishing in the drawer for her Holtbury pad. 'I swear I won't tell anyone else – but it could save lives.'

'All right, but Colonel Scott must never know, nor anyone else for that matter.' His housekeeper took a weary breath, then set down her cup and folded her twitching hands. 'He's only interested in money, you see.

Me and the others he took on were never paid more than a pittance. But then that's not the reason I'm here, is it?' Her old eyes searched Abbie's face before she continued. 'You see, he doesn't want anything that smells of trouble locally, anything that might lower the value of his assets.' She glanced out of the window, and its light showed her nose translucent, her neck worn into deep dry folds. 'You watch it here, now. He'll be trying to buy this site up again if things get out of hand, just like the Scotts snatched everything off the poor folk here during the Enclosures.' The old woman took a deep rasping breath to enable her to continue. 'Of course, when he originally sold it to your firm he was rubbing his hands with glee, wasn't he? But not for long, the way things are going round here money can't keep secrets hidden forever . . .' Her voice suddenly sounded more Lincolnshire than Dutch, her tone becoming ever more bleak . . .

'What secrets do you mean? Go on, Mrs Schaap,' Abbie urged, as one of the plasterers, sporting Union Jack shades went by smiling in at her, thinking she'd at last pulled a punter.

'I can't.' Her visitor glanced out at plot 2 opposite. 'I'm in fear for my life, as it is.'

'You should come and stay at the hotel for a while,' Abbie offered, disguising her frustration, but not wishing to upset the housekeeper any further. 'At least you'd feel a bit safer and have someone to talk to. Sheila Livingstone's great company if you don't mind sharing space with a walking chimney.'

'Thank you, I'd like that.' Mrs Schaap unzipped the front portion of her hold-all and put all the items back inside. 'I don't think I could stay in the Hall another night – not after what I've done. As you can see, I've come prepared.' She indicated the bag.

'That's right.' Abbie thought the woman was looking better already and went to switch the kettle on again.

'I did like your young man,' the widow said suddenly when Abbie reappeared from the kitchen. 'Where's he now?'

'He's had to go back to Germany. He's an army lieutenant.'

The housekeeper paused, then said, 'Oh dear, dear.'

'Why do you say that?'

'Well, look what happened when my Pieter left me that last time. There was nothing wrong with his ship, the *Koning Willem*, it was almost new, the sea was calm, nothing around, no wind, no threat of any storm in the North Sea, but suddenly, there came a wave which welled up high as a mountain . . .'

My God. Abbie listened with fear quickening her pulse.

'*She* took him. I know it.' Mrs Schaap's bony fists thumped the desk. 'She wanted to punish him for being happy. For having the son *she* couldn't have . . . He was only twenty . . .'

Just me and my boy? So what did that mean? Abbie spooned sugar into the cups, trying to make sense of it all as the old woman carried on speaking.

'That's why Lilith Leakes gave me your name just before she was killed. I think in some strange way she could foresee she was going to die and she wanted me to make contact with you. But of course I couldn't risk it, what with Colonel Scott already suspicious of me, so I asked Mr Stimpson instead. He lives out of the area, you

see . . .' Her voice tailed away as suddenly the daylight
outside dimmed, the short bursts of sunlight surrendered
to an eerie darkness that crept like an eclipse into the
Show Home making the old woman indistinguishable
from the furniture. Abbie screamed, and forgetting the
boiling kettle tried to reach the old woman.

'Mrs Schaap!' she shrieked. 'Where are you?' Her
arms thrashed about, trying to find her, but they encountered nothing familiar. No desk, no flowers, no filing
cabinets or chairs. It was like being on some empty coast
at night with just the sound of waves, the slurp of silt
being sucked underneath and the terrible smell of death
everywhere.

'Fucking hell.' The plasterer, back from an early
lunch, ventured to the doorway then stepped back in
horror. He bent down to take a closer look at her, his
tuna sandwich rising in his throat. 'Abbie? It's me, Tom.
Can you hear me?' Then his attention was distracted by
something over on plot 2, where, although the black
liners were pinned down, a vast dark shape spiralled over
the foundations. Not just a figure or even a shadow, this
seemed powered by some huge cosmic energy and was
coming towards him like a tornado. He flung himself to
the ground, feeling the evil in it touch his whole body
and, worse, the mad laughter deep within it threatening
to unhinge his mind . . .

The power was mysteriously down – no phones, not
even mobiles, and no electricity either, so in a state of
terror the roofer Handel Myers ran to the newsagent's.
Never before had he witnessed such a thing, or felt a
storm like it, though used to working outdoors for over
thirty years. The shop owner put a cold towel on his
forehead, then tried phoning 999. She tutted about

everything going wrong in Black Fen ever since that building site had commenced.

When Tom Nicholas, the plasterer, opened his eyes, he found everyone else had done a bunk, just left their equipment lying around, while on plot 16 the Kumatsu's engine was still running. He watched a young woman in a navy suit emerge from the office, her feet and legs seemingly covered in green slime. Behind her, the same muck oozed down the steps and on to the path.

'Jesus.' Abbie had almost lost her voice. 'I can't find her.'

'Who?'

'Mrs Schaap. You saw her. She was with me – in there.'

The big man sat up. He couldn't remember anything.

'Shit, man, who the fuck am I?' He sprang to his feet and beat his head with both hands. 'Who the fuck am I?' Then, still yelling, he belted out of Kingfisher Rise.

Abbie picked up his shades, wiped them clean and began to weep.

'Then shall ye do unto him, as he had thought to have done unto his brother: so shalt thou put the evil away from among you. And those which remain shall hear, and fear, and shall henceforth commit no more evil among you. And thine eye shall not pity; but life shall go for life.'

Fifty-four

AFTER HER HARROWING interview with Aldreth and O'Halloran in the Portakabin, in which she could barely make herself understood, Abbie tried to contact the rural dean, but even his answerphone was off. She looked in despair at the Show Home, its façade now hidden under sheeting and the neat drive awash with stuff too thick, too green, to be just marsh water.

She walked past its putrid smell, much the same as from Lilith Leakes's bags, and only when she reached the Punto parked outside the site did she let herself breathe freely.

Half an hour later, after a long hot shower at the hotel, careful to keep out of Sheila's way, she decided to call in at Snutterwick General now that Vallender was on the mend. When she found him, he was sitting up in bed with a bowl of jelly in his lap.

'Your flowers were lovely. Thanks, but you shouldn't have.' She couldn't say they'd actually drowned in filthy water that had come in from nowhere. 'I'm sorry these aren't in a bottle.' Abbie laid a bunch of grapes on his locker, 'but we'll have some of that too when you're allowed.' She glanced at a photo of a chubby little girl on a pony and thought of the missing Rosie. 'Is that Gemma? She looks really sweet.'

'She is.' He blew Abbie a kiss. 'Hey, it's great to see you.'

His wounded shoulder was padded out like a baseball player's, and Abbie noticed how his pyjama sleeve had been slit to accommodate it.

'So, any news?' he asked.

'Not sure where to start, and I've been told not to get you worked up.'

He grinned. 'Please, feel free, any time.'

'They closed the whole site for three days, just to get things back to normal. Has Holtbury's said anything to you?'

'Not a bloody whisper. Three whole days? Why, what happened there?'

'I'll tell you later. It's just that my office is still a stinking mess and half the men have cleared off.' The details of Mrs Schaap's disappearance and the plasterer's apparent fit of derangement could wait.

He frowned, then reached for her hand as the bed pan trolley began its rounds, fortunately passing him by.

'Is it that Martha Robinson thing again?'

'Yes. And we need to do something. Urgently.'

'Such as?'

'Digging up plot 2 for a start. To find out if there's anything to do with the past hidden there . . .'

'Don't be daft. It's just getting sorted.'

Abbie leaned towards him. He smelt of Dettol and liniment. 'OK. An exorcism then. And if you're better by Sunday, will you come to the church with me?'

'You're joking!' It was loud enough for other patients to notice.

'I'm not. I've got to pester the rural dean about it

again, and I need moral support, especially as you're my line manager.'

He spooned some jelly between his lips, just like a five-year-old all over again.

'What about that boyfriend of yours? Won't he do?'

Abbie turned away, that message in the Visitors' Book engraved on her brain. 'He's away at the moment. And he's my fiancé, actually.' Omitting to mention that she'd not yet replied to his proposal.

Vallender stopped eating. 'Since when?'

'Since Saturday.'

'Oh.' He lay back on the pillow. 'Does that call for congratulations?'

'If you like.'

'OK. When I'm better.'

'Now, say you will come along with me.' She pressed both his hands. They felt warm, brushed with fine dark hairs.

'Look, the last time I passed through holy portals was to marry Carol Ann Smallbone, spinster of Ecton Brook. Never again.' He licked the spoon and set it down. 'Wrong guy, I'm afraid.'

'It's not just for me,' Abbie pleaded.

'No way. Far as I'm concerned, the way things are going, I'll be lining up with all the other dole scabbers in about six weeks. How will seeing some bloody vicar help?'

'Please!'

The nurse advancing towards the next bed with a rectal thermometer gave Abbie a stern look.

'OK, OK. But only if I'm feeling better, mind. It sounds too much like a bloody health hazard.'

'We can take along my notes and a site plan . . .'

'Whatever you say, boss.' He looked at her intently, his eyes the blue of warmer seas, and she felt she was sinking with every second. Simon had gone. Rosie was still out there somewhere. Her mother too was unreachable beyond anywhere – unlike Martha Robinson . . .

'Have you any idea how long they're keeping you here?' she asked.

'Should be Friday evening, fingers crossed.'

She pecked his cheek. 'I'll check the exact time so I can collect you then.'

'Excellent.' He smiled, swung his legs from under the sheet and, as the nurse watched, hobbled for the bathroom. Just to show her he was immortal, Abbie thought, waving after him. But he was gone.

'How you doing, kid?' Sheila let her into the empty lounge bar.

'So-so.'

'He must have nine lives, your dishy friend. Is he married?' Her smoke got into Abbie's face by mistake. She was trying too hard to be cheerful and Abbie didn't need it.

'They're splitting up. He's got a little girl.'

'Why is nothing in life ever bloody simple?'

'Because it isn't.' Abbie sighed, not looking at all like someone who'd recently received a proposal of marriage.

'Well, hang on in there. I think he's a babe. God knows, we could do with a bit of light relief round here. How long's he staying?'

'The hospital said he needs at least a week's convalescence. After that I'm not sure. But he's hardly light relief, Sheila, I can tell you.'

'Well, he's a nice change of scenery, whatever.'

Scenery?

Abbie thought of dark wet gulleys, the suck of the marsh inside her office. She shivered. No amount of cleaning had managed to lift the muck off her suit, even her watch face was still ringed with green.

'I'm really scared, if you must know.'

'Join the club.' Sheila turned away to exhale. 'That weirdo'll be coming in here in disguise next, and how will I be able to tell? He might walk up to the bar and order a bloody drink.'

'Couldn't you shut up shop for a bit after next Friday when Vallender's out of hospital? Go and visit your ma? We'd look after the place.' Abbie said bravely. The 'we' was unplanned.

'No, but thanks all the same.'

'Well, think about it. At least I'd have company here.'

Sheila smiled. 'Ah, I get it. A little love nest while the cat's away . . .'

Abbie blushed deep to her roots. Had she been that obvious? She who was unofficially spoken for? She felt such a traitor that she went upstairs with her mobile to phone Simon and make reparations.

Number engaged. She clicked off. This was the third time. Maybe they'd already gone into the war zone, but there'd been nothing about that on the news. Maybe his CO didn't want his men pestered by next of kin, for that's what she was now. He'd said so, himself.

Abbie lay rigid on the bed, suddenly too nervous to close her eyes, and when she heard water gushing in the cistern her heart thudded in her chest. She kept the mobile under her pillow, just in case, as the night deepened. And not far away a distraught Michelle Pick-

ering cried herself to sleep in her daughter's little bedroom shrine.

At three a.m. Abbie's phone rang under her ear. She
reached for it and pulled up the aerial, her first words
to Simon ready. However something looked different.
Instead of a normal phone number, the luminous panel
showed 666. And when she finally pressed 'Receive',
Martha Robinson's victorious laugh reached her ear.

Abbie wanted to yell in fury, but held back. She'd
learned one thing: to respond was to let the Demon
think she'd won. Look what confrontation had done for
poor Mrs Schaap, she thought, groping her way down
the corridor past Simon's empty room to Sheila's, where
she climbed gratefully into the other woman's bed.

'Does that feel the right place?' Thomas Gloatby enquires of me without a shred of irony. He moves the knot to one side and then the other, until I tell him it will make no difference. It will still take me to the last darkness ... I remember saying years ago if I had my time again I'd have slipped Moeder's coat cord around my neck tight like a mooring knot. And so my time will come again, and I'll see to it that all the worms will be drowned like before ...

Fifty-five

ON FRIDAY AT seven o'clock in the evening, Snutter-wick General waved goodbye to one of its more charismatic patients. He'd left behind more than one broken heart and puzzlement among his nurses as to why the lucky Miss Parker, who'd come to collect him, hadn't seemed more demonstrative. They stood at the door of the A&E unit as the Fiat bore him away, waving until he was out of sight.

Vallender turned to Abbie and grinned. 'I've decided, your lieutenant is forgiven.'

'And me?' Abbie asked.

'What for?'

'If I hadn't booked you in at the Sails, you'd never have even met him or got yourself shot.'

Vallender leaned over, still smelling of antiseptic. The dressing was smaller now, but she'd bought a shirt one size larger than normal to cover it.

'I wanted to be there, remember?'

Abbie smiled. It felt good to have someone next to her, driving back towards the Wash, but as they passed the Kingfisher Rise development a familiar shiver triggered up her spine.

'I'll help you clear up in there tomorrow if you like,'

he offered. 'Do you want to take a look now and check on what we'll need?'

'No, thanks. I couldn't face it.'

The gates to the site were closed but not locked, as the police were regularly in and out, talking to those still left on the workforce and taking samples from the Show Home floor. It was the last place she wanted to be just now – with or without him.

When they reached the hotel, they found Sheila had left a welcome note, saying she'd put a bottle of Chardonnay in the fridge. She had to go to Lincoln to replace her car and have dinner with an old mate from her schooldays.

'Are you allowed to drink?' Abbie had brought two glasses over to the window table, but not before she'd taken the Visitors' Book into the kitchen and torn out the page with Simon's message.

'Yes, please.'

After two glasses each, a mellow warmth embraced them as the light outside turned to dusk. They sat close together, arms and legs touching, aware of a frisson from flesh to flesh, which grew stronger every minute without either speaking.

Suddenly he stood up and held out his hand. Together they climbed the stairs and she unlocked her bedroom door. As she closed the curtains she looked out to the quayside, where the *Constanza*'s security beam probed shore and water in ever-widening arcs of light, while the old wherry *Juliana*, emptied of coal, lay up-river and breathed with the waves as her watch nodded into sleep.

She had helped Vallender undress, then he watched her, ready, his smile like an arc of moon as she slipped out of her clothes. Abbie felt she'd remember all this for ever. This turning point just ten steps away. He held out his arms and she floated like a spirit into his eyes. When she woke, she found his body hard against hers and afterwards they lay silent, buried in the room's dimness. Then he spoke.

'Abbie?'

'Yes?'

'I need to tell you something.' He touched first her arm, then her hair. She rolled away from him so even that little space would make it easier. She knew what was coming. When had she known anything else?

'It's Gemma.'

'Oh?'

'In hospital, when they were uncertain if I was going to make it, they asked me about my family and if there was anyone in particular I wanted to see . . .'

'And?' She could read the script even before he'd written it. In the old days she might have made things more difficult for him, but now she just wanted it over with – out in the open. Now, she'd got Rosie to think about. It had been far too long with the child missing, out there somewhere in the dark . . .

'So I said Gemma. But no way was the bitch going to bring her. Then I realized I could have died there and never seen her again . . .'

'It's OK. I understand. I hope you get things sorted out.'

Abbie got up and went into the shower. It took two minutes to wash him away, then she put on her tracksuit bottom, pulled on one of her father's old shirts and let herself out of the front door of the Sails. She needed to feel the night, the bigness of space, and to sense that, between the fields and the quiet sea, another little girl – whom she now knew better than anyone – was waiting in safety . . .

I am lifted up as an eagle and my strength knows no bounds since I left the sufferings of earth, and like a blacksmith I will forge a chain which will bind up all those hardships and banish them deep in this greater darkness. Until then, and only then, will my dues be paid. But first I must hold my son again in my arms . . .

Fifty-six

IT WAS TEN P.M. and the Xantia had gone. Her bed was empty but still warm. Just as she was about to hide under the sheet again, Abbie heard a car pull up outside. Not the Cortina, but something smooth and new. She peered through the curtain gap, breathing a sigh of relief, but instead of Sheila, it was a man. In the brightness from the security light, he clicked the central locking on a silver grey Audi saloon and picked up his bag.

Simon? Was it possible?

She checked again, in case Quinn might have copied his posture, his clothes, but it was definitely Simon and Abbie drew back when he suddenly looked up at the window. She had a choice, but the alternative loomed like an infinitesimal black hole. Rosie would need both of them. They had to be there for her, and that certainty swelled in her heart as she ran down the stairs and unbolted the door.

'What on earth?' she gasped, seeing pain dull his eyes.

'I went back, signed off for all my stuff . . .' he paused, watching her eyes widen. 'Then I resigned my commission.' But before Abbie could respond, he continued. 'I then drove back home to Wales and told my father where his pathetic notions about me being a professional fucking soldier had got me. I'm sorry.' His lips, his arms, devoured her, his breath warm on her skin. 'So if you don't want to see me again, just say and I'll go.' He waited expectantly for a kiss, an embrace, anything, but for Abbie there was no room for joy or relief. Too much had happened . . .

'I do need you, Si. It's been so terrible . . .' was all she could say.

'Tell me.'

'I will, but first I want to know something. Did you mean what you wrote in that Visitors' Book?'

He stared at her for a moment, his expression more purposeful than she'd ever known. Then he put a hand into his jacket and produced a tiny box studded with garnets and put it on the bar.

'Now do you believe me?'

Abbie's eyes widened as she opened the lid and saw the ring.

'Go on then,' Simon whispered. 'It won't bite. It's pure Welsh gold.'

As she reached out, she felt her arm stiffen. Suddenly it seemed dead, from the shoulder down. She rubbed at it, then tried the other arm – no feeling there either.

'What's up?' He looked worried. 'You all right?' But before she could explain, a sharp gust of icy air swept into the room and towards them. When they looked again at the mahogany bar top, the little box had gone.

'Holy shit.'

They searched together, turning all the lights full on, trailing their fingers in vain along the polished wood, inspecting the floor. Then, realizing what had happened, they stood facing each other, fear reflecting fear.

'You fucking bitch!' Simon bellowed at the ceiling. 'Leave us all alone. What have we done to you?'

Abbie grabbed his arm, panic choking her voice. 'Don't say that. Don't say anything. It's what she wants, it gives her a reason . . .' Simon shook his head, looking dazed, and when he sat down she told him about Mrs Schaap and the photographs.

'When's that Jarrold next due at the church here?' he asked impatiently.

'On Sunday, the day after tomorrow. I went to check.'

'Right, we'll be his first bloody customers.'

Sheila's shock at seeing him back soon turned to a welcoming smile, but the moment she picked up on the atmosphere of fear she put down her beaded bag and sighed. 'Oh no, not again.'

'So what d'you think of Simon's new car then?' Abbie cut in. But Sheila wasn't biting. She'd had a good evening and Black Fen was spoiling her mood again. She hung up her summer jacket and poured herself a Cointreau.

'What make did you get for yourself?' Abbie tried, aware Simon was telling her to leave it.

'A bloody sports car, if you must know. To get me out of this hellhole double quick.'

I remember Moeder with her last breath begging me and Annie to visit her in Heaven with Mary, Abigail and Lazarus, but how can that ever be? For such a place lives only in the minds of fools, and Gloatby, who's selling off my rope for five shillings a foot without a conscience, will soon know something quite different . . .

Fifty-seven

SATURDAY WAS SPENT clearing the Show Home office using a wheelbarrow and a gallon of bleach. Simon attacked the floor while Abbie scrubbed at the resurrected furniture, trying to lose the obstinate slime scum marks. However, the spot were Mrs Schaap had once sat was respectfully covered with one of Sheila's old sheets and Abbie laid a single rose in the middle. Nothing had remained of the old woman's bag or its contents.

None of the workmen came in to help, despite the lure of overtime. Word had leaked out about Tom Nicholas's fit of dementia and the strange goings-on in the office, so the few who were still working further up the crescent stayed there, and their knocking-in of fencing posts echoed eerily in the stillness.

Abbie wondered about Vallender, whether he'd gone altogether from Holtbury's head office and who would now replace him, but neither Sheila nor Simon had mentioned his absence from the hotel and that's how it was left.

Simon was looking serious as his Audi hit sixty down Walsoken Road towards the church looming in the grey Sunday drizzle, his wipers set so they could see the few parishioners summoned by bells leaning into the weather, with that gargoyle projecting unnervingly overhead.

'It's half dog, half man, creepy bloody thing.' Abbie hated the stone protrusion's expression and the depressing dribble of water from its mouth.

'We know a few like that, don't we?' He slid the saloon into the kerb, instinctively looking out for Quinn. 'Look, I'll say it again in case you've forgotten, I'm not a believer, OK?' He set the car's immobilizer and quickly raked his fingers through his short hair.

'What do you go for then?' she asked, herself keeping an eye out for Avril Lawson. 'Druids and Arch-Druids?'

'Hell is other people.'

'Seconded – you excluded of course.'

'And you.'

Inside the porch there were further notices about the new arrangements for worship in the parish and the regrettable cancellation of Helen Quinn's Young Wives' Club. They were signed by the rural dean of North Sand.

'Welcome to St Mary Magdalene.' He looked surprised to see them as he handed each a hymn book, and even more surprised when they declined.

'You know what we've come about, don't you?' Abbie blurted out. 'I'm really begging you now. You've got to come over to our building site. It's getting worse . . .' As her voice broke, Simon gripped her hand, and other parishioners filed past staring at them.

'I have explained to you already,' Jarrold said anxiously, observing the tiny choir settling in the stalls, 'it would be a serious breach of my ministry, much as I would like to help . . .'

'Look, how long does a ritual like that take?' Simon

fixed him with urgent eyes. 'I mean, who'd bloody know for a start?'

The cleric put down the hymn books and sighed. He looked unwell, his cheeks blotched by livid patches, his lips in drought. But Simon didn't care about that. He felt Abbie's body slump in desperation.

He suddenly snatched up a hymn book and hurled it into the darkness, its tearing pages echoing their sense of utter futility as the man they most needed walked away from them.

She'd called out the name Vallender in her sleep – and again at dawn the next day. This other man who needed her lay alive in her grasp and drew her tight. Contour to contour, bone to bone, and slipped inside her for the second time as the sun lifted over Herringtoft Water.

'I'm Cresswell, remember. Shoe size 10, collar 15, shall I go on?'

His voice, his body, blocked out everything, and the immediacy of love, the sudden desire that cocooned them, kept the other child's eyes out of her sight and mind . . .

'I'll get you another ring,' he said suddenly.

'No, it doesn't matter.'

'OK. I'll make one out of my own hair.'

'It'll need to grow a bit more first.'

'So?' He took her nipples into his mouth in turn and played with them – until Sheila knocked on the door.

'Sorry, folks, but there's a Detective Superintendent Aldreth on the phone.'

'Shit.'

Simon scrambled into his jeans and ran downstairs, and Abbie followed. Sheila stared after them in surprise. As he listened to the message, she knew it was serious.

Apparently unnoticed by anyone, mid-afternoon yesterday, the Very Reverend Derek Jarrold's off-roader had skewered into the bank of a lay-by near North Sand. He'd died of a massive stroke and drowned on his own bile.

I am at one with the Greater Spirit more completely than ever before. I am his chosen messenger, lighter without my heart that had turned black as a drowned potato, or my old soul grown heavier than Three Fingers' sand. The pity of it is my sissen Annie has taken it upon herself to name the dolls she stole from me as Lazarus, Mary and Abigail. Poor murdered children she says. Oh, how little she knows, and when she at last heaved the sickly William from her body, it was only natural I should claim him for my own. And didn't I always say Clench-toft would kill her too, but at a time to suit myself. . .?

Fifty-eight

THE REVEREND PETER QUINN felt it safe to remove his woollen hat. It was making his head uncomfortably hot, even though there was no sun. His coat too, rescued from a British Heart Foundation shop in Gosdyke, was weighing him down, but at least it gave him good cover while all this police activity was taking place. And thanks to that throwback's carelessness, he'd found his gun and acquired a decent watch. So all in all his sortie had been worth it.

He slowed down, using his ears more keenly than he'd ever done before when listening to the responses of his tiresome inbred congregation. How he'd despised them for all those years, with their petty problems, their mean self-interest. How easy it had been to fool them and the Church hierarchy. He had a good voice that resonated with study and scholarship, a manner at once dignified and concerned. *Oh yes it was almost too easy. Too easy . . .*

His daughter was still visible, like a little marsh flower on the move in her yellow and green. She knew where the police dogs were, where the action was, and he knew she had no wish to be seen. He could tell the way she was crawling along past Seal Point – far beyond her usual hidey-hole – but as he followed her progress his head began to throb.

He tried the mini self-exorcism, but again, like all the other times, it proved useless. Whoever or whatever was feeding on his psyche was beyond the reach of any God. There was nothing he could do to shift it. He was now the proverbial empty vessel which this woman felt at liberty to fill any time she chose. And, like before, he offered no resistance.

His quarry stood up, saw him coming and ran off down through the reeds. At one point she fell, giving him an advantage, but then, being lighter, more nimble, she took herself off again, screaming, this time towards the sea.

Quinn too began to run until he felt hot, faint with exhaustion. To end it all, he pulled out the Walther and pointed it at his target.

The bullet met the mud, throwing up a spray of blinding silt, but Rosie was sinking without a sound, just like her mother, drawn to the peace and silence of the deep, and when he looked for her again there was nothing. Just the silent salty world of the marsh dead.

But still that voice urged him on, back along the Wenn, with even greater insistency. To anyone passing he was just an ordinary walker out on a Monday stroll, until he dropped down to the north side of Hick's fields like a fugitive and headed for Canal Farm.

By now, despite the worn and folded verse in his pocket, he was the complete puppet, the chief instrument of her power, and as the chosen one he was now very clear in his mind as to his next move. It was logical and rational. The Buckleys had let her down and their descendants were still blackening her name. Why should she allow this to continue unchecked?

'I saw to it her *boy didn't last after I'd placed my hand on its fontanelle, but she kept trying to breed twice more, oh yes, like the fat sow she is . . .'*

Quinn made an involuntary grunt of concurrence, then noticed there was neither Range Rover nor dog outside. The farmer was obviously not around. In the old days when he'd called here on parish matters, the cur had almost taken his leg off. Now the place was deathly quiet, with just a couple of flies cruising round the duck shit on the path.

He rang the doorbell. It was always best to be upfront and open. No use sneaking round the side, that just set up hostilities.

'Victor,' he heard her calling. 'Someone's at the door.' But she didn't fool him, stupid garrulous woman. There'd have been no hangings on the bank if the likes of her had kept quiet. Always too ready to put their neighbour down – them and Zillah Watts.

She'd be easy too, he thought, checking his new Breitel. Give or take half an hour . . .

He rang the bell again and stepped back to see a bedroom curtain flinch. Nervousness excited him. He pointed to his badge and waved a piece of paper from his pocket. Better, with hindsight, if it had been in a plastic wallet or attached to a clipboard, but too late for that now.

'It's a survey on Genetically Modified Crops,' he shouted, 'rather important and more than topical these days . . .'

Her slippers sounded on the lino, flop-flop, fat ankles full of pastry, and veiny feet.

'Yes?' She clearly half recognized him, but he wasn't deflected.

'Sorry to intrude, but I've been round to all the other farms. Your answers will help shape government policy for the next year or so . . .'

'Oh? We've already done one questionnaire.' Amy Buckley stared at his crumpled sheet of paper, the knitted hat, but by then he had the advantage and, with the strength of five men, pushed her into the parlour and on to the sofa.

She was surprisingly quiet for such a large woman, and his tie was very useful being woollen and rather thick. Just three tight turns around her leaping Adam's apple, then she was all his. Still as a dumpling, her mouth gaping in fixed horror as he made his escape.

Quinn then crept along the Buckley boundary, blessed by a line of uncut grass which harboured clumps of hawkweed and things blown down from the bank above. Things he himself had no use for, but where half his teenaged mothers had begun their road to penury and their deserters' dried seed lay in shrivelled rubber pouches.

Then over Breakwell Track and across Slave's Drain via a wooden footbridge. No one stopped or even noticed him, even though the sky was busy with helicopters near Lethe Island. They really were a bunch of incompetents and good job too. He allowed himself a tight smile as the widow's wreck of a dwelling showed above dock and foxgloves.

His hassock mender was round the back picking at something, wearing rubber gloves. That's it: nettles. It was going to be nettle soup with a dob of butter. He licked his lips as she let out a startled cry.

'Ministry of Agriculture, Mrs Watts. Just doing a survey.' He was blithely reassuring and she wiped her gloves on her apron. 'This Genetically Modified Crops issue's going to be affecting us all, sooner rather than later.' His Scottish accent was thinning, and the hassock mender cocked her little head, thinking hard, sensing danger.

'Bugger off!' she suddenly screamed, scuttling down to the end of her garden, through a gap in the hedge she'd been meaning to block up. Then into the ploughed field behind Rievely Hall. 'Help! Help! Help!'

The tall man loped behind her, his hands outstretched to grab her brittle legs.

She came on to gravel and round to the entrance, panting and pressing the bell simultaneously. 'Oh, please God, answer!' Mrs Watts could hear Quinn's steps, crunch crunch, and a sudden panic made her wet herself. 'Mrs Schaap? Where are you?'

'She can't help you now.' Quinn had his long white fingers round her neck, relishing his power, but sweating, his grip beginning to slip. 'She was another meddler like you who couldn't leave things alone.'

'What?'

Two astonished eyes turned up on him and then, with unexpected bravura, she spat in his face.

The surprise of it loosened his hold, and in that split second she was off down Tithe Lane to the Whiplash, where, by God's mercy, she saw Sheila Livingstone passing in her new MG.

Quinn clutched his head and ran as he was instructed, north towards Clenchtoft Farm, where a police cordon still stretched across the gate. Two barns there – he had to choose, and dived into the bigger one, nice and dark and dry. This would do until things died down, until his next move. He raked up what straw he could find to lie on, and, when settled, closed his eyes. Meanwhile Martha Robinson's vengeful orchestration continued, for his ears only, long into the night.

And now after all this time, though it seems no more than an hour ago, whenever I know any sort of peace, He calls again 'Lilith Leakes!' How her name rings in the air, spinster of Clenchtoft and only issue of Thomas Leakes and Elizabeth Willing, deceased, but I've never yet seen them in this other world. There's not one soul I recognize. It is as if He has made a special place for me, where I can gather all my earthly strength for Our common purpose . . .

Fifty-nine

EIGHT-THIRTY A.M. AND Sheila had just brought Zillah Watts tea in bed. When she'd gone in, the old girl was still half asleep, but occasionally she called out, reliving her ordeal with wide staring eyes.

WPC O'Halloran had agreed the Sails was the best place for Zillah's own safety. At least she'd have someone with her there, and an array of security devices to prevent the man who had chased and terrorized her from having another go.

So a room had been hurriedly aired and some soap and a fresh loo roll installed in the nearest bathroom. The hotelier's sympathy had also extended to a posy of rosebuds on the walnut dressing table and three complimentary sheets of hotel notepaper with matching envelopes. Not that Zillah had any family left to write to, Sheila knew that, but somehow it always made guests feel at home.

And then there was Sheila's car seat. Mrs Watts's 'accident' had left a dried stain on its grey cloth, and even first thing in the morning after several washes it still smelt of pee. Her posh new MG. Then she reminded herself what the poor old duck had just been through.

'I'll bring you up some bacon and eggs when it's ready.' Sheila checked through the curtains in case anyone was lurking about. 'You have a good rest now.'

As she went past Simon's room she heard the shower, reassuringly normal. But Abbie's door was open, her work suit and blouse still on the hanger.

'I can't face it, not today, not ever.' Abbie still sat in her dressing gown at the bar, when normally she'd have been dressed and ready for work.

'I don't blame you, kid.' Sheila found her cigarettes and lit up.

Abbie finished her coffee. It was the thought of that ruined office, the horrible lingering smell no matter what sprays were used. Besides, the men were different now, surly and preoccupied, the buzz and cheerful banter all gone. That was the worst part.

Even any last-minute efforts to tempt a 'biter' now seemed pointless, with mail shots and advertising not worth a light. Her gut feeling was right. Olaf and Anya Martinsen had been their last hope and with their going the place had died.

She jumped as the phone rang. It was Aldreth, sounding well sorted by comparison with herself.

'The reason I'm calling is to warn you. It's bad news, I'm afraid.'

Abbie glanced at Sheila, who was listening.

'What is it?'

'Mrs Buckley's been found dead in her own home. She was killed there yesterday afternoon.'

Sheila stubbed out her dimp as Abbie whitened. 'Was it Quinn?' The name felt foul in her mouth.

'It may well have been. There was no sign of a forced entry or of any struggle, which leads us to believe it was all *very* cleverly planned.'

Cleverly? The word seemed an odd choice, but there

was already too much else to take in. Abbie gripped the
bar edge, remembering Amy Buckley, her apple cheeks,
her kitchen full of cooking . . .

'Where was the dog?'

'Died a few weeks ago, I gather.'

'So she was there on her own?'

'That's right. Victor Buckley found her later that
evening. I can't go into details but it wasn't very nice . . .
Not nice at all . . . Still, I'm glad to hear her neighbour
Mrs Watts is at least safe with you . . .'

Abbie stared at the receiver – a creeping unease made
her heart beat faster.

It was Aldreth's turn of phrase, or something in his
voice. Something wasn't quite right about it.

'Well, thanks for letting me know anyhow,' was all
she managed before putting the receiver down.

She tried dialling 1471 straight away. The caller had
withheld their number. She looked at Sheila, panic in her
eyes.

'Is that door locked?'

The hotelier checked while Abbie dialled Snutterwick.

'Yes.'

'And the windows?'

'OK. I'll take a look.'

'Detective Superintendent Aldreth please. It's urgent,'
Abbie began, listening to the old sash windows being
rammed down and fastened.

'I'm afraid he's in a meeting.'

'Where?'

'I'm afraid I can't say. Who's calling?'

Abbie jabbed the thing down and swore, just as
Simon was coming down the stairs, new jeans, new shirt

and his growing hair with a side parting, making him look younger.

'Abbie? What's up, for God's sake?' He stared at her.

'What have you been doing?'

'Chucking out old clothes, why?'

'I think Quinn's just been on the phone.' Her voice was quiet with shock. 'Pretending to be Aldreth and boasting that he knows Mrs Watts is here.'

Before Simon could try 999, the phone rang again.

'Yes?' he said in a tense bark, then he passed the receiver to Abbie. 'Vallender.' He then made a show of rechecking the lounge bar windows so he could listen in.

'Hi.' The line was poor.

'You all right?' the sales director asked, remembering her smooth skin, the sheer pleasure of those few hours . . .

'No, but go on.'

'Just to say I'm on the site. Few things to sort out – pretty crucial really.'

'Such as?' She couldn't care less and maybe it showed.

'There's a full briefing at nine-thirty – see if we can put some turf down, plant some trees round the finished plots, you know, the icing on the cake . . .'

'Then?' Aware of Simon thinking the worst, not trusting her.

'I need to see the replacement foreman when he arrives, point him in the right direction, check on his trainees . . . Abbie? You still there?'

'Sort of.'

'Not bad for an almost has-been, am I, eh?' He laughed to himself. 'I'm feeling a bit more positive now . . .'

'That's good.'

'Funny thing though. Old Colonel Scott's come in with an offer for the site. Far more than he bloody paid for it, *and* allowing for appreciation. The letter was delivered by hand at eight-thirty this morning.'

Hardly surprising after what Mrs Schaap told me . . .

'Look at it this way, it's still a nice investment. OK, one or two little intangibles to consider . . .'

One or two little intangibles? This is unreal . . .

'Work in progress, decent profit once the house selling starts again.'

Sheila looked drawn and tired. Abbie watched as Simon followed her into the kitchen.

'And yeah, I've already got Pitts organized. Next it'll be his new mate and the Ratcatcher, what's his name?'

'Handel Myers.' She'd almost forgotten it.

'Thanks, as I was saying, they can go on to plot 2 asap and start putting some windows in.'

And pigs will fly . . .

'By the way, I've missed you.'

She glanced at Simon, now back and sitting at a table toying with a knife and fork.

'I'll be there.' She put the phone down as Sheila came over with a tray carrying three breakfasts.

'Brilliant, thanks.' Simon grinned up at her, hunger now taking precedence over his 999 call.

'Anything to please.' She noticed Abbie was leaving her breakfast untouched. Suddenly, from between the spirits and the maraschinos, the phone rang for the third time. Sheila listened to the call, covered the mouthpiece and shouted over to Abbie. 'It's for you. Vallender again.'

Abbie took it with a frown. Forgetting his feast, Simon leapt up as he saw her free hand cover her face in shock.

'Greg Pitts? When? God in heaven! Hang on, I'm on my way.'

She hurried upstairs, threw on the first clothes that came to hand and ran, with Simon in the lead, down Walsoken Road into an enclave of spinning blue lights.

A cordon was already set up, with an ambulance nearby, as onlookers from the council houses opposite were being turned away. She recognized the fat local reporter, beige slacks under his bulging paunch. 'Piss off!' she hissed at him quietly, while Simon was already sprinting on towards the dereliction of plot 2. Then when she spotted Aldreth coming out of the Portakabin she told him about Quinn's scary impersonating phone call to the hotel.

Immediately Aldreth phoned Sheila to warn her to stay indoors, then radioed for a car to go over to Canal Farm. Within ten seconds two of his team were in the Sierra parked nearest the gates and heading north-east.

Meanwhile on plot 2, the concrete skim lay heaped up like broken glass around the retaining walls. Mud and peat lay everywhere, darkly filling all its unbuilt rooms, and in the middle of what would have been the Martinsens' dream kitchen a huge hole filled with brown water lay open to the sky.

Simon steadied himself, hypnotized by its moving liquid surface that reflected the clouds. He was nine all over again at Llangorse Lake with his brother, Matthew, and their little boats. He'd not remembered where his mother and father were, just that Matthew had put stones on his craft to make it sink and, as it sank, the cotton sails took it further and further away . . .

He'd gone after it, his favourite toy *The Bounty* already half under water, sliding to oblivion. And so was he, getting deeper, colder, with reeds easing him into the lake's murderous depths and something or somebody trapping his arms so he couldn't swim to save himself. It was Matthew – wanting Mummy all to himself. Matthew who wanted him dead . . .

'Simon?' Abbie took his arm. 'Don't look at that any more.'

He turned, and for the first time she saw a terrible unspoken fear in his eyes. One day he'd tell her. When he was ready.

Meanwhile WPC O'Halloran was trying to keep Vallender back.

'Where's Pitts?' he yelled.

'We couldn't reach him,' she said falteringly.

'We've got to!'

Aldreth came over and took his arm. 'We're doing our utmost.'

A Eurocopter drafted in from Three Fingers Beach drowned the rest of his reassurances, stirring the dirt as it hovered over the far end of the site. Simon held Abbie close, fascinatedly watching the water continue to rise, wondering where the hell the police divers were.

Abbie uttered a private prayer, but soon more news reporters and someone with a camcorder were adding to the general din. Meanwhile, Vallender had joined the gang of workmen who huddled like cornered sheep by the Portakabin steps.

'No more now.' The Detective Superintendent advanced on the photographers, waving his arms. 'You can have the details later, thank you.' He was grimly hanging on to his habitual politeness, despite the horrors the day was revealing.

The sunlight had passed from sea to land, too soon

for shadows but not bright enough to disguise the brooding turmoil of plot 2. Aldreth signalled to his men. Three brought ladders across and waited for a volunteer. Mark Knowles stepped forward, then tested his weight before crawling along one to lie flat at the edge of *her* world. Black upon black. The stuff of nightmares.

Abbie remembered the marsh. She wanted to cry out, to stop him. But this was man's work, with four more on stand-by, including Simon.

'Steady, for Chrissake.'

Up to his elbow now, the chief pipe layer inched forward, every muscle tuned to survival, feeling around, as deep as he dare. The sound amplified around the site as his foraging became a different labour – of iron on peat, digging, digging . . .

'Jesus, man!' he suddenly yelled.

Aldreth, with the safety cord cutting into his trousers, craned forward.

'I got something here,' Knowles panted.

'Take your time.'

'Feels like, I dunno, kinda weird . . .' He eased back, his big hand full. But as he held the small skull for the surplus water to sluice away, his arm stayed rigid. Then he began to shake, his thumb and fingers loosened as if by some huge force he couldn't resist. The whole site darkened as clouds scudded over and then hung, waiting above, forcing the helicopter to move away.

The relic fell, but instead of landing with the expected splash of an object hitting water, it vanished silently into the vaporous mass that now covered the plot. When the cloud lifted, great needles of icy rain glanced down from the sky.

*

When the freak storm had passed, WPC O'Halloran sat at Abbie's desk. She'd recovered her composure and dialled with her pen.

Abbie watched with her tray of coffees ready as the policewoman tried again, let it ring for a while, then put the receiver down with a sigh. She looked drawn and grey, dialling for the third time. Again no luck: the workman's widow clearly wasn't at home.

Abbie waited for her moment before taking the tray outside. 'I've got to phone another vicar, if that's OK.' The other young woman looked up. 'The job needs to be finished properly.'

'I don't follow. What job?'

'An excorcism. Here.'

'Good Lord.'

'Yes, and I hope *He's* bloody listening.'

Abbie noticed Vallender standing outside with Simon, both looking pale and subdued.

'It's urgent. If you'd seen what I have . . .'

Abbie located a Kingfisher Rise information pack. Apart from St Cecilia's and the St Mary Magdalene, there were two more churches listed in it. She tried one after the other, both responding with answerphones.

'Shit shit shit.'

Suddenly Vallender's head showed round the door. He had no more Little Chef breakfast left to throw up, his mouth now dry and acid. No more ambition either.

'The big guns are on their way,' he said. 'That's all we bloody need!' He leaned towards the mirror, adjusting his tie.

The WPC stood up. Her tights were newly laddered, like a scar on her calf. 'I'd better get over to Bankside Cottages before the gossip starts.'

When she'd gone, Simon came in, pulling Abbie close. He sniffed her hair, stroked her hand. 'I won't let you down.'

'Nor me you.'

She then distributed the coffee mugs to grateful recipients, except for Mark Knowles, who, wrapped in a survival blanket with his eyes rolling and his speech blurred, was in another world. Vallender held the man's mug and tried to get some coffee into his mouth but there was no coordination, no attempt at swallowing. Abbie thought of Tom Nicholas and her stomach turned over.

The ambulance took the big brave man away, its siren fading, while back at the Show Home they both faced the renewed sunlight. Warm bricks behind them, in front a scene of ever-changing chaos. The Eurocopter returned and whipped the sand and cement to a whirlwind that stung their eyes. Through grit and tears they saw a diver dangled from the winch before disappearing into the hole of Tartarus.

Abbie's hand stayed in Simon's as the nightmare paraded its spectres before their eyes. So detailed, so haunting, was the procession that she missed hearing the phone. It was Simon who leapt to it, and was answered by the Reverend William Dole of St Bede's in Slatterton, who'd just finished an early lunch. The clergyman consulted his diary, Schubert in the background. 'Today, I've got a remarriage and a baptism . . .'

'You'll have some more burials soon if you don't come over here quick.'

'More? What do you mean?'

'Look, we're desperate.'

'I do have other obligations, Mr . . .?'

'Cresswell,' Simon said. 'One man's dead already. You just fax me the whole ritual and I'll do it my bloody self!'

A gasp, then silence. 'Give me thirty minutes.'

'Cheers.' Then Simon looked round. 'Abbie?'

But she'd gone. He went to check outside as another ambulance lumbered into the site. Even her scent was missing. Squinting, half blinded by the sudden bright-ness, he called out for her, but nobody noticed. Backs were turned, waiting like a human fence around the pit. Waiting for two men to reappear as the sun, burning towards midday, scorched the site to an instant desert.

Simon felt a knot in his stomach. Abbie was still nowhere to be seen and Aldreth and his team were busily gathered around the car just returned from the Buckleys. As he left the site, two silver BMWs almost ran him over, their sunroofs up like operculi as they stalled to a halt.

Stanley Potterton the managing director of Holtbury baled out first, looking pink and crumpled. His chauffeur hovered silently deferential as Allan Holtbury Junior, company chairman and his secretary, Dina McRae, step-ped out of the second car, she in a black suit, her hair slicked into a French pleat. They all looked grim and worse when they spotted Vallender. Stanley Potterton's bulk made quick progress.

'What the fuck's going on here?'

'We're getting it sorted, believe me.' Vallender held open the office door and sucked himself in to let the other pass. 'Just a minor hiccup.'

'Is the lavatory here working?'

'Sure.'

The fat man fingered the various dusty knick-knacks on his way to the cloakroom. The lock screamed shut, then came his voice from inside, above the extractor's hum. 'The shit I'm about to dump is nothing compared to what you're in.'

'Me?'

'You said it.'

Vallender felt panic. He put two fingers inside his collar and tugged, tearing off the top button. Neither Abbie nor Simon was anywhere to be seen. Her desk was now a dereliction. Dina gave him a death stare as Holtbury Junior's long legs brought him closer . . .

Wherever Vallender looked, the same message rang out in his mind. There was no place for him now. North, south, east or west, it was all the fucking same. He smoothed down his hair and walked to his car.

'Hey, Vallender!'

Holtbury began to jog after him, but the sales director had the advantage of speed. The constable waved him through the site exit, his car almost clipping the Reverend Dole's wing mirror. The minister hooted in protest, but Vallender's heel was already to the floor, pushing the speed up to fifty by the turning for Snutterwick and the road leading back to little Gemma and the rest of his life.

Suddenly the helicopter lifted, its passage vibrating the flimsy building struts and rafters below, as the diver emerged mummified by mud and by trauma, his empty hands as if sealed to his sides.

*Lilith Leakes . . . how she resembles me
with her length of thin hair and the
figure that sends Gedney Stimpson's
heart a pounding. Yes, she could be
me all over again, with her swelling
boy-belly from that whelp of a sailor,
and it is this which gives me true
comfort . . .*

Sixty

THE WENN LAPPED against its banks, pushing cartons and wood remnants against the campshedding.
A bull-nosed barge from Ostend lay newly stacked with
feed stuffs, while its crew, forgoing the drama in Kingfisher Rise, cooled off in the shade of a stack of pallets.

After checking the Sails and a nervy Sheila, Simon
passed by the harbourmaster's hut, oil and nitrates in his
lungs as he slung his jacket over one shoulder. Someone
on the weighbridge smiled at him. A bit like finding
treasure in all this shit, he thought, angling his face to
the sky and all its possibilities.

Herringtoft, once lined with workers' cottages,
stretched bare to the Wenn's wide mouth. The mud
path was dry, with ballbearing stones, and as he strode
towards the intermittent gunshots out on Cortlever Low,
he knew from now on Kosovo and Albania would just
be names on a map. Anxiety neurosis was something
they ran a bloody mile from, so here he was, only with
more anxiety, more neurosis, and sweat trickling into his
ears.

'Abbie!'

This was where she'd often been and might be again.
God, if he had one wish, it would be to find her and
never let her out of his sight. Not even for the blink of

an eye. He'd sit out on the marsh all night if need be and maybe, who knows, even Rosie might show up.

Sounds from the site faded into the vastness as he went along Judas Canal and over the footbridge to Seal Point, his arms burning, his head a cauldron in the silence. Water like cat-licks, greening over, slowing his heart.

Suddenly he saw someone sitting, curled up against the day. Her bob of hair burnished like a conker ... Relief made him laugh and carried his legs down the bank to its deeper quiet. Their warmths joined and melted, his shirt the go-between, until the moment.

Afterwards they lay sated and sunstruck under the lilt of lark song until other voices drew nearer from a slow line of people against the sky.

In his hurry, Simon got his boots mixed up, but the procession ignored him, fixed with its own grim purpose. He took Abbie's hand and together they approached the final stragglers and the attendant stench of rotting fish.

'What's going on?' Simon tried the one who'd smiled at him on the weighbridge, a man sunburnt from bird-watching, his hat brim down on his nose.

'Can't rightly say. Ask one of them.' He pointed further along the line as Abbie quizzed a German tourist with a limp who was in front.

'I have not any knowledge, pardon.' The lederhosen-wearer refolded his map, letting Simon pass to try a woman in a lime-green tracksuit.

'What's that lot up ahead carrying?' He was growing impatient.

'I dunno. I was just taking bird shots for my Steven's project when along they all came.'

'It's not a body?'

'Simon,' Abbie said, holding him back, 'don't.'

'Wouldn't be surprised,' the woman went on, unfazed. 'There's drownings every month round 'ere. Usually some drunken tramp or other. I'd never let my lad out here on 'is own. Not now.'

They left her behind and tried to reach the front of the procession. Abbie's thoughts growing bleaker the closer they got. On the bank side of the shipway a small crowd followed parallel. Word had already reached the farms and dog barked to dog across the watery divide.

'It's not that vicar's wife by any chance?' Abbie asked the sunburnt man again, keeping to his shadow, stride for stride.

'Like I said, we don't know.' This was said with annoyance as they passed some marine biology students from Norwich, all uniformed in yellow cagoules.

Neither she nor Simon spoke further as the party prepared to join the lane. They heard a distant ambulance's ominous wail. That same fish smell was growing, choking her.

Four men from the *St Ursula* held each corner of the sail to stop its load from slipping, their faces rough and dry as old rope. Abbie caught a terrible glimpse of their burden. If it was Helen Quinn, she must have shrunk by at least a third – how, she dared not imagine. If, on the other hand . . .

O Jesus, help us. Rosie, Rosie . . .

The bearers continued without further stoppages. Someone at the front started to sing a snatch of hymn and the sound swelled after initial hesitancies until the track met the tarmac. A team of paramedics scrambled over, ready with a stretcher, then slammed the ambulance doors on the watching crowd.

With whispered questions, ears gleaning information, the watchers stood as though this last journey was also theirs. No one felt moved to leave, except the bird-watcher, who slipped away and headed back towards World's End Marsh.

'Listen!' Abbie tugged Simon's arm. 'Can you hear something?'

They both looked up at the sky's deepening blue, now streaked by a smoke trail moving west. But Simon shook his head.

'She's laughing, I tell you.'

There was no disguising that sound again – the same as she had heard in her car. The same as everywhere. A penetrating malevolent mirth that seemed to roll and ululate on the very clouds looming in again from the sea.

I only saw that whipster Pieter Schaap the once and could tell there was no pleasure in his rutting. A fortune-hunter in sheep's clothing if ever there was, and now on this ninth day of February, she is near, and so am I. Waiting until I am summoned. Until the moon draws the sea south into the mud channels and her waters into my hands . . .

Sixty-one

B Y MID-AFTERNOON the CID had formally requisitioned the lounge bar at the St George's Sails and within a couple of hours this had been sealed off from both the saloon and the snug, while the room's two windows which overlooked the yard at the back were darkened with blinds.

Sheila observed the whole transformation with more cigarettes than usual. Spare sockets and lights, some grey office furniture and a Home Office Large Major Enquiry System was installed, whereupon her shuttle service of tea and chocolate mini-rolls began. Zillah Watts remained upstairs with a gardening programme and her hair in curlers.

The deal for this requisition was lucrative enough for Sheila to have sent off for several holiday brochures: ideally inland hills and picturesque villages with not an ocean in sight, and silver service thrown in of course. Besides, she thought, doing some last-minute dusting, it was no mean thing for her one-horse hotel to be a crucial help in this dreadful business, and pride made her shine up the remaining tables like mirrors.

The lounge bar wasn't ideal, but it was spacious enough for the team to function. As the Senior Investigating Officer, Aldreth had been allocated the area next

to the bar, with his deputy, James Stock, alongside him
– his clothes now immaculate and a trial moustache
making him look older.

After a private briefing with Stock, Aldreth came out
to address the small audience waiting in the saloon bar,
his shoulders stooped, his large hands working their way
round his sheet of paper. Three pairs of eyes took in
every nuance of his movements, already knowing something deadly serious was up. He coughed and drew a
hand through his hair.

'Unfortunately, the skull found at the construction
site hasn't yet been recovered for examination. We can
only assume it dropped back into the water and when
time is on our side another attempt will be made to
retrieve it.' He glanced at Abbie, Simon and Sheila in
turn, then coughed again in the continuing silence.
'There will also be another attempt to find Mr Pitts,
but we cannot let our divers face unacceptable risks until
the right equipment is available. We must just hope
against hope.' He sat down with the latest print-out in
his hand.

Stock took over from him, as though standing to
attention.

'I'm afraid this next news may be more distressing.
We have appreciated your help and your deep concern
throughout and are satisfied that everything that could
have been done has been done—'

'Bollocks!' Simon stood up, his jaw jutting.

Abbie saw him working up to a fight and tried to
calm him. 'Let him finish, Si, please.'

He shrugged her away and stepped out to face them.
'If you'd moved your butts when we first told you what
was going on, we wouldn't even bloody be here now . . .'

WPC O'Halloran moved over and escorted him back, under Stock's hostile gaze, then placed herself at Abbie's shoulder.

Stock continued, picking over his words as if treading on the bomb-strewn sand at Mickleton. 'However, we must inform you that the body picked up from the sea by the *St Ursula* crew near Lethe Island was in fact that of little Rosie Quinn.'

Abbie gasped, then began sobbing loudly, so his next words were drowned, like the myriad other creatures who had made up the fishermen's gruesome catch along with the child – no more than a rag doll, pale and bloated from the North Sea's womb.

'Her body's been taken to Snutterwick General, and there'll be a post-mortem of course.' He paused. 'The head teacher of Black Fen Primary School has already made a formal identification.'

The WPC moved closer, but Abbie elbowed her aside, her cheeks on fire. 'Why couldn't I have done that?'

'Miss Parker, please. There was a note covered in polythene found in her pocket. From you, Lieutenant Cresswell.' His look was unsettling. Whatever he wanted to imply was still under wraps.

Simon, too, broke down, his head bowed, his shoulders rising and falling in a rhythm of helplessness. Sheila passed him a hotel napkin. She couldn't cope with men crying – especially him, the fearless one.

'Rosie knew that marsh better than anyone,' Abbie shouted. 'Her father killed her!'

'That's something to be investigated,' Aldreth said, 'but we're all aware nevertheless that the strong anticlockwise current out there is treacherous – apart from the sand bars and channels on that area of coast. Anybody could have—'

'She wasn't anybody.' Abbie interrupted, her face wet with grief.

Simon drew her head against his and felt her whole being lurch with pain and guilt.

Sheila flicked her lighter. 'Do we get protection now? Or poor Mrs Watts? And you've not mentioned Mrs Buckley at all, not once.'

'We've no proof of anything yet.' Aldreth and O'Halloran glanced at each other. 'And the search goes on – be assured of that. The only positive link to him is with the axe found at Clenchtoft Farm, and that's by no means 100 per cent certain.'

'So what *are* you fucking well doing? Waiting till everyone's dead?' Simon burst out.

You will all die . . .

'Surely to God he should have been noticed by now.' Sheila lit up, frowning. 'It's hardly Piccadilly bloody Circus out there.'

'No chance,' Abbie murmured. 'He's very clever and *everywhere* at once.'

'I repeat, we are doing our very best.' Aldreth stared into space as though space was his only refuge.

Simon once more raised his voice. 'What about that nutty cow Lawson? She hated Rosie's guts more than anyone.'

'We've no reason to suspect she's involved in any way.' The WPC said.

'So where does that leave us?'

'We take one step at a time.' The SIO carefully folded his paper, suddenly looking weary as his fingers sharpened its crease. 'By the way, two things. Another Reverend turned up at Kingfisher Rise this morning, but then Mrs Pitts and her family suddenly arrived. It was a difficult situation, to say the least.'

'That must have been Dole,' Abbie murmured, still in shock.

'And?' Simon asked accusingly.

'No choice. We had to ask him to leave.'

'O Jesus. So he didn't do it?'

Aldreth deflected. 'He said you'd asked him to come over, correct?'

'Correct. And he knew exactly what to do. It wouldn't have mattered who else was there, for fuck's sake.'

Abbie felt her anger rising. 'The place still needs cleansing – more than ever now. And if my dear boss had taken any notice of me in the first place, we could have had it arranged sooner and all this wouldn't have happened.' She smoothed back her hair. 'I was trying to protect the site as well as ourselves. I had a job to cling on to, but it's impossible now.' She shrugged, then for the first time, as the clock marked out the afternoon, she carefully revealed everything that had happened there and as much of the dead woman Martha Robinson's bleak history as she and Simon had managed to piece together.

The air around them seemed to grow colder even though the sun blistered the bricks outside. Everyone fell silent as Abbie recounted verbatim each of the site labourers' experiences, then Amy Buckley's and Zillah Watts's accounts. Afterwards an uneasy stillness filled the room.

Simon took over. 'If, as his wife's Pentateuch seemed to suggest, Quinn was hearing some demonic voice, then this Martha Robinson could be the one behind it. Only a guess, mind.' He looked at Stock, who shook his head.

'That's all guff. I have to say it. Some people are just born evil.'

'Precisely,' Julia O'Halloran agreed, catching both her superiors off guard. 'But I think we're into something pretty big here. I mean, what about those other poor kids dying, and now Darren Greenhalgh being so ill. It could all be tied up somehow, if only we could prove the link.' Her lip was trembling as she looked over at Abbie and Simon sitting closer together in the cold, suddenly unable to respond. Then the policewoman left the room and no one tried to stop her.

'Well, anyhow, we'd better have that account of yours in writing, if you don't mind.' Aldreth finally said. 'As soon as you can provide it.'

'To get mislaid just like the last time when Abbie's letter and Lilith Leakes's *Secrets* simply vanished?' Simon hugged her with both arms, long enough to whisper in her ear, 'No way, Abbie, don't waste your bloody time.'

Aldreth didn't think it the best moment to confess that Helen Quinn's Pentateuch had also disappeared from their strongbox.

'I've got to go now.' Abbie pulled away from him. There was something she had to do, something private and necessary, so she could get on with what remained of the rest of her life. Then she was gone.

Simon rose to follow, but hesitated, hearing the same treacherous sound of moving water filling the saloon bar that he had listened to before on plot 2.

Aldreth and Stock went out and stood in the sun by the porch, as if its warmth and brightness might expunge the atmosphere that had settled inside. They watched without speaking as Simon Cresswell ran off, his face like a mask of grey terror. In just three leaps he was up on Herringtoft. Meanwhile, Roy Kettle the indexer was receiving news of a mysterious find off the Deeps of Lethe.

14 February 1954

She has cut the cord with her poppy knife and bound it with a piece of her hair, but, unlike the sickly William Leakes and all those others who succumbed before time, this one is heavy from a full term and has left her so weak she can't prevent me taking him to complete my business. But her plea for me to lift my words from his soul fell on stony ground, because if there's one thing I learned in that life, it was to cling to what was rightfully mine . . .

Sixty-two

S NUTTERWICK GENERAL WAS quite different the
second time around. Without Vallender *in situ* it
seemed cold, impersonal. Even the hospice in Banbury
where, four years ago, her mother had stayed had at
least been welcoming – a giant bungalow stuffed with
pastoral pictures and decor not unlike that of the Show
Home. Hilary Parker had died at St Stephen's under
a pretty duvet with matching pillows – pink yet again,
like prisons of contentment and calm at the door to
eternity.

Now the hospital seemed dulled by tainted chrome
and puke green, and full of labyrinthine corridors. The
plastic trellis and vines did nothing to make the waiting
area any less grim and a smell of stewed tea and lavatories
pervaded.

Abbie tried to get her bearings.

'Yes?' queried an Indian in stark white standing near
the outpatients desk. 'Can I help?'

'Detective Superintendent Aldreth said I could come
and see my friend, little Rosie Quinn. She was brought
here dead earlier this afternoon.' The words felt wrong,
too terrible to say without faltering.

The brown forehead frowned. 'I'm afraid we have
procedures, Miss . . .'

'Parker. Abigail Parker.' Abigail carried a bit more weight, she thought. Besides, she was desperate.

'Have you any written authorization?'

'Look, she was very special to me. I was the only one who really bothered about her.' Fresh tears welled up, but this man had seen it all before. Every hour every day. She could tell.

'We don't allow members of the public into the mortuary.' He was showing impatience now.

'I'm not just a member of the bloody public! I was going to take care of her . . .'

People waiting for radiography stared as Dr Vishna-varna moved smoothly away from reception, his face serious. He disappeared through a swing door labelled DANGER. Before he could return, Abbie sidled further along E corridor, with the wind buffeting the half-open Velux windows above her. In between shift lists and ambulance rosters she found a map peeling at the corners: 'You are here' was marked beside a black cross.

She memorized the route she needed, then strode back outside into the stabbing overhead sunlight, to steps down alongside the hospital wall and a solid double door below ground level. She went in, aware of an intestine of galvanized pipes overhead, and of how cold and imper-sonal the whole place seemed. A red sign on the wall read 'Strictly No Entry for Unauthorized Personnel'.

Forgetting how to read, she pushed on through, her stomach heavy like lead, her breathing as shallow as a herring out of water. She wished Simon were there, with his warm propelling hand in the small of her back. But the lonely landscape of corridor remained all hers and the dead child was waiting.

Suddenly voices, then loud sneezing.

She crouched by a row of waste bins as two chattering nurses took a left turn. Chill, and light without windows, the passage's recirculated air possessed its own eerie song. Then came another door with a rota list attached, this time simply initials, most slots ticked off.

This door was of iron, different from the others. Her heart stopped. She blinked. It was in the process of opening, opening just enough to allow a tall white-coated figure to emerge. A mask left only the eyes visible. But they were eyes she could never forget: pale and reptilian, lined with red – and fixed on her.

Icy cold gripped her legs. She and the white coat were almost face to face. A sliver of a scalpel glanced in his hand and blood edged his shirt cuffs, carelessly wiped clean.

Turning abruptly, Abbie moved first, not daring to look round but hearing him give chase, grunting for breath. Screaming loudly, she charged back outside and up the steps again into the bright main building, where she spotted a group of police officers, not all recognized. Most distinctive was the mannish DI Irene Pringle, short-cropped hair and, unusually, in combat fatigues. She'd just been brought in from Cambridge to reinforce the operations. And, after hearing Abbie's sobbing plea for help, she was soon tearing to the mortuary, with Aldreth close behind to witness the Devil's handiwork.

Simon stood on the highest point of Morpeth Bank, close to the gallows stumps, feeling total despair, remembering the little skull, the stench of inundation . . .

He watched as a gull cruised the shore to land on a tuft of grass. Abbie had left him again. He didn't know what was what any more, and there wasn't much left of him to care. Wherever she was, she was there without him and it hurt.

The sea barely shifted, as if conspiring in the silence that enveloped him, yet underneath its bland calm, he knew, lay histories of human tragedy, blighting the years and the lives of those trapped at its edges. He could feel its malevolence seep through his pores, he wasn't fooled by it, and Helen Quinn, too, was out there somewhere, part of its ebb and flow, the meaninglessness of it all.

Suddenly something nudged the clouds to the south. Too large for a bird yet definitely aloft. He squinted, using both hands to blinker out the rest of the sky and focus, and realized a helicopter was dropping and rising near Lethe Island, winching black morsels aboard and transporting the bigger pieces to a waiting boat.

There was nowhere he could stand to get a closer look, for the marsh below had a skim of thin mud where the gulleys had overflowed. Sweat fringed his forehead as he stayed rooted in that empty open place. He thought back to Brecon and Dan Y Parc, with its fine views towards Pen y Fan, then of Leicester and the first time he'd ever seen Abbie, looking for her college room. Those were all the things he loved and yet he was fixed here, joined almost symbiotically to an evil already fully hooked into his side.

> This Gallows Tree hewn by stout hands
> In true and honest toil,
> Now stands as black and fearsome still
> Upon our tainted soil.
> Its shoulder held the savage rope,
> Its sides the wind's long moan,
> And in between, old Joseph hung

Till death stopped up his groan:
The drunken folk who'd come to view
This husband face his end,
Think twice afore offending God
For fear of what He'll send.

It was something he'd read in one of Abbie's books once, and for some reason memorized, like other gobbets of her study subject, so far outside his own – little knowing then its future significance. He looked at what lay around him here, what others in that same spot must have seen the moment before their death. World's End Marsh, how apt, how terrible. His fists clenched and unclenched, as if ready to fight the unseen enemy.

The helicopter drew away from its preoccupation, growing larger and larger over his head, stirring the grasses, growling towards the Wenn. And as he glanced up he noticed something black and wet streaming from its belly.

Next day, while Abbie was still upstairs, too upset to face anyone, Zillah Watts had chosen the table closest to the TV and invited Simon to sit next to her. She sipped her ginger beer, as the six o'clock news trumpeted into the saloon bar, and occasionally glanced sideways at the young man who'd just downed four Budweisers in swift succession. No Kosovo, no floods in Colombia or a Third World island earthquake, this time the disasters were all just outside their door. In Shitland.

When Home Office pathologist Nick Burrows came on the screen, the former seamstress fell silent, her wrinkly hands clutching her skirt as he relayed the findings on the little girl's mutilated body. This was only his second case and his eyes said it all.

Dr Gerald Myerscough, the local police surgeon, could only hint that what Rosie Quinn had suffered even after death had come from the outer darkness and was not of this world . . . Reading between the lines, it seemed that Quinn had tried in the crudest possible way to get rid of any evidence of his previous abuse. It was now an even more urgent matter of public safety that he be caught . . . The bulletin ended with a brief report that police divers had discovered human remains off the Deeps of Lethe while searching for the missing Helen Quinn.

Simon opened another can. He couldn't listen to any more of it. That bastard Quinn was still free and there they were, sitting fucking ducks, with no protection except for Kettle manning the computer next door.

'You go up and see your girlfriend.' Mrs Watts nudged his arm and pointed upstairs. 'There's no joy in grieving alone, I can tell you.'

So he went to her room and sat close to the only thing that mattered to him now – the one person in this whole shitty world he must protect.

'We'll go somewhere,' he said, Budweiser breath in her ear. 'Anywhere you like. Just say when.'

'It's not as easy as that.'

'It can be. We could go to Cornwall or Wales. I can do some forestry work. I've still got some contacts near Abergavenny and you—'

'What *about* me?'

'You could have babies . . . something decent to come out of all this. And I'll put a ring on your finger in indelible ink if I bloody have to.'

Suddenly the phone rang downstairs. Sheila had trailed it through from the kitchen and now it perched incongruously on a spare stool. It was DI Pringle, her tone urgent, and she wanted to speak to Abbie.

An hour later, they lay together in Abbie's room among their packed luggage which, like canvas and leather rocks, sheltered their bodies, while outside the clouds that had sneaked up and buried the earlier sun now darkened to rain.

To break the news gently, Abbie began with the end of Pringle's message. That the sister of Goosefoot's late landlord would like to meet them both while she was still in the UK.

'Why? You've got nothing to do with that pigpen any more, surely?'

Abbie hesitated, bit her lip. 'You're not going to like this.'

'Try me.'

'She wants us to hole up in there from next Monday afternoon onwards. Said it might be their last resort to catch Quinn, now the child is gone.'

Maggots . . . Worms . . .

Simon's breath stopped. He stared at her close up, her eyelashes curving soft on each cheek, her mouth awaiting his response, and the more he looked, she grew stiller, almost waxen, then alabaster, heavy in his arms.

Sheila Livingstone's paper towel had been busy round her eyes and with two mascara blurs dominating her face she looked ten years older.

'What's all this about you two leaving?' She found

things to fiddle with as Abbie and Simon waited for the right moment to go.

'It's not through choice, believe me.' Abbie put her arm round her and noticed the sleeper holes that had closed up in her ears, the unplucked hairs on the woman's chin.

'What the hell anyhow.' Sheila pushed chairs under tables as if she really didn't care any more. 'D'you know, I really fancy living in a big city. I mean a big, big city: Glasgow, Leeds, London . . . At least I'd get a life again.'

'You'd be great anywhere.' Abbie kissed her. 'But don't do anything rash meanwhile. Wait for us to get back.'

Sheila wagged a finger at Simon. 'You look after her. She's one in a million.'

'One in a million million, which is why we're having to go away for a while.'

'This is meant to be very secret,' Abbie whispered. 'So if anyone round here mentions it, make out you don't know.'

Sheila stared at her, waiting.

'We're meeting old Mr Mower's sister in Wisbech this afternoon. Goosefoot's hers now after all.' She was trying to break the news as gently as she could, but this wasn't going to be easy. Just seeing Sheila's expression change was bad enough. 'We'll only be staying at the cottage for a bit . . .'

The hotelkeeper's mouth fell open. 'You *what?*'

'Don't worry, we'll be getting full police protection.'

But in her shock Sheila had knocked a glass to the floor and left it there.

'They'll arrange all our shopping, postage, whatever.'

Simon tried hard to make it all sound normal, as if it was some place of refuge or a retreat.

'They think my presence there can lead Quinn into a trap.' Abbie was holding back tears by now.

'I don't believe this. What about your dad? Shouldn't he know?'

'*Nobody's* to know. If he does get in touch, we've just bummed off for a break somewhere. OK?'

'OK.' Sheila's hands covered her mouth.

'Do nothing and say nothing. That way we'll have a best chance. Promise?'

'Promise.' Sheila hesitated, then went over to the letter rack, where the second post had just left two envelopes. The first, a letter from her bank inviting her to take out a loan, went straight into the wastepaper basket.

'What's in the other one?' Simon was curious because of its Legal Aid franking and the pinky red letters reading 'Sanderson Boyd & Rickard, Solicitors'.

'Later. We'd better go.' Abbie pocketed it before going out to meet the blowing rain.

Simon stopped his new Audi at the construction site for one last glance at Kingfisher Rise.

'Hey. See that?'

The new barred gate bristled with barbed wire on which hung a Chinnery & Arkle auction notice. Beyond it, the place looked deserted, deathly still. Plot 2 lay smothered by a green tarpaulin that seemed to inhale and exhale with the wind, while parked diggers and dredgers lay lashed together and thickened by mud. There were no other vehicles, not the smallest signs of life, and the blinds were all down in the Willoughby.

'She's won,' was all Abbie could say to herself. Locating her Holtbury pen in her pocket, she flung it high into the air and watched it sink into an earth-yellow puddle. She also dug out the Ace of Spades card which she'd long since kept in her bag, and with one press of her toe, made it disappear under the surrounding mud.

'Why are you doing that?' Simon asked.

'We don't need any more bloody bad luck do we?' she replied.

During the drive to Wisbech, a strange sense of detachment lingered. Her job, her steps up the Holtbury ladder, had all ended and yet it didn't matter. For worse had happened, in fact the very worst, and having experienced that, nothing else could seem as bad again. She wondered about the other letter, so made an excuse to Simon that she needed a wee.

It wasn't until she was safely ensconced in the Ladies of the Little Chef near Fitton End, while Simon went to buy an Ordnance Survey map of mid-Wales, that Abbie finally opened the envelope. After reading the letter she stared at herself, whitening, in the mirror. Her whole body was stiff with fear. Every word spelt out disaster.

Why me, *for God's sake? Why* me?

And other travellers devouring their early teas who'd earlier seen a striking young woman pass them by, now saw a different person emerge from the toilet.

Eric Mower's sister was tiny – even more diminutive than the schoolgirl waitresses who plied backwards and forwards, their youthful faces pinkened by teapot steam. Her smile, when it came, covered her whole face, brown as a maple nut and weathered like hide. Abbie, still feeling aftershock, moved her chair nearer to the woman, as if she were the sun itself.

'Course my brother never really looked after that little cottage.' The woman from Denver, Colorado, played mother, spilling not a drop. 'He had no business letting it out to you in that state. You poor girl.'

'I was OK.' Abbie gratefully put her hands round the warm cup, while Simon still wondered what Abbie's letter was about. She'd not said a word in the car, just stared at nothing. It was as if he hadn't existed.

'Eric had too many other goslings in the pie, I guess,' Gwendoline Benning went on, chuckling to herself. She took no milk, no sugar, just a nibble of biscuit. 'I couldn't abide the place myself, I have to say.'

'Why's that?' asked Simon, passing Abbie the cakes, which she refused.

'I just got bad feelings there. It was weird. Still, it could make someone a nice litle vacation home, so my lawyer says.'

Abbie asked the older woman if she'd seen or heard any news of Black Fen and received an emphatic shake of the head, its white hair smoothed impeccably into a knot.

'My dear, there's too much news from everywhere. Me, I keep things simple. Age does that for one at least. Makes one more selective, I guess – and I sure select. But I have to admit that when the police got in touch with me about them having to occupy the cottage for a while, I did panic.'

'Did they say why *we* needed to be there?' Simon managed to tweak the envelope corner from Abbie's pocket and pulled it free.

'No, and I didn't ask them. Just as long as you two take care.'

'It'll be a couple of weeks at the most, but we've both been through quite a bit lately.'

Gwendoline Benning looked at him over her silver frames. 'I can see that, but hang on to the key and stay as long as you like. Do it good to be lived in again. Only thing is, it'll be up for sale beginning of July, once I've sorted out all his affairs. Probate shouldn't take long after that, or so they tell me . . .'

'I hope you don't mind my asking – ' Abbie felt now was the best time for this – 'but what did your brother actually die of?'

The American visitor paused, uncomfortable, then dabbed her lips with a napkin. 'In the bath. He'd had a stroke. Poor Eric.'

Jesus. Water again.

Simon finished his tea and stood up.

'Are you sure of that?'

The woman looked puzzled. 'Well, I should know. I am his sister, after all.'

In the silence that followed, Simon excused himself and went off to the Gents. Once he'd gone, Gwendoline Benning leaned forward.

'Maybe you shouldn't be going there at all.'

'We have to. We have no choice.' Abbie suddenly shivered. 'Anyhow, what do you mean?'

'Oh, nothing really, just that he wrote to me something about some strange prayer book.'

'Was it black, with the name Esmond Downey inscribed in the front?'

'Lord knows, but he also said that one day some very odd dolls appeared . . .'

'Dolls?' The pit of Abbie's stomach turned to stone.

'Yeah, three of them. And he told me that every time he tried to get rid of them they kept coming back.

'You mean he actually handled them?'

Gwendoline Benning didn't follow her drift at all and frowned. 'I guess he must have done.' Her eyes narrowed. 'Why do you ask that?'

'I don't know, forgive me.' Yet, recalling the old man's tremulous voice, his frail fear, she knew with greater certainty than ever that it was just a matter of time before she herself joined him.

Gwendoline Benning passed her the scones.

'Well, there we are. Eat up now, girl. Lord, if my steers had bones that stuck out like yours I'd never have afforded the air fare.' She ordered another pot of tea, then opened her handbag. 'Here's my card. There's a map on the back. My own little patch of the US of A. Eight hundred acres including a stretch of old railtrack. It's yours if you'd like to come on over.'

'Thanks, Mrs Benning.'

'Gwendoline, please. The Cool Dude Ranch ain't exactly four star, but our bar's never dry.'

Simon returned, his face set hard, even though he tried to behave normally.

He watched silently as Abbie wrote the St George's Sails phone number on a menu back and handed it over. 'Just in case.'

The American then tidied herself, picked up her saddle-leather bag and put her working hands into theirs in turn.

'The Home Office is paying me the rental for your stay at the cottage, so no worries. Good luck with whatever it is you expect, and thank you for coming along today – it's been good to meet you.'

They exchanged waves before she was lost among the busy tables.

The moment she was gone, Simon leaned forward. 'What's this then?' He brought out the solicitor's letter and held it up. Abbie's expression was the strangest he'd ever seen and she could barely speak. He slapped it on to the table. '*Do* you know what this means?'

'It's not my fault, for God's sake. I'd no idea Lilith Leakes wanted to leave me that shitty dump of hers. Anyhow, it's my private business. It was addressed to me.' She snatched the letter, stuffing it in her bag as if it was contaminated.

The sunlight boring through the window was forgotten, their table rapidly cleared as others hovered, waiting.

'Better go,' he said, his hand clutching a map of the Cambrian Hills and the Ceredigion coast, sensing with a bleak heart that bloody Wringland wasn't done with them yet.

Her boy is little Walter all over again and I can hardly bear to look at his fine clear eyes that met mine in a far better communion than I ever knew below. 'I am your Valentine,' they seem to say, and if I could cry I would . . .

Sixty-three

THE PREMISES OF Sanderson, Boyd and Rickard, Solicitors and Commissioners for Oaths, were situated in the middle of a long Edwardian terrace to the north of Gorrington. What had once been front parlours of respectable middle-class villas with names such as Mountview and Albany were now curtainless offices of accountants, insurers and the like. There was nowhere to park.

'How they do bloody business, I do not know.'

Simon finally left the Audi in a used car lot at the end of the road, ready to pose as a prospective punter upon their return if necessary. He was quiet, preoccupied, and held Abbie's hand tightly as if they were walking towards another unspeakable tragedy with the inevitability of night following day. She too felt foreboding and had got dressed in black that morning like an automaton, forgetting about her make-up. Her new Ray-Bans had left dents on either side of her nose, so she fumbled with her foundation and got an overload, staining her sleeves.

'You look fine.' He squeezed her hand. 'Anyhow, once you're a farmer's wife, it won't matter.'

'What?'

'Sorry. Sick joke.'

Then a deadly seriousness returned as they reached

the entrance, his thoughts churning with possibilities that germinated like seedlings with no light.

'There is a bright side, I suppose,' he said at last. 'The old girl may have been a closet millionaire – you know the sort of thing, living on crusts and cat food while stashing all the loot away.' He bent to kiss her while she was thinking hard, anything to resurrect this girl he'd fallen in love with.

'Mr Boyd'll be with you in a minute.' The receptionist looked both of them up and down, then smiled at Simon. 'Hot, isn't it?'

Jarvis Boyd's head showed round the door. 'Do come through. Melanie, can you check Mr Rickard's got the Clenchtoft file for this meeting?'

'Will do.' She obviously enjoyed her work and Abbie instantly resented her. The girl had a proper job.

The lawyer arranged an extra chair in front of his desk, which was littered with family photos. Boyd next cleared a space on his blotter and placed a box file marked L.A.L. in front of him. 'Curiouser and curiouser.' He snapped it open. 'The deceased certainly knew her own mind about things.'

'What do you mean?' Abbie asked, wanting him just to get on with it.

'Let's say it's doubtful there'd have been any will if she'd not met you, Miss Parker. Obviously you enjoyed a special relationship with Miss Leakes. Otherwise, as you probably know, the Crown would have had the right to her whole estate, unless any other claimants could be traced. Here it is.'

He detached a small photograph of the farm which Abbie took and passed to Simon. It looked grim even on a small scale.

Had the old woman somehow known what would happen to the Kingfisher Rise site? Known that she would soon be without a job? Abbie tried to recall her only conversation with the hermit, but Boyd had started to speak again.

'Her property consisted of Clenchtoft Farm, with fifty acres of land and forty thousand pounds in cash, which was, wait for it, found on the premises. According to the police, whoever murdered her either knew about the money but couldn't find it or had some other motive altogether . . .'

'My God,' Abbie turned to Simon.

'Sorry about the print, by the way. Melanie was trying out her new camera.'

'Doesn't matter. It's a stinking place,' Abbie said, noticing Lilith Leakes's request for burial at St Mary Magdalene and Melanie Smith's signature as witness.

'Have you actually been to the farm?'

'Indeed. Miss Leakes sent a note, via the late Mrs Buckley, for me to visit her there. With hindsight, I should have taken my mop and bucket. Must admit, I've never seen such squalor.'

Abbie started to read the will with Simon breathing in her ear. The words, slightly smudged, conspired with a future she was aleady dreading . . .

1. I, LILITH ANNIE LEAKES of Clenchtoft Farm, Black Fen, Lincolnshire, appoint JARVIS BOYD of Sanderson Boyd & Rickard, Havenden Road, Gorrington, to be the Executor and Trustee for the time being hereof . . .

2. I DEVISE and BEQUEATH all my real and

personal estate and effects of which I have power to dispose of by WILL (hereinafter called 'my Residuary Estate') in trust for my said new friend ABIGAIL PARKER and in the event of her decease in trust for my other small friend ROSIE URSULA QUINN attaining the age of eighteen years . . .

Simon and Abbie grew pale in the shaft of morning sun, their fingers touching then separating as Boyd continued.

'Of course, it would have been more conventional for her to leave her estate to *your* issue in the event of your death, rather than name another beneficiary,' Boyd added. 'But maybe she wasn't sure of your situation in that department.'

Abbie spun round. 'What do you mean?'

The lawyer shrugged. 'It's all hearsay, I know, like so much local gossip there, but Lilith Leakes did regard herself as something of a psychic. At least that's what Mrs Buckley told me when she and her husband last came in here.'

'So you're their solicitor as well?' Simon enquired, thinking what a small strange world this was.

'Oh yes. Like most of the other land-owners there, they'd been feeling Colonel Scott breathing down their necks for some time. Someone has to help protect their interests, and now that Mr Buckley's on his own, poor chap, we need to be extra vigilant.'

The young couple looked at each other, recalling the old man's undisguised greed.

'Anyhow, as I was saying,' Boyd continued, 'apparently Miss Leakes had forecast a quite uncanny incident some years before . . .'

'Oh?'

'Something along the lines of Mrs Buckley never having a live birth—'

'Ugh.'

'And we know now that's exactly what happened. Three late miscarriages, I gather.'

So *that* might explain those three angels in her cabinet . . . Abbie thought as Simon now gripped her hand, felt her pulse jumping in her wrist. She looked totally distraught.

'That's dreadful.'

The money vanished from her thoughts. All Abbie could see now was the farm's monstrous dark, still harbouring the ghost of Martha Robinson. She looked at Simon. At least Rosie'd been spared this inheritance. That's what she'd really wanted to say.

Jarvis Boyd rang his bell and, when Melanie obliged, asked for three coffees.

'Obviously, it's your own decision as to what you do, Miss Parker, and despite the farm's tragic association, the site itself could have many uses, subject to planning permission, of course.'

He nodded as his assistant passed round Portmeirion cups. Simon first.

'Are you sure there are no other claimants?' Simon asked suddenly, ignoring her attention. 'We've heard rumours that Lilith Leakes may have had a son.'

'And we actually met a Mrs Schaap from Rievely Hall several times. She claimed that her son was the child's father.' Abbie waited expectantly for Boyd's response.

The solicitor plopped a sugar cube into his coffee and stirred it for what she thought was longer than necessary.

'Mrs Schaap, God bless her, was not exactly – how shall I say? – entirely *compos mentis*.'

'What do you mean?' Simon leaned forward in consternation. 'She was lucid enough when I talked to her, and Abbie here—'

'I may be speaking out of turn, but didn't you know the poor woman had been in and out of hospital for years?'

'You mean a nuthouse?'

'Exactly. So let me re-emphasize, Miss Parker is now *sole* beneficiary, except . . .'

'Except?'

'I think it would be wise to keep all this under wraps for the time being. To save unpleasant speculation.'

'Can't I tell anyone?'

'I wouldn't recommend it.'

Simon frowned, not giving up. 'So there was *definitely* no son?'

'I repeat, no contender has come forward, despite all the publicity from news coverage, and by the way – ' Boyd softly reshuffled his papers – 'in case you're wondering, Miss Leakes's funeral's already been taken care of.' He coughed. 'As no relatives had made themselves known, I acted as her personal representative. It saves a lot of misunderstanding if it's someone from the legal profession.'

'I could have done that,' Abbie objected.

'I'm afraid not, Miss Parker. However, as the coroner released the Order for Burial last week, everything is in order.'

'The burial was last week?' Abbie was stung by this second exclusion.

'It was of necessity a strictly private and purely official affair, after a short service in the chapel of Broadlands Hospital near Gorrington. No voyeurs or vultures, you understand?' He gave Simon a knowing glance.

'Where's the grave then – or whatever?'

Jarvis Boyd finished his coffee and stood up.

'St Mary Magdalene. A very quiet occasion, as I'm sure you can appreciate.'

'You mean just her and the gravedigger?'

The lawyer nodded evasively, then looked at his watch.

'No police to see if her killer was hanging around then?' Simon asked, incredulous.

'That I'm not at liberty to divulge, but shall we just say that the burial took place – ' he hesitated – 'under cover of darkness.'

Abbie shivered.

'Now if you'll excuse me, I'm expecting another client at twelve.' Jarvis Boyd packed the documents away and pinged the file shut. 'The good news is, of course, that probate couldn't be simpler. No stocks or shares to deal with and no inheritance tax either. The actual dwelling was valued at only fifty thousand, but, as I've already implied, it's ripe for renovation.'

Simon was deep in thought as Boyd shook their hands.

'The inquest has been set for 27 July. Not a particularly good time as school holidays tend to take over. However, it will be public and a jury will be appointed. You're more than welcome to attend, to witness the coroner's verdict. I'll send you details nearer the day.'

'Thank you.'

'Of course, until the head is found, any findings are doomed to be incomplete. But a start must be made . . .'

'Head?' Abbie was aghast.

'You're joking.' But Simon knew he wasn't.

They lurched into sunlight, fresh after the mist, yet shadows sharp as knives had already entered Abbie's soul, and that dreadful laughter, never far away, was now like an oath of vengeance on them all.

*Those Baldwins spare nothing at Heck-
wardine to make him into a proper
farmer's son with a good eye for store
cattle and for when the land should be
turned, just like Ben Robinson before
him. But in the dark moments when
the herds are at rest, he is mine again
and it is as if he waits for me to touch
his shoulder and speak in my Master's
tongue . . .*

Sixty-four

Humberwell Crematorium, eight miles north of Walsoken and barely three years old, served an increasingly ageing local population. Set in lawns smooth as skin, new brick, new rosebeds and burial plots had been laid out like bleak war graves. Everything sanitized, even shining on that bland June morning.

The car park was full by eleven o'clock, and a representative of the Education Authority plus some hospital staff and local tradespeople filled the pine-clad room. A single spray of cream lilies stood by the lectern, giving off a funereal smell.

Abbie stood near the door, gazing through a sea of mourning hats, just to be there for the little girl's last journey. And to see if Evil was among them, paying his respects.

A few people, including the head teacher, glanced her way, their faces wet and swollen. WPC O'Halloran was there, without lipstick, and both Aldreth and Stock were solemn in their uniforms. Sheila and Simon had simply accepted that Abbie wanted to attend the ceremony alone.

She wondered if Helen Quinn's elderly parents would be there, but they obviously had no intention of travelling over from Wisbech for a granddaughter who'd remained unforgiven for her one act of retaliation against her own mother.

The solitary bearer left his damp footsteps on the cord carpet. Then everyone sat down to face a small ivory-coloured casket with the new doll placed on top and a wreath bearing two pink wellingtons, which had been Abbie's idea. She cried out at the sight of it and someone touched her arm, all lavender and mothballs.

'It's all right, me duck.'

'No, it's not,' she whispered back, as yet another stranger began to speak of the love of God for all his children.

'Bloody fairytales,' Abbie murmured.

'Hush!'

Suddenly Abbie felt a finger in her back that stayed there. A quick glance at the veiled onyx eyes, the red mouth, told her it was Avril Lawson, a smiling reveller at the feast.

Abbie broke away and pushed through the late-comers and out into the rain, just as 'Jesus Wants Me for a Sunbeam' began, and Lawson's be-suited, be-wigged companion followed her with his red eyes.

'You all right, miss?'

Someone was setting a marker into the perfect geometry that was to be Rosie's spot. But she ran past him, feeling the rain meet the tears on her face.

I tell him his mother was a whore with the young men from the North Sea, and it's a wonder he wasn't diseased when he met the world. I also tell him that to know one's place of birth is everyone's right, and after I've finished he will return there. I know.

Sixty-five

MONDAY'S DRIZZLE had eased to a whisper, setting everything out of focus. Goosefoot Cottage was almost invisible from the end of Smithy Lane and before dark the mist would steal over the sea like a wraith.

Simon's Audi was hidden in one of the Sails' garages, but the Fiat stood like a come-on outside the gate. Irene Pringle had decided it best to advertise the fact they were there, even to leave a chink of light showing between the drawn curtains.

'We see the bait.' Those were Captain Oliver's words during the last unit briefing he'd attended. So what was different? For Goosefoot Cottage read snare. The two of them trapped in a diving bell waiting for the predator's teeth . . .

Simon had unpacked a crate of Fosters and a box of dried goods, and was standing by the door casting a wary eye over the gloomy garden when he heard the rustle of reeds. Someone was approaching. 'Who's that?' He was supposed to be getting a gun for protection and felt useless without one now.

'Only me. DI Pringle. I wasn't able to give you final details earlier, sorry. Everyone's chasing their own tails at the moment.'

Abbie'd said she was tall, but this was different. The

woman with a crew cut was taller even than Aldreth. Maybe the height requirement's gone berserk, he thought, as the senior officer emerged with an Oddbins carrier bag and a small portable electric fire. She was dressed in cords, navy jumper and a quilted jacket – the universal country woman unlikely to attract attention. 'Right. We've got two in the barn, Keegan and Biddell, plus a portaloo. They're disguised as farmworkers by the way, and both tooled up.'

'Armed latrines? The mind boggles.'

Pringle allowed herself the merest smile. She liked him, an army man – maybe what she should have done years ago, but it had puzzled her more than once that he'd opted to give it all up.

'And here's yours.'

A discreet 9mm. Beretta with a nice bit of weight. Plus the ammo.

'Thanks.'

'Let's hope you don't need it.'

Abbie came out, drying her hands, still grieving and unable to put Rosie's coffin out of her mind. She saw the gun and felt an instant knot in her stomach. This wasn't going to be mothers and fathers together in a cosy cottage. This was life and death, where other deaths had preceded. Her eyes wandered to the bedroom window above. No way would she ever go up there again.

Pringle turned to her. 'I'm sorry there's no fridge, and we couldn't risk the hassle of bringing a generator in but, as I explained earlier, you'll manage, and we'll try to get fresh supplies in as discreetly as possible. Now, as far as outside is concerned, make your gardening efforts convincing, Abbie. Don't keep looking up from what you're doing and, above all, come straight in the moment you see or hear anything unusual. Understood?' Her trained eye roved over the misted scene around the cottage. 'DC Mansfield will be staying here with you as well. He won't invade your privacy, least he'll try not to.' She checked her watch. 'Should be here in five minutes, OK?'

'Sure.' Simon led the way back indoors, thinking that Irene Pringle was nothing if not thorough.

'Can I make a fire?' Abbie suddenly asked and the DI looked thrown for a moment. The grate's black emptiness allowed a thin draught from the chimney to chill the room. 'It'll warm us up at night and – ' she looked at Simon – 'it may be important.'

Pringle shook her head absently. There'd been something else she'd meant to say. Something *more* important . . .

'It's our only defence.' Abbie said simply. 'To keep Martha Robinson's spirit away. She used to live here, for God's sake!'

Simon put his arm round her. She smelt of soap and Jif. If it was anywhere else, he'd be upstairs, getting used to her again, but now desire was a luxury.

'Point taken, but no,' Pringle said. 'We don't need a fire risk. Now, where was I? Ah, yes. We saw Miss Lawson, this morning, running along Tithe Lane, in some distress. She told us someone was following her and gave us a description. Said he was a bird-watching type . . .'

'Wind-burnt?' Simon asked, seeing Abbie start. 'Hat? binoculars?'

'Don't know about that, but he was certainly talking to himself.'

'It's him.' Abbie remembered the procession along Herringtoft. 'Shit.'

'We did warn her not to go out alone. She knows about Mrs Buckley and Mrs Watts, but she still won't hear anything against him and insisted it was her duty to keep an eye on the rectory and the church.'

'Can't you bring her in, make her tell us more about him?'

'We've already thought of that, but it might make things worse – for us, I mean. If she's still protecting him in any way, it'll make her more determined. Could still be an option though,' she added, seeing their look of dismay, 'if push comes to shove.'

'The woman's a bloody nutter.'

Pringle ignored that. Victim stress was part of the job.

'Is there any news on Mrs Schaap?' Simon was trying to keep cool.

Pringle shook her head. Some things seemed beyond human logic, including the fact that Colonel Scott, as the missing housekeeper's long-term and supposedly caring employer, was proving a surly and obstructive witness.

'We're piecing one or two things together. The flood in the Show Home for example. Would be different altogether if it had come from the mains—'

'What was the cause of it then?' Abbie interrupted.

'It was sea water.'

'Are they sure?'

'Yes. Now, just one more thing.' She tried not to look at their stricken faces.

'Neither of you step outside that gate.'

When she'd left, they both stood in silence. Abbie stared at the unlit, useless grate, the borrowed chairs imported from the Sails and the couch where she'd lain that first night and dreamed of the man who was now standing

next to her. What a place to die! What a sick twist of fate
that she was here again, with her one remaining hope of
happiness. She put her ear to the boarded-up window,
where the fisherman's shots still echoed through the
gloomy afternoon.

Simon knew what she was thinking. 'This is for Rosie,
remember?' His voice seemed far away. 'We mustn't
forget that.' He tried to draw her close to him, but Abbie
had heard something else. Another noise from outside,
then a gentle tap on the door.

Simon's hand went to his gun. 'Who is it?'

'Mansfield, CID.' He showed his ID, the photo taken
after a severe haircut.

Simon let him in and shook hands. 'Sorry, I forgot
you were coming. Hey, why aren't you eight foot three?'

'What d'you mean?' The detective looked puzzled.

'Nothing. Here's Abbie, my friend for life. Fiancée,
actually.'

She blushed, straightening her top.

'Shithole's not the word, is it?' said the policeman.
'Give me a French camp site every time.' Mansfield made
for the stairs. 'Remember, be patient, be vigilant. Got to
keep our eyes on the ball.'

'Yes – sir.' Then Simon saw Abbie look at the fireplace
and go white.

'What's up?'

'It's impossible . . .'

The same little prayer book with its worn black
covers. The one she'd chucked into the foundations of
plot 2 after it had appeared on her desk. She remembered
the cigarette lighter left on the draining board and coaxed
a flame from it, but the book wouldn't burn. Then she

stamped on it hard, twisting her foot, but nothing would alter it, make it die.

'Let's take a look again.' Simon ran through the pages like a pack of cards, expelling dusty air, then looked again inside the flyleaf, where now a smear of dried blood covered Esmond Downey's name.

'Shit.'

'I've had enough,' she groaned.

Simon took it outside and tried to tear the pages from their sewn spine, but despite its flimsy construction it stayed intact. Then he had an idea. It would only take *two* minutes if he ran as he used to in the old days. That same two minutes might just save their lives – but he hadn't reckoned on the mist. It was thickening in from the sea, disguising the different levels at the end of Smithy Lane and the knee-high beet crop in Buckley's field.

Morpeth Bank was slippery with wet grass, and for every step forward he slid back part of the way, until finally he reached the top and ran to where he'd uncovered the stumps.

No stumps now. He stopped and stared, his heart beginning a different beat. There was just the smooth semi-dried mud of the track to see. He knelt down and traced with his fingers where he was sure they'd been, but someone had removed them and filled up the holes. Someone who obviously didn't want his discovery spoiling things.

Simon looked round, shivering, his breath coming in short gasps. Abbie would be worried sick, never mind the police. He'd wanted to put the bloody book here, in a significant spot, where people had suffered and prayed, not just discard it anywhere. He then thought of Colonel

Scott, who'd put an offer in for the Kingfisher Rise site. Maybe the greedy sod was going to try his luck at the auction, demolish the lot and create a retirement complex complete with mini-golf course. The remains of a gallows nearby would hardly be appealing. But maybe there was another explanation . . .

That's what the mist does. It disorients and turns a man's mind . . .

Undeterred, he began to scrape at the same ground, forgetting the time and what needed to be done at Goosefoot. Under the earth's skin lay something hard which almost took his nails off. It seemed concrete and inviolable. Then a touch on his shoulder. He spun round, nearly toppling over.

'Mr Cresswell. Well, well.' The voice was rougher but recognizable. 'We have unfinished business, in case you've forgotten. Now move.'

Simon felt the gun prodding his back and stood up. Army training took over and he kept his movements slow, deliberate, so he could gauge what was going on, so his muscles could prepare themselves.

'Down there.'

Never argue. Let the cunts think they've got the upper hand. Just think, think, think . . .

He thought of the Wenn only steps away. He was a good swimmer. That was one thing he'd sorted out after Llangorse. No one would ever do that to him again.

He took a deep breath, filling his lungs as if for the rest of his life, then sprinted and dived, the biggest dive he'd ever performed. Quinn's shot slewed past him as he hit the water.

It was cold enough to slam his whole body into instant rigor mortis, so all he could do was float with the current into the river's mouth, past the old clinker-built barges, until he could angle into the Wenn's timber side.

There was nothing to grip on to, just oily wood. No rope or wire, not even any grass. He felt weak, his chest barely working, his arms sticking out like dead fins, and his legs, weighted down by his boots, were unable to stop him sinking.

Suddenly he felt something beneath him. Not sea-weed, it was too solid for that, yet a certain substance that moved when he nudged against it, rising and falling, obstructing his progress. He tried to kick it out of the way, but the object lay stubbornly across his thighs. In his delirium he remembered a bin-linered dog he'd once found in the River Usk, how without the connective tissue its bones had shifted and poked against the plastic with a life of their own. This was a corpse, he knew it.

He thought instantly of Helen Quinn. His mouth filled with oil as he screamed and threshed the water, both the prayer book and the gun sliding from his pockets to be lost in the silt below. By some miracle he reached the side of the lugger *King John* and hauled himself up by its mooring rope, past the hold full of stinking fish and on to the deck.

Meanwhile Quinn, who could not risk being spotted by barge crews and the like, disappeared among the sugar beet, his head full of reprisals.

'Where've you *been*? I've been going mad.' Abbie dragged Simon in and bolted the door. 'Mansfield was going to give you another five minutes, then they'd have sent someone looking for you.' She looked at his hands. 'And where's that prayer book?'

'I've got rid of the bloody thing.'

He was a shivering spectre of himself, his new black jacket layered with oil. She peeled it carefully from his back.

'The gun's fucking gone as well,' he added miserably. 'And he's bloody out there still, took another pot at me.'

Abbie went to the stairs, her legs trembling. 'Ian?' she whispered. 'He's back.'

Mansfield stayed resolutely by the landing window. 'I know, but I didn't want to break up the happy reunion.'

Happy? What was that word, for God's sake? Stupid man.

'Listen, mate, stay put now, eh?' he warned, while Simon crashed on to the couch and let Abbie undress him, her hands warm on his skin.

'Quinn was up on the bank, larger than bloody life,' he panted. 'And another thing, I think there's a stiff in the river.'

He was down to his vest and boxer shorts, which Abbie made him step out of before wrapping him in a towel.

They heard Mansfield speak into his two-way, then he raised his voice to address Simon. 'You were lucky to get back in one piece, I'm telling you.' His eyes were still hunting through what was now fog outside, sensing things might get busy by nightfall.

'Would you like a beer?' Simon called out by way of apology. The cans were waiting and his mouth needed a serious antidote to the water of the Wenn.

'No, I can't. And if I were you I'd go easy on it.'

Abbie didn't like the sound of that. She pulled some clean clothes from Simon's bag. 'Get these on, quick.'

After gulping from a can, Simon went to check the kitchen cupboards. A sudden hunger had invaded his stomach, but instead of miniature bangers in baked beans or meat balls, he found pasta tubes, rice, dried peppers and tins of haricots verts.

'Who got this shitty stuff in?' he demanded.

'Not guilty.' Abbie was following him round, trying to dry his hair.

Abbie then filled the kettle, set out three unmatching cups and pulled a spider from the sugar bowl. She listened in dread for an encore of that childish singing, the hideous laughing, the reappearance of those rough red hands, and whenever the floorboards suddenly creaked overhead or the lavatory flushed, channelling cistern water down behind the sink, she almost fainted.

Then by ten o'clock all was quiet, with Simon and Abbie sleeping on the settee, the hatches battened against the deepening sky and the tide crawling over the marsh. When he woke again, it was completely dark. He turned towards her, drinking in her breath, his hands cupping her breasts, but in the hushed aftermath, like all the hunted creatures in a dangerous world, he strained to hear each murderous sound.

Abbie brushed her hair, staring at the spotted mirror, then ran some water into the sink to clean her teeth. The toothbrush seized up in her mouth as she noticed blood staining the bristles. Her teeth were, like the rest of her, falling apart. Besides, her period was two days' late. She knotted the laundry bags: mostly Simon's things, still damp and oily, still reeking of the river. The new leather jacket now resembled the skin of Peat Bog Man, on its own, as if in quarantine, though the smell seemed to snake through the knot however tightly she tied it.

Through a crack in the warped wood of the front

door she glimpsed Constable Wickling arrive with fresh groceries. He slipped round the side of the cottage to notify the men in the barn of his presence before he knocked. At least the food was now more interesting than on his first forays since he'd discovered a new deli in Snutterwick, but Abbie wasn't eating much. Nor were the Fosters touched. The former soldier knew one can of the stuff could slow him down. And now wasn't the time to be slow.

Each day the overgrown garden succumbed to shears and the scythe. Swathes of cuttings lay heaped around the cottage walls, while inside its ceilings seemed to have lowered even further on their airless tomb and each sound was a possible introduction to murder.

Abbie's breathing seemed tense and shallow in the sour air, even during their noiseless lovemaking on the couch. Afterwards she'd lie coiled against him, conserving his moist heat, then, while Simon slept, she'd listen to Mansfield settling to his watch upstairs.

A former navy man, he preferred the floor, and he kept a photo of his wife alongside him in a heart-shaped frame. He whistled through his teeth whenever he took a piss and kept his clothes smart. At six every morning, he'd roll his sleeping bag into its pouch and take his first cigarette.

In the evenings, Simon laboured over his army fitness routines and then tackled crossword puzzles, something he'd never bothered with before. At least they kept his brain going, while she, feeling worn as driftwood, left him alone, only touching him in passing with a weak smile.

Minutes seemed hours, and by the fourth night, Abbie

knew every crack, every ancient corner and its wildlife. She counted woodlice, keeping the bigger ones aside to identify with Tippex, and noted how the living fed from the dead, leaving only shells. She pondered how they could swim and scale heights, and if she was feeling generous gave the winner freedom of the garden.

Now it was twenty past five and she felt as though she'd never experienced anywhere in her life other than this stale yellow darkness.

At six o'clock, Mansfield confirmed that Simon had guessed right. The tide had indeed delivered the reverend's wife back to Black Fen.

The next day brought a fog so intense that Abbie couldn't even make out the garden gate, and as the Friday afternoon wore on its intensity grew to isolate the cottage in a deadly vaporous shroud.

'It's getting bad out there.' Ian Mansfield hovered on the stairs. 'Can't see a tinker's arsehole.' He stretched his arms out like a bat. 'Anyone making a cuppa?'

Simon looked up, distracted from his crossword clues, but Abbie got up to oblige and the water spewed from the verdigris-encrusted tap into the kettle like Angel Falls.

Suddenly Mansfield ducked to one side of the landing window. 'Turn it off!' he yelled. 'Something's going on.'

Simon threw down his crossword and leapt up the stairs two at a time. Abbie followed from the kitchen, but not quickly enough.

As steam rattled from the spout and mist suddenly curled round her ankles from the now open back door, she was aware of a tall figure in police uniform coming closer. Either Brad Biddell or Phil Keegan must have left his post, she thought, or maybe Constable Wickling was making a rare call. But no. Under the glow of the bare light bulb she could see that *this* officer had veins in his eyes like blood in the sea and gave no word of greeting. It was Quinn.

Abbie tried to push past him, but the Devil had given Quinn the extra strength to drag her from the kitchen and then carry her bodily out into the dark blanket of fog.

The back door was left swinging behind them as finally Simon and Mansfield gave chase, following her screams, but the taller man tripped and fell like a length of timber, obstructing the other's progress.

'Phil? Brad?' Mansfield yelled into the fog as he picked himself up, nettles rashing his hands with a terrible pain. But there was no reply.

He and Simon hurried on, stumbling over oil cans, scrap-wood and nests of old wire at the rear of the cottage, until they reached the broken-down fence bordering the Buckley's fallow field.

Too late. Quinn and Abbie had vanished.

'Jesus!' Simon listened for the faintest sound coming from the emptiness around him as the police torches played their misty beams in all directions. Then he left Mansfield and turned to run back, groping along the cottage wall with his hands so that he wouldn't fall. Yelling out Abbie's name, he vaulted the front gate, catching his boot heel and lurching to the ground in Smithy Lane as the sudden lights of an approaching police car pierced the veil of fog.

Now I am angered. He's bending his ear to that other voice which abandoned me in my time of need and he prays to it most hours of the day. While he's milking, whenever he's alone and thinks no one is listening, he offers prayers which in my life only cursed me. I can see I shall have to be more insistent and when he begs for peace make myself more easily heard . . .

Sixty-six

'I ALWAYS KNEW YOU had pretensions as an historian, Miss Parker.'

Hideous with false black hair and whitened features, in chilling contrast, Quinn busied himself with the attic door. 'The pity of it is, you were never straight with me,' he snorted. 'No one's ever called Stella these days, and what a dissembler you were, pretending I was your uncle . . .'

He crossed two sections of stout battening and hammered them in, then dragged over a chest of drawers to wedge the door tight. 'Not only are lies sinful, but yours have wasted much of my time and made it impossible for me to continue my ministry here . . .'

The bat room?

It was barely light, with shit on the beams and walls of unrendered brick. Too high for the reassurance of trees, too low for the secrecy of clouds. No tokens of other lives. Just Rosie's prison.

Abbie looked desperately for a way out, but there was none. If only Simon hadn't charged up the stairs. If only she'd realized sooner who'd come into the cottage. She felt anger with herself, with everyone . . . If she could only get hold of his gun, wherever it was, she reasoned, she might stand a chance of escape.

'There.' Quinn straightened up and slithered out of

his uniform jacket to reveal a bloodstained vest whose armholes sagged to his waist. He hunted through a small CD collection on the shelf, but even his pleasure in his only congregation's feeble efforts at escape was spoilt by that same voice filtering into his head.

'Sick bastard,' Abbie muttered having seen no tell-tale bulges in that jacket's pockets, nor any other clues as to his weapon's whereabouts. She turned to face the window, suddenly and ferociously intent, but whitewashed strokes hatched out the misted tops of yews and the graveyard below.

Quinn scrutinized his music collection, then deliberated. He slotted in a disc and fast-forwarded to the Requiem and Kyrie.

'Verdi's my man, you know. Heavenly, just heavenly. Are you familiar with his work?' His lips looked parched, his fingers like bleached bone.

She sensed that the air was thick with death and in that moment could feel what Rosie had experienced. But for her there was no distant light, no embracing glow or come-hither angels. Dying was not coming unknowingly. It was giving her plenty of notice.

'*Dies irae, dies illa, solvet saeclum in favilla,*' Quinn sang in a deep bass. '*Teste David cum Sibylla . . .*' His wig swaying separately to the rhythm. '*Quando judex est venturus, cuncta stricte discussurus . . . Quantus tremor est futurus . . .*' Then he came closer, breathing heavily into her hair.

There was only one window, its smears of whitewash blocking out all events below. Abbie wondered whether she could distract him enough to get a chance to open it. That seemed the only way. But no, he was coming over.

'Tell me truthfully now.' He drew up the only other

chair so she could smell his long-unwashed body. 'Did
you enjoy the funeral?' His knees bored against her thigh,
as if to make his whole being at one with hers. 'I thought
you looked quite fetching in black. And how about your
little pleasure cruise? D'you know, I've always wanted to
make more use of all this sea we've got round here. Bit
of a botched job though, you'd have to admit. Better if
I'd done it myself, rather than giving that halfwit *carte
blanche* . . .'

Abbie felt more than sick with fear now. She tried
to express her loathing for him and what he'd done to
Rosie, to claim she'd survived the sea to help put him
away for the rest of his evil life. But nothing came.

'Go on, go on, I do like to see a little anger. Especially
in the fairer sex.'

Abbie lowered her face and whispered what she
thought of him.

Quinn tutted. 'Oh dear, I'd show a little more respect
if I were you, Miss Parker. You don't seem to understand
anything. My daughter was born for me. She knew that,
and so did her creator . . .' Suddenly he began to beat his
head, as if to shake whatever had lodged there out
through his ears.

Abbie tried to swivel away, but his boot savagely
found her leg.

'And talking of the Almighty, you might well be
asking yourself when it was I first found Him. When
indeed? That thing that gives shape and meaning to our
rancid little lives . . .'

Abbie's chin now hung on her chest.

'Are you sitting comfortably?' As another blow from
his shoe made her lips crunch in pain against her teeth.
'Then I'll begin. The trouble is, God is never without his

shadow. One day I walk in the light, the next in darkness. So it is with everyone. Just like chiaroscuro. Byers taught me that word.'

Abbie sucked in her breath. It was time to fight back. She pretended to be Simon in his fearless days. It helped a bit.

'What about those other words you keep hearing? Looks like they're doing your head in most of the time.'

Warm blood flooded her mouth after he struck again, and in her mind she saw Rosie's eyes unblinking, then nothing.

The Offertorio brought her round and for a dizzy moment Abbie thought she was still in hell.

O Jesus, help me, help me . . .

What else did he have in mind for her? She saw him by the door, putting his jacket back on.

'Unfortunately, I have other problems to attend to now. I need to clear my mind, to recall something of my past. That is priority number one, because my past can *never* be taken from me.'

He switched off the Sanctus. She swore at him, then listened to the miracle of muffled voices outside, which started her praying desperately. Quinn seemed to notice nothing, as if back in the private dark of the Baldwins' Heckwardine Farm, deep in the green folds of Herefordshire.

Abbie rocked in her chair, waiting for her prayers to be answered, but she couldn't hear anything now beyond the rectory and silently screamed. Quinn's trance ended. He began pacing back and forward to a trap-door lid placed in the far corner of the attic room.

'And what, you may ask, about my beautiful Miss Lawson?'

Abbie's ears pricked up at the woman's name and she listened as he murmured on. 'My Dame aux Fleurs I called her after I'd first set eyes on her walking down the aisle on the day of Saint Luke, framed by her own *Chrysanthemum morifolium.* My favourite flower, although our French cousins allow them only for funerals, which seems such an awful pity. But tell me, Miss Parker, have you noticed her eyes?'

His voice was obscenely mellifluous and seductive, yet Abbie was desperately trying to recall Simon's voice instead.

'I asked you,' he said, interrupting her thoughts in a more menacing tone, 'have you seen her eyes?'

'Yes.'

'What colour are they then?'

'Black.' How could she ever forget?

'Ah. But that's not all.' Quinn smiled with teeth like a set of ochre shells shining with spittle.

'They burned like planets on the dark side of the moon – just for me. No woman has ever done that before. Not even my wretched mother, and I really ought to say God forgive her, but I cannot. Not even my wife. So you see, the world is truly full of wonders. Now where was I? Yes, my flower, Miss Lawson.' He smiled. 'But I'm afraid she has lately become more like the *Helleborus niger,* full of showy blooms but bearing a poison that has begun to taint me. So you see, I have no choice.'

He began to sing anarchically, waving his hands as if conducting himself. 'Blest are the pure in heart, for they shall see our God, the secret of the Lord is theirs, their soul is Christ's abode ... Not that you'd know much about that, Miss Parker, but at last I have both her *and* the one who forsook me.' His windmill arms beat the air, then struck his chest with a hollow sound. 'And talk of the Devil.' He pulled open the trap door to uncover ten blood-red, varnished fingernails frantically clawing the air. Quinn promptly ripped the cowl from the face of his prisoner in the storage area below.

The stench of decay was overpowering, almost solid, as Avril Lawson stared helplessly from one to the other, her mouth a square of masking tape and half her forehead bald from a missing eyebrow. Abbie gasped, but no words would come.

'And what do we do with the Devil, pray, Miss Parker? Have you been listening? How do we best dispose of God's leavings?'

'Go to hell!' Abbie's instinct was to reach down and pull the woman to safety, but Quinn stood too close, ready to spring.

She willed Simon to be on his way, his boots already on the stairs, as the crazed fugitive bent towards the false nun.

'Exactly. See how great minds conspire, Miss Lawson. I'm afraid the vote goes against you.' He moved closer to the opening that boxed the woman in, his feet crushing her pleading hands. 'But first we must purify, must we not, Miss Parker?'

Abbie half turned, to see him urinate into the opening, and despite another wave of sickness she tried to offer her some words of comfort.

But Quinn kicked the trap door shut on Avril Lawson's pitiful wailing and that split second gave Abbie her last chance. She attacked the window with desperate strength, seeing the mist was lifting and trees glinted silvery in the little sunlight. It was her turn soon, she knew. Like all the others lined up in his madness.

The old glass was easy, weak in its frame, and it was as if she wore armour, feeling nothing as she hurtled through it into the air outside, until the crushing pain of landing on some lower roof, she didn't know where, and smelling, feeling, blood warming her skin. She heard a shout, then more sounds of glass splintering. She twisted round to see Quinn scrambling down from the sill, his dark trousered legs dangling in space until, with a deep cry, he fell beside her and clamped his hands round her throat.

His arm cut off her air supply as he began to haul her through the undergrowth towards the track leading over Buckley's land. Despite her injuries, Abbie tried to fight him off, bite his hand, anything, and he struggled to keep his grip on her as he ran.

'Give yourself up!' Pringle roared, poised to fire, but not taking any risks as a bramble bush had sprung back making them invisible. 'We'll get him. Stay clear!' she shouted to Simon, who'd charged on ahead of her. They found Abbie lying abandoned, seeing a hundred faces in the sky, and not one was her dead mother's ... They covered her with a blanket, then let the dogs run free.

Simon held her hand and never once let it go. 'I'll make it up to you, Abs.' He choked back his tears. 'I promise.'

As Quinn slithered, eel-like, away from his pursuers, heading towards Canal Farm.

So, despite all my intercessions, he is to go and kneel at the feet of God, my other betrayer. Damn him and everything he touches. When he next prays I'll put the gapeworm in his gullet and turn his mind. But that won't be the end of it. The strength of four men is still mine and he will know it. He will know it . . .

Sixty-seven

SIMON'S EYES WERE the first thing she saw when she woke. Two blue fires burning into her confusion, his arm close round her neck. He tried not to look at her cheek, where they'd stitched the wound into a long ridge, where blood pricks bubbled to pink through the new dressing.

A saline drip snaked from a bag over the bed into her hand, limp on the sheet next to a morphine pump for whenever she needed a boost. On the locker stood flowers from Aldreth and Pringle, with a basket arrangement from Simon himself and its accompanying card wreathed in kisses.

Her eyelids half opened. 'Does Quinn know I'm here?' Abbie asked suddenly. She would never forget that white, mad face as long as she lived.

'Nobody does – not even your dad. They couldn't risk it.'

The ambulance had been disguised as an ordinary van in case someone in Black Fen had managed to follow it to Wisbech, to the Sancta Maria Clinic.

'Nor Sheila?'

'No.'

At the end of her next check-up, while Simon had gone to sit in the waiting room, Abbie had asked the nurse to do a pregnancy test to confirm what she already knew.

However, an hour later, with Simon out looking for a coffee machine, the nurse pronounced the result negative. Taken aback by her patient's vehement disagreement, she tried, in her soft Suffolk accent, to explain that to be six days overdue wasn't abnormal, given Abbie's recent trauma. But not for one minute did her words ring true.

And now as Simon sat close, his breath mingling with hers, Abbie felt different, strangely alienated, knowing that nothing from now on would ever be the same again . . .

There was a wistfulness in his gaze she'd not seen before and it was unnerving. He stroked her hair, and made to kiss her, but Abbie gestured with her free hand to be left alone, and he retreated. 'Look, when you're better we'll start a new life away from all this evil shit . . .'

Her eyes glazed over. It didn't mean anything, not any more. She winced at the sudden spasm of pain inside and pressed the morphine button while he stood by, helpless.

'And we'll take that Mrs Benning up on her word.' Simon looked out beyond the gauze curtain to a summer sky edged by trees. 'Why not? Just think of all that space, that wildness, you and me under the stars . . . Would you like that, Abs?'

She nodded, almost asleep again, and he cradled her in his arms, imagining they were already there.

True to his word, he'd bought tickets to Denver and organized a hire car so they wouldn't be dependent on Gwendoline Benning and her husband for any trips out from the ranch. He'd even chosen a new set of luggage for the occasion, in matching green – His and Hers – with each case boasting an interior courtesy light. Plus maps of course, sometimes the only language he really understood, all now stored in Abbie's room back at the Sails, the room they'd decided to share – thus halving the rent – once she was well enough to return.

After Quinn's fatal shooting of Keegan and Biddell at Goosefoot Cottage, Sheila had begged Aldreth to find somewhere else to house the Incident Room, so two days later an empty council house in Smithy Lane was occupied, restoring the hotel to its former quietude.

The hotel keeper had welcomed Abbie back with not the usual commiserations but anger that they'd not told her earlier of the ordeal, and at Simon in particular for letting Abbie stay at the cottage in the first place. She was secretly appalled by her scar, the present state of her friend's once pretty legs, and more than once had retreated into the kitchen to hide her tears.

'For Christ's sake, Simon, do you want her dead too?' she reproached him as he helped get the lounge bar back to normal. 'Hasn't there been enough death round here, what with those coppers and now that poor Darren Greenhalgh?'

'What?' Simon silently put down the chair he was carrying and perched on the window seat, feeling the warm sun on his back. 'We didn't know that.'

'How could you, stuck in that bloody hole? Even I wasn't allowed to phone you.'

'Sorry.' He'd never seen her looking so upset, her hands continuing to wring out her cloth until there was not a drop left in it.

'You'd better get away from here, I'm telling you,' she continued. 'God knows, you need to.'

'Course we will. It's all fixed.'

So how could he tell her about Abbie inheriting Clenchtoft? It was that horror which lurked behind his every thought, every waking moment. That place of the headless corpse no doubt waiting for its young owner, for yet another unwitting victim. New blood on the land . . .

Each night, to the Wenn's rise and fall and the nudging of its vessels against their berths, Abbie and Simon lay plotting their future and asking questions to which, then, there were no answers – only the small sounds of ensuing dreams and nightmares.

Meanwhile, Goosefoot Cottage stood boarded up with a 'For Sale' sign behind its front wall. Apart from the fast-regrowing garden, it was as though no one had set foot there for years. Even those buried under the mounds near the smaller barn would remain until such time as a warm North Sea bore their little bones away to its plundering bed.

Sheila had then shut up shop, entrusting Mr and Mrs Turling to call in on Saturdays to check the place over. She'd taken a ten-day coach trip with Mrs Watts, up to York, beginning with the sealess, sheltering Vale of Pickering.

'It'll do Sheila and the old girl the world of good.' Simon stared across at Abbie out of the window as their United Airways flight UA907 angled upwards away from earth. 'Christ knows we could all do with a bit of normality.' He summoned one of the hostesses and asked for two vodkas, but Abbie declined hers.

She was too busy watching the M25 and its network

of feeder roads, choked already even though it was only seven a.m. Who'd want to bring another life into this bolted cabbage of a country, she thought, seeing the endless developments haemorrhaging out from the London suburbs. Four, five, six each to a house, plus cars and yet more cars ... Her hand rested on her stomach under her denim jacket. Not her, not anyone in their right mind, would want to add to it all, but here she was with the decision already made for her.

'I think I'm pregnant,' she announced suddenly.

'You're what?' His plastic cup of vodka tilted precariously by his lips.

'I'm two weeks late.'

'Shit, Abs. You sure? Why on earth didn't you tell me?' Simon squeezed her hand, his mind racing ahead. It was everything he'd dreamed of. Him, a dad, and intending to be a better one than his own had ever been. 'That's fucking amazing! Oh, Abbie ...'

A man sitting nearby with an antiques magazine looked up and smiled as Simon placed his outspread fingers on her stomach.

'Are you sure it's OK for you to fly? I mean, to America?'

'No problem. Everything's fine.' But she lied. There'd been moments at the Sails when sudden pain had made her double up and nausea had driven her to crouch staring into the loo bowl ... They were secret, private moments never free of knowing that the Sancta Maria test had proved wrong and all was not well ...

She watched those same motorways and housing estates now become a smudge of browns and greys, diminishing into nothingness as the Boeing's height increased. Besides, it was another excuse to keep the left side of her face less exposed, for incredibly her scar seemed to have grown to match Martha Robinson's in shape and colour, and no amount of make-up altered it. Between her and Simon, the disfiguration became just another taboo subject, along with Clenchtoft and the remains of the gibbet discovered on Morpeth Bank.

Turning greyer and greyer, the altitude seemed to suck out her very life, leaving her mindless, weightless, with his cheek on hers. New blond stubble on his skin and now a second vodka making not the slightest difference.

'Cheers. Here's to the three of us.'

Simon leaned closer to the window, his third leather jacket, brown this time, smelling appropriately of the Wild West. She'd bought it for him out of her redundancy money, then put the rest away for the blur that was the future. He noticed she was fingering her scar and tried to draw her hand away.

'It's my memento and it'll protect me – I mean us.'

'Abbie, don't.'

'Lilith Leakes told Rosie once that a scar stitched up would keep out the Devil.'

'And you believe that crap?'

'She *knew* things.' Abbie's lips drew in with the awful realization that Clenchtoft Farm was now all hers – ready and waiting, in all its rotting isolation.

The Boeing continued its climb over the land of the Celts, heading west not east, and somehow that felt all wrong. Something was pulling her back. It was as though Martha Robinson's drain-digging hand was clamped on her living soul, her fingers worming their way down to her deepest places . . .

Abbie looked round at everyone else, many nodding

towards the edge of sleep, as *Notting Hill* came on the screen. Simon too was dozing until she nudged him.

'I want to go back.'

'For God's sake, Abs, what's the matter with you?'

'I've got to think of the baby.'

Simon buried his head in his hands. 'We can't go back now. Not now.'

'I'll be catching the first flight I can.'

He reached out, took her hand and stroked her fingers, lingering on the fourth where he'd drawn a ring with Sheila's laundry marker.

'Think of the ranch, the sun . . . This is crazy.'

'I've no choice.'

Abbie looked over at their neighbour's magazine – a page filled with portrait miniatures. There were ovals filled with taffetas and curls, exquisite blushing flesh. She had no willpower left, and what little she had of anything had to be carefully saved if she wasn't to end up supervised by white coats . . .

'OK. You win,' he said simply.

It's not me who's winning . . .

All at once the 747 lurched. Once, then again, sideways as though a rudder had swung.

'Holy Jesus!' Their neighbour tried to grasp his magazine as it slid to the floor, and found something else instead. 'Hey, is this yours?' He held out the Book of Common Prayer.

For a second, all the blood left Simon's face. He tried to think quickly.

'Sorry, never seen it before,' Simon answered. 'Looks old though.' The man studied the flyleaf, pocketed the book then spread his magazine back on his lap.

'I couldn't look at it.' Abbie whispered, her colour also gone. 'Is it never going to end?'

'It might do, now the bloody thing's gone to someone else,' he whispered.

At the cockpit end of the aisle, two hostesses rocked together as they advanced on their rounds amid a murmur of fear. First, an eerie suspension, then a drop like a faulty lift, as the speakers crackled.

'Ladies and gentlemen, this is Captain Brian Usher speaking. I would like to reassure you that we are experiencing minor turbulence only and would advise you to fasten your seat belts for the duration and to please remain calm.'

A chant of dread and sickness rose above the engines, suddenly one scream, then another. The cabin crew swayed and clung to seat backs as the film vanished, leaving a vacant screen. Abbie squeezed her eyes shut against Simon's chest.

'It'll soon be over.' His lips stirred her hair. 'I've been in a few of these before now.'

'This one's different.'

Another neighbour had put his hands in the prayer position. 'O God our help in ages past, our hope for years to come,' he intoned, while loose brochures and business papers drifted into islands under the seats. Then sudden darkness, followed by someone's torchlight veering in a wild dance as hand luggage hurtled down the aisle.

Screaming now, as icy air swept through the aircraft.

Simon's face also screwed up, as Usher's voice came to a halt, and his co-pilot took over the reassurances. To no avail, for someone else was now speaking more loudly, in calm and measured tones. It carried the faint but recognizable burr of the Fens.

'*You will all perish as my children perished*' – the silence stayed frozen – '*unless the one who knows me swears to return. I must hear her speak!*'

Nobody moved, nobody spoke, as a spectral vapour intensified their terror. The Boeing tilted and twisted in one persuasive diabolic motion. Abbie remained dumb with fear, but Simon, sweating despite the chill, suddenly took a deep breath.

'Damn you, Martha Robinson!'

'*I am that already and I'm waiting . . .*'

'For God's sake, spare us, whoever it is!' someone cried, and then the clamour deepened while the aircraft was tossed about in the cosmos – a nothing in the void.

'*Mention God again and you'll meet me in hell . . .*' This invisible threat brought more cries of dread.

Abbie sobbed, while the stink of burying soil engulfed her, its weight slowly crushing, deadening her brain. She knew she had to say it.

'It's me!' she yelled. 'And with the stomach pain intensifying more than she could bear, she lolled senseless out of Simon's arms.

Good Friday 1992
*   And the only good thing about it is he's mine. Finally mine. He has put the lies of that other God behind him. Now all things are possible . . .*

Sixty-eight

REPORTERS SWARMED ROUND the Boeing even while it taxied to a stop on the wet tarmac. Abbie and Simon slipped through the cluster of waiting ambulances and makeshift customs at RAF Braddleham and, in their desperation to escape, forgot to claim their luggage.

She was white as the moon, her usually smooth hair in chaos, and he was six vodkas the worse for wear. They hurried towards a line of waiting cabs. Simon grabbed the door handle of the last in the rank, its driver dozing oblivious.

'Sorry, mate.' An eye opened. 'They go first, at the other end.'

'Shit.'

On past a group of cleaners at the end of their shift to an E-reg Cherry. It was different from the rest, engine at the ready, with Andy Williams crooning from the speakers. The driver's gloved fingers drummed on the wheel in time to 'Almost There'. as his saloon touched eighty heading north back into Wringland.

Abbie woke with a hollow feeling as Snutterwick's lights shone into the car. She saw Simon's eyes flickering in and out of sleep and nudged him.

'I've just realized, Sheila's not going to be at the Sails and she's got our bloody room keys.'

Simon groaned, the thoughts of bed, the bar, slipping away to nothing. And even their cars were locked in the garages for safekeeping.

'Fuck it.'

The driver looked his way.

'What about Mrs Turling?' As Abbie spoke she felt a bleak darkness, now covering the Fens, enter her thoughts, bringing the word Clenchtoft to mind. The farmhouse key was in her hand-luggage – big, rusty and wrapped in clingfilm to protect her other things – as if subconsciously she'd known they might soon need it. And sooner rather than later . . .

'Where does she hang out, for God's sake?'

'Walsoken Road somewhere.'

'That's two fucking miles long.'

Abbie leaned forward towards the driver. 'Could you take us to Clenchtoft Farm please? It's first on the right after the Whiplash Cross.'

The Nissan pulled in by the gate and the driver switched off the engine. Simon stared out at the black shape of the farm ahead, the stuff of nightmares. His wallet stuck in his pocket as the man's knitted hand stretched out.

'Thirty quid to you, sir. Bit of a favour and all that, considering . . .' He clicked off the tape. The resulting silence seemed deafening.

Abbie waited while the notes were handed over, feeling the night breeze find her skin. She shivered, clutching her bag close to her stomach, feeling that what was inside needed all the protection she could give it. She watched the car pull away, its lights diminishing, then she hunted among her make-up bag and scarf for the key.

'Do we have to do this?' Simon wasn't happy with the prospect of a night in this filthy hole.

They held hands, trying to pick their way over the huge grass tufts and general detritus strewn around at the front of the house. Neither spoke as the place loomed large against the moonless sky. It was a hideous prospect, but, as if discouraging second thoughts, the key turned grudgingly in the lock.

Its emptiness was like hell's extension, as its tinged air of decay and squalor hit their nostrils. Memories of their last visit and the prospect of encountering Martha Robinson again sent violent spasms of fear, like an electric charge, from one to the other. The spectre of Lilith Leakes's missing head seemed to hang over them. Was it possibly in the house somewhere, overlooked by the police? Was it under the floorboards beneath their feet? Hidden in a cupboard? For there were plenty of those still crammed with stinking old clothes and other delectable souvenirs.

Now, at midnight, this prospect made the place seem even worse than Goosefoot and, try as he might, Simon couldn't block out the awful truth that it was now all Abbie's – grafted like some disease on to their lives. And her return had been an order impossible to ignore.

'Let's get out of here, Abs. There's bound to be somewhere else.'

'Where, at this time?' She was already groping her way towards what had once been the parlour. 'It's only for one night and at least we've got each other. In the morning, I'll get it put up for sale.'

'Don't go wandering off, for Christ's sake. Stay with me. We're going to kip right by this bloody door and nowhere else. If we want to pee, we'll just have to do it on the floor somewhere, sod it. House rules.' His mobile suddenly rang in his pocket. The gun came out first, then he got organized.

'Yes?'

'Irene Pringle here. Just checking on you. You were on that flight that was abandoned, yes?'

Simon breathed relief. It was good to hear a familiar voice. Someone on their side.

'Are you and Abbie OK?'

'We need to chill out for a bit, that's all. The whole lot of us could have been stiffs in the sea.' He watched Abbie's dark shape move into the kitchen. 'And our bloody luggage is still there, somewhere.'

'Don't worry. We'll sort that out for you. Now, tell me where you . . .'

Simon frowned as the voice suddenly faded, the line just a burr of sound.

'Shit.' He tried recall, 1471, but with no result. He banged the thing on his thigh. 'Come on, you bastard!'

'Does she even know we're here?' Abbie was now standing close, sharing his panic, thinking of the construction site when Mrs Schaap disappeared. When there'd been no phones, no faxes, nothing that worked. Only water and more water, thick and green . . .

'I was just about to tell her.'

'O God.' She covered her stomach with her hand again. 'What shall we do?'

Simon hugged her, his mind turning over the few possibilities. He now wished he'd left the drink alone, because clarity and logic were going to be his best allies from now on, and in his bones he knew this was the lull before the storm.

They listened hard, but Lilith Leakes's legacy was

giving nothing away. It was uncannily quiet, with no birds trapped in its chimneys, no voles scrabbling for cover underfoot – only Quinn and Martha Robinson biding their time.

'We'd better stay here then,' he announced suddenly. 'If that pervert's out there somewhere, we don't want to go bumping into him. At least in here we've got walls to protect us.'

He crouched down to lay his new jacket on the cold uneven flags. That was for her. He'd manage some other way. On manoeuvres it had been the forest floor or on a straw bale in some barn – and her then so far away. Now at least Abbie was with him, Abbie and their child.

As the bell of St Mary Magdalene tolled one, and the tail lights of some business flight winked across the sky overhead, dreams of water and drownings descended on them.

And now we have the meddlers who have come to stir the foul waters. I must remind my helper of his obligations – that certain places in Black Fen are mine, and if he doesn't act for me, I must act for myself, my good name, one of the few things I had, remember? And the memory of my children . . .

Sixty-nine

THEY WOKE SORE and unrested. Simon's throat felt the same constriction as at his medical and no amount of coughing would clear it. His brain too seemed as if it had been pickled in brine. Abbie felt no better.

She'd dreamed of her womb, her last place of safety, yet saw her child swimming for its life in that amniotic sea, had seen its pulsing lidded eyes, its tiny prawn fingers searching to escape. Subconsciously, in sleep, she'd wrapped her drawn-up knees in her arms to give it greater protection – from what she didn't know – but while Simon tried again to contact DI Pringle, she'd gone into the scullery to be sick.

It was as if her whole insides wanted to abort, yet nothing appeared, just gargles of air and the salt taste of the sea, and when she ran the trickle of bog water from the one old tap to wash her face, she felt as dead as the mobile phone itself.

Is this what Amy Buckley must have felt – not once, but three times? And Lilith Leakes?

She missed her mother the midwife, for Hilary Parker had known more about babies than anyone, and she'd be helping her now, assuring her that a morbid fear of loss wasn't unnatural. That it was every pregnant woman's nightmare. But what about morning sickness so early on?

And why the sudden cramps, as if there was a battle taking place inside her?

Without telling Simon, she'd go and get a scan, and if they insisted it was too soon to reveal anything, she'd pay to go private instead. With every last penny if necessary.

Abbie watched him continue punching numbers till she screamed at him to stop. 'Why don't we call in at Smithy Lane, for God's sake?' Her eyes were dull, her hair flattened from the floor. Tensions were high, both of them nearing the limits of endurance. 'At least there's two of us, just in case . . .'

'Good thinking, Mrs Cresswell.'

But the moment the front door closed, exposing them to the day's possibilities, a collective fear embraced them, and every person out walking in the renewed sunlight was Quinn.

'Shit, I miss my wheels.' He walked in front of her down Walsoken Road, aware of the creases in his best jacket and the pallor of his face. 'Why didn't the stupid cow at least leave us duplicate keys?'

'Don't talk about Sheila like that.' Abbie snatched the *Morpeth Record* he'd bought and aimed it at his head. 'She's been like a mum to me.'

He spun round, gripping her wrists.

'And what am I then?'

A woman with a shopping trolley stopped to stare, and the newsagent, arranging postcards of bulb fields outside her shop, tutted to herself.

'Nothing but trouble's followed those two around,' the newsagent commented to the next customer. 'No good'll come of it. And I tell you what,' she added with a sly smile, 'folks say she's been left Clenchtoft.'

The old man sighed and took his fruit pastels. 'More funerals then.' He popped one in his mouth.

Number 8 Smithy Lane was just another council house from the outside with the one car in the garage at the back. It had a path swept and trimmed, but Venetian blinds instead of curtains, and an entry phone by the door.

The equipment once installed in the Sails now filled the front room: all magnolia and beams boxed in with polystyrene, over the hum of computers, and the same team consisting of statement reader, indexer and researcher.

Aldreth switched on the kettle to make his visitors a cup of tea. They looked in need of something stronger, especially that girl with the weal on her cheek, but rules were rules.

'So you were at Clenchtoft Farm last night? Mmm.'

He began dialling Pringle and, when she answered, he spoke to her in a way they couldn't quite gauge. Something was being cooked up, that was obvious, but when Simon asked to speak to the policewoman, Aldreth waved him away. Still, when tea was delivered, he personally passed round the sugar.

'Look, both of you,' he began, 'we need your co-operation again in trying to draw Quinn out of the shadows. Nail him once and for all. This might be our last chance.'

Simon scowled. He was pissed off big time, as everyone could see.

'Why can't you catch him on your own? You've got bloody choppers, men on the ground, dogs. Besides –' he glanced at Abbie – 'she's pregnant.'

A fleeting look of concern passed over Aldreth's face.

'Well, rest assured no harm will come to either of you.'
But, a certain desperation entered his voice as he drew
his chair closer. 'This is vital to everyone's interest – and
I mean everyone.'

You will all die . . .

'What about our safety, for fuck's sake?' Simon
flushed, his fists working in his lap. 'Look what happened
to Abbie last time?'

'That will not happen again. I give you my personal
assurance.' The tall copper leaned back, his chin propped
on a spire of fingers, the clock behind him suddenly very
audible.

Abbie looked at Simon, her eyes welling up. 'Remember what you said? We must do it for Rosie? We've got
no choice.'

Simon slumped in his seat, his tea untouched. 'How
long? Or are we talking about a piece of bloody string
here?'

'A week at the most. Once he knows you're at
Clenchtoft Farm, he'll want to get on with it.'

A chill seemed to encircle them despite the warm
room. Abbie shivered visibly. Simon's hand found hers.

'OK,' he said to Aldreth, 'we'll do it. But I want DI
Pringle in there with us. That's my one condition.'

'And the other is, we get the place exorcized –
immediately,' Abbie added.

Aldreth stood up and reached out to shake their
hands. Neither of them moved. It was obvious and
terrible to them. They were being sentenced to death.

Neither spoke of their decision as they walked along
Smithy Lane, past the church and the rectory, where
there were already new signs of residence.

'I've got to get hold of my Audi.' Simon locked his arm in Abbie's as they crossed over to the newsagent's. 'And I bet you a tenner this nosy old cow knows something.'

He was right. Mrs Clapman told them it was a Sunrise Tours coach from Norwich which had been waiting outside her shop to pick up Sheila and Mrs Watts. While Simon attempted to contact the tour operator, Abbie made her way over to the Quinns' former residence.

Its new incumbents, the Reverend William Dole and his wife, Marjorie, had almost gutted the interior, and turned night into day.

Peeled-off wallpaper arched into umber seas on all the floors and the banisters bubbled like treacle toffee under the paint stripper. Rolls of ravaged carpet lay like rotten hay bales on the path outside, together with the other scrapings of the Quinns' existence heaped into tea chests.

Abbie picked her way through the rubbish, each step a personal hell. But she had to do it, because this was where her little friend had lived and suffered . . . A round-faced woman leaned out from the window above and waved.

'I'll be down in a mo.'

Close up she resembled a home-made biscuit pocked by freckles, her thatch of hair held by two unmatching clips. Behind her, a sander whined over the floorboards in a flurry of dust.

'I'm Abbie Parker, Clenchtoft Farm.' The last two words felt strange and heavy, and for a brief moment the incomer paused.

'Marjorie Dole.' She held out a paint-spattered hand in lieu of any comment about Abbie's introduction, or the dark scar on her cheek. 'What a job this lot's turning out to be.'

'I'll be doing the same myself soon,' Abbie said without enthusiasm.

'Really?' Her eyes took in the young woman's paleness against that wound, her slight build. 'Well, good luck.' Meanwhile she peeled a fragment of old paint from the door. 'I say, if nothing else, the Quinns were fond of brown.'

If nothing else. My God.

'Do come in then.' The amateur decorator looked over at her husband, who had stopped his noise. 'This is Bill, busy working miracles as usual.'

'Oh, I hardly think so.' His smile showed a set of vivid acrylic false teeth.

'It's amazing what he's done already.' Marjorie Dole patted her husband's shoulder, but their visitor could look no further than the stairs.

'Coffee?'

'No, thanks. I just needed to come and lay some ghosts.'

'Oh?' The couple exchanged puzzled looks.

'You do need to do all this, believe me.' Her voice sounded odd even to herself.

'Need to? Why?'

'Don't you know what really happened here?' Thinking of Rosie again, and Avril Lawson.

The Reverend coughed, embarrassed. 'Let's just say we're determined to make a fresh start. Aren't we, Marjorie? The Good Lord knows that Black Fen could do with some stability.'

'There won't be much of that till Quinn's finally caught.' Abbie's body started to shiver despite the warm breeze. Why couldn't she mention Martha Robinson as well? What was keeping her back? But however hard she tried, that name stayed unspoken. 'I'm so scared,' was all she could manage.

Marjorie Dole laid a practised hand on her shoulder. 'Oh, come on my dear, he's long gone from here. Anyhow, the police have wonderful technology on their side these days.'

'What about God then?'

An uneasy laugh followed. But Abbie didn't look relieved.

'Him as well, of course.'

'That's a relief.'

The Reverend Dole wiped his hands down his boiler suit. 'Oh, by the way,' he said as he went through into the scullery. 'We found these things in one of the attic rooms just after we'd moved in here. Pretty revolting, I know, but maybe with a bit of disinfectant . . .'

Abbie's heart suddenly raced, vomit rising again. She recognized the bedspread but it was too late to say, '*Don't touch, put them down and run a mile.*' Too late for her as well . . .

'Somehow we couldn't just throw them away,' he added. 'They must have belonged to the little girl who lived here.'

He can't say her name and neither can I.

Abbie gingerly undid the old candlewick bedspread and gasped in horror. That same beetle she remembered from Goosefoot Cottage now settled on Lazarus's hand.

Abbie grimaced, covering the dolls up again, holding them tight in her grip.

'What are you going to do with them?' Dole asked, relieved to see the things on their way.

'Lay them to rest.'

Abbie then said goodbye. These two were just two turnips nourished by a cloying mutual affection, and perhaps a useless faith, but she kept up her smile all the way to the graveyard, keeping the dolls well away from her stomach.

The grave she sought had nothing save L. LEAKES crudely pyrographed on a plank that jutted above the earth. Compared to the neighbouring grave, the soil here seemed rougher, less finished off, as though it had been recently disturbed. As though someone else had got there first . . .

She scanned the trees as a flight of crows suddenly darkened the sky like a funeral veil and in that moment pure terror gripped her. Again her benefactor's empty eyes, that lipless smile. But economic freedom hadn't been her gift at all. No, the woman had delivered her into the very snare she had herself escaped: Clenchtoft, deep in the mire of Wringland.

Abbie first made sure she was on her own, then pulled out Lazarus, the sailor doll, by its head and laid it along the burial ridge. Mercifully, that vile insect was nowhere to be seen. The cruel daylight showed porcelain cracks etched by dirt, the mouth even more sullen, and when she stepped back it was like a little old man who rested there. Old lying upon old, lullabied from above by a lonely bittern's cry.

Suddenly she screamed.

The beetle had transferred itself to her sleeve as if she herself was a corpse already and frantically she prised it off, before scraping out a nest in the ground and filling it with the other two dolls: Abigail and Mary, silk and muslin yielding to the soil. Then she looked up. 'Damn you,' she cried to their sister in the sky. 'You're not bloody well going to stop me this time.'

Abbie went back to the rectory, where Dole was stacking paint cans outside, and, having made sure his wife wasn't around, she approached, feeling that same deep ache hit her insides. She doubled up, gripping her stomach.

'Are you all right?' He stopped what he was doing and stared.

'Never mind that,' Abbie panted. 'There's one more miracle for you to do.'

'What's that?'

'You must get over to Clenchtoft as soon as you can. Forget the building site for the moment. Come to us first, please.'

'An exorcism?'

'Yes.' It would take a blind man not to register the look on her face. The terror possessing every part of her.

'I'll see what I can do. Leave it with me.' He looked around, checking they were alone. Marjorie was nervous of this aspect of his ministry and most certainly would have tried to prevent him going. He'd even had to lie to her about the Kingfisher Rise business, pretending he was seeing someone in hospital . . .

'Before tonight if you can,' Abbie urged.

'I'll try.'

She needed to sit down, so went back to the graveyard and chose a spot near her benefactor. A mound just next to an ancient stone proved perfect, and the sun too, between the high clouds, seemed to lessen the pain. She closed her eyes to the backdrop of starlings in the leaves overhead and farmer Hick's perpetual tractor. She put her silent questions to the old woman. *Should they go or stay? Whose baby was she really carrying? Would Quinn be caught? And Martha Robinson expelled for ever?*

But when she opened her eyes again and looked over towards the hermit's plot, the sailor doll had vanished and the nest of earth that she'd made for the two girls lay open and empty.

The meddlers have gone too far. They think they can see me off with a few words which I reason are no more than sounds, like the wind or the gulls. And as for him, *with his withered seed, he's as useless to me as a wherry without its sail. Worse, they have disturbed my Walter's place of rest, even that of my own dead body which the Charybdis took out to Lethe Island. So I am violated even in death and allowed no peace. But know this — all that which has been taken from me will be given back. In good measure, be sure of it . . .*

Seventy

THESE SAME HIGH summer clouds cast intermittent shadow over Clenchtoft's dilapidated acres and the offshore breeze teased the Reverend Dole's cassock as he stood with a cup of tea trembling in its saucer. He looked drained after the short intensive service conducted in the farm's hallway with just one candle lit on the stairs.

'Good of you to make it. Thanks.' Simon shook the man's free hand then patrolled the small group with a plate of wafers.

Jim Morton, a builder from North Sand, who'd called in that afternoon on the off chance to give an estimate, took three of them.

'D'you know, it feels different already.' Abbie stared up at the infinite blue above. Never had the whole place appeared so harmless, so free of other energies, and for the first time in weeks her face radiated cheerfulness.

'This could be a grand home for you both.' Morton munched the biscuits and threw bits for his dog, whose mouth lay permanently open, slavering on to the ground. 'And worth a fair bit, I'd say, when it's all done up.' He watched the exorcist pick up his case, glad he didn't have to wear a dress like that.

'I'd best be going,' the Reverend announced. 'You'll be all right now.' He placed his teacup on the step and, as he left, Simon slipped his arm round Abbie and she let her fingers burrow under the waistband of his jeans to feel the reassuring warmth of his flesh.

But their kiss was short-lived. It was Morton again, his papers flapping in the wind.

'Sorry to interrupt your good selves, but can we just check through these figures again, so's I know when we can be starting?'

'Hey up. We've not decided anything definitely.' Simon saw Dole's Clio reach the gate, his aerial sliding up. 'We've got other plans too, haven't we, Abs?'

'Have we?'

'Yes. Remember what I'd said about Wales.' Simon took another wafer and lowered his voice through the mouthful. 'You can find a cottage to renovate with a bit of land for about forty thou.' The sum she'd been left by Lilith Leakes, now in a joint building society account. He'd worked it all out – his little dream. 'Anyhow, it's a safer bet for a kid, I reckon.' He turned to the builder. 'There's been too much dark stuff going on round here for our liking. Do you know what the car hire people said?'

'No. What?'

'That this was the most haunted place in England. Good recommendation, eh?'

'I wouldn't know about that.' Morton brushed pink crumbs off his sleeve.

'Anyhow, I've got roots over the Severn myself.' Simon looked at Abbie for concurrence, but she was thinking about something else – thinking that with Quinn out of the way and the place back to normal, a new kitchen, a new bathroom, all tidied up, it wouldn't be too bad after all.

'I don't know, Si. It's not that simple. Besides, this house is mine. It's the first time I've owned anything really.'

Simon sat down on the step, ruffling his hair with both hands. Abbie knew what that meant, but before she could discuss it further, the large half-breed dog started barking and tore off to the gate.

Simon sprang up on the alert, then his shoulders dropped in relief. Irene Pringle's filthy Range Rover came into the shabby drive, followed by a cloud of dust. Once more wearing her combat fatigues and with an even shorter crop of hair, the Detective Inspector looked more masculine than ever. With her were two DCs in jeans and sweatshirts, casting long shadows over the ground.

'Thank God.' Simon grinned at her. 'I feel I can breathe again.' But when he noticed the groundsheet and a sleeping bag that she was carrying, alarm took over.

'Aren't you going to be in the house with us?'

'That's DC Owens's and DC Skelton's remit. Sorry, Simon, but I always work best outside.' She looked over to where Abbie was putting up a makeshift washing line, then made phone contact with Aldreth and Stock to say she'd arrived.

After asking Morton to give them five minutes alone, she waved Abbie to come over to join them. Still peeved, Simon challenged her about their two cars still at the St George's Sails – whether a locksmith could be sent over there to somehow open both garages, and while Pringle was still shaking her head he relayed how Sunrise Tours had refused to pass on what they'd felt was a non-urgent message from him.

'That's down to me I'm afraid. For everyone's security.'

'Oh bloody great. What about when Sheila's back?'

'Sorry Simon, but you and Abbie have just got to sit tight. Things are beginning to move.' The DI squinted into the sun. 'We've had another sighting of Quinn, near Canal Farm, and we know our crazy friend'll stop at nothing now. Victor Buckley heard him shouting curses in the farmyard, but by the time he'd fetched his rifle, not a whisper. By the way – ' she checked that Morton couldn't hear – 'I'm sorry to spoil such a beautiful day but there are things you need to know. Let's go inside.'

'Such as?' Abbie's smile left her face as they entered the dark hallway.

'We made some pretty grim discoveries over at the rectory, after you were rescued. We didn't want to remind you too soon of your ordeal.'

'O Jesus.' Abbie clung to Simon, gripped by fresh guilt that she hadn't ever enquired further. That terrible stench, those fingernails frantic to get free ... What could she have done? What could anybody?

Pringle hesitated. Aldreth had told her once that she lacked a way with words. Now she could prove him wrong. She took a deep breath. A bit like diving into ice, she thought: you never knew.

'As well as Avril Lawson, we found Lilith Leakes's head.' She paused, checking this wasn't a traumatic overload. 'Both together under the trap door.'

Abbie let out a stifled scream. Lilith Leakes's gaping mouth seemed to fill her brain.

'But at least I have her and the one who forsook me ...'

She gripped the banisters till the blood left her fingers. Was that what Quinn had really said, or was her memory playing tricks?

'Are you all right?' Pringle asked warily.

'Fine,' she lied, sitting on the bottom step, trying to remember.

'Why there of all places?' Simon asked pointedly. He was thinking of Wales again with a sudden extra longing.

'We don't know. The man's deranged.'

'It may be significant, though,' he said frowning. 'Odd that he had Lawson a prisoner as well, unless she was some kind of sick trophy. After all, he did have a close relationship with her.'

'She sheltered him too, when he was on the run. We know that now,' Roger Owens said in the doorway. Pulling out a packet of Camels, he offered it around, then, with no takers, lit up. 'Very obliging of her, I must say.' His smoke veered away from the farmhouse and on impulse Abbie wondered again if she would need to light a fire. Wondered if she should be there at all.

Pringle managed a smile. 'He may even be spying on us now.'

DC Skelton turned his eyes towards the shallow fields and poplars darkening to silhouettes. 'He knows this place like the back of his hand.'

The back of his hand . . .

Abbie remembered that first time she met him, recoiling from those veined white fingers. Now they were red with Rosie's blood and more . . .

'But so do we.' Pringle led the two of them deeper into the farmhouse and, after a brief recce, gave Simon a replacement gun. Then, on her map unfolded against the wall, she showed them where she'd be hiding.

'No dogs available?' Simon asked her.

'Not yet. And neither of you is to leave the house for *any* reason. There'll be no need to answer the door, or even open a window. And stay together at all times. Abbie, I know you're expecting, so try and take it easy.'

Abbie laughed to herself at the irony, then felt a twinge inside. 'Julia O'Halloran and Constable Paul Matthews will bring you food etc. No one else. I repeat, no one else is expected, so if you see anyone, even a meter reader, whatever, it's a no-no to admit them. Understood?'

'What does this Matthews look like?'

'Same height as Owens. About six feet, with reddish hair and a war wound on his chin.'

'War wound?'

'A white scar – received in the line of duty.' She was trying hard to reassure them, but the longer she stayed, the worse their anxieties became. 'Now, good luck, and thanks for helping us.'

They watched her slip off, crouching round the side of the farm, nimble as a creature of the wild, until she disappeared.

'It's all happening here then?' Morton now had his dog on a short lead. He saw their tense faces, read their body language. 'Shall I call back tomorrow?'

'Leave it for a week, that's best,' Abbie said. 'Then we'll know for sure.'

'Fair do's. Here's my card if you change your mind.' He pulled the dog closer, then ambled back to his van.

'A week?' Simon's eyes said it all.

'I had to say something.' She slipped the card in her jeans pocket.

Simon shrugged. It was still early days, he thought. Besides, once she'd seen photos and plans of longhouses built of river stone all with mountain views, she'd change her mind. That would be his next step, when this was all over.

Those simpletons who received him all those years ago and turned him towards the church have passed from that wretched life with their mouths full of silage, their ears deaf to each other. Even to the one they believed in, which is no surprise to me. Grass to burning treacle grass and too late now for them. I should have acted sooner, that is obvious, but now more pressing things are needing my attention . . .

Seventy-one

SEVEN DAYS PASSED. Seven days in which Simon not only informed Boyd that they'd be away for the inquest, but he also postponed the builder for another week, as Abbie's stomach cramps had grown more frequent, her dreams more disturbed and convoluted, leaving her drained and inert. In the mornings she'd sit staring into the mirror, trying to connect with the reality of life before working for Holtbury's, and Kingfisher Rise, when she and Simon had seemed on equal terms, working for their degrees and supporting each other with the intensity of new love.

Now all that had changed. The baby seemed to be the only thing holding them together, as if its forming umbilical cord was somehow entwining them outside her body in a common destiny she couldn't control. Yet Simon wanted out, while she wanted peace: a chance to see what the next weeks, the next months, would bring with things at the farm returning to normal.

So far the Reverend Dole's efforts seemed to have succeeded. Even Simon admitted that. No reappearance of the prayer book, no dreadful laughter, not even an echo of anything strange or a temperature change. And, apart from the presence of Owens and Skelton, who kept themselves quietly apart and had spent part of the time clearing up the house, it was getting easier to imagine Clenchtoft as a perfect family home. Given time, anyway. But she knew time was running out.

'That Quinn, he's a clever fucker, I'll give him that.' Roger Owens sat with Simon in the kitchen that Tuesday morning, having a break from his look-out duty and checking over the two-way radios that Pringle had left for Simon and Abbie to use. 'He could trot past done up as a bloody fox and we wouldn't know.'

'Well, that's encouraging.' Simon opened a second Budweiser and gulped it down. 'So when's the DI going to get more bloody back-up out there?' Everything suggested he couldn't take much more waiting. The waiting just like at Rheindahlen, holed up here watching Abbie lose weight, lose her spirit . . .

'There's a team of four over with Victor Buckley now, poor sod. Still, it'll all be over in the next few days, I reckon.' The DC lit up again. 'Want a bet?'

'No thanks.' Simon felt sweat trickle from his forehead, the flies, big ones, coming into the house with the weather change. It was hot and close, brewing up for something.

'By the way, next time tell that builder chappie of yours to give you a miss.' Owens put his feet up. 'We don't need him around here at the moment.'

'What?'

'I said, give him the heave-ho. He called by while you were still asleep.'

Simon put down his can, went to the window and moved the grubby curtain to one side. 'He's not due till a week today. I bloody phoned him.' He stared at Owens. 'Shit, what's going on? Did he have the van with him or his dog?' Sweat was now salting his eyes.

'No. He came on his own. Legging it.'

'That's mad. He lives in North Sand.'

Owens shot out of his chair, his voice brittle as he contacted Pringle out near Snake's Mouth. Simon didn't stay to listen but ran upstairs to check on Abbie, as Owens and Skelton barricaded the front door and the first roll of thunder echoed from the sea.

'The cheeky bastard must have seen Morton close enough to copy the sort of gear he wears.' Simon pressed himself close to her, his stomach on hers, the only protection he could give. 'Christ.' He thought of KFOR still picking up the pieces in Kosovo. Surely anything was better than this.

Abbie could smell the beer again. O'Halloran, feeling sorry for him, had left two more crates by way of encouragement, while all Abbie had were her demons, busy by night and resting by day.

Three more days followed. More waiting and listening to the Twin Squirrel's drone over the marsh and sea, and the shadowy figures of Skelton and Owens, still strangers, moving round the farm. As minutes grew to hours, a curious lull descended in which Abbie, whose cramps had eased, began cleaning up two of the dingy bedrooms, then turned to the kitchen and scullery.

That old black dress which had harboured the *Secrets* had been hung up in a rickety wardrobe in the boxroom until she decided what to do with it. Abbie could tell by its details that it was much older than Lilith Leakes herself and, like some other antiquated finds, would some day be a useful piece of real history.

The motion of wiping and scrubbing somehow dispelled the fears of the night before, and as each window pane let in more light, each floor tile showed up its true terracotta colour and each board its own subtle grains, she felt ever closer to this place and the lonely woman who'd once lived there. However, one room still remained unopened: Lilith's 'laboratory' – the place where she had been murdered.

Simon occasionally watched as Abbie worked, her hair tied back with one of the scarves intended for Colorado and retrieved with their luggage by the police from the RAF base at Braddleham. Her jeans were loose around her hips, her elbows jutting through the skin. He couldn't actually force food down her, but to see this weight loss reinforced just how powerless he felt.

It was as if he were back in the army mess again, his nerves dulled by the pleasures of beer and whatever other distractions lay to hand. He stretched out over two chairs, his body losing its tension and its energy. He wasn't interested in crosswords any more, and the newspapers fetched in with the groceries stayed unread. He just wanted out of here and spent the whole afternoon clinging to his new dream of reliving days on the Black Mountain, with its smell of damp fleece and the sight of the Towy winding through the ancient way of the saints.

The heat was increasingly enervating. The ever-present clouds hovered just above the roof, bloated with rain that wouldn't come, and by nightfall he and Abbie lay like sardines in oil, listening for the silent sea, willing Quinn to come.

A van, a dog and Jim Morton a day early – not a drop of sweat or a smear of work stained his immaculate beige outfit. These were the sort of clothes to inspire confidence, like she herself used to wear, Abbie thought, putting the kettle on after he'd reluctantly let Skelton frisk him. He'd had enough grief from Pringle and the rest already, about a visit he never actually made, but Clenchtoft was potentially a big deal, worth all the hassle.

'I still say this is a cracking good building,' he continued as he sipped his tea, choosing to ignore Simon's irritation at his zeal. 'You could be talking two hundred thousand when it's sorted.'

Abbie put her arms round Simon's neck and kissed his ear. 'Couldn't we give it a try?' she pleaded. 'Look what I've done already.'

'I've got to hand it to you,' Morton said, looking round, 'you've worked wonders, you really have.'

Simon scowled, knowing what the old flanneller was up to, but when he saw Abbie's face, his defences crumbled.

'OK, you win. But promise me one thing in exchange.' His eyes seemed even more desperately blue.

'Go on.' She was aware of Morton listening as he took a piece of paper from his inside pocket.

'You've got to start eating, not just for yourself . . .'

'But for the baby – I know, I know. And I will. Oh, Si, thanks.' She kissed him, but the glow of it was short-lived.

'So where do we start?' Morton returned his mug to the kitchen sink.

'Abbie?' Simon gestured that it was her call.

'What do you suggest?' she asked the builder.

'The roof's in the worst state. No roof, no home, that's what they say.' Morton's gold ballpoint was poised, his fingernails pink with perfect half-moon cuticles.

'How much?' Simon tried to read upside-down as the man began to write.

'Including VAT, four grand, and that's on the tight side.'

Faraway thunder reverberated round the kitchen. Morton frowned out of the window. 'There's summer storms coming up, and don't forget that tornado up in Yorkshire last week. You need something doing quick.'

Abbie chanced a look at Simon. He reached out and took her hand.

'Well, we've made the decision. Let's just go for the lot. Roof included.'

'Fighting talk, that's what I like to hear.' The contractor scripted more figures, his tongue between his teeth. 'I'd say twenty-five thousand would cover it all. Nothing posh, mind, just basic. Barns as well.'

'Fine.' Simon remembered the axe and the stinking carcasses. 'Will you be removing all the shit that's in them?'

'Course, part of the deal. I'll get you the estimate in tomorrow, all typed up proper by the wife.'

'I've just thought,' Abbie suddenly said. 'We might be able to get a better price than that.'

'Oh yes? Who from, might I ask?' Morton's pen stopped. His mouth tightening.

'An old contact of mine from Holtbury's. Say twenty grand,' she said.

Simon looked at her with a mixture of admiration and embarrassment. Sales and its attendant wheeler-dealing had never been part of his life, except for observing his father, driven by bonuses and commission.

The fifty-year-old builder thought for a moment, picking something off his cuff.

'OK. It's a deal.'

Abbie smiled.

'When can you start?' Simon was visualizing a torrent pouring through the rafters.

'There's four of us. Think you already know Myers from Kingfisher Rise. He's glad of any work at the moment after all that business. Say next Wednesday?'

Simon shook his head. In his mind's eye, water was already drenching their bodies, curling round his ankles. 'Why not tomorrow?'

Both Abbie and Morton stared at him.

'It'll take a few days,' the builder said, thinking aloud, 'still, leave it with me.'

They shook hands, two of them sweaty, one cool, then the prisoners watched him push his dog into the van and drive off, mindful of the ruts.

'You're Vallender's clone, that's what.' Simon held her close, trying to feel the other life inside. 'Still, that got us a bit off.'

Then in lingering dust the van was gone, echoes of Morton's barking dog mingling with new thunder over North Sand.

'And let me tell you something.' She checked neither detective was around, then put her hand on his fly. 'The day you start wearing gear like that will be your last.'

They collapsed laughing, and then the new occupants of Clenchtoft Farm hauled each other upstairs for their own private house-warming until the sky grew dark.

On the following wet afternoon, the day of Lilith Leakes's inquest, Abbie and Simon began in earnest, to clear the old woman's cluttered shelves.

'I don't know about you, but I feel really shitty doing this.' Abbie was thumbing through old annuals, autograph books, farm diaries, drainage manuals and tidal charts in what had once been the parlour and was the next room to be made habitable. 'I'm surprised the police weren't interested in these.'

'Are you really? What, with their one shared GCSE?'

Wondering if Owens or Skelton had heard that, Abbie shut the door.

'Look at this. *Fenland Dictionary*, 1951. Carvel . . . caulk . . . clinker . . . clough . . .'

'Mmm. Interesting.' Simon took the tome and thumbed through it, smelling its pages. He'd always done that, first thing, even as a kid, and the older the book the better.

'And this is all about Daniel Leakes, 1840–1902.' She held up a small bound volume, privately printed, listing his accomplishments, the frontispiece showing a portrait of a rotund figure with a cunning expression. On the flyleaf was stuck a facsimile of a congratulatory letter from Disraeli. 'A well-connected lot then,' she observed, searching the pages in vain for any evidence of a wife or child.

William Tapper Leakes?

'Keep all the old stuff.' Simon hefted two bin bags into the hall and then rejoined her. 'You never know, ours might be interested in it one day.'

Ours?

Abbie shot him a doubtful glance. 'Look, how about *Herbs for All Seasons* . . . Or this – *Dutch for Beginners*.'

'Hey,' Simon nudged her, 'read this It's a bit of a weird coincidence.'

Abbie leaned closer to see the inscription inside the front cover. 'Voor Pieter, veel liefs, van Hanneke Schaap.'

Simon's finger traced round the already familiar names, but the ink was smudged, almost lost to the page. 'Could have been a gift for her son,' he said.

Abbie wasn't convinced. 'Why, if he was Dutch already?'

'OK. Perhaps the sailor brought it with him, to help teach Lilith Leakes the lingo. I don't know.' Simon studied it again, confused. 'Unless it was for her grandson, who might *also* have been called Pieter.'

'What's the publication date?' she asked.

'Difficult to tell.'

'So let's just get Pringle on to it.' Abbie suggested. 'Because at the moment we're the blind leading the blind.'

'Good thinking.' He left the text book on the mantelpiece, as more and more of the hermit's other reading came to light.

Palmistry and Tarot Readings. Abbie flicked through it. 'That's what she wanted me to get involved in ... *Sabbath Rites ... Blood Sisters ...*' Her unease grew as more such works joined the pile. 'They're weird. I'd rather you take them.' No baby of hers was going to share the house with this stuff, so book after book was hurled to oblivion, until only one remained.

'Shit. What's this?' Simon stopped.

'Looks like some kind of diary.'

It was slender, black, with a gull's feather stuck to the cover. The yellowing pages showed signs of being well thumbed over the years, and in parts the poor writing was almost unreadable. But, unlike in *Secrets*, there was at least distinguishable writing.

'Any name on it?' He turned over the page to see.

'Doesn't look like it. D'you think it's hers too?'

'Dunno. Let's take a butcher's then . . .'

At first glance, some entries seemed vaguely chronological, the rest just a mish-mash of reminiscences and doodles. Until they studied it more closely.

'Whoever did this obviously never sat in a classroom.' Simon shared the floor with Abbie, peering at the cryptic images, the blurred words in dialect, and as the sky outside grew even darker and the first drops of rain began to slap the window, the pieces of the strange puzzle fitted together all too clearly. Lilith Leakes, with typical foresight, had shared it all.

the gilimot eg   a werld ful of ilands

clenchtoft 10 februry
i dont ned
no visiters now apart from stimpson
                                    hoo is at lest helpful with repars
the
uthers are too nosy for me liking
                besides
                        i have annie leakes
        dols and thay sit wer thay
usd to

sit with her with a
gilimot eg betwen   werlds ful of
ilands i tel them
and beter than this
wun as i wat for me tim

    such pane such pane I endur

ive now told stimpson to stop plaging me

im not lonly i keep teling him
                now that hes movd the nests and cleerd the
drayns thers no ned for him on the dorstep evry uther day
hes wiling i grant ya
                but i now what his wilingnes mens   iv told him id
be mor intrested in his padle if he can kep a secret
                my secret the duchmans child is big
bilt lik his father i can tel   and he is fiting inside me fiting
to liv

the yung salor wil be bac i now, tird of the sea and hell be
luking for some acers for his old ag
                mebbe then il be hapy   hoo nows

stimpson ses
im entitld to things

 to kep me and me child wel fed   but that wud meen showing mesen to the grub
 sissens and al the uther gosips her
wen the only help i want cums from me best frend
the popies   besids i kep a tidy pach for mesen owtsid and the
frisyns ar ful enuf of milk
       so i dont ned any artifishal stuf
               even thow he ses the orinj jus has got môr

vitamins

he also tels me
          one of the land gerls the ministry put on at brakwel
in the war is to mary
stanly wats
i cant see his sissen madge being to hapy at seing new blud
cum into things even tho
she has shard his bed for ten yers

the ministry also wanted clenchtoft as wel from wot he sed tho
I never herd of it
          but samwel scot
declard nowt wud grow
                    no worms and to much inundashon even
thow grandfathers drayn is the finest in the cuntry

  stil, it sewted me but when this is al over, il show
him

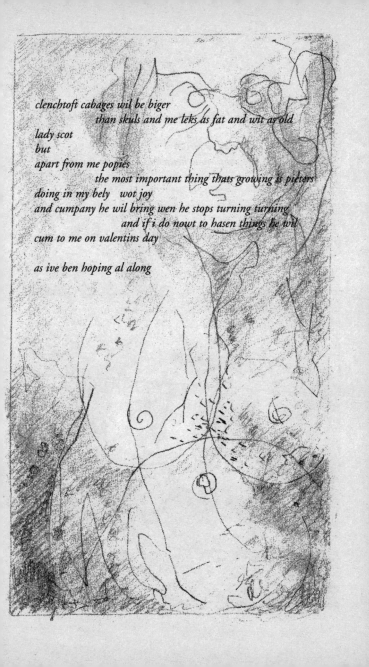

clenchtoft cabages wil be biger
            than skuls and me leks as fat and wit as old
lady scot
but
apart from me popies
            the most important thing thats growing is pieters
doing in my bely   wot joy
and cumpany he wil bring wen he stops turning turning
            and if i do nowt to hasen things he wil
cum to me on valentins day

as ive ben hoping al along

faros dust is evrywer
and stil the red sand is faling

stimpson ses it brings gud fortun
but i now beter that the wurst is yet to
cum
hungry magots
wen they hav gorgd to much on us

is it to much to hop we wil rise from ther
vomit

it is so dep cold

the grownd so hard i canot dibl in any new seed
            stimpson has come over from revly to help

 even he is defeted   he asks about me helth   luks at me bely
as
 he always dus
he wud take me if he cud but i bring up me shorl for shelter
            i have no mor ters   the man from the see
has drunk them al and he is the last man
i shal now

the wind devowers wot is left
of me iys, and
            if i am not to die of solitude i must sek sum cum-
fort
me nit on the coningwillem wos al solt   see solt and
  semen
        we are born of blud and semen
i have livd to long alown

hoo wil cumfort me now

such cold befor she cums...

the payst is redy my sun aslep
i see oryon trawling the erth for
                    new sowls so i must content mesen with his lev-
ings
i set to work with me bit of gren glas
        me finger a pesl on me
to bluds   then i fil me pipe and jurny to the

owter reches   this lonly begar canot chose and from far away
            i her me boy sudenly wak and cry to the wind
sumwun is eger to find a herth i can tel
for such a winters cold is cum upon this rum
and the fir has
  dyd

evil is upon us

and to kep it away i try to rekindl the flams
          blakning me fingers
splintring my parms

she is taler than any marsh alder stronger than any specter of the
brocen   she nows
                    i am stil wek and weker in this chil and
thin of blud

i want your child
                        she ses in a voys deper than
leth and i ofer her bac her dols insted
but she punches them
to the flor

giv the boy saylers sun to me she showts
                    but unlyk hers and anies por wek
thing

mine wil liv and i push her awa   she
trys again with the strongest wuns ever betwen
 blak fen and the see.

wer is solomon and his jugment now
me child stifens and way runs from his
                                mowth   she is ther
            furst with
al her teribl strength
and taks
                    him from me wispring into his
                    soft part until my own werds tak efect   but
i now i am to layt   to
layt

new yers day
and i have ben in me bed a wek sins   i new wen me breth
met hers
that i had abusd me gift   that me
rongdoing

                        had put me in the presens of evil   i had
rakd
up the ashes

                        not of the denshiring dun befor the berth,
but of the damd hoo had layn with esmund downy
                me sun is
cursd
i wil never bery dep enuf the
seeds she has sown   like the bindwed tha
wil giv shoot and flurish as sure as deth folows lif
                        me hands ar stil cwivring so

help
me

al fools
stimpson nows of a family from the

old days on the estat.
                        tha kep a smal farm ner the wy
althow ther felds ar fertil thay ar not
stimpson ses thay are reglar cherch goers and kep a statu of
jesus
                        in the frunt parler   besids I hav no mor
milk it has dryd in my brest and me sun is

ayling
                        he must never now hoo i am.
stimpson wil mak them promis that much
and besides thay wil hav me
letter

sunday
this morning
i rapd him up over his new

salor sewt
id mayd agenst the wether and
                              wen stimpson wos redy as the bels
struk eleven i pasd my fuchur over into his hands and sed
his nam shud be

pieter

thersday
i can

no longer tak a com
                 thruw my hayr so now it lys soft
arownd me fet and no man wil luk
at me

agen

no dayt
　　　　for the days are al the
saym

i spend mor time than ever with the dols

thay hav becum me children and lyk a gud muther
　　　　　　　　　　　i hav sown a new sewt for
the boy dol, exactly like i mad for pieter   I fed him beter
than I do
 mesen and this givs
　　　　　　　me sum consolashon   sumwun has to show them
luv i am al thay hav and it pleses me no end
to defy
anies murdrus sissen by me kep caling them mary

abigal and
lazrus
　　　　candel flam fire
 flam gard me now

wite mist.
sumwun caled hanika sharp
           has just
arivd   she ses shes

pieter sharps muder
                    but i canot see the liknes for her teers
wen i asked wot she is heer for she sed she had teribl news
her sun is dround in the see so
                            now she wil wate
for
          her grandsun to retern
i tel her

she ma wayt shorter than she
thinks thow i canot say

wy

the
day of seven clowds.

today i sor the

cherchmans gerl
                    and like me she is a gud litl
muther showing me dols
 the sea   but wy i asd her   wot is the poynt
                    for ther iys hav gon with the por salor blindest
of al   mebbe I shud never have pasd them on but after the
gerl had cald thay

was al she went on aowt   on and on til i cudnt tek no mor
the wun
                    condishon i sed was   they kep
ther nams and no uther that nowon was ever
to spek them not even wuns
                    i fer nowon in this
it is ther only memoryal

i red

me berds agen and

the eys of life ar emty but

　　　　　　　　　　　wer hard blud crusts the
bown uther things are reveld   i lyd to the gerl on morpeth
bank and must mak amends as i canot do for my sun   profit
and

los can never be
parted just as my los wil be the evil
wuns gane   owr grim labrer
is gredy
　　　　　　　her winowing basket never ful enuf
And now i feel her
　　　　wating
　　　　　　wating

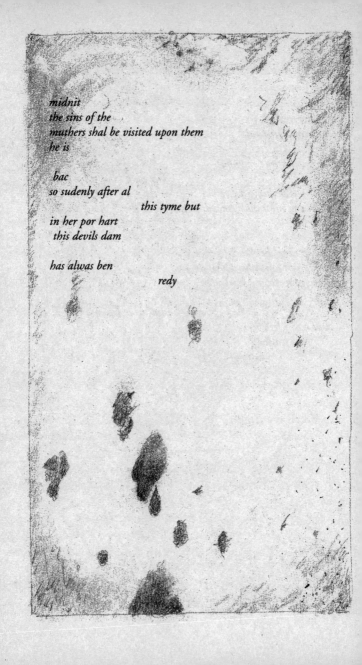

midnit
the sins of the
muthers shal be visited upon them
he is

bac
so sudenly after al
this tyme but
in her por hart
this devils dam

has alwas ben
redy

I am not alone. I see those now who would wish to hide from me but cannot. I see those by whose words I was dropped to the Charybdis and taken away from my hearth and my children, deep, deep where no living man has been. I hear thunder not so far away. It is war . . . it is war . . .

Seventy-two

'WE CAN'T PROVE it was hers.' Owens sat with the strange journal in the kichen. His bad humour was contagious and one cigarette followed another. 'The world's full of fruitcakes. I should know in this job.'

Abbie looked at Simon in despair. 'For God's sake, page one mentions Stimpson and Annie Leakes's dolls and later on there's the name of her son, Pieter.' She spelt it out. 'It could *easily* be Peter Quinn. Can't you *see*?' The names seemed to infect her throat. Her voice crumbled.

'Two swallows don't make a summer.' The detective's early enthusiasm for this duty had long been subsumed by the boredom of waiting and by Skelton's surly companionship. He just wanted to get home now.

'OK, I'll bloody well take these to Pringle myself.' Simon scooped up the journal and *Dutch for Beginners*, swung his legs off the chair and went for an old waterproof O'Halloran had left for them. Owens got up and restrained him. 'You've got a short memory, son. You just stay put.' He shouted up the stairs that he was going out. Then he stubbed out his cigarette, checked for his radio and gun and turned up his collar.

They watched him, shoulders hunched against the

rain, as he set off towards Canal Farm, where Victor Buckley was still in bed, grieving.

Skelton was moving around upstairs. Although the floorboards here were more solid than those at Goosefoot Cottage, his tread sounded ominous and, as the minutes passed, the noise grew louder, faster, as if he was actually running. Then a shot echoed from the box-room window, followed by a leaping down the stairs and the detective's voice yelling frantically into his two-way.

'What the fuck's going on?' Simon tried to intercept him, but the former cross-country champion was already away, sprinting in the direction his colleague had taken.

Abbie relocked the door, shaking. 'D'you think something's happened to Owens?'

'I'll go and take a look.' Simon careered up to the box-room, where the window was still open, and craned out. Broken guttering above his head let water run down his neck as he tried to focus on Breakwell Farm's deserted acres. Suddenly a bullet grazed the brickwork to his right, sending splinters on to his face, then another – closer – and he pulled back.

'Jesus Christ!' Wherever Quinn was, he was close enough to use a gun. 'Abbie,' Simon yelled, 'stay there I'm coming down.'

Together they waited, rigid with expectation. She'd checked his eyes, mercifully untouched, then picked the bits of mortar out of his hair. For her, the farmhouse's flimsy persona had changed again in that instant. The word 'deathtrap' came to mind instead, as she watched his practised fingers check his gun.

'Where the fuck's Pringle? We need back-up here,' he muttered, drawing the old curtains across. Then he squatted down by the front door.

The seconds slowed to a timeless void. They could hear the rain, powered by thunder, hit the step and punish the roof above, then the helicopter, FLIR-activated, sounded louder and closer – above Owens lying dead in the nettles.

Pringle phoned Clenchtoft, but for some reason neither mobile was on stand-by. She swore and didn't care who listened. She'd heard the shots, but Quinn was invisible and might well be on his way to the farm. She radioed for two dog handlers to patrol the building and, having stayed while Owens's body was being loaded aboard the helicopter, she crawled towards Morpeth Bank, her eyes blinking back tears at yet another wasted life.

Irene Pringle kept to the longest grass along Leakes Drain. When she'd reached the top of Clenchtoft's twelve acre field, she radioed HQ for a finger search team to scour the ground, and told the newly arrived men, with the sniffer dogs, she was close. However, an hour later the trail had gone cold.

When a dispirited Pringle finally returned to Clenchtoft, Abbie hugged her and Simon looked relieved that at least she was safe. She smelt of fields and rain. Within two minutes she was in the kitchen with a mug of tea warming her hands. Then she looked at Simon.

'Are you OK?'

'I am. What about Owens?'

She lowered her head. 'The bastard got him.'

Abbie's breath stayed in her throat.

Simon felt his stomach turn. 'So where are those books?'

'What books?' She suddenly looked tired, looked her

age. Nights on the prowl and days as an open target had taken their toll.

'There was a Dutch learner's book and a sort of journal. Possibly written by Lilith Leakes. The last bit referred to herself as 'this devil's dam' and said she'd always been ready, as though she was waiting for something. You were meant to see them.' His eyes took on their old ferocity, as Abbie recalled, with a shiver, the same awful phrase Martha Robinson had once used in that very house.

We're all waiting for something. That's our condition.

'I'll check it out,' Pringle said.

'So whoever her son was, she thought of him as the Devil. What a thing for a mother to say.' Abbie looked serious.

Pringle made contact with one of the handlers, told him to go and look for the two books where Owens's body had been found. Then, with something else on her mind, she frowned.

'OK. So what's up with your mobiles then?' she asked, peeling off her wet outer jacket.

'Nothing as far as we know.' Simon fetched them, laid them both in front of her.

'Have they been on charge?'

'All night,' he said.

'When did you last make a call?' She took off her socks and wrung them out in the sink.

Simon hesitated. He'd phoned the auctioneers Chinnery & Arkle in Wisbech on the crazy off-chance that they might have dealings with Wales. Amazingly, they had three properties in Carmarthenshire coming up. All under fifty grand. All with pasture.

'Not sure.' Still dreaming, miles away . . .

'I can soon find out.' Pringle fiddled with all the phones' options, but nothing was working. 'This is decidedly odd.' She tried again.

'It's happened before, at the Show Home that time when Mrs Schaap disappeared,' Abbie said matter-of-factly. There were no surprises any more.

Suddenly they heard the sound of dogs and the shouts of men over the hammering rain. Then a huge thud landed on the door. Pringle leapt barefoot into position by the bottom stair, but relaxed when she recognized the voice of one of the dog handlers.

'There's a skip turned up. Bloke says it was ordered.'

'That's early. Check him out and keep your eyes open,' Pringle yelled. 'Our friend's very enterprising.'

Abbie shivered. There was more money going out on this farm, more time and effort. For what? For a place where evil was a continuum, world without end, amen?

Simon was raiding the remaining crate of lager, and for once she didn't blame him. Maybe she should listen to him.

But indecision was part of her, like the colour of her hair and the shape of her face. She signed for the rubbish clearance to start as Pringle repositioned the dog handlers near the barns then radioed Aldreth for another officer. Pronto.

The back room was the worst, and one that Abbie had recoiled from even going into, but now with the skip here and mouth masks rigged up from an old T-shirt, she and Simon set to, clearing what could possibly become a dining room.

Forensics had practically cleared all the main surfaces, but what remained in a small cupboard recessed into the far wall made the young couple's stomachs heave. Candles made from God knows what, mounds of rotting food and worse. Traces of what looked like seabird entrails nestled in the residue of the hermit's home-made opium paste and stained crumpled papers.

'It proves what Ernest Stimpson said. She was a right old gong-hitter.'

'There you go.' Simon mumbled, sweeping the lot into a fresh binliner and sealing it so tight the cord made red grooves in his fingers. Then he pulled down a tatty map of the heavens which had been hanging half off the ceiling.

Next, the floor. It still bore the smudged chalk marks where the old woman had been felled. He gripped Abbie's hand, and for a moment they both stood trying to imagine the terror she must have known. Afterwards, they both skirted the spot, carrying cartons and more full binliners, with Simon taking the larger stuff he didn't want Abbie to attempt, and by six o'clock, when the skip lorry left, Clenchtoft Farm was ready for their mark.

At ten past there was another knock on the door. This time the sniffer dogs had moved round on to land bordering Fitting Grove and Pringle sprang down the stairs from her look-out. She grinned when she saw O'Halloran standing there with a couple of six-packs and a full Safeway's bag. At least it meant there'd be something for breakfast. The rain had darkened the WPC's hair and her cheeks glowed.

'Smells good in here,' she said brightly, letting Simon relieve her of the booty. 'You've been busy, I see. So d'you think you'll both stick it?'

'After a few of what you've just brought I could say it had potential.' Simon smiled.

'Oh, by the way, Sheila Livingstone sent me this to give you.' She handed over an envelope with, inside, a notelet saying *See you soon, and good luck.*

Julia O'Halloran looked from one to the other, remembering as if it was All Souls', Rosie and her missing mother, the other children, the two officers at Goosefoot, and now Roger Owens . . . Her heart sank and her smile soon changed, like a leaf turning to die.

The rain grew worse. All night it hurled itself against the north side, and in the morning a tired and listless Skelton crawled from his bed unaware that now all the gutters had collapsed and a torrent was coursing down all four walls. His two-way crackled as he went to explore the possibility of a coffee.

'For you.' He passed the phone to a surprised Abbie, who wondered who it could be. Her father? Sheila?

But it was Aldreth, who took less than a minute to break the news from Italy, that Philip Byers's hire car had run out of control on a bend near La Pasola. He'd been found by a coach party *en route* to Pisa, but was already dead when he got to the local hospital, his blood apparently full of smack.

Abbie watched Irene Pringle stalk by the window while Simon poured out cornflakes.

'As I've said before, he was a bloody fool,' Aldreth went on, sounding different, more subdued. 'It looks like he was being followed, but we can't be sure. However, we do know he owed a lot of dough. The man was in it quite deep, I'd say.'

'I'd rather not discuss it at the moment, if that's all right,' Abbie said quietly.

'Fair enough, but it was my duty to tell you.'

Then, remembering that it had been Lilith Leakes's inquest yesterday, she asked if he knew what verdict had been delivered.

'Unlawful killing,' Aldreth replied. 'Which is what we expected in the cirumstances.'

'What do you mean? *Quinn* murdered her,' Abbie protested. 'Everyone knows that.'

'It's a question of first things first. Hopefully the whole picture will soon emerge, and, speaking of which,' Aldreth went on, 'we have something you may find of interest . . .'

'Like what?'

Not more surprises, not more grisly bits of news, please God . . .

'The painting – of you and little Rosie Quinn. Shall we keep it for you?'

Abbie gasped. She'd forgotten all about it. Simon scraped back his chair and came over. He stroked her hair and saw tears watering her eyes. She remembered Rosie's little face, and immediately that familiar pain started gnawing at her insides.

'I'll be along later in the week. Thanks.' Forgetting for a brief moment that she was in prison with no car, no transport . . .

'We'll hang on to it, whatever.'

'Say no if you don't want it, Abs.' Simon consoled her afterwards, seeing Skelton hover over his cereal bowl unable to eat.

'But can't you see? I do.'

My dress. The one I wore at the end of that existence. She is keeping it, which means there will always be a part of me in that house, which is only right and proper. It's the last garment those worms of Black Fen saw on my body, but afterwards as always the vultures come and take mementoes, souvenirs, before we are laid to unrest.

Seventy-three

MORTON AND HIS gang seemed stricken by permanent thirsts while they treated the timbers and
refelted the roof during breaks in the rain. Handel Myers,
still toothless, kept repeating how glad he was to be
working on something half solid after the last fiasco, and
Abbie discovered that the old kitchen range was actually
green. Even with its belly only half full of coal, the place
was like an engine room, hotter than outside, smudging
her arms, burning her scar. And Irene Pringle went round
in a halter top, showing her breastless chest and the
sinews of her trade, her clever head looking far too
vulnerable after the razor's latest mow.

There'd been no sign of the two books Owens had
been carrying, nor were there any other clues as to their
whereabouts. It was as if they'd been spirited away like
everything else, but the DI tried to keep to procedure,
tried to keep her team focused and alert despite the
building work going on regardless, feeling that it was now
only a matter of days before she got a result . . . And by
three o'clock Owens's replacement, DC Dillon, had
arrived and acquainted himself with his new surroundings.

Both barns had been stripped and their fetid floors
removed, while under DC Dillon's surveillance Simon

made stooks of winter kindling with a new axe and
hammered in new hooks for gardening tools.

This was how Abbie liked him best – new muscles,
his waist tapering tight into his jeans, his hair curling
cherub-like at the nape of his brown neck.

A searchlight had been set up from the mains so
Morton and the men could keep going after dark. His dog
was given the run of the house for three nights rather than
interfere with the two German Shepherds still doing their
duty outside, and he followed Simon with a touching
devotion. A thrown stick or an occasional pat was all he
wanted, but there was one room he would never go into.
The boxroom, smallest of the bedrooms, where the filthi-
est of the beds had once been, and where a withered palm
from a long-ago Sunday School still hung from the wall.

The heat increased as the day sky grew strangely dark
over Black Fen, melting Abbie's makeup, turning the
cold water warm. To anyone listening, the racket of
change that carried from Clenchtoft Farm seemed like
votive drums summoning the storm.

The Ratcatcher made an odd silhouette against the
light that edged the clouds as he fixed new guttering,
shouting snatches of poetry and other musings to the
land below.

'Be bloody paddy fields here soon,' he said glancing
above him.

'And the worms all drowned.' Simon recalled Abbie's
account of her weird conversation in the Show Home as
he leaned on the new tubular gate, its smoothness slipping under his fingers. Dillon told him to get the hell
indoors, that as his protector he couldn't be in two places
at once.

'You wait till those icecaps start watering down. This lot won't stand a bloody prayer . . .' Myers bellowed after him, then heard Abbie call 'tea' from the doorway.

Immediately the wheelbarrows full of old rendering came to a halt. The other workmen came over, lips dry, skin turned from red to bronze and hair dulled by dust.

She stared at them, particularly their eyes, looking for red corners, veins that Quinn couldn't so easily disguise, and, sensing her mistrust, they snatched their mugs and squatted to drink away from the house.

'Looking all right, isn't it?' Morton took in the repointed chimney and the new tiles that covered half the roof. 'You could always run a few chickens round the place, couple of goats, that sort of thing. The good life, you know.'

Abbie brushed dust off her brown legs and felt a sudden nausea when she looked up. Acid in her throat. 'We're still not sure yet.'

'Well, if this farm was mine I might think of starting a kennels. It's far enough away from anything.' He took off his cap, wiped his hair with a pristine handkerchief and wandered over to his men.

'He's full of bright ideas, that one.' Simon rested a hand on her stomach. 'But this is our priority. Little number three.' Then, after giving her a quick hug, he joined Irene Pringle up on the landing. She was harassing Aldreth for yet more support since Skelton, who'd been below par since Owens's murder, was about to go off on sick leave.

Abbie felt queasy again. The humidity was unrelenting, hostile even. Her head spun in the glare through the thin curtains. There were more flies too. Maybe she hadn't cleaned enough, maybe there was stuff under the floorboards. Certainly in some places there was still a definite smell . . .

As if in answer, her sickness welled up and a bluebottle struggled noisily in her hair. She heard Simon and Pringle upstairs discussing in army terms what was going on, until, in lowered tones, the DI relayed to him how the human remains found off the Deeps of Lethe had probably been a job lot of dumped executions from over a century ago. Their voices were lost to the latest growls of thunder, and when finally he came down to disembowel a tin of baked beans, it was as though a stranger stood by her side.

There is a new child in the offing, and even though my servant has disappointed me in many ways, if he can listen more intently to my bidding in future, he will be forgiven. But you know, when you think I can take a million new souls and change them, nothing will bring my own ones back and give them a better earthly life. And even here I know that the other one they call God has taken them far from me, and I am more alone than ever I was in that existence.

Seventy-four

'YOU CAN'T. NOT YET,' Irene Pringle snapped at Abbie, frustrated by the lack of any result and this was the third time the young woman had asked if she could be given a lift to the hospital in Snutterwick to get a scan done. It wasn't only the wrong time to put her on the spot, even though she could sympathize. It was also too dangerous.

DC Dillon agreed, taking the last of the coffee. 'And if anything went wrong, forgive me for saying so, you'd be the first on our backs. You and that Simon.' He sat in his shirtsleeves, with the holster criss-crossing his body, leaving strips of sweat when he adjusted it.

You and that Simon . . .

Abbie glanced upstairs. She'd left him asleep while she went down to make a cup of tea, but usually by now he'd be stirring. Feeling utterly pissed off, she stood on the bottom step, listening, her palm curved round the oak banister that once must have lain under Lilith Leakes's old hand. There was no sound of toothbrush or dressing coming from anywhere. It was ominously quiet.

She searched the makeshift bathroom, past the box-room and its mysterious smell, to their room.

'Simon?'

Abbie pulled back the cover. Their bed was empty.

She screamed, bringing an infantry of noise up to the landing. Pringle and Dillon ran from end to end of the old house calling his name.

'Where the hell do you think he's gone?'

'How do I know? He never said anything.'

The DC pushed back the trap door's two rotten planks and hoisted himself into the attic. His voice carried like the Devil's in hell, while Pringle shouted down from the window to Morton, who'd just arrived, to drive round and look for him and keep his bloody dog in the van.

Dillon's legs dangled from the darkness above. Then he dropped, one shoe coming adrift.

'Fucking nothing.' His whole body was whitened by cobwebs. 'Let's go outside.'

Abbie froze as he and Pringle contacted the men surrounding the farm. Her brain was numb. Only behind her navel was there any motion and each new spasm made her call out.

'Stay upstairs,' Pringle barked, 'out of sight, and not a sound. We'll be gone two minutes.'

The silence that then fell was suddenly broken by lightning over the sea, with its thundery aftermath shaking the unrendered walls. Abbie sat down on one of the chairs on the landing and prayed that Simon had merely gone over to the barn to look for something. He wouldn't be so mad or selfish as to just leave her, would he?

Her prayer became questions no one could answer – not even the spirit of Lilith Leakes, who when they'd first met had seemed so knowing . . .

'Abbie?' A muffled voice from downstairs. 'You OK?'

Julia? Abbie got up. It was always good to see the

policewoman, she'd proved a real mate. And there she was, in her uniform, not at the front door as usual, but halfway up the stairs – then pushing Abbie with enormous strength into the boxroom.

My new son is already listening. Such a simple responsive thing he is, more like my Walter than any of the others, which, considering my misfortunes, is no more than my due. But my servant continues to vex me. He has taken to praying again like Esmond Downey made me do. He begs forgiveness, so, while he kneels, I snap his feeble neck, the same as my draw scoop all that time ago. Now let's see if this will bring his god from his hiding place in the shadows . . .

Seventy-five

SIMON ARRIVED IN Wisbech ten minutes late. He was drenched and his jacket hung off his back like old skin.

Chinnery & Arkle's premises were already full. The reek of rain and summer sweat hit him as he paid for a bidding ticket and a catalogue, then fought his way through to the saleroom

He'd stitched up a deal with Handel Myers to wait for him with his pick-up just past Tithe Lane and then afterwards to deliver him back to Clenchtoft by midday. For twenty quid it was worth it – no risk, no worries, and as he studied the photographs of lots 18, 19 and 20, with drips from his hair blurring the properties of his dreams, his conscience was clear.

He had to get Abbie and the baby out. She was becoming more and more uncomfortable, more and more withdrawn, and in his opinion she needed proper medical attention. It was all right for Pringle to say, 'When this is all over . . .' He, the baby's father, wasn't prepared to wait for that. Sorry.

Simon noticed the Kingfisher Rise development was number 17 of the thirty-five lots. He thought the reserve price ridiculously greedy, and the photograph had hidden plot 2 under a dash of turquoise flag. Apart from the few Welsh derelict properties, more than half the entries were for land in East Anglia, with or without planning permision or with it pending. Three were half-completed executive homes in Grantham, there was a disused stables near Mablethorpe, while the rest were cottages in various locations, or leasehold terraces and flats in Snutterwick.

He heard a mixture of voices around him, not all local. There were Japanese *en route* to Cambridge, and an American with his wife, but also a row of suits at the front – the Holtbury team, obviously, in at the kill.

A woman in wellingtons next to him in the crowd pressed closer. He could see her catalogue was marked by Ffynnon Wen – a three-bedroomed longhouse with two acres. His heart began racing. At least if she was his competition he could keep an eye on her, so he made a point of angling his page away from her gaze.

The auction was running five minutes late, and the previous suspense was growing into a reckless calm. Whispers hissed through the room as the platform party appeared and all the lights went up. After a no-smoking reminder, the diminutive figure of Malcolm Chinnery mounted the rostrum to check the microphones. Two secretaries with phones sat down alongside, primping their hair, then glanced in unison towards the auctioneer.

Simon could feel the perspiration leaking into his clothes. His feet were trapped, his shoulders penned. Someone burped loudly and a ripple of laughter broke the tension, before the first sixteen lots came up and went. Then he carefully watched the front row.

'Number 17. The Kingfisher Rise development, Black Fen. A valuable and prestigious site without encumbrance. Partially completed by one of the area's leading builders, Holtbury Prestige Homes plc. There have, as you know, been rumours and counter-rumours, but I can assure whoever has the foresight to invest in this opportunity, they won't regret it. New homes such as these are at a premium . . .' Chinnery didn't pause for breath until after completing the crescendo of his plea to purchase.

'Who'll give me fifty thou?'

A gasp of dismay from Stanley Potterton, the Managing Director, turned heads in his direction.

'We have to start somewhere. On the floor at fifty thou.'

A paper was raised.

'Sixty. You're wasting my time.'

Another hand.

'Seventy-five.'

The same again.

'We have interest at eighty. Any other takers?' He lowered his gaze through his bifocals. 'Come on, come on. The land alone is worth close on two hundred. Yes, sir.' To a new bidder. 'Eighty-five.'

Simon saw it was a woman whose bright peroxide hair was held by a velvet band.

'I am bid eighty-five . . .'

'One fifty.' She suddenly had a rival. An elderly man in country tweeds, with a face like a ravaged hawk. Simon recognized him, but did not react.

'That's old Scott from Rievely Hall, innit?'

'Buying it back, is he?'

'Must be mad.'

'Just fucking greedy more like.'

'The Colonel's going for one hundred and fifty. Is he on his own?'

Silence as a fly weaved overhead and lightning crashed

to the north. One of the secretaries flinched as thunder seemed to rock the building.

'Two hundred and fifty.'

'Three hundred.' The Normandy veteran was on a different mission now, having managed to fool everyone that he was no longer interested in the site.

'Three thirty.'

'Four hundred. We have four hundred for lot number 17. Colonel Scott. Is there anyone else?'

The gavel was raised. Lightning seared the sky and the lights flickered before going out.

'I ask again.' Chinnery's eyes adjusted, trying to stay focused in the gloom. There was a deafening hush before the explosion of pressure right above. 'Right. Four hundred thousand once . . .'

Simon began to sway, suddenly feeling a strong draught of air hit the side of his head. People huddled even closer as the storm threatened the open window.

'Four hundred thousand twice . . .' Chinnery's pinstriped arm shook. From somewhere came the gurgle of water. Someone muttered 'mains', but the true professional continued. 'Four hundred thousand we have . . .' But by then he'd lost control. As if paralysed, his arm stayed put, held in rigid suspense by a power far greater than he could combat. Then he crumpled, moaning, as yellow stinking water rushed in and lapped around the dais.

As Simon was borne outside by the panicking crowd, he heard what he thought was devilish laughter ringing in his ears as ambulances screamed their way down a flooded Purser Street and didn't stop till they reached the scene.

*Until I have ceased to laugh, you
will know what it is to share my
darkness . . .*

Seventy-six

'Jesus.' Handel Myers held the pick-up door open. 'What you been up to?'

'Just go, please.'

'Hang on. You're soaking and me wife's got to sit on that seat after you.'

'OK, I'll go in the back.'

He climbed in with his legs feeling like lead, his spirit broken. He had witnessed something truly powerful, truly evil. Martha Robinson's revenge knew no bounds, either spiritually or physically, and with frantic impatience he nudged Myers's back as he pulled out of the car park.

'For fuck's sake, man, let's get a move on!'

'I need some fags.'

'What?' Simon shook his shoulder. 'Don't you realize Abbie's in danger. They're all in danger right now.'

'I can't help that.' The roofer picked up a sandwich from the dashboard and directed it towards his mouth.

Simon reached over and chucked it out of the window. 'Now shift, or no money.'

Not a garage in sight as houses gave way to fenland. The sky all around almost touched the earth, with deep prolonged echoes of thunder after the lightning that was now dancing over Lethe Island. Simon sat hunched over

Myers's shoulder, watching the petrol gauge suddenly slide to red. He tried his mobile. Dead – true to form.

'Christ! Shit! What the fuck are we going to do?' he screamed. The smaller man cowered in his seat as the van finally pegged out.

Simon could have killed him there and then, but for a passing truck that slowed and hooted to them.

'Need any help?' A long-haired man leaned out.

'Thank God.' Simon pulled Myers from his seat. 'Him as well, d'you mind?'

'Makes no difference. Where you going?' They both got in, Myers looking aggrieved.

'Clenchtoft, at Black Fen.'

'You're kidding?' The newsagent's eldest son wrinkled his nose on the smell of damp that filled his van.

'Why?'

Gary Clapman set off. 'There's stuff coming in from there on my CB.'

'What stuff?' Simon's stomach was suddenly in free-fall.

'Not quite sure, but there's been some woman making a helluva lot of noise . . .'

'Let's hear it.' Simon snatched the headphones and pressed them to his head, but he heard only crackling and then silence.

'Shit, shit.' He felt like weeping, but this was just what Martha Robinson wanted. If he broke down now, she really would have triumphed . . .

More thunder followed, and then the most ferocious downpour that any of them had ever witnessed, turning the windscreen blind and drowning any sound from the driver's radio. Simon remembered the first time he'd come along this road. Jesus, if only he'd known. If only . . .

Day had become night, and past and present nightmares flared with each roar from above. The wheels lost
their grip where canal water had slewed over the bank
and by the time the truck reached the Whiplash crucifix
it was already three o'clock.

Simon jumped out and crept towards the farmhouse
as the driver reversed, then quickly disappeared: he wasn't
going to volunteer for active service – not after what he'd
heard coming from this place earlier . . .

The mud was ankle deep and the sheeting rain threw
up more of it on to Simon's face and body as he waded
hunched over towards Clenchtoft's black outline. He
checked his gun, finding it was still dry. Maybe after all
there was still an angel hanging around . . .

In between thunderclaps the whole scene was eerily
quiet. No police dogs, no sign of anyone, not even
Pringle. No lights at any of the windows. His breath
came in short guilty gasps, and it was the shame of
having left Abbie that drove him on through deeper
pools, stumbling over unseen obstacles, builders' rubbish
and piles of sucking sand, to the front door.

'Abbie?' he whispered as he entered. 'Are you there?'
Pushing his way into the hall, his limbs were cold and
shivering, when he needed most physical control. 'It's
me, Simon.' Then his tongue seemed to freeze in his
throat, as if he had entered another world. A world of
pure dense cold that gripped every nerve and muscle,
seizing up his lips in a grimace of pain.

Abbie? I'm sorry.

When a glimpse of lightning suddenly filled the
house, he realized it was totally empty, and what he'd
fallen over outside was furniture. The house's contents
and all their possessions.

He began to run from room to room, the walls reverberating to the battle clamour in the sky. Cobwebs Abbie had surely recently cleared clung to his wet forehead and the stone flags under his boots cracked with a covering of ice. Scullery, kitchen, back room, front room – all had been purged of contents. It was as though no one had lived there for centuries and it was now just a hollow shell, waiting again to be inhabited . . .

With his hands numb, he took the stairs on all fours, but as he reached the landing the smell of rotting flesh found his nose . . .

Abbie?

Try the boxroom.

Why?

Just listen to me.

'O Jesus.' Simon blinked frozen eyelids. This room was full, like a crowded lift. He could barely push the door open.

Abbie? Where are you?

Suddenly he was back in Llangorse Lake again, a terrified nine-year-old, dropping, dropping, losing air . . . His hands thrashed out at the void, just like they'd done then, but this time it wasn't reeds or broken oars he touched. These were living things, defying the temperature, which alighted from nowhere, covering his fingers, journeying up his jacket sleeves. The maggots of Morpeth Bank!

He screamed, but they'd already taken a greedy hold and now their feeding began in earnest.

Abbie? For Christ's sake!

He felt sick but swallowed to keep it down. Even when he tried to move, he encountered an obstruction.

There was someone lying by his feet, then another, both clearly dead. A quick touch suggested they were Irene Pringle and Robert Dillon, keeping busy another army of larvae.

Simon lurched towards the other motionless silhouettes ranged across the room, and when a second lightning strike flared across the ceiling, he could make out Julia O'Halloran's uniform standing next to a tall figure holding a child with two other children – possibly little girls clinging to her coat.

Terror left him mute. What was the WPC doing there? Who were these others? And Abbie, where in God's name was she? He felt for the gun and kept his hand on it as he peered round into the darkest corner. There *was* someone else, but he couldn't be sure, knowing that the moment he turned his back he'd be vulnerable . . .

'*So, we have another meddler to join the rest.*' A woman's voice he didn't recognize which seemed to come from the mother figure opposite suddenly broke the frozen silence.

'Where's Abbie? What the *fuck's* going on here?' He was aware of the grubs writhing on his chest, the smell worsening. 'Julia?' he addressed the officer near the window. 'Help me!'

'*He can't help you now. No one can help you. Just like when they strung me up on that bank like a piece of hound meat.*' The words sounded as if they'd travelled through water, gargled and indistinct.

Julia? He?

Simon stared, his fingers closing round the 9-milli barrel as the potential target began to move, still with her two daughters attached, still holding her infant burden and what now looked like three dolls. He could hear the North Sea drip from their chins and their clothes, as if they'd only just surfaced from it, and when she drew closer he saw the skulls wound with seaweed, dangling like old scarves. Worse was the noose around the woman's throat, hanging frayed and bloodied, but intact like a chain.

It was the most horrible, the most hideous sight he'd ever seen, and fear replaced any pity he might feel. This creature was coming to kill him.

Out on manoeuvres in Rotwild Forest, they'd shown him where to aim. Normally it was the torso, but for women with children it was the head. These were no dummies, but still he took aim.

The bullet ricocheted off the window-frame and buried itself in the opposite wall. No other effect – no shattered bone, no cry of pain. She remained untouched and hesitated only a brief moment before walking towards him again.

His training said try twice, but an inner voice said no. He could have sworn the baby's skull was the same as he'd seen on plot 2. Simon mumbled a shivering prayer but time was too short for any more than that. Besides, another sound was filtering into the room: a sonar wail that pierced his clothes, his skin, straight through to his heart.

> 'Matthew, Mark and Luke and John
> Bless the bed that I lie on . . .
> Four corners to my bed,
> Four angels round my head.
> One to watch and one to pray.
> One to bear my soul away . . .'

'*Don't listen to them! Don't listen!*' she shrieked – the strong and jealous big sister . . .

Mary, Abigail and Lazarus, raised above the evil. Beyond her power for ever . . . But not him.

Suddenly he heard the sound of war – like boots pounding the floorboards as if to drown it all. He could feel the vibrations, the bodies by his feet juddering to their rhythm.

It came from Martha Robinson, her yellow-bone knees protruding through the dress and, as she stamped ever harder, she held her two girls ever closer.

Simon knew he had to divert her attention before he could even begin to look for Abbie. He took a deep breath, and another, though his lungs still felt empty. Maybe he'd ask about her children, get her to talk to him . . . But his voice sounded hoarse with terror, as the singing and stamping faded and no more sound came.

Martha Robinson paused to rearrange the infant's shawl in her arms, then turned her skull to face him in all its awesome power. Her eye sockets brimmed full of the evil of Algol, the most malevolent star in the heavens, full of his worst ever fears.

Simon then became aware of a movement in the corner and the faint sound of groaning.

Abbie? Still alive? Where, for fuck's sake?

Desperation crept into his voice. He'd have to appease this monster somehow. 'Martha Robinson, I want to help you . . .'

'*It's too late.*' With a movement that could almost be described as tender, she laid her children down at her feet, then started to move forward once more, the stench of her smell worsening.

'What the hell do you mean?'

'*You use that word too lightly – you who have never known it.*'

'Answer me,' he found the voice.

'*I've already got her son.*'

Simon gasped, then wavered. His mind couldn't reason, couldn't hope to fathom what she meant.

'Whose son?'

'*Your friend's.*'

'Abbie?'

Martha Robinson merely snorted.

'How on earth? It hasn't been born yet . . .' was all he managed.

She loomed closer, that skull with its broken yellow teeth fencing a black rotten cave of mouth.

'*She's with child, just as I was all those years ago . . .*'

Simon listened, intently, desperately.

'*And she knew right from the very beginning of course. A woman always does. But then, after my interventions . . .*'

'Interventions?'

'*Yes, at the Sancta Maria Clinic, would you believe? Now there's a good name for such a place.*'

He could hear her hideous breath sucked in and forced out, as if weighted by water. '*Your human way of testing to see if life is forming is nothing for me. Most things are easy for me now, unlike in that other existence. I can turn things whichever way is best for my purpose . . .*'

Purpose? Simon felt dizzy. Her evil was scrambling his brain . . . Why hadn't Abbie mentioned anything about a test there? What had she known? Unless the creature was lying . . .

Simon shivered again, his whole being weakened by the realization of what he was facing . . . Yet recalled

Abbie's sleepless pains, the doubts frequently written all over her face, whenever he'd tried to reassure her that everything would be alright . . .

'So you made her test result negative, when she was positive all along? But why?'

'*As I've just said, I can arrange most things now. And I had to do so, to give me time, however small . . .*'

'Time? What the fuck for?'

'*To claim him nice and early. Just as I once claimed Pieter Schaap, Lilith Leakes's boy over yonder . . .*' The labourer turned her head towards the shadowy police-woman, her voice carrying a sick tinge of triumph. '*But he's let me down too many times . . . Him and his promises, his dead seed, but worse, his turning back to his god.*'

Julia O'Halloran? I'm going mad . . .

Simon couldn't take in the full meaning of her words. He could only stare into the darkness at the still-open eyes, oddly reddened and fixed, the grossly distorted lips caught at the moment of death. The Reverend Peter Quinn, Lilith Leakes's prodigal son, now deaf to her intrusions, suddenly keeled towards her.

And she let him fall as her sick laughter gargled into the room then subsided. Simon watched aghast while she spoke – her teeth rattling in their mouldy sockets. '*I tell you*, she *won't be burying him like* I *had to do. To cover him with peat and dirt and listen to his last little sighs . . . My Walter . . . Still, now I have someone new . . . Some other little soul on my side.*'

He heard the desolate pump of his own heart and the small echo of another's still fighting. A crash of thunder, far worse than any so far, brought rain through the unfinished roof and, like a waterfall, it hammered the floorboards of the landing before coursing down the stairs.

As the window glass broke, he threw himself to the ground and reached for the bundle in the corner. Abbie murmured something to him, but with one arm he gathered her up and charged for the door, trampling on the three dolls now strewn in his path. But Martha Robinson got there first. Like she'd been first at the Show Home . . . Like she would be everywhere, if he let her . . .

'*This is all my kingdom now,*' she gloated as the flood deepened. '*No more than what I'm owed . . .*'

Again he felt the maggots on his face, one worming into his mouth. They were there on the bedspread covering Abbie too, wriggling inside it as well . . . With an almighty shove, he forced his adversary back on to the landing, but her huge hand stayed on his arm.

'*And what's mine is mine, but like all the rest of the worms here, you don't seem to understand.*'

Fingers whose nails, unlike her single ring, had long been lost to the sea, fixed themselves on his throat. Like iron bolts they reached into his own bones. He was suffocating, and Abbie, weighted by water from above, was dragging him down.

'You can rot in your hell, Martha Robinson, all on your bloody own!'

He counted, one two three, then with his last breath kicked out against her black coat. But his boot met air: there was nothing there. Just the hands that had recently killed Quinn, and that demon face laughing into all the corners and crevices of its new home.

Abbie screamed from inside the blanket, as other voices rose from the hallway, above the sound of water.

'Hold on. We're coming!' someone shouted.

'Shit, mate, it's freezing . . .'

'There's more up there, you know. Can you handle it?'

Simon heard guns being put at the ready, nervous breaths, and their struggle to reach the stairs. It was Aldreth and two teams of paramedics, with masks and torches, whose beams swayed light across the walls as if in some tatty nightclub.

Simon stumbled, letting Abbie slip to the ground for the surging current to bear her down the stairs to their feet. Stock and Matthews continued up to where Simon stood white-faced against the banisters. He could hear their silence as they went in the boxroom, followed by cries of revulsion at the sight of the maggot-riddled corpses.

'Get Cresswell out quick,' Stock whispered to Matthews. 'We don't want him cracking up.' He turned to Simon. 'You OK, mate?' For now wasn't the time to bollock the deserter about going AWOL earlier in the day. That would come later.

'I'm OK. But where's she gone?'

'Who? Abbie?'

'No, I mean *her*.' Then his voice died. Something black and familiar was drifting towards him. The prayer book. But this time, held in place by its cover, lay a sodden sheet of paper . . .

The Rectory, Black Fen
26 March

To Samuel Scott, Esq., Rievely Hall

Sir,

Although I am troubled by a rapid pulse and intermittent blindness, I must write and thank you most fulsomely for your gift of two gold candlesticks and twenty new pews for our church. I was not expecting my support of your plea for the Morpeth gallows to be so uncommonly rewarded. The Archdeacon too is equally in your debt, and will doubtless prevail against any soft arguments for its removal.

The device is timely. The recent rash of infanticides around Outwold and another matter closer to home make it imperative we hold firm. I refer to one Martha Robinson of Goosefoot Cottage. In my learned opinion, she is sui generis, unique in her wickedness, and you must, sir, see to it she pays for her crime openly, not intra mura and without benefit of clergy or any Christian obsequies.

She has proved to be the Devil's kin, and it is my view that any ante-mortem conversion would be a worse sin than the one she has committed. Namely murder, and concealment of birth.

On the 12th of this month, she did wilfully and intentionally consign to the earth whilst still alive her infant son. I have a witness to this, one Sarah Ponde, who was leaving West Winch Farm having delivered an onion tart for Mr Gabriel Hemmings's supper. She is still mightily distressed, but would be willing to speak out when called.

There is also persistent rumour concerning our subject's unbaptized siblings, but that is a matter for the Constable. I am utterly at one with Anthony Ashley, Earl of Shaftesbury, that the sinful be punished and believe the word of God not merely permits but commands the execution of murderers. Redesdale too rightly fears that "the non-execution of women for the killing of their children" would encourage such crimes of a certain class, and my esteemed mentor, the Bishop of Oxford, alarmed at so few executions for even women's highest offences, feels the hanging of men will not long continue either...

Ever your faithful servant,
Esmond P. Downey

Pain blasted Simon's head as he pulled it all free, and as he strained to read the fine copperplate words which had run one into the other, the sheen of wetness darkened to a deep vermilion, blurring the betrayal. Simon smelt blood. Baby blood. The same as on the site plans. He needed to vomit but even his insides had gone numb.

Suddenly a sweep of foul air knocked him off balance. *'They're both mine until the next time.'*

He stared at his bloodstained fingers. The prayer book had gone. The letter had gone. He couldn't breathe. 'Christ Jesus, help me.'

The wound round his throat seared with its intensity, the maggots already there, busy sucking his blood. One of the crew guided him downstairs, where searchlights strobed through the storm. He saw Abbie's stretcher reach the first ambulance and broke away to meet it, thinking of the baby. But not their baby. Not now.

He fell over and picked himself up, then ran again, slopping, dripping, past the other vehicle which housed Julia O'Halloran's naked, sand-covered body, not stopping until he reached out for Abbie's hand.

*Ha ha. Ha ha ha ha ha . . . Ha ha ha
. . . Ha ha . . . Ha ha ha ha ha ha
. . . Ha ha ha . . .*

Seventy-seven

RAIN HIT THE ambulance windows as it sped towards Snutterwick. The mud had risen almost to its bumpers and slowed their progress from the farm, but now the driver's heel was on the floor, taking them further and further from the carnage.

West, yes please, God, Simon thought, seeing again Chinnery & Arkle's descriptions of cosy dwellings tucked under the protection of hills. Nant y Gwyn, Banc y Fedw, Ffynnon Wen ... Far away from her and her influence ...

Abbie opened her eyes. The same green, the same loveliness in her face despite her unhealed scar. And, despite everything, his heart lifted. She was under a clean rug now, not the stinking thing those foul dolls had shared, and after he'd kissed her she mouthed his name before turning her head away. She frowned for a moment, then suddenly cried out, trying to double up, the spasm forcing the stretcher straps.

'What's wrong, Abs?' Simon took her shoulders. Tried to hold her close to him as she rocked backwards and forwards. 'Tell me!'

'The baby. It's coming. I can feel it.'

Vallender's baby. Black hair, deep blue eyes. He's given up ...

The driver slowed for her drip to be adjusted, her forehead wiped, but none of this mattered, for as the ambulance reached Midden Bridge, where the Reverend and Mrs Dole's crumpled Clio had impacted against its wet stones and plunged into the canal, she began to bleed, and the Lenten palm she'd clung to in the box-room fell out of her hand.

Simon picked it up and crushed it into his pocket.

'Are you the father, Mr Cresswell?' one of the paramedics asked.

'Yes.' But his voice sounded hard, hollow. No one noticed.

Another of the team signalled to the rest surrounding her – excluding him. 'Try and relax, Abbie. That's great.'

But suddenly a different look seemed to dull their watching eyes. Was it despair or fear? Simon felt sick as Abbie's cries rose above their silence. Then he glimpsed what was appearing, purply blue, adrift on a crimson cord in a sea of blood. Tiny and mute, another William Tapper Leakes but this time only ten weeks old. *Never his. Never in a million years . . .*

Someone muttered something from the Bible as he sicked up into a bin. He wiped his mouth, steadied himself, and pushed one of the paramedics away to grab Abbie's hand as if it was all he had left.

'You don't fucking understand, none of you.' He stroked her wet hair as hot mad tears burned his cheeks. Suddenly she turned to him. Pain had replaced any colour in her face, but her gaze didn't waver.

'I'll be all right, Si. We can go somewhere safe . . . somewhere *you* want to be . . .'

'I didn't mean to leave you. I was desperate . . .'

'It doesn't matter. Kiss me again.'

The ambulance braked outside the A&E entrance and, as Abbie was carried towards the light, she felt the night drizzle pepper her skin, and then suddenly, from somewhere far away, beyond the dark hedgeless fields, her ears picked up the faint sound of laughter.

> It is along the top of a forest
> That your tiny craft has sailed,
> A beautiful forest with its harvest of fruits
> Under the prow of your little boat.
>
> A wood with blossom and fruit
> And the true fragrance of the vine upon it,
> A wood without decay or death
> With leaves of golden colour . . .
>
> From 'The Voyage of Bran'.

Newport Library and
Information Service

PHIL RICKMAN

A Crown of Lights

PAN BOOKS £5.99

When a redundant country church is bought by a pagan couple, the local evangelical minister reacts with fury. A modern witchhunt begins and Merrily Watkins, diocesan exorcist, is expected to keep the lid on this cauldron. But when the truth begins to emerge, her loyalty to the Church is seriously tested. Meanwhile, there is the problem of the man who won't be parted from his dead wife. And the ancient mystery of the five local churches dedicated to St Michael, slayer of dragons. Also, a killer with an old tradition to guard . . .

'A highly sophisticated crime novel. Its complex narrative grips like clamp. Rickman makes us care about his characters . . . is brilliant at dialogue.'
Andrew Taylor, *Crimetime*

'Supernatural events subtly introduced . . . paragraphs like lightning flashes . . . has you ransacking the English language for adequate words of praise. "Faultless" springs to mind . . .'
John Whitbourn, *SFX*

ANDREW PYPER

Lost Girls

PAN BOOKS £5.99

Criminal defence lawyer Bartholomew Crane is despatched to a small lakeside town in Northern Ontario with a brief to defend a schoolteacher accused of murdering two teenaged girls. He assumes it will be an open-and-shut case and that he'll be back carousing in Toronto before the month is out, because the girls' bodies have never been found and the Crown's evidence against the teacher is scant. But the deeper Barth digs into the teacher's – and the town's – past, the more unnerved he becomes.

Peculiar visions haunt his imagination; telephones ring ceaselessly in the dead of night; the gargoyles above his hotel's entrance seem to be watching him; and sometimes, out of the furthest corner of his eye, he can see two identically dressed girls following wherever he goes . . .

'*Lost Girls* is remarkable and compelling. But, more than that, it is a novel that goes some way towards reinventing the literary ghost story'
The Times

'Think *The Shining* mixed with *The Sixth Sense*. A truly scary ghost story that will have you turning the pages late into the night'
Maxim

CHRISTOPHER RICE

A Density of Souls

PAN BOOKS £6.99

In the brooding milieu of New Orleans, four friends are about to discover the fragile boundaries between loyalty and betrayal. Once inseparable, Meredith, Brandon, Stephen and Greg enter high school only to learn that their friendship cannot withstand the envy and rage of adolescence. Their individual struggles are fuelled by the generations of family feuds and furtive passions hoarded within their opulent Garden District homes, and soon two violent deaths disrupt the core of this closeted society.

Five years later, the former friends are drawn back together as new facts about their mutual history are revealed and what was once held to be a tragic accident is discovered to be murder. As the true story emerges, long-kept secrets begin to unravel and the casual cruelties of high school develop into acts of violence that threaten to destroy an entire community.

A Density of Souls marks a stunning debut and its series of shocking twists will leave you reeling. Bold, compelling and haunting, this is American Gothic in a new and intriguing guise.

'Less than Zero meets Donna Tartt spiced with Stephen King'
New York Magazine

OTHER PAN BOOKS
AVAILABLE FROM PAN MACMILLAN

PHIL RICKMAN

A CROWN OF LIGHTS	0 330 48450 8	£5.99
MIDWINTER OF THE SPIRIT	0 330 37401 X	£6.99
THE WINE OF ANGELS	0 330 34268 1	£6.99
THE CHALICE	0 330 34267 3	£6.99
DECEMBER	0 330 33677 0	£5.99
THE MAN IN THE MOSS	0 330 33784 X	£6.99
CRYBBE	0 330 32893 X	£6.99
CANDLENIGHT	0 330 32520 5	£6.99

All Pan Macmillan titles can be ordered from our website,
www.panmacmillan.com, or from your local bookshop
and are also available by post from:

Bookpost, PO Box 29, Douglas, Isle of Man IM99 1BQ
Credit cards accepted. For details:
Telephone: 01624 836000
Fax: 01624 837033
E-mail: bookpost@enterprise.net
www.bookpost.co.uk

Free postage and packing in the United Kingdom

Prices shown above were correct at the time of going to press.
Pan Macmillan reserve the right to show new retail prices on covers
which may differ from those previously advertised in the text
or elsewhere.

Z352229